PETER BUWALDA

BONITA AVENUE

'A dazzling family saga' The Times

'One wild ride' *Sunday Telegraph*

'An instant literary classic, loaded with suspense'
Herman Koch, author of *The Dinner*

PUSHKIN PRESS

'Great European art: the Dutchman Peter Buwalda explodes the bourgeois family saga: the narrative pyrotechnics alone are a tour de force' *Die Zeit*

'One of the first great European novels of the 21st century' Jonathan Ruppin, foyles.co.uk

'Buwalda's magnificent first novel offers proof of Tolstoy's dictum that "every unhappy family is unhappy in its own way"' *Publishers Weekly* (starred review)

'Extraordinarily gripping. A dream debut' *HP/De Tijd*

'A brilliantly constructed story, with complex characters tested to the limit' *The Lady*

'A literary sensation. *Bonita Avenue* is no less than a phenomenal masterpiece' *tip Berlin*

'A bold and assured debut, *Bonita Avenue* deftly alternates between narrators and settings to keep readers morally unsettled and in suspense... both sprawling and meticulously constructed... a satisfying, psychologically nuanced read'

Huffington Post

'A dazzling family saga... [Buwalda's] brilliance is unique'

Kate Saunders, *The Times*

'Addictive bedlam... deserves to be a book, not just a debut, of the year'

James Kidd, *Independent, Best Debuts of the Year*

'A robust dark farce... Whatever literary benchmark you use, the book's hyperbolic excess and willingness to plunge recklessly to the depths are what make it work... The plot orchestration and lively character renderings of *Bonita Avenue* are dazzling'

The New York Times

'This award-winning debut novel is flat-out extraordinary. The rich layer of detail would be impressive if applied to one topic, but Buwalda creates multiple complex worlds around vastly different subjects... An outstanding literary suspense story that will appeal to a wide range of readers'

Library Journal, (starred review)

'Dazzling... [A] giddily twisting family drama'

Penthouse

'Buwalda's debut... becomes increasingly compulsive reading as it nears its dark close... This tumultuous saga of a family breaking down... is an international bestseller and award winner. A significant literary achievement'

Booklist, (starred review)

'A considerable achievement for a seasoned writer much less a newcomer, *Bonita Avenue* is an entertaining end in itself, and evidence that Buwalda is just getting started'

James Kidd, *Independent*

'A new writer as toe-curling as early Roth, as roomy as Franzen and as caustic as Houellebecq'

Sunday Telegraph

'Buwalda writes with ferocious dexterity'

New Statesman

'The Dutch answer to Jonathan Franzen'

NRC Handelsblad

'Peter Buwalda's impressive family saga is a genuine page-turner, with a forceful, precise style'

Jury report, Libris-Prize

'Buwalda's debut novel [is] daring in its linguistic power and freedom, and impressive, even frightening, in its psychological sharpness and precision… great and outrageous'

Frankfurter Rundschau

'It's a fantastic debut which, at over 500 pages, doesn't outstay its welcome'

Glasgow Herald

'Racy, rip-roaring, rich, suggestive, sensitive and succinct. Impossible to put this book down'

Jury report, Academica Literature Prize

'The strongest debut in years'

Vrij Nederland

'Puts the reader in a headlock and drags them from climax to climax'

Jury report, AKO Literature Prize

'Highly, highly recommended reading'

Savidge Reads

BONITA AVENUE

A NOVEL

PETER BUWALDA

Translated from the Dutch by
JONATHAN REEDER

PUSHKIN PRESS
LONDON

Pushkin Press
71–75 Shelton Street,
London WC2H 9JQ

Bonita Avenue first published in Dutch
as *Bonita Avenue* in 2010

This translation first published by Pushkin Press in 2014
This corrected and revised edition published in 2015

Nederlands
letterenfonds
dutch foundation
for literature

This book was published with the support of
the Dutch Foundation for Literature.

ISBN 9781782270713

Book design by Barbara Sturman
Offset by Tetragon, London
Printed in Great Britain by the CPI Group, UK

www.pushkinpress.com

"I'm a natural. I know, don't blow your own trumpet, but that's just how it is. Judo is a ruthless, cold-blooded sport. I've let myself be taken for a ride often enough in life and I'm naïve, but on the mat it's another story. Then I'm a calculator."

—Wim Ruska

"Y'know, I am to you what a gladiator was to the Roman citizen."

—Sasha Grey

1

When Joni Sigerius first took Aaron to meet her parents at their converted farmhouse one Sunday afternoon in 1996, her father's handshake was so firm it hurt. "You took that photo," the man said. Or was it a question?

Siem Sigerius was a stocky, dark-haired fellow with a pair of ears that you noticed immediately; they were lumpy, they looked deep-fried, and Aaron's judo past told him they were cauliflower ears. You got them from chafing against coarse cotton sleeves, from letting the flaps get scrunched up between hard bodies and rough mats; blood and pus built up between the cartilage and the baby-soft skin. Not doing anything about it meant being stuck with hardened, swollen lumps for good. Aaron had a pair of perfectly normal, unblemished, peachy-soft ears; cauliflower ears were reserved for champions, for the monomaniacs who scraped themselves across a tatami night after night. You had to earn ears like that, man-years had gone into it. There was no doubt in his mind that Joni's father wore them as a badge of honor, as proof of hard work and manliness. Aaron used to dread coming face-to-face with a similarly ear-marked beast at a tournament; a cauliflower ear on the horizon was bad news, as a competitive judoka he was useless. To hide his awe, he replied: "I take photos all the time."

Sigerius's ears quivered. His frizzy hair was close-cropped like felt against his broad, flat head. Despite his wardrobe—suits or corduroy trousers and Ralph Lauren polo shirts, the garb of the employer, the arrivé—you'd never take him, judging from the ears and that buffalo body, for someone who ran a university, let alone believe he was the Netherlands' greatest mathematician since Luitzen Brouwer. It was a physique you expected to see at a construction site, or on a freeway at night in a fluorescent vest, trudging behind a tar-spreader. "You know full well which photo," he said.

Joni, her sister, Janis, his wife, Tineke, all of them in the spacious living room knew which photo he meant. It had been printed full-page about a year earlier in the newspaper serving Tubantia University, the small college whose campus was tucked into the woods between Enschede and Hengelo, and where Sigerius was *rector magnificus*. He was standing on the bank of the Amsterdam-Rhine Canal, wearing nothing but a necktie, legs planted wide in the muddy, trampled grass, his genitals clearly visible under his cautiously rounded fifty-plus belly. The next day the photo had found its way into nearly every national newspaper, from the *NRC* to *De Telegraaf*, and ultimately even to the German *Bild* and a Greek daily.

"I have a hunch," Aaron conceded, wondering whether Joni had told her father who he was, or if Sigerius simply recognized him: the tall, bald photographer from the *Tubantia Weekly* who buzzed around the rector during public appearances like a horsefly with a single-lens reflex. The latter option, he thought, was more flattering, just as anyone on campus would feel flattered to be recognized by the charismatic man who at this very moment was crushing his hand to a pulp.

Simon Sigerius was, since his appointment in 1993, the Helios of Tubantia University, a blazing sun around which 8,000 students and hard-working academics orbited in calm little ellipses, surprised yet grateful that he would bathe *their* campus, of all places, in his warmth, and not the Binnenhof in The Hague, where he had turned down a plum government post, or one of the big American universities that vied for his favor. The first time Aaron had seen Joni's father was on television several years earlier, when he was still living with his folks in Venlo. The August following his final exams, something possessed him and his brother to become fanatical *Zomergasten* viewers, and one of those exhilarating, reflective Sunday evening marathon interviews was with a mathematical judoka—or was it a judo-practicing mathematician—anyway, a man whose "ideal TV evening" selection alternated video fragments of judo star Wim Ruska, edgy jazz, the Tokyo 1964 Olympics, and a Dutch comedian with documentaries about prime numbers and Fermat's Last Theorem. Aaron recalled a clip where a talkative physicist succeeded in giving sworn art majors like him and his brother the impression that they actually understood something of quantum mechanics. ("Richard Feynman," Sigerius said later. "We'd just buried him.") The man himself rubbed his stubbly jaw and talked about computers, about the universe, about M.C. Escher, as though anything else was a complete waste of time. It turned out he'd also judoed against Geesink and Ruska, but owed this television appearance mainly to the fact that he'd been awarded a Fields Medal, a distinction the host called the Nobel Prize for mathematics.

Since then Sigerius had grown into the national poster-boy scientist. Their rector would regularly, after a full workday on campus, pull up a seat on the evening news or a talk show and offer scientific commentary on current affairs, dazzlingly intelligent yet at the same time remarkably down-to-earth, never a word of gibberish. As photographer for the *Weekly* Aaron was front and center when Sigerius set up shop in the university's administrative wing, and what his camera saw, everybody saw: this was exactly the man

Tubantia needed. Just by being himself, Sigerius had liberated this overlooked and underrated university from its Twents timidity and inferiority complex. In his inaugural address he vowed to turn Tubantia into the Netherlands' premier research institute, a phrase that was broadcast that same day on the national news. He was a media magnet: no sooner had somebody uttered the word "university" than the cauliflower ears appeared on air, and *their* rector gave, on behalf of *their* university, his opinion on the competitive position of Dutch research schools, on girls' technical ability, on the future of the Internet, you name it. Sigerius just as effortlessly attracted top international scholars. Maybe it was a pity that the Fields Medal wasn't a genuine Nobel Prize, of course that was a pity, but his aura of mathematical genius still mesmerized investors in pure science, dyscalculaic MPs with education portfolios, communications giants and chip manufacturers whose labs sprang up around the university. And perhaps even schoolkids, they too recognized Sigerius's stubbly mug from TV; don't forget the precious progeny, each year the little brats had to be lured to that godforsaken hick town in Twente, how do you entice them, how do you hook them?

The pied piper of Tubantia, bare-assed in the daily papers. "Nice work," he said, and released Aaron's hand.

He'd taken the photo on a Sunday afternoon in Houten, just after they had finished rowing the Varsity, the traditional student regatta between boats from various universities. Blaauwbroek, the editor-in-chief of the *Weekly*, had assured Aaron that something special was on the cards: the Tubantia boat had an Olympic skipper on board as well as an oarsman with the Holland 8 Atlanta crew. Still, it was unusual for a university rector to sacrifice his free day to accompany a busload of boozing fratboys all the way to the Amsterdam-Rhine Canal. During the minor events he observed Sigerius out of the corner of his eye; the man stood on the soggy washland grass between the bar and the wooden bleachers, surrounded by a rat pack of hard-core Siemsayers, fawning undergrads who went out of their way to claim the rector as their own. Sigerius appeared to take pleasure in these boys' company. He had sucked them out of their big townhouses, they came swarming to the campus, hankering after a part-time job at the policy office or with public relations, flattering themselves on being invited to Sigerius's annual barbecue at his farmhouse. Aaron felt a pang of jealousy. Was the guy acting or genuinely enjoying himself?

Blaauwbroek's instinct was right: it was a historic Sunday afternoon for Tubantia. An "Oude Vier" from Enschede won the race for the first time in its 112-year history. Aaron was standing on the windy bleachers when the crowd around him roared, an explosion of hoarse cheers mixing with the crackle of plastic beer glasses. And because fratboys will always do the predictable thing, the gang of fanatics down at the water's edge tore off their clothes and swam, stark naked, out to the boat—at which moment he caught sight of the rector, who did something totally *un*predictable: Sigerius flung his half-filled beer tumbler into the grass and crossed the mudbank toward the water—Aaron had already clambered down from the bleachers, his camera lens followed the grinning rector as he removed his suit—everything came off, his shirt, his socks, his underwear, all except the necktie, a rowing tie, of course he'd let them foist a team tie on him, he was an honorary member of every club with a beer tap—and just before he broke into a sprint toward the canal to dive in after them, Aaron shouted his name, "Sigerius!," and snapped a photo of him from about four meters away, in all his glory.

Joni's dad was right, it *was* nice work, it was in all respects a fantastic photo. There was speed: his subject, filling the frame, stood on the balls of his feet, his arms thrown into the air, and while his torso appeared to already be heading for the glistening strip of water in the background, his bellowing mouth and furious eyes looked straight at the lens. The late-afternoon sun floodlit his naked body, the composition seemed meticulously arranged: Sigerius's outstretched left hand pointed more or less in the direction of the boat off in the canal; like a stylized sporting photograph, it resonated with a Greek-Olympian buzz. But this was all photographer blahblah—it was obvious why the newspapers wanted the picture. Even before Aaron left Houten he spent a quarter of an hour squabbling with a PR girl from Tubantia University, who insisted the photo had to be run by her department for approval, which of course would never be granted. On the contrary, the next morning the editors treated him like he was Robert Capa. "You bet I'm going to print that photo," snorted Blaauwbroek. "It's going to the printer's in an armored car, and I'll guard the presses with my life if need be."

After that the naked rector surfaced everywhere, blown up above the bar in the rowing club canteen, on a local debating society's T-shirts, on a poster announcing a massive summer festival on campus. Aaron saw him taped to dormitory bathroom doors. And, coincidence or no, Sigerius was increasingly the subject of wild speculation, in the fraternities on the Oude Markt, at parties in the campus housing. The rector was said to have traveled with Ruska through the Soviet Union and China en route to Japan, trashing Russian eateries on the way; he was purported to have been given electroshock treatment in an American madhouse after his big mathematical breakthrough; there were allegedly children from an earlier marriage who had come to no good. You only had to take a better look at the photo, and all doubt melted off the paper onto your lap. Everyone could see that Sigerius's ears were representative of the body hidden beneath those immaculate two-piece suits, mostly monotonous dark blue, sometimes light-gray pinstripe; the body, so crudely exposed, appeared surprisingly tough and sinewy, hard, unbreakable—"dry," to express it in sports terms. It was difficult not to have an opinion about that body, or about the clearly visible tattoos on the left side of his chest, over Sigerius's heart: Aaron recognized the inscription, in cheap, dark-blue sailor's ink, the pair of Japanese characters—"judo." It evoked conflicting reactions: in 1995, not only were tattoos relatively rare, they were downright tacky. But at the same time it tallied entirely with Sigerius's physicality, the apeman who would tip back his chair during meetings, balancing on the back legs until he had to grab the edge of the table, who rolled his shoulders loose like a trapeze artist during the coffee breaks, looking around to see if there was anyone who needed a thrashing before the meeting reconvened—murky keyholes through which the campus could catch a glimpse of another, discarded Sigerius, a thug, a he-man whose dream career had begun with two European judo titles, a fighter for whom the Munich Olympics should have been the highlight of his life.

In interviews they read that their rector was, like Ruska, tipped for a medal in 1972, but that a month before the Games, fate intervened: hungry for a custard donut, Sigerius crossed the Biltstraat in Utrecht, and just as the soft, creamy custard made contact with his mouth he was sideswiped by a motor scooter, whose metal footboard drove straight through his shin: *crack*, goodbye athletic career. What no journalist, no student, no scientist could get enough of was the idea that without that uneaten donut, the real miracle of Sigerius's career would never have taken place. The Miracle of the Antonius Matthaeuslaan, as he himself called it, after the street in Utrecht where for eight months he was confined to a bed in a tiny upstairs apartment, encased up to his groin in plaster. In the dark winter following the '72 Olympics, as Joni's father, bruised and broken, lay thumbing through a cardboard box of back issues of waiting-room magazines, he came across a stray exam booklet from the Dutch Mathematics Olympiad—a pamphlet full of uncommonly difficult problems for uncommonly brainy high-school students—and out of sheer boredom started scribbling sums in the margins. The next morning he was finished.

Exactly what happened in those twenty-four hours, which doors were flung open in Sigerius's traumatized athlete's head, is anybody's guess, but the fact was that within three years he had graduated summa cum laude from the Utrecht Mathematics Department, produced an alarmingly brilliant doctoral dissertation, and in the early '80s moved with his family to Berkeley, California. And there, at long last, he reached his Olympian peak. The Ramanujan of Utrecht forced a breakthrough in knot theory, a branch of mathematics that attempts to understand the number of ways in which a piece of rope can be tied—there is no conciser, simpler definition of his work—which earned him the Fields Medal in 1986 at the quadrennial congress of the International Mathematics Union.

All this shot through Aaron's mind when he recognized the woman sitting diagonally across from him. Despite her metamorphosis he knew straightaway who she was. There, next to a gum-chewing girl in the crimson sales uniform of some chain store, sat Joni's mother. He was blinded by a stroboscopic shock of white light.

He had been jolted out of a dreamless doze, and although he was still sitting in the express train to Brussels—they'd already passed Liège—his situation had altered drastically in the half hour he'd been sleeping. The carriage was now jam-packed, the evening light that shone through the windows appeared heavy, leaden, it was Belgian light, refracted and made turbid by the undulating landscape. Tineke Sigerius, he saw in a glance, leaned with her temple against the window and stared absently at the receding Walloon hills and single-steepled villages. His first reflex was to bolt, make a run for it, but his escape route was blocked by standing passengers—so to get up and move to the other end of the compartment was virtually impossible. His body acted as though it were racing up a steep slope in blind panic. He sat like this for several minutes, sweating, hyperventilating, exhorting himself to calm down, in anticipation of the confrontation.

Nothing happened. Whenever a bump or unexpected noise jerked Tineke Sigerius away from the view, he felt her eyes glide over his jittery body without stopping. *She pretended not to see him.* They were in the same boat, he realized, she didn't want this any more than he did. Happenstance had forced her to sit across from him, she was glad to get a seat in the overfull Sunday evening train, and only once she'd settled in did she recognize him. She must have been relieved to see that he was sleeping, a lucky break that allowed her to catch her breath and devise a strategy. She had boarded in Liège, which surprised him more than that she was heading for Brussels. What was Tineke Sigerius doing in Liège? He hadn't seen or spoken to her for eight years, of course plenty could have changed since then. Maybe she and Sigerius had left Enschede, maybe Sigerius was a European commissioner by now and they had moved to Belgium. This coincidence struck him as overwhelmingly unfair. Perhaps they had split up and she was living here alone? Of course someone else would have taken his place by now; she'd have a real son-in-law, a rich, successful one. Wallowing in self-pity, he fantasized that Tineke was not on her way to Brussels after all, but to Paris, the city of her grandchildren, where Joni now lived and worked (her American adventure could only have lasted a couple of years, he guessed) and ran a family together with some French moron, a guy with a fat face, greased-back black hair, and platinum cuff links, he could just see him opening their lacquered front door, his welcoming arms spread out for his mother-in-law on the granite doorstep.

Or was he mistaken? He glanced briefly in her direction in the hope that his conscience was playing tricks on him. No, that was Joni's mother all right. But look how skinny she'd got, it was like she'd been halved; her surreally narrow hips were wrapped in brown slacks with a neat pinstripe, she wore a tailored jacket and under it a cream-colored blouse, on her feet were boots with thin, elegant heels that on the old Tineke Sigerius would have bored straight through the chassis of the train carriage. Her mid-length hair was graying, not unflatteringly, and lay in a studied knot above her weirdly sunken face, which radiated something most people would describe as decisive, independent, and even sympathetic, rather than what he suspected even back when he was still Joni's boyfriend: ill-tempered, or downright nasty. And now it dawned on him: along with all that fat, the last bit of kindness had been boiled off, apparently for good. Although she had gained a certain femininity, the effect was undermined by an excess of loose skin around her cheeks and chin, by her baggy, pink-smeared eyelids that hung dejectedly over her lashes. She looked, in a word, bitchy.

Sigeriuses did not belong in Belgian trains, Sigeriuses belonged at home in Twente, where he had left them nearly eight years ago. It was precisely to avoid this kind of encounter that he had skipped town. It wasn't the cuisine that had drawn him to Linkebeek, a dump just south of Brussels where, he'd thought until five minutes ago, a person could start afresh as inconspicuously as in Asunción or Montevideo. He had imagined himself sheltered and unseen, Linkebeek was a village where the trees outnumbered the inhabitants, every lopsided thing that human hands had built was concealed from view by rustling, crackling, snapping wood.

He stole a glance at Tineke's hands. They lay in her lap, strangely fine and bony, emphatically segmented. How many tables, how many chairs, how many chests had those hands produced by now? Joni's mother made furniture in a workshop behind the farmhouse, she did back then anyway, chic and pricey interior furnishings that found their way into villas, offices, and stately canal houses across the Netherlands. Now, the one hand took hold of a finger on the other, one after the other, and gave each a little—bitter, he presumed—tug.

They had never hit it off, he and Tineke. They didn't gel. He thought back to the first time he and Joni slept at her parents' house; he, as usual, lay awake for hours on end, yearning desperately for Sigerius's wine cellar, and finally crept out of the narrow guest bed and down the open staircase, through the cool front hall and into the living room. From the kitchen he descended—routinely, he knew the way—the creaking cellar stairs and removed one of Sigerius's self-tapped bottles from the cast-iron rack, determined to uncork it at the kitchen counter and guzzle as much of it as possible in the hope that it would knock him out. But on his way back up the stairs he heard footsteps in the living room and had to duck back into the opening. Someone entering the kitchen, cupboards being opened and shut. Standing on his tiptoes, he peered over the edge, and what he saw was shocking and repulsive: he looked out onto a hideous back, a mountainside like you saw in nature films about South Africa or the Arizona prairies, but this was a mountain of flesh. It was Tineke. He counted six deeply pleated rolls of fat between her armpits and her backside, on which, halfway down, hung a sort of orange awning, which even with the best will in the world you couldn't call a "panty."

Joni's mother tore open a cardboard packet and poured its contents into her gaping mouth, half of it skittered off in all directions, chocolate sprinkles rained across the floor tiles. Once the package was empty she wrung it out, squashed it flat and shoved it deep into the trash can. He recoiled at the fleshy thud as she fell to her knees. She gathered up the spilt sprinkles with spit on her fingertips and palms. By then he had forgotten his cover, and as she sat there licking off her fingers she suddenly swung her head a quarter-turn and looked at him. "Hey," he said, once they had both got over the initial shock. "I was thirsty." She did not answer, she could at least have said, "I was hungry"; instead she hoisted herself up and stumbled out of the kitchen without a word, and only after he heard her bedroom door close down the hall did he return to his own bed.

And now? What could they possibly say to each other now? The train was too full, he reassured himself, for a scene, and he therefore tried to imagine how a controlled variant might proceed. So, Aaron, how are you these days? God, now that was one question he did not relish. He would rather continue his journey on the roof of the intercity than give an honest answer. He'd just spent the weekend at his parents' in Venlo—doctor's orders, just as everything he did was on doctor's orders. It was awful to have to admit he was sick, that he was tethered to neuroleptics and antidepressants. How do you tell someone you're a five-star basket case? How was he to tell this woman he was insane? That's me, Tineke: nothing but doctor's orders.

After the debacle in Enschede he worked briefly as a photographer for the better Brussels newspapers, but after a second severe psychosis in the winter of 2002 nearly did him in, he and his mental health counselors decided he should quit. Since then he had been driving around in a VW van refitted as a photo studio, taking individual and class pictures of primary-school children in Brussels and its surroundings. He would trace a numbered silhouette of each group photo on a lightbox. On his meticulously maintained website, fathers and mothers and grannies and grandpas could order reprints by clicking on a variety of formats, frames, and captions. The rest of his time—the hours, days, weeks, months that other men his age spent breeding, chasing careers, or maybe even raising idealistic hell somewhere—he just loafed about like some retired geezer, shuffling up the mossy steps to the town square, buying a newspaper in a secondhand bookshop appropriately called Once Upon a Time, picking up his meds in the pharmacy across from the ancient sycamore. Sometimes he snacked on a satay in the bistro at the end of the square, and then shambled back to the ridge, scuffing behind an imaginary Zimmer frame, and allowed himself to be swallowed up by his oversized, mortgage-free house.

According to his doctors he was a patient who "identified and acknowledged" his own condition, which meant he took his capsules voluntarily and thus was capable of living on his own. But that was about it. He led an entirely aimless existence. His motivation in life was avoidance: avoid stimulation, avoid excitement, avoid motivation itself.

He looked at his knees. What if he were to blurt it all out, right here in this chock-full train compartment? A detailed, concentrated, no-holds-barred monologue on his misery, on his psychosis-induced fears? A lecture, a short story, an epic poem on the immeasurable, irrational terror he had endured. The commuters hung cheek by jowl on their ceiling straps, no one could get away. If he really put his mind to it, if he were to wax eloquent, who knows, maybe the fear he described would spark over to his listeners, first to Tineke and the girl in the too-tight outfit, and then to everyone in the seats and aisles. And they would all be scared to death. His fear became everyone's fear. Frenzied panic, as though the Semtex in his brain had finally exploded.

He and Sigerius gelled just fine. In the winter of 1995 he had latched onto an intelligent, headstrong, beautiful girl named Joni, and Joni turned out to be a full-blood Sigerius. Two months later, to his amazement, there he was paying a house call to this guy and his family. And then the truly improbable happened: the man whom the entire campus sucked up to, the man whom he, the Venlo dropout, gawked at on the TV, *that* man extended him a calloused judo hand. And he accepted that hand, eager but also surprised. They became friends, and he took care not to wonder too often why.

Once a month, on a Saturday, he and Joni went to dinner in the refurbished farmhouse on the edge of the campus, a completely renovated white-stuccoed residence so utterly desirable that passersby slid "if-you-ever-decide-to-sell" notes through the mail slot in the dark-green front door. Although he teased Joni about her clingy attachment to her parents ("Now don't just call Daddy," he said when a blown fuse suddenly left her student flat pitch-black and deserted), he always enjoyed those visits. As they cycled out to the farmhouse, downtown Enschede would melt into the Drienerlo woods, which in turn flowed seamlessly into the campus, the backdrop for their four-year relationship. On those Saturdays, Tubantia seemed heavily pregnant. The humming meadows looked grassier than on weekdays, in his memory the wooded paths rolled gently, they cycled through an undulating landscape that smelled of pollen and where the ponds seemed inevitable. The shimmering water had collected at the lowest parts, just as hundreds of scholars and thousands of students had flowed precisely here in order to shine. You could hear their brains rustling, the fields and the trees and the berm seemed statically charged by the billions of bits and bytes that zoomed through the campus network under their feet. And when they returned home late in the evening, a prehistoric darkness enveloped the route, the gentle hills had become shallow dells, the greens and woods lairs for slumbering academic buildings. Applied Mathematics lay like a brontosaurus in its lake, the Tyrannosaurus rex of Technical Physics stretched up to the highest treetops, its slumbering head among the stipple of stars.

Sometimes they'd spend the night, and the next morning they would eat warm croissants with marmalade and drink jumbo glasses of fresh orange juice Sigerius squeezed for them after doing his forty laps of breast stroke in the campus pool, with the music of the Bill Evans Trio, the Modern Jazz Quartet, Dave Brubeck in the background, easy-listening Sunday morning jazz, which, he said, worked like salve on their morning moodiness. "Can you turn the salve down a little?" Joni complained, but Sigerius ignored her. With a raised index finger and one eye shut, he would call out: "Listen!" His wife and two daughters fell silent, dutifully stopped chewing and concentrated, just to indulge him in something that bored them, and after about ten seconds Sigerius released them with words like: "Beautiful, how Scott LaFaro plays *around* Evans. Hear that? *Around* him. Yeah, *now!*, this, that meandering bass, listen."

"Dad, I *hate* jazz," said Janis, or Joni, or both.

"Just listen to this, it's unreal! It's foreground and background at the same time, accompanist *and* virtuoso. No way am I turning this down."

At moments like this, Aaron was the one—and this was the basis for their bond, the simple fact that he was a boy, and not a girl, although there are also certain breeds of boy that get the creeps from jazz, for whom jazz is a complete waste of time—who remarked how tragic it was that Scott LaFaro smashed himself up in a car crash, and that Bill Evans, after that dramatic loss in 1961, never found another bassist of that caliber, although Chuck Israels of course did come close, certainly on *How My Heart Sings!* And before he'd finished with his little spiel, another heart sang: that of his father-in-law, who divided the world into jazz lovers and ignoramuses, and who had often announced, even in company, that he'd never met a young person so clued-up about jazz as Aaron, a feather in his cap that he not only left there but also, now and then, when no one was looking, stroked.

The Saturday evenings usually began in the sunroom, which was then spanking-new and, since the wall was taken out a year earlier, ran directly into the kitchen with its cooking island where Tineke prepared simple but tasty meals. After supper they retired, arguing or joking, to the old living room, and Tineke followed, carrying a tray of buttered *krentenwegge* and jittering coffee cups, and Joni opened the cabinet doors concealing the so-called unimportant television, and Sigerius kept up his end of the bargain by not answering his cell phone for an hour. The times when Janis went off to meet friends at a café downtown (usually right after *Frasier*, watching the end with her coat already on) and Tineke and Joni decided at around ten to watch a Saturday evening film, and Sigerius would ask: "How 'bout some tunes?" and he would not say no but yes, and they would disappear like a pair of schoolboys with a bottle of whiskey to the "music room," a space on the ground floor fitted out with two dark-red Chesterfields, an expensive NAD amplifier and CD player, a Thorens turntable, and two man-sized B&W speakers on spikes and bits of NASA foam rubber that Sigerius had wangled from Technical Physics; and there, seated among framed photos of Bud Powell and Thelonious Monk and Bill Evans, they listened to democratically chosen records (with bilateral veto power), original American LPs that Sigerius kept in tall, narrow, waxed beechwood cabinets designed and built by his wife.

Boys' stuff, just like that judo of theirs. In the farmhouse entrance hung a blown-up photo of five hulking, bare-chested men dragging a tree trunk up a hill: Geesink, Ruska, Gouweleeuw, and Snijders, and there, second from the left, with the tensed pecs and cropped dark curls above the flat face, was Sigerius himself. The Dutch national judo team in training for a World Championship, it must have been '65 or '66. Geesink, coach as well as teammate, sent his line-up into the woods near Marseilles; according to Sigerius he was a slave driver, but when tree trunks had to be dragged uphill, he was out in front. Up on top, while the others lay gasping for breath, Geesink grabbed the trunk at one end and, palpitating, shoved it out in front of him ten or so times, tore the clothes off his steaming body and jumped in a mountain creek. "If we offered him a water bottle, he refused, thought it was a waste of his thirst," said Sigerius, who soon discovered that Aaron had practiced judo until he was nineteen; and when he learned that he was even a black belt, Sigerius coaxed him into taking it up again, first in the senior group he coached on Thursday evenings at the campus athletic center, and when Aaron had regained, as they say, his old "feeling," Sigerius asked if he felt like going for a dan exam together.

Judo is a strangely intimate sport. A couple of times a week for a good two years, he and Sigerius rolled around the judo mat in each other's arms. Intensive, concentrated hours with the gym entirely to themselves. Talk was kept to a bare minimum. They gave themselves one year to hone their throwing and grappling techniques, Sigerius going for his fourth dan, he for his second. Each training session closed with the savage bouts he often thought back on, even now. And after each session he climbed into bed, occasionally in her parents' guest room, next to Joni, Sigerius's painstakingly raised daughter, the apple of his eye, and then Aaron noticed that Joni smelled vaguely like her father—maybe it was the washing powder Tineke used, he couldn't say. And while he mixed pheromones—he was a messenger of bodily scents, a bumblebee that traveled between two bodies of the same make—he felt that his strange happiness was doubled in their careful lovemaking after the training sessions, their muted groans in Sigerius's guest bed, his hand sometimes firmly over Joni's warm mouth to keep her from waking his strange friend a floor below.

The train rolled through Leuven. Tineke had closed her eyes, she pretended to sleep so that they would not have to acknowledge each other's existence. He admired her cold-bloodedness. He hadn't seen a single Sigerius since late in 2000, the year everything was blown to pieces. Nevertheless they roamed stubbornly through his subconscious, he still had recurring dreams—nightmares mostly—of Enschede.

Twilight was falling, the sky was purple, silvery on the edge of the wispy clouds. He caught the reflection of his own bald head in the window. He felt himself become calmer, and somber. A village unfurled itself alongside a canal, a wafery moon hung curiously early in the sky. Soon he would walk home through the moldy dusk of Linkebeek. The deadness that awaited him, the cold, high-ceilinged rooms he had longed for back in Venlo. He was just thankful that it was Tineke who sat there ignoring him, and not Sigerius himself.

It had never been completely relaxed. In Sigerius's company

he could freeze up, literally, becoming dramatically paralyzed: his jaws clamped shut, bringing about a barely controllable tension that spread from his neck vertebrae and his shoulders throughout his entire body. He was, for hours on end, a statue of himself fighting against total paralysis, desperately talking all the while, praying his voice would continue to function. If Sigerius were to give him a push during one of these moments, he'd have fallen over and smashed to bits like a Chinese vase.

He experienced their friendship as magical—before he'd come to the campus to take up photography, he had flunked out of the Dutch program in Utrecht, was chucked out on his ear, and here he had simply walked right into the inner chamber of the academic heart, just like that—but mendacious as well. He made himself out to be more than he was. It all started with the jazz. One Sunday at the farmhouse, not so long after their first meeting, they slurped hot coffee from slim-handled mugs. Sigerius, distant, his mind on other matters, got up and went over to a hypermodern metal cabinet housing a record player and put on an LP. Jazz. Even before he'd sat back down on the long, pale-pink sofa next to his wife, Aaron recognized the music. He waited a bit just to be sure, but he was right: the theme, the round, slightly coquettish piano-playing, this was Sonny Clark, and the LP was called *Cool Struttin'*. He could see the classic Blue Note jacket before him, a pair of woman's legs strolling over (he presumed) a New York City sidewalk. Over Joni's and Tineke's heads he said: "Nice album, *Cool Struttin'*."

Sigerius, with his amazing morning stubble (it would take Aaron a whole week to cultivate such a shadow), opened his brown eyes wide. "*Cool Struttin'* is a *great* album," he said, his voice more strident, higher, as though a piano tuner had taken a wrench to it. "So you know it. *Cool Struttin'* is by far Clark Terry's best LP."

Clark Terry? Aaron got it at once: Sigerius was mistaken, he was confusing Sonny Clark with Clark Terry, an amusing gaffe, but he decided not to rub it in. It was hardly tactful to swoop in like a schoolmarm and rap your new father-in-law on the knuckles, but to just play dumb, no, he was too proud for that. "I'm with you," he said, "this was Sonny Clark's best band, Philly Joe Jones, for once, holding back on the drums. Not going at the cymbals like a hooligan."

Eyes like saucers, briefly, then suddenly shut. "Terry. It's Clark Terry."

"This is Sonny Clark on piano," Aaron said, more decisively than necessary. "Terry's a trumpet player."

"You sure about that?" Joni asked.

Sigerius bolted up off the sofa and slid past his wife, his heels ticking as he marched over to the novel metal cabinet which, he learned later, Tineke had made herself. He pulled out the record jacket, glanced at both the front and back cover, propped it up next to the turntable and closed the cabinet. He returned, painfully slowly, to the sofa and sat back down.

"You're right. Of course you're right. And damn, I even saw that Terry in the Kurhaus. And in Boston too, later. Ladies, I'm going to have to watch my words from now on."

That is precisely what Aaron did for the remaining quarter of an hour; Sigerius didn't catch that his knowledge of jazz was wafer-thin after all, that the Sonny Clark album was pure luck. He knew *Cool Struttin'* so well because of that pair of legs, he'd picked up the album at a flea market because of the jacket, it spent a few years taped to the door of his wardrobe, the vinyl disc collecting dust on the turntable. Sure, he liked jazz, but to be honest, his heart lay with blues and rock 'n' roll.

But honesty was not his speciality. Now that Sigerius had promoted him to jazz expert, to someone with an encyclopedic knowledge on, of all things, his own turf, to a kindred spirit, he needed to get to work. That same week he let a nervous guy in a black turtleneck at Broekhuis bookshop talk him into the *Penguin Guide to Jazz on CD*, a 1,500-page jazz bible that, according to the turtleneck, not only contained the entire history of jazz, but separated the wheat from the chaff with a handy system of stars. Across from Broekhuis, at the discount-book warehouse, he bought a biography of Miles Davis, a *Jazz for Dummies* and a book called *Billie and the President*. In his wallet he had the business card of a retired dentist in Boekelo, a silver-gray man in red trousers who had been standing behind him one day at the campus record library as he checked out a Bud Powell record. The man told him he had 800 original jazz LPs at home—American pressing, thick, pitch-black vinyl, sturdy cardboard jackets—"you can have them for a guilder apiece," at which Aaron nearly hit the roof with fermented craving. "Give me a call," the man said, and he did just that, the very same evening, and he kept on calling him, twice a week at first, then twice a month, brief, hasty exchanges in which the man was always too busy, or he was about to leave for the States, or he was ill, or was about to be; "call me again soon," but "soon" gradually became more of an obstacle, a testiness crept into the exchanges—until Aaron stopped believing him. Stick your LPs up your retired old ass. But now he decided to take the plunge and cycled out to Boekelo, on the other side of town. He rang the bell at a seniors' apartment that corresponded to the address on the tattered card. A Turkish man answered the door.

So he plundered the record library and, when Joni wasn't with him, studied jazz history as if he had to program the North Sea Festival that summer. He perused the artist entries, concentrating first on the big shots who got the most pages—the Parkers, the Ellingtons, the Monks, the Coltranes, the Davises—and after that, the rest of the '50s jazz greats: Fitzgerald, Evans, Rollins, Jazz Messengers, Powell, Gillespie, Getz. He listened to all their records, jotted down biographical particulars in a notebook, etched it all in his memory, Blue Note, Riverside, Impulse!, Verve, Prestige. It was like his former studies, only that fucking *Kapellekensbaan* had taken him three weeks and *Giant Steps* just thirty-seven minutes and three seconds. Books had dominated the first half of his 1990s, he read like a maniac, entire evenings, at bus stops and in waiting rooms, when he lay awake at night: tallying titles, keelhauling oeuvres, five years of forced labor to recoup his humiliating comedown in Utrecht—now it was "mission accomplished" in just five *weeks*. Then he knew it was safe to go back in the water. Another five weeks later, he stood next to Sigerius in De Tor listening to the Piet Noordijk Quartet, sipping whiskey and putting his faith in a silicone-implant jazz knack.

Deceitful? Of course it was. But everyone in that farmhouse lied. They were a family of prevaricators. Although he knew this was a lame excuse, he told himself that all of them had secrets—Sigerius, Tineke, Joni, him, they all had something to hide. How long had he not known that Janis and Joni weren't Sigerius's real daughters? Long. And they'd have been quite happy not to tell him at all. Not a word about the real genetic set-up. Sometimes he had the impression that they'd forgotten it themselves.

It was at least a year before Joni told him, during a weekend in the woods in Drenthe, that her "procreators" divorced when she was five. More than the news itself, he was surprised that she waited so long to bring up something as relatively ordinary as divorced parents, but she was so dead serious about it, uncharacteristically earnest, that he didn't let on. They were staying in a secluded clapboard cabin about twenty kilometers south of Assen, and the cloying romanticism of isolation and a wood-burning stove apparently gave her that little extra incentive to share. During a crisp winter walk in the woods she challenged him to guess which of her parents was the "real" one: Come on, Siem or Tineke? Good question, he said, but in fact it was a piece of cake. Sigerius, of course.

"Why d'you think that?"

"Just because. It's a wild guess. You don't look much like him, but not like your mother either. You're both athletic. Athletically built too."

In truth, they didn't look at all alike. Sigerius was dark and swarthy, had eyes like cold coffee, he looked like a gypsy, almost sinister. His beard growth would make an evolutionary biologist's mouth water. Joni, on the other hand, was fair and blond, butterflyish, had a face so smooth and symmetrical that Sigerius couldn't possibly have had anything to do with it. And yet he detected a common denominator: their drive. Father and daughter possessed the same compulsive energy, wouldn't tolerate dallying or doubt, hated the thought of giving up, and couldn't understand it when other people—he, for instance—did so. Joni, like Sigerius, was smart and tough and decisive. Maybe it was genetic.

"So you think Siem is my real father because I'm not fat."

He'd never really given it any thought, he realized, there had been no reason to. "Yeah," he said. "No . . . Also the way you interact. You and Siem are in cahoots, you can see that within ten minutes. Janis is a mama's girl. You're more like your father."

"But Janis and I are blood sisters. So there goes your theory."

"Just tell me then."

"So you think it's Siem?"

"Yeah. That's what I think, yeah."

"Nope," she sang, laughing. She kicked some dead branches and rotting remains of fallen leaves, as though the gravity of her disclosure evaporated at once because he'd been wrong. She didn't say so, but her odd excitement told him she was glad he'd guessed Sigerius; he even suspected she would just as soon have left his illusion intact. And he had to admit feeling a bit disappointed—it was a pity there was no genetic tie—but of course he didn't let her see that. Maybe Joni felt the same way, because even before they had returned to the clammy cabin her high spirits had dissipated into an inwardness he had not seen in her before.

While he silently warmed up chocolate milk on the two-burner stove and she sat on the moth-eaten sofa with an old issue of *Panorama* on her lap, leafing through an article on skating, he thought about the natural easiness with which she and her sister called Sigerius "Dad." They said "Dad" with a teasing or admiring smile, wheedled him with "ple-e-e-e-ease Daddy" in his ear when they wanted something, groaned "Da-haaaad" when he irritated them. When he asked her about it, she said with a certain pride that it had been like that since day one; from the day in 1979 when Siem Sigerius and Tineke Profijt married at city hall in Utrecht—without hoopla, without tuxedo, without Rolls or Bentley, without a reception—they had addressed their stepfather as "Dad." She was six, Janis was three. From that day on, Joni called herself Joni Sigerius. Her real surname, Beers, a word that she only grudgingly revealed, had been encased in cement and dropped to the bottom of the Vecht River.

Later, back in her student flat, she showed him ochre-brown Polaroid photos of an implausibly tiny Joni, her head sprouting two intensely blond ponytails, a surprisingly ordinary-looking little girl, an almost homely six-year-old, sticking out her tongue as she hung on the leg of a youthful Sigerius—the leg of her new father, who had let his beard grow wild. Her mother, still trim, not skinny like now, but just trim, in a sober dark-green pants suit, the snot-nosed Janis cradled in her arm, wore large brown sunglasses in all the photos because an ophthalmologist had scraped a cold sore from her left eyeball a week earlier.

Keen to put the past behind them, mother and daughters accompanied their new chieftain to America, to Berkeley, where Sigerius had been appointed assistant professor in the Mathematics Department. Not there, nor at any subsequent campus, did Joni Sigerius volunteer any information about her biological father. Aaron had to press her just to learn the man's first name. "Theun." "Theun," he repeated. "Theun Beers. OK. And what did he do?" Her real father was a traveling salesman in tobacco articles, the nameplate on their front door said "smoking accessories" and behind two small doors in the tall china cupboard were cartons of cigarettes, arranged by brand, that Beers had acquired surreptitiously and sold duty-free to smoke-logged characters who appeared in their living room at all hours, usually after Joni's bedtime, to place their gravelly voiced orders. Her father often only got home after nine, he ate his meatballs and schnitzels in salesmen's cafés and roadside diners. Even at the weekend they seldom saw him, she said, because then he rehearsed or performed with his band, a not entirely unsuccessful blues band where he sang and played guitar.

"Blues? Did he make any records?"

"How should I know? I think so, yeah."

(*Blues?*—he would have given anything to race off to his house on the Vluchtestraat to pore through his three editions of *Oor's Pop Encyclopaedia* in search of Theun Beers. A blues band, Jesus, *now* she tells me. And sure enough, the next day he found, in his oldest encyclopedia, under the heading "Netherblues," a three-line piece about Beers and his band: Mojo Mama, "blues-rock formation with lead singer and guitarist Theun Beers, who enjoyed a brief cult status"; once "Utrecht's answer to Cuby + Blizzards," cut "three LPs of varying quality," was "famous primarily for its live act." When he read this he pictured Tineke, Joni's mother, as a groupie, at about the weight she was today, flower-power hat, platform shoes, sitting backstage on big Theun's lap.)

Although uncles at birthday parties liked to joke that Theun never had to say "I'm going to go get some smokes . . . don't wait up," he had vamoosed long before the divorce, leaving a heavily pregnant Tineke and a toddler behind. She could never remember him even sleeping in the same house, which of course couldn't have been true, but never mind.

"Do you ever think about him?"

"Never. Only during this kind of conversation. Only if somebody asks if I ever think about my real father do I think about my real father."

The times he pressed her on that mantra of hers, if he asked "but *why* don't you ever think about Theun Beers?," for instance when they were at his place watching *Long Lost Family* on TV, she assured him that it was not out of pique, or out of vengeance, or some kind of reproach, and no, she hadn't "suppressed" him; the fact was that her begetter had simply vanished from her life without leaving a single impression, and that was that.

On the last day of their weekend in Drenthe, rather late actually, it was such an obvious question, he asked if Sigerius had also been married before. "Yeah," she said drily. They had just giggled their way through a dolmen museum and were cycling side by side along a bike path parallel to a provincial road. He slammed on the brakes of his rental bike. "Why didn't you say so earlier? Why don't you ever tell me stuff?"

"I'm telling you now, aren't I?" she shouted, without stopping. "And he's got a son too."

"Say *what*?"

"He's got a son." Without getting off, she did a wobbly 180-degree turn and rode back to him. "A son named Wilbert. Wilbert Sigerius."

"So you and Janis have a stepbrother?"

"If you want to call it that. We never see him, he leads his own life. Just like us."

He bombarded her with questions, but she couldn't or wouldn't tell him much about this Wilbert, except that in her youngest days she had been his downstairs neighbor. ("Downstairs neighbor?" he cried. "OK, explain.") She told him a complicated story that took him a while to get straight. In the early '70s the two families had lived on the Antonius Matthaeuslaan in Utrecht, Sigerius with his first wife, a certain Margriet, and their little boy, that'll have been Wilbert, at number 59B, the upstairs apartment. Below, at 59A, lived Tineke with this Theun and their two young daughters.

She remembered the fights between Sigerius and Margriet above their heads, altercations they could literally follow word for word as they sat at the kitchen counter, she and Tineke, with Janis in her high chair, eating sweetened yogurt, just as she recalled Wilbert's menacing tirades, frenzied, thunderous stomping, Margriet's histrionics. Within a few years, that neighborliness culminated in the classical three-way marital drama: Tineke and Siem, she downstairs and he upstairs, fell in love and were caught in the act by Wilbert's mother, that Margriet woman, although Joni wasn't privy to the details.

"Cheating rats," said Aaron.

Prior to the marital meltdown, the racket-making ruffian from upstairs would often traipse through their house to the paved courtyard out back, trampling strawberry plants and knocking over pots. He smelled of sweet soap. After the divorce, Wilbert came to see them just once, she seemed to recall. When Sigerius took them with him to America, that was the end of that.

In the photo album from that period Aaron spotted an overgrown gnome with jet-black hair, the same widely spaced, inky eyes as his father and unpleasantly full lips, insolent as hell, you could just see it. Only later did Joni tell him that he had been the neighborhood bully, a boy who easily terrorized even the older children. Forced them to eat toads he'd caught. Fabricated small bombs with petrol he had siphoned out of parked cars, peed through old people's mail slots. Coerced the daughter of people up the road into stealing money from her mother's wallet. Joni's only first-hand memory of Wilbert's antics concerned one warm evening when he showed up with one of his cohorts, having found the downstairs front door open, and suddenly stood there in her bedroom. They each carried an enormous green rubber boot, probably Sigerius's rain boots (when he was still just the upstairs neighbor), that they'd filled to the brim with sandbox sand. The boys poked a yellow PVC pipe between the bars of her bed, goaded her into crying, and when her three-year-old mouth went wide open, they dumped the sand over her face. The grainy taste, how the sand found its way into her throat like a fist, clammy, cool, and dark in her eyes and nose. She'd nearly choked, she said.

A freight train rumbled along the parallel tracks. Startled, Tineke opened her eyes, and for two deafening seconds she stared at him. In Venlo he had taken his oxazepam, but he could feel that the straitjacket around his heart muscles needed an extra tug. So much was evident in those serrated blue irises: condemnation, contempt, disappointment. Arrogance. With a shudder she folded down the collar of her jacket and closed her eyes again. He collected saliva in his cheeks and wriggled his wallet out of his back pocket. Focusing on Tineke's closed eyes, he slid out a strip of oxazepam and pushed two tablets through the foil. The girl in the red shop uniform watched him, it was the first time she deigned to look at him, she stopped chewing momentarily. A thin line had been traced around her lips with black make-up pencil, vulgar, dated, "a black-belt blowjob," Joni used to call it. He put the pills in his mouth and sent them, riding on the gob of spit, off to his stomach.

Not long after Joni's unbosoming, he and Sigerius were sitting at the corner of the long bar in the athletic center's canteen, both of them slightly woozy from the hot shower following their usual Thursday evening training, he with a mug of beer and a cigarette, Sigerius on tonic water as he still had work to do. His father-in-law was casually dressed: a pristine baby-blue lambswool sweater over a button-down shirt, calves bulging inside ironed corduroy trousers, his wide, loafered feet resting on the bar stool, against which his corpulent leather gym bag leaned like an indolent beast. Every few minutes Sigerius raised his hand to greet a passerby. Aaron felt the slight awkwardness of being in the company of the rector in public.

The canteen was large and 1980s-bleak and reminded him of the Pac-Man playing surface, half-wall cement block partitions that prevented the potted plants from getting enough light, foosball, and two pool tables. The low-rise flannel-upholstered seating units were empty at this late hour, chlorine fumes from the indoor swimming pool somewhere in the belly of the sports complex mixed with the odor of deep-fried bar snacks and the linoleum floor. They recapped their training session, chatted about the university, about the Student Union, which was a thorn in Sigerius's side, this is off the record, he kept saying. Aaron had been beating around the bush for a few weeks, but now he said: "By the way, Siem, d'you know, I had absolutely no idea you have a son."

Sigerius was in the middle of a gulp of tonic water. He set his glass down on the bar, wiped his mouth and after a few seconds' silence said: "Well, well. So she told you. Couldn't keep it under wraps forever."

"I was really surprised. I had no idea."

"Are you shocked?"

"A bit. A bit. It's kind of unexpected, of course. You're all such a happy family. I'd never have guessed."

"I completely understand. I really do. It's no joke either."

Aaron, struck by Sigerius's grave tone of voice, chose his words carefully. "Of course . . . ," he replied, "these things happen. Statistically speaking. Every day, in fact."

Sigerius rasped his hand over his stubbly chin, he took a deep breath and exhaled through his nose. "That's kind of you," he said, "but I don't think that's true."

"Divorce isn't common?" Aaron asked, surprised.

"*Divorce?*" Sigerius grimaced at him, his ears trembled with surprise, but his eyes suddenly grew tired, he aged on the spot. Grinning, he plucked a loose hair from his sleeve and let it flutter to the floor. Then he stared straight ahead, as though he were weighing something up.

"Aaron," he said, "I'm not sure what you're getting at, but I'm talking about manslaughter. About a brutal murder that the lawmakers oblige us to call manslaughter. The bastard killed a man. He's been locked up for four years already. You didn't know that part, did you?"

It was nearly eleven at night. About ten meters away the beanstalk behind the bar stood rinsing glasses, his shirtsleeves rolled up; with the exception of two sweatsuited chinwaggers at the pool table, the canteen was empty. Everything they said reached into the pores of the cement blocks. The brief silence he was forced to drop was a thing, a heavy object. A murderer? Blushing, he said: "Siem, you're joking. Please tell me you're making this up."

"I wish I were." In a forced attempt to remain offhand about the hard facts of his life, Sigerius told him about his one and only offspring, a guy about Aaron's age. Nothing to write home about. A life of misdemeanors, drug abuse, relapses. The very same Wilbert whom Joni had so dispassionately described became in Sigerius's version a criminal who had twisted himself like a corkscrew into a life of wretchedness. One weekday in 1993 Wilbert Sigerius hit rock bottom by beating a fifty-two-year-old man to death. "The Netherlands is a wonderful country," said Sigerius. "No matter how dysfunctional you are, there's a great big professional circle of friends ready to help you. Anyone who doesn't have the balls to just get out and work is given a nice subsidized job, even if they've got a criminal record."

He sounded unexpectedly bitter, and a damn sight more conservative than usual—this scenario was clearly way too close to home, something that forced him to throw his liberal principles overboard. Aaron was glad Sigerius did not look at him, perhaps out of shame, so he could let his own emotions cool off, that usually worked best; he was overcome by a strange exhilaration that consisted partly of delight, grateful to be taken into another's confidence, and partly of discomfort with this sudden intimacy. It felt as though they were dancing across the canteen together.

"They gave him a pair of overalls and a decent salary, so he had somewhere to show up in the morning with his lunchbox. After grief followed by even more grief that we won't go into right now, he was given the chance to start over again—what more could a person want? At the Hoogovens steelworks, of all places. An excellent company, tens of thousands of Dutch men and women have earned an honest living there for the past 100 years. A sporting chance, you'd say. But the first spat he gets into, the kid picks up a sledgehammer and beats his direct superior, a foreman looking forward to a gold watch from the head office, flat as a pancake. I sat in the public gallery when the prosecutor described what various witnesses had seen. What happens to a person when you bash them with a four-kilo sledgehammer."

Sigerius wet his mustache by pulling his lower lip over it, pressing it flat with his thumb and index finger. Aaron didn't know what to say. This was not your average revelation. It was a fucking bombshell. He thought he knew a thing or two about Sigerius, he thought he understood what this man, whom he looked up to despite desperately trying not to, had dealt with his entire life, understood the path to success his life had taken, the essentials of that life, and now he discovered he knew absolutely nothing. (That sensation of ignorance, he realized later, was something he should have just got used to: it was the story of his life in Enschede. He never knew anything.)

"Eight years," Sigerius said loudly; the bartender, quite a bit closer to them now, was scrubbing the draining racks. "The prosecutors demanded ten plus mandatory psychiatric treatment. But he impressed them at the psychiatric observation clinic . . . yeah, there, he did well," and here he lowered his voice, "entirely compos mentis. My son is not at all stupid."

As though it were a stiff drink rather than tonic water, he put the glass to his lips and drained it. He set the empty glass down with gentle precision on the broad cherrywood bar.

The train slowed down, the suburbs of Brussels slid into view, the passengers standing in the aisle peered out, craning their necks at the gray, haphazard urban sprawl. Tineke, who had reopened her eyes, brought a small mirror and dark-red lipstick out of a red-leather handbag, painted her wrinkled mouth with a steady hand, repacked the accessories and stared, scowling, at a point just between Aaron and the man next to him.

Wilbert Sigerius. He had never met the fellow, after all these years the fascination had long since faded. Still, it occurred to him that everything he had found out about her stepson over the course of his Enschede years must have been just as awful for Tineke as for Sigerius. She had contributed two healthy daughters, girls to whom they had given a wholeheartedly devoted, not to mention an indulgent and privileged, upbringing; Joni and Janis had both grown into outgoing, stable, at times maddeningly rational adults. Sigerius, on the other hand, had saddled her with that viper.

The train trundled into Brussels Central Station and shuddered to a halt. The crowd in the aisle moved slowly toward the still-shut doors: waiting quietly for salvation, a hundred silent heads in isolated prayer. Tineke didn't budge. He could just as easily stay in the train until Brussels South, although there was a train to Linkebeek from Central as well. The girl removed her chewing gum from her black-lined mouth and reached across Tineke's lap toward the metal rubbish bin. Then she stood up, brushed against his left knee, and joined the current of disembarking passengers. Now Joni's mother stood up too and, her back to him, removed a tartan roller-suitcase from the luggage rack. Seen from behind, with those slender, pointy hips, he would never have recognized her.

On an impulse, he decided to get off, he wasn't sure exactly why. Should he let this complete coincidence simply evaporate into nothing? All he had to do was stay put, and the meeting wouldn't even have taken place. His heart pounding, he left the train, the stony smell of the platform filled his lungs. Almost against his will he pursued Tineke, maintaining a five-step distance, as she trotted up the stairs toward the central hall. Once in the light-brown marble open space, she set the valise down on its back wheels and dragged it into the bustle. Just inside the main entrance she took a cell phone from the pocket of her maroon wool overcoat, punched in a number, and started to talk. He saw her step into Brussels, she was gone, and again he hesitated.

Instead of returning to his platform, instead of *not* living, he ran after her, into the open air. He scanned the shadows cast by the streetlamps. She was not part of the throng at the intersection leading to Brussels' Grote Markt. He walked to the edge of the sloping sidewalk and looked around. There she was, she had turned right onto the Putterij; quickening his pace, he closed the dark gap of twenty meters, and before he knew what he was doing he placed his hand on the heavy fabric of her coat. She stood still and turned around. She looked surprised, startled. Her meticulously made-up skin covered her jaws and cheekbones like wrinkled paper.

"Tineke," he mumbled, "I . . ."

"I beg your pardon?" she asked kindly.

"Tineke," he said, more forcefully this time, "I don't know if this is the best . . ."

This time she really looked at him, he could see she focused. She stuck out a hand that briefly touched his arm, as though that extra tactile assistance might help. "Weren't you sitting across from me just now in the tr—?" Her face changed again, she raised her droopy eyelids as far up as possible, her mouth became an astonished, scarlet "O."

"Aaron!" she cried, "of course! Aaron Bever. But my boy, what . . ." She let go of the handgrip on her suitcase, it toppled over. She took a step toward him, grasped his shoulders, and gave him two kisses. Over her fragile shoulders he saw a car pull up to the curb, a sporty dark-blue BMW that flashed its headlights twice. She turned and waved. When she looked back at him, she said: "We're in a hurry. I have to be going. But Aaron, I absolutely didn't recognize you. You've . . . changed. Enschede was so long ago . . ." She clutched his lower arm, looked straight at him. "Oh dear . . ." she said, "but how are *you* . . . things turned out so badly . . ."

He was too flabbergasted to reply. Any moment the door of the BMW could swing open and Sigerius would come walking their way. He gasped for breath, felt dizzy. Since he could think of nothing else to say, he stammered: "Say, Tineke, how's Siem? Is that him?" He gestured feebly at the impatient car.

She let go, just as abruptly as she had grasped him. She took a step back, her face slammed shut like a lead door.

"*What?*" she spat. "You must be joking."

"No," he said. "Why?" He felt his eyes go watery.

"You rotten kid," she said. "What do you want from me? What are you doing here? Are you stalking me?"

The car door opened. A small man of about forty-five got out, his wavy black hair and trimmed beard glistening under the street lights. They looked at each other. The man, who in an unnerving, aggressive way was not Sigerius, smiled politely. Another car swerved around them, honking, and behind the BMW a minibus switched on its flashers.

Tineke reached for the handle of the passenger door.

"You don't know?" she said. "You really don't know, do you?" She laughed awkwardly, her face a scrawny grimace of disbelief. "Siem is dead." She shouted over the traffic. "He's been dead for eight years. We buried him in early 2001. Or are you just trying to upset me?"

"No," he said.

Then she got in.

2

According to his résumé, Sigerius has a pretty good understanding of coincidence. In his Berkeley days, and later in Boston, he taught practical courses in probability theory and stochastic optimization to first-year math and physics students. He was paid to impart the sensation of mathematical order amid chaos to classrooms full of emotionally stunted number nerds. These were chess players, ZX-spectrum scholars, Rubik's wizards, not one of whom claimed a place on a university athletic team, no basketball, no baseball; they had come to Berkeley to serve quantum physics, to unleash the digital revolution. Before he bombarded the boys and that single stray girl with discrete stochasts, probability space, and Bayes's theorem, he challenged them to relate the most spectacular piece of coincidence they'd ever experienced. Let's have it, your most outrageous twist of fate, your spookiest fluke. As a teaser he made a probability analysis on the blackboard of the most remarkable of the students' anecdotes.

Sigerius was reminded that he was dealing with quick-witted young adults when, once, a pale, severe-looking boy at the back of the lecture hall raised his hand and launched into a story about his grandparents' honeymoon in the 1930s. They are on a cruise to South America and just off the coast of Chile, his grandmother drops her wedding ring overboard. Sixty years later, celebrating their diamond anniversary, the couple takes the same exact cruise, and the two of them are there when a fisherman reels in a tuna and flings it onto the deck. Gramps insists that the fish be cut open, and what do you think? (Even though it's been a good fifteen, nearly twenty years since those classes, he still recalls, at that "what do you think" and the kid's serious face scanning the classroom, the smell of pulverized blackboard chalk. In his memory, the orange curtains he always drew halfway right after lunch billow in front of the wide-open windows. His stuffy classroom was located on the ninth floor of Evans Hall; summers there lasted six, seven months.)

And? No ring.

When he told that joke to Aaron Bever recently, Aaron nodded, got up, took a novel out of the bookcase and showed him where Nabokov had pulled the same stunt half a century earlier.

Coincidence is at its most striking when it manifests itself as executioner—he and his students agreed on that. When the chuckling subsided, the same translucent young man told a story about an altogether different excursion. About his brother, who was planning to travel through Europe with his girlfriend, from the northernmost point in Scandinavia down to Gibraltar in three months. They flew to Kirkenes, a town at the very tip of Norway, rented a car and made their way toward Sweden along a flat two-lane road. During that tranquil, snow-white leg of the journey they encountered just a single oncoming vehicle, a lurching Danish Scania towing a heavy trailer. Just as they pass the truck—or actually, a few seconds before, or maybe the coincidence had kicked in several minutes earlier, no, it was probably a matter of long-term metal fatigue that had been eating its way through the nuts and bolts—the truck loses its trailer. The shaft comes loose. The deep-frozen shaft that juts perpendicular to the steerable front axle turns, like a jouster's lance, in the direction of the rental car and bores through the windshield. The trailer flips over, flinging the car into the snowbank like an empty beer can. The girl is decapitated. The brother, at the wheel, escapes with a bruised wrist.

The boy was restrained and controlled. He sat straight up in his seat. Siem looked at him from the blackboard, he was wearing a button-down shirt with a large, pointy collar and while he talked his hand kept flattening out the same sheet of graph paper, densely scribbled with formulas. "Coincidence, huh?" Siem said. In the weeks that followed the boy never returned to class. Speculation around the coffee machine had it that the brother was himself.

What did Sigerius want to teach them? And what is he trying to tell himself now? That the probability of the improbable is huge? That so-called bizarre coincidences happen all the time. That a mathematician's job is to judge the bizarre on its quantitative value, that is: to strip the coincidence down to its bare probability instead of assigning it some magical significance. He stares at the rain as it runs down the windows of the restaurant where the task force has convened. The brightly lit space is narrow and feels like a city bus in a car wash. The lobsters and crabs in the unappetizing wall of stacked-up aquariums next to the entrance are secretly hoping for a deluge that will upset the balance of power. Their claws are spotted with rust-colored freckles, sometimes one shifts as though it's got an itch.

He tries to concentrate on his conversation with Hiro Obayashi, seated to his left at the Formica table where the eleven-man group of scholars is eating. Every Saturday evening following their afternoon session at Jiaotong University they meet at this table in this restaurant on Huaihai Zhong Lu, it's a long-standing tradition. And usually he enjoys it, just as he enjoys these junkets to Shanghai, because that's what they are, of course, pleasure trips. His membership in the Asian Internet Society goes back long before he became *rector magnificus*, and one of the conditions of his appointment was that this "valuable Asian connection" would remain intact. Of the utmost importance to the position of Tubantia University, he had argued, and so forth. Why of course, they agreed, absolutely, it goes without saying. As he wished. Complete bullshit is what it was, but even then he knew he'd be needing them, his jaunts to Shanghai. Just to get away from the campus for a bit, away from the glasshouse.

"To be honest," he says, "I found the puzzles a bit . . . how shall I put it . . . a bit boring."

Obayashi, Professor of Information Technology at the University of Tokyo, opens his eyes wide; his skin stretches like a mayonnaise-yellow mask over his broad skull.

"But maybe I'm not the right person to judge them." Sigerius wipes his mouth on his napkin and, in an attempt to avoid Obayashi, looks around the room. Like every other decent restaurant in China, this one is ugly as sin. The lighting is merciless, certainly now that someone has thrown a blanket over Shanghai, the decor is haphazard: no two tables have the same shape or height; even the flickering and humming fluorescent lights, which radiate X-rays down on steaming dishes of—it must be said—fantastic food were made in different state-run factories and date from different decades. At the next table, a boisterous group of Chinese men are gorging themselves. Businessmen, undoubtedly: shirtsleeves with sweaty armpits, loosened neckties, lip-smacking, belching, bones tossed aside, loud, throaty shouts.

Obayashi nods. He lays his chopsticks on the table and stares silently into his plastic bowl of rice.

"What I mean," Sigerius says, more tactfully, "is that other

Dutch people, and therefore Europeans, might think they're really good puzzles."

Obayashi raises his close-cropped head, looks across the table where John Tyronne is in conversation with Ping. "But maybe you know of a publisher?" he drawls. "Siem, just put me in touch with a publisher. I've got high hopes."

At the last meeting of the Asian Internet Society, in 1999, this same man took him aside to discuss what he termed a "private matter." Obayashi's son-in-law was the commercial director of Nippon Fun, a Japanese enterprise that marketed a successful puzzle book in Japan. One of the games, Number Place, was all the rage in New Zealand, where someone had developed a computer program capable of mass-producing the puzzles, as for a daily newspaper. Unfortunately he hadn't any with him, but Obayashi wanted Sigerius's opinion on the Number Place game and promised to send him a few copies. He was convinced, even more than his son-in-law, that the world was ready for Number Place. A little while later, an envelope from Tokyo landed on his Enschede doormat: two Japanese booklets, each with sixty puzzles and an accompanying letter explaining in toy-English that the one with the five chili peppers was called "kamikaze," he'd see why soon enough.

Only during the flight to Shanghai, when he'd driven himself crazy with all his theorizing and brooding, did he take the puzzle books from his carry-on and give them a closer look. Like so many number puzzles, he saw directly, they were derived from Euler's Latin Squares. They comprised a nine-by-nine matrix of cells, a few cells already filled in with a whole number from 1 to 9. The challenge was to complete the remaining cells so that in each row and each column, the numbers 1 through 9 occurred only once.

Additionally, the matrix was subdivided into nine three-by-three blocks which likewise had to contain the digits 1 through 9.

Perhaps, he thinks now, it was unkind to be so brutally honest with Obayashi. "I've still got one book left," he says, suddenly mild. "I'll give it to my wife."

The truth was, he had finished them within fifteen minutes, after five or six puzzles he could whip through them as fast as he could write. His mind wandered. How did these grids work? Did Number Place become more difficult the fewer numbers you were given at the outset? Often it did, he reasoned, but not necessarily. The beginning digits themselves were more of a determining factor, although he suspected that you needed at least eighteen to start off with. Or seventeen? He set out an indirect demonstration, assuming a puzzle with sixteen starting numbers. After a certain amount of juggling he concluded that you needed to start with at least eight different digits. After that he tried to work out how many correctly completed puzzles were possible, an interesting problem that he sunk his teeth into for some time without realizing it (arriving at a number somewhere between a 6 and a 7 followed by twenty-one zeros, but to what extent were those trillions of puzzles all truly different? the grid contains natural symmetries and mirroring), because when he was startled by a gentle female voice in his ear, it was dark in Business class. Would he like something to drink? Around him, eye-masked businessmen were sound asleep.

It had been wonderful: for a few hours he'd been aware of nothing apart from the deeper mathematics behind those puzzles. As though he were flying in a small private jet above the Singapore Airlines 747, at the edge of the stratosphere. Mathematics was always good medicine. But even before the stewardess had returned with his whiskey, he had slipped back into restless melancholy.

"If you can help me find a publisher," says Obayashi, "we can discuss a cut for you. Just for the Dutch market, of course. But even from that, Siem, you'll get rich, I guarantee it."

After Tineke dropped him off at Enschede Station, the moment when the strain of the anniversary week slid off him, he started fretting about what he had seen. On the way to Schiphol he'd asked himself questions, absurd questions (were they the same size? the same age? the same build?), after which he reprimanded himself (it just can't be, it's too much of a coincidence, this is what psychiatrists mean by paranoia), checked in relatively calmly, and, without slipping into outrageous fantasies, browsed through the bestsellers in the bookshop display, only to catch himself asking himself even more absurd questions while boarding (is she capable of this? is this *in* her? in her genes?)—a steady tidal motion, panic and calm, panic and calm, that has possessed him for the past three days.

Tubantia's fortieth anniversary celebration had gone as this kind of public event usually did: it washed over him, it was as though he had dreamed the past few days; and just like in a dream, there was no opportunity to look either forward or back. Pampering four honorary doctorates and their spouses; rewriting, rehearsing, and reciting his anniversary speech on nanotechnology, not the meatiest of subjects; breakfasts, lunches, and dinners with his guests, the endless chit-chat, all that bullshit, he felt like he might drop dead in the middle of his speech.

It was Thursday afternoon, during the closing reception, when things started coming undone. After he'd draped the Tubantia regalia onto his four honorees at the Jacobuskerk, the whole circus moved to the Enschede Theatre. He, Tineke, and the four honorary doctorates and their spouses mounted the raised black-velvet platform in the foyer, ready to be fêted by the hundreds of schmoozing guests who grabbed glasses of wine and fancy hors d'oeuvres from silver platters, or took their places straightaway in the discouragingly long reception line. He must have stood there for three hours, shaking hands, exchanging witty repartee, the long strand of patience reflected in his patent leather shoes.

About an hour into the handshaking he spotted Wijn. Menno Wijn, his ex-brother-in-law and former sparring partner, towering head and shoulders above the hundreds of students and almost exclusively robe-clad professors, inconspicuous at first, clearly ill at ease, glancing around awkwardly with a mineral water in his fist, almost, it seemed, on the verge of leaving. When he looked again five minutes later, Wijn was standing in the queue like a golem. "Psst, look, two o'clock," he whispered to Tineke. Her chubby hands released the arm of a professor's wife and she turned toward him. "To the left," he said. Mildly amused, she scanned the queue and froze. "Well, I'll be goddamned." She lifted her shoulders and shook her freshly coiffed hair that smelled of cigarettes and pine needles.

Wijn had the expression of someone sitting in a dentist's waiting room. Before he had arrived the foyer was the picture of diversity, so many different people, so many nationalities, but since noticing his ex-brother-in-law Sigerius realized that every academic looked like every other academic. Back when he and Wijn were in their twenties, he had a rough but rosy face and a ready laugh, finding the mistakes in others especially funny—until those mistakes started to close in on him. The mistakes belonged to his sister Margriet and nephew Wilbert, but most of all to him, Siem Sigerius, traitor, the root of Margriet's undoing. According to Wijn. What on earth was he doing here? He hadn't been invited, he must have read about the reception somewhere. Had he come all the way from Culemborg for this?

While Sigerius planted kisses on powdered cheeks and endured flattering small talk, he could feel the brother of his late ex-wife gaining ground. Vengeance and venom filled the foyer like fumes. It was twenty-five years ago, damn it. In the first few months after the divorce, his old pal had just ignored him, but once Margriet and Wilbert had moved into the attic of Wijn's sports school in Culemborg, things turned bitter. Hostile. For years, Margriet let her stable but angry brother do her dirty work for her: sis needed money, sis had to go to the liquor store. And for Wijn—by that time landlord, lawyer, and foster parent all rolled into one—what was one more nasty telephone call? Sigerius was already in America with Tineke and the girls when, right around Wilbert's birthday, an envelope arrived with a greeting card—"congratulations on your son's birthday"—accompanied by a typed sheet of expense claims: bills from the glazier, medical fees, sessions with the juvenile psychologist, fines, you name it, and at the bottom the bank account number of Menno Wijn Martial Arts Academy. It was the prelude to a few phone calls per year, collect calls of course, fault-finding tirades in which Wijn, in his crude redneck lingo, filled him in on what that "punk" had got up to now, which school he'd been kicked out of and why, about the pulverized licorice cough drops the "fuckwad" sold as hash, how Menno had to throw out the "scum" that came to the house for payback, about the brawls at the carnival, the shoplifting—so when you coming back to Holland, Pop? Menno was down on that whole America thing. But when Sigerius himself phoned, Wijn shut him out, let the deserter know in no uncertain terms that he had no business with them, and banged on and on about how Wilbert had settled in just fine with his dutiful uncle. "He ain't a bad kid, you know, all of a sudden he got twenty-four canaries up there in the attic. Loves 'm, y'know. Gerbils too, guinea pigs, it's a regler zoo up there."

He always just let it go. Of course he was worried. You're here now, Tineke would say. We are in California. Menno only quit haranguing him after Margriet died. After that they had only the occasional telephone conversation, Menno moaning and groaning about his role as Wilbert's guardian, he as the disillusioned father trying to get out of his alimony obligations. Businesslike exchanges, the enmity of the past electrically dormant on the phone line.

Here he comes. His ex-brother-in-law, backlit by the glare that cut in through the tall front windows of the theatre, stepped onto the dais and stopped in front of him. You'd almost expect to see him holding a UPS clipboard, or wonder whose chauffeur he was, what was this guy doing coming after his boss? Straight as an arrow, arms dangling alongside his bony body, his weight on the balls of his feet, just like he used to take his place on the mat: here I am, just try me. No handshake.

"Menno," said Sigerius.

Wijn pulled in his chin. "Doing all right for yourself, I see," he said in the same tacky accent they spoke back in Wijk C, forty years ago. "I was passing by. I've come to tell you your son's free."

Sigerius cleared his throat. "*What?*"

"Reduced sentence. On accounta good behavior. He's already out."

At times, language can have a physical effect on him, ice-cold water being dumped over him from meters above his head. "Aw no," he muttered. "Now that is news. Bad news."

Wijn picked at a penny-sized scab on his cheek, no doubt the remnants of a blister he'd got himself from scraping across a judo mat, a self-conscious gesture that made him look, for a brief moment, like his dead sister. His middle finger was missing its nail. A blind finger.

"Just thought I'd let you know. And tell you that I wash my hands of 'm."

"He was supposed to be locked up until 2002." Tineke. She stood glowering at Wijn with eyes like pistols, but he ignored her, just like he'd been ignoring her for the past twenty-five years.

"Where's he going to live?" Sigerius asked.

"Dunno. Don't give a shit."

Then they stood there looking at each other in silence, the rector and the gym coach. Two guys in their fifties who used to stand in the shower room together, three times a week, year after year, after having mixed their sweat on dojos all over the west coast of Holland. It hadn't been of any use. Suddenly, without provocation, Wijn brought his hand to Sigerius's forehead and gave him a rough little jab with that mole finger of his.

"Dog," he snarled.

Before Sigerius could realize he *mustn't* respond, before he realized he was *not* in the position to pick the man up high and crosswise by his polyester collar, hurl him back down and, growling, yank him back up—strangle him on the spot, as big and nasty as he was—Wijn walked off. Without looking further at anyone, he shambled in his cheap, ill-fitting suit past the row of laureates and stepped off the podium with a hollow thud.

Later he thought: maybe this is all Wijn's doing. That claw of his, that dirty stinking finger. That it made him start looking at things differently. A cue of flesh that put a spin on his thoughts.

The fact was, not a minute later he spotted Joni and Aaron in the receiving line, his daughter beside her bald boyfriend, admiringly and attentively listening to him. What did he notice? Nothing in particular, at first. That she looked gorgeous, she had a stunning profile. That she knew exactly what to wear when her old man was up front. Today she had chosen a white wool turtleneck sweater, snug but classic, white gold sparkled in her ears and around her wrists. He was struck, not for the first time, by how smartly she could dress, more expensively, more well-put-together than other students—never prim, you couldn't make Joni prim even if you buried her in pearls, but chic, *classy*. She had tucked her entire head of hair under a cap, a sort of Russian Nikita thing, so only the back of her neck betrayed her blondness.

The next moment he leaned over so he could hear the soft-spoken, silvery-gray wife of an ex-rector. His eyes wide open and his head alongside her elongated ear, he caught sight of Joni, more or less by coincidence; he smiled and winked but she did not see him. Her beautiful face was concentrating on something else, probably on her mother next to him.

Then he sees it. The dark-brown Siberian cap above Joni's face jogs something in his memory. Apparently his mouth produces a sound, a sigh or a groan, or something, because the woman whose ear it enters shrinks back. He straightens himself, nods absently, opens his mouth wide and snaps it back shut. The resemblance penetrates his consciousness as something hot, as a liquid that attempts to smother him. Boiling lead. He is dizzy. The phenomenal ability of the brain to recognize faces, effortlessly, unhesitatingly. It has always fascinated him, but now it is killing him. It is not even recognition, it is far more, on all fronts. What he experiences is . . . *identification*. Joni's attentive expression, five, six meters away, the dark fur hat whose brim lies across her smooth forehead so that he sees her, for the first time, as a *brunette*. The make-up, heavier than usual, the glossy lips parted in concentration. All her features, the broad purity of her compelling, self-assured face, everything that determines the way his daughter looks, shifts over that *other* face, a face that he, in a sense, also knows like the back of his hand—until his perspiring brain goes "click." *It's her.*

"Siem, darling—are you OK?" Tineke's cool hand grabbed him by the wrist, she made an effort to look at him. He didn't focus properly, he saw the grainy structure of her purple eyeshadow, heard her say that he looked pale, that he hadn't been getting enough sleep the last few weeks. She gave his shoulder a squeeze, took a step forward and said something to the woman in front of him. He stared at Tineke's broad back, wrapped in the purple gown she'd had specially made for this afternoon.

"Tomorrow you'll be sitting on a plane to Shanghai," she whispered, once she was next to him again. "We're in the home stretch. You're doing great. You were just thrown off by that news about Wilbert. I can tell."

His protectress, the lovingly bowed second violin, it is the role Tineke has been playing ever since he lay like a shipwreck on the Antonius Matthaeuslaan and she came upstairs to join him for coffee. Then, too, she talked him through his depression, consoled the inconsolable with cheerful empathy. And now, once again, that endless understanding, although this time, thank God, she didn't have an inkling as to what it was about.

"Yeah," he mumbled. "It worries me. I hate that man. And I hate my son."

"I know you all too well," she said. "Forget that boy. Forget both of them. That Menno is nothing but 100 kilos of rancor. He came here deliberately, just to rile you. They've released Wilbert because he's ready to return to society."

Of course Tubantia University's anniversary celebration was bigger than himself, a figurehead is attached to the prow, and the prow to the ship; everything else went as planned that Thursday, starting with the ceremonial dinner in Koetshuis Schuttersveld, where he found himself, smiling, once again at the head of the table. *Calm down!* hissed a pinched voice in his head during the toasts to the academy, during the supper of red bass, during his own speech. He thought: it's impossible. It's statistically impossible, it's morally impossible, it's logistically impossible. He knocked back goblets of white wine to drown out the heckling in his brain. He and Tineke arrived back at the farmhouse, reeling, at half-past one in the morning, and when he flopped down beside her in bed, his back to her, he sank into a raccoon-like slumber. He hadn't given his son's release a moment's thought the entire evening. All he could think about was Joni.

There was no opportunity to verify his suspicions. Tineke brought him to the train station early the next morning; the first computers he saw were being hogged by a group of backpackers at the airport Internet café. He waited indecisively for one, but walked off before it was his turn. He didn't dare. The newly opened Shanghai Pudong Airport, he discovered eleven hours later, did not even have an Internet café.

After a taxi had jostled him through the driving rain, through rundown concrete suburbs into the heart of the metropolis, more or less catapulting him into the lobby of the Okura Garden Hotel, and even before unpacking his bags, he unplugged the telephone cable in his hotel room and tried to connect his laptop to the Internet. When that didn't work, he shaved, put on a clean but wrinkly shirt and took the elevator down to the lobby. He crossed the mausoleum of gold-veined marble, slid his key across the reception desk, and requested a quarter of an hour online. A uniformed girl led him to an area with colorful table lamps and outfitted with three communist Pentiums, the cubicles separated by frosted-glass partitions in walnut frames. He seated himself in front of the farthermost computer. The girl gestured for him to wait, leaned across him (sweat and something sweet), and set a digital egg timer. Next to the keyboard—nerve-rackingly non-QWERTY—was a ballpoint pen on a chain and a cube-shaped memo holder. He found, with some difficulty, a working search engine but subsequently ran into what is gradually gaining worldwide notoriety as the Great Firewall of China. He cursed out loud. The pen stayed put when he gave the table an irritated shove, but the plastic cube tipped over with a smack. He couldn't even get onto the site, and although the irony wasn't lost on him (he had been summoned to this backward dictatorship to instruct his repressive yellow friends in how to reinforce their nefarious firewall; they wanted to know about everything—broadband Internet, the future of video graphics—only to nip new technology in the bud, that's what it came down to), he was vexed by being stymied for the umpteenth time as he scooped up the little square memo sheets from the marble floor.

"I don't need money, Hiro," he says, "I've already got money." Maybe he is taking out his frustration on Obayashi because now, two days after the reception, he has still made no headway. Taking his tone down a notch, with a forced smile: "And, to be honest, I don't think your puzzles will be much of a success in the Netherlands. Do you remember Go? We don't. The ever-thrilling board game Go. Now only available at the flea market." He has no idea if it's true, but if he doesn't make himself clear now he'll be spending this summer as a traveling game salesman. His colleague appears, momentarily, to doubt his understanding of the English language, and then says: "Nippon Fun has a computer version of Go. I can send it to you. Two CD-ROMs."

At a neighboring table, a waitress is going around with a teapot with the beak of a tropical bird, a slender, curved spout at least a meter long, from which the woman refills teacups from a distance. John Tyronne, the young Stanford professor, beckons her with a flourish of his arm. Tyronne, talented but naïve, was brought aboard the task force with a certain amount of fanfare, primarily because of his early and technically well-argued papers on the millennium bug, but he'd gone overboard and had done himself more harm than good with his increasingly apocalyptic Y2K articles that had sprung up in American newspapers the previous year and where he had more or less predicted the end of the world. As Tyronne refused to set foot in an airplane after December 31st, 1999, the first meeting of 2000 had been postponed. "Ah, there's our doomsday prophet," smiled task force chairman Gao Jian at their first reunion in the unravaged world. "Still eating canned food?" This afternoon, during the paper Sigerius had presented on haptics, he teased Tyronne that he would never have to fly again. "Soon we'll plug a rubber hand into your laptop, John, and when you squeeze it at home, your PC will send your pressure profile to a special rubber Johnny Tyronne task-force hand here in Shanghai: the cyberspace handshake! Minor problem with that fraction of a time delay, though"—and here he gave Tyronne, who was sitting up front, a dead-fish handshake. "Not so nice, is it?" A second later he squeezed—too hard.

"Wouldn't a Japanese name be a better idea?" he says, trying to humor Obayashi. "Something other than Number Place?"

Obayashi mumbles an answer that escapes him entirely. For a moment he hears nothing, it's that idiotic comment about the Go CD-ROMs that ignites, in delayed action, a phosphorus flame in his brain. Here he is, eating Peking duck, while his laptop is lying on his hotel bed. *Maybe that CD is in the laptop bag. Maybe you've got the photos with you.* He has to restrain himself from jumping up from the table, marching straight through the wall of seawater and lobsters, and making a beeline for the Okura. Instead he smiles at Obayashi, wipes off his greasy fingers on the paper napkin and closes his eyes. *Think. That disc full of photos: is it in your laptop bag?* No idea. He imagines himself in his study, the familiar smell of paper and fallen dust, the tranquillity of his monk's cell. He pictures his desk in front of him. The disc could also be lying in a locked drawer.

He checks his watch, pulls his cell phone out of his inside pocket. Without looking at Obayashi any further he unlocks the keypad and stares pensively at the illuminated screen for a few seconds. "Excuse me," he whispers, laying a hand on the pudgy Japanese wrist. Although he has only the contours of his pretext ready, he gets up and buttons his sport jacket. An image flashes through his mind: the police phone him here in China with the news that Wilbert has been decapitated. The shaft of an uncoupled trailer. Dead as a doornail. Without finishing the thought, he clears his throat and says: "Gentlemen . . . sorry to interrupt . . . but I'm afraid I have to be going. I've just received word that . . . something is up in Enschede."

"Anshkieday?" shouts Tyronne, whom he perhaps teased too much this afternoon. "Ansh-kie-day . . . Sigerius, where is that university of yours, Atlantis?"

Gao Jian stubs out his cigarette and lights another, smoke escapes from the corners of his mouth. He looks inquisitively at Sigerius. "Colleague," he says earnestly, "what seems to be the matter? Can I be of any assistance?"

"I'm afraid not," Sigerius hears himself say, and, thinking of the torrent he is about to step into, says: "I've just heard that the campus has flooded. Terrible weather in the Netherlands, heavy rain—just like here, but worse."

"You'll miss the evening program."

"Tomorrow's another day. They're expecting me to make a statement in Enschede concerning the, er, damage."

The tepid downpour shades the Shanghai twilight. Gurgling, the rainwater seeks out drains and sewers, sloshing against the Huaihai Zhong Lu sidewalks, over which hundreds of Chinese tread hurriedly with precise steps, shielding their straight hair with umbrellas or briefcases. Occupied taxis spray fans of glistening water; shoppers, their arms ending in clusters of purchases, take cover under awnings or in doorways, staring into space or conversing in their secret language. The usually thriving, vibrant, pulsating avenue with its high-priced shops, malls, hotels, and restaurants almost looks covered, it is so dark.

Jaywalking against a red light, he crosses a flooded intersection, dodging the aggressively advancing taxis and rickshaws. His suit jacket is drenched, lukewarm rainwater soaks the toes of his shoes. He takes large strides, a curious disquiet steers him toward his hotel. On the one hand he believes his suspicions say more about himself than about Joni, that what he has seen is a projection of his own fears; but on the other hand he is just a bit too familiar with adversity to be entirely sure. As different as his daughters are from each other, he has never doubted their respectability, their decency: it is a question a man with a son in the Scheveningen penitentiary never gets around to asking. He would put his life on the line for Tineke's daughters, Janis and Joni, whom he regards as his own—the elder, who has everything going for her, who will breeze through life: she is quick on the draw, witty, ambitious, above all engaging—"take the plunge with me," it's written on her forehead in glittering gold letters—and on top of it those damned good looks, her extraordinary beauty, so no, the father of a criminal does not worry about a daughter like Joni. If they have any worries about Tineke's girls they are for Janis, who is altogether another matter. The younger daughter has made it her life's work *not* to engage, she harbors a programmatic, often intolerable, loathing for everything that in her eyes is not genuine, she fights a one-woman guerrilla war against everything that is insincere, fake, hypocritical. That is why she refuses to diet, that is why she wears boys' clothes, that is why she so vehemently abhors money, meat-eaters, Hollywood films, saddled horses, universities, vacations. She shreds Christmas cards sent by aunts and uncles. Deodorant: Tineke had to force her to use deodorant, as a teenager Janis insisted it was a lie to mask your own odor, it's deceitful, deodorant is bourgeois. At least she's honest, he and Tineke told each other.

The heavens open, downpour turns into hailstorm, the deafening drumroll is so loud that the traffic appears to glide noiselessly forward. Sigerius has no choice but to take refuge under a sodden awning. Packed together with other pedestrians, he picks up a scent that reminds him of the sweaty judo mats of long ago. One of the men points to the bouncing ice balls, maybe he's never seen hail before, at least not on May 13th.

For a couple of years he was the jogging coach for Joni's gymnastics class; after returning from America she joined a club in Enschede called Sportlust, and one day she asked if he felt like coaching them. Sounds good, he said, and it did sound good: a weekly run with thirteen thirteen-year-olds through the Drienerlo woods. Shortly before his summer holidays, the chairwoman and the head coach sat in his living room discussing the details; soon thereafter, every Wednesday evening the farmhouse overflowed with beanpoles with braces and tracksuits, an arrangement that Joni soon regretted because all the girls canceled now and again—homework, illness, being under the weather—something she could never get away with. He laid out a not-too-girlish route of about four kilometers. They ran southward down the Langenkampweg, cut across the campus, including the motorcycle club's dune ("Oh, *noooo*, sir, not the loose sand!"), after which they continued through the woods until coming out at the farmhouse, where Tineke served them glasses of elderberry cordial.

Joni was still young enough to be proud of her athletic father, and he too would have looked back with pleasure on the training if it hadn't been for that incident. Sportlust participated, as it did each year, in a door-to-door fund-raising drive for cancer research, and Joni and Miriam, a small but pert girl who jogged with her blond curls flattened under a headband, spent two long afternoons canvassing the houses and apartments in Boddenkamp for donations. "A neighborhood where you can expect them to be generous, just like in previous years," remarked the chairwoman the evening he phoned her because Joni had come home from try-outs and—first stammering, then crying—told him she'd been accused of stealing money out of the collection can.

While counting the takings, the woman told him, the Sportlust treasurer noticed that Miriam's and Joni's cans didn't contain a single banknote, and that their proceeds were not only less than a quarter of the previous years' but also the lowest of all the other cans, even the ones from what she called the grotty neighborhoods. Miriam was in the Tuesday evening gymnastics group; they took her aside and within ten seconds she had confessed. According to her, she and Joni managed to fish out all the paper money with a geometry triangle and then divided the loot—a little over 150 guilders—between them.

Joni was furious. What a bunch of lies. She had nothing to do with it! How could somebody be *so* mean. She *hated* that Miriam, she always knew she had a mean streak, she should never have trusted her. When they had finished their rounds, she told him through her tears, it was already dark and dinner time and Miriam had offered to turn both cans in to the treasurer at the central collection point, near where she lived.

Sigerius was livid. "My daughter is standing here in the living room bawling," he said to the chairwoman. "I know Joni inside out, your accusations are premature and totally out of line. I guarantee you my daughter is not going around plundering charity collection cans." They agreed that he and Joni would go together so she could tell her side of the story, a suggestion she accepted with a pout, but she backed out just as he was about to leave for the gym. She was afraid she'd burst into tears. Or explode in anger. So he went alone. It was an onerous meeting; the woman insisted that it was Miriam's word against Joni's, and he was adamant that Joni's name be cleared. When he returned home at ten-thirty that night, he told Joni he'd given them the choice: either take her word for it, or that was the end of the training, and then we'd have to see whether she stayed in the club.

He can still remember exactly where they were standing: in the front hall, he with his coat still on, right foot on the open spiral stairs; Joni halfway, holding her toothbrush with toothpaste already on it. He'll never forget the moment she broke. After he'd finished his report she went quiet. Then she slumped down onto a step, dropped the toothbrush, tick, tack, tock, onto the slate floor. She hid her face in her nightie and said with a drawn-out sigh: "Dad?"

He raised his eyebrows.

"Listen, Dad, don't freak out or anything. I, um, what I mean is . . . well, actually, Miriam's telling the truth."

• • •

He walks under the dribbling plane trees toward the Okura. He deliberately bangs against the shoulder of a phoning businessman, steers clear of the vegetable stalls on the sagging sidewalk and the garbage bags ripped open by stray dogs. A little group of Chinese, maybe five of them, dart out of a side street and spread a large purple tarp on the sopping wet pavement. In a wink they've laid out their wares: leather bags, Ray-Ban sunglasses, Gucci pullovers, Adidas T-shirts, CDs, DVDs, video games. Fake. He pauses for a moment, his shorter leg—the scooter one—hurts, he massages his hamstring. One of the hawkers accosts him in snarly Mandarin.

"Fuck off," he says with a smile.

What's worse: selling imitation Gucci or robbing a collection can? What about the gray area? Is it logical or worthwhile to worry about Joni, about a hypothetical problem—as long as he doesn't know for sure, it doesn't exist—while he also knows that Wilbert is free? Navigating his way between cars, he crosses the four-lane Huaihai Zhong Lu, turns left forty yards farther on and passes in front of the ramshackle Art Deco façade of the Cathay Theatre, where a horde of Chinese cinema-goers is waiting to see *Mission: Impossible* 2. What will happen now that the kid is free? What does six years in the slammer do to a man like Wilbert Sigerius?

"Hitler knew the answer to that," answered Rufus Koperslager back when he asked that question incessantly, though usually guardedly, to anyone he thought might offer him an educated answer. "Hitler saw prisons as a university for criminals. Didn't you know that? An indoor gutter, where the rookies learn the trade from the pros." He is reminded of his first private conversation with that eccentric Rufus, a meeting he would rather forget. "Do you know Hitler's Table Talk?" No, he hadn't got round to Hitler's Table Talk yet. God, yes, Koperslager—a law enforcement chief with a knighthood and the petulant candor of a policeman—was made dean at Tubantia in late '95. The appointment went against the grain, a cop on campus, a man perhaps a bit too straight-from-the-shoulder, impatient, used to giving orders and to a braided-steel chain of command. But a realist. Sigerius pricked up his ears when Koperslager told them during the selection procedure he had been director of not one, but two prisons in the early '80s, an achievement that intrigued him enough to take advantage of the sandwich reception to confide in his new colleague about his criminal son. He was like that back then. Heart on his sleeve. Wilbert had been in for just over a year and in that time Sigerius had developed a not-so-subtle obsession with everything that took place behind bars: he devoured every newspaper clipping, every book, every television documentary, anything that could tell him about correctional regimes and jailhouse norms. "I understand you have a prison background? My son, he's doing time."

"Where?" Koperslager also had a considerable affinity with the subject; a dark shroud fell over his policeman's face, he touched his clean-shaven chin ever so slightly, Sigerius saw him descend into an underworld that excited him more than he would care to admit. Without twitching a muscle, Sigerius named the three penitentiary facilities where they had been stowing Wilbert thus far. "Transfers?" asked Koperslager.

"I believe so."

"Do you want me to be frank with you?"

"Please," he said, giving the go-ahead for Koperslager's both convincing and dispiriting sketch of Wilbert's "career," which, in his humble opinion, Sigerius's son was building up "on the inside." "They only transfer the ringleaders," he said. "Transfers are expensive and cumbersome, I was never keen on it, but sometimes you have no choice." Wilbert was probably a kid with clout, was his analysis, a key player within his block, a power-broker, one of the "sharks." We always plucked 'm out, Koperslager said, they're the ones who undermine authority, intimidate and bribe the wardens, they're forever making deals, both inside and out. "So they're shunting your boy around. Sheesh. Maybe he's got talent. Judging from his father: not at all stupid, physical and tough—yeah, he'll be learning the tricks of the trade."

Koperslager's favorite criminologist had an interesting take on prisons. "Hitler repeatedly advocated corporal punishment over detention. You're better off beating the crap out of a twenty-year-old, or cutting off his hand—he says that in 1942, and it's probably true. Jail only hones their skills. Prisons, Siem, are criminal academies, aggression workshops, testosterone laboratories. Masculinity flows like water, it's machismo at its meanest, everyone hates everyone else. Divide and conquer, 24/7. Gangs, protection. There's no feminine perspective, there's no such thing as consideration—only power. Blackmail, beatings, sexual abuse, it's all part of the game. You go in as a weenie and you leave as a gangster. Chop off a guy's foot, I say."

It was just the nightmare scenario he had been tormenting himself with, and Koperslager was clearly not the man to allay his fears. Without telling a soul, as though he was going to a whore on a houseboat, Sigerius drove by the local prison every time he needed to be in The Hague, or Amsterdam, or wherever, on university business. It was an obsession: he stood in front of Scheveningen Prison at least five times, staring at the infamous gate with its medieval battlements, and felt awful, disheartened to the core—so miserable and depressed that one day he decided enough was enough. Quit wallowing. Basta! The penal dissertations, the magazine articles, the pamphlets full of prison stories, the video documentaries—he put all that paranoid crap in a gray plastic garbage bag and dumped it on the curb.

And sure enough his mind cleared, sooner than he had expected.

He appreciated the truth in "the only thing we have to fear is fear itself." He had to laugh at his readiness to accept Koperslager's tall tales, at his latent *Telegraaf*-conservatism, and felt his faith in the rule of law return, his faith in mankind itself.

He is nearly there. It will be dark soon, the lanterns in the Okura's formal French gardens are already lit. A hundred yards off, the hotel looms like a white stone-and-glass peacock, in front of it an unstaunchable fountain. (The student cafeteria at Tubantia has a cook who asks every student in his dishwashing room the same dead-serious question: Tell me, you're the student, aren't you afraid that one day the water will just run out?) He is still taken by the Art Deco grandeur, even though, in one of the hotel's 1,000 rooms, a black box is waiting for him. On his way up to the fourteenth floor his body fills with the fervid hope that the CD-ROM is not in his bag. His stomach keeps rising even after the elevator has stopped.

His room smells of steamed towels. The bed, where he tossed and turned for a fruitless hour this morning, has been made, his shirt and the suit he wore on the plane are hanging in the open cupboard. The laptop is no longer on the bed, but on the oval desk next to the sitting area. He plugs it in. Hoping to quell the butterflies in his stomach, he takes a shower. He washes himself with gel from a purple packet he has to tear open with his teeth. Anything is possible, he's well aware of that. You can be going to the Olympics and then not go after all. He dries himself with the largest of the three towels and puts on a bathrobe. You can father a rattlesnake.

He adjusts the air conditioning to nineteen degrees. Takes the laptop case and sits on the edge of the bed. He feels around in the side pockets and digs out an etui with just three CD-ROMs in it.

Two of them are clean as a whistle, on the third is written in black felt-tip: "Minutes, U Council." Bingo. That's the one. He takes a deep breath and clenches his hands. He gets up, goes over to the window, draws the heavy curtains, sits back down and inserts the CD-ROM into the drive. Windows start-up is complete, he enters his password, at first incorrectly, he fumbles with the capital letters. The program asks if he wants a slide show. No, no slide show. Windows lines up the JPEG images, icons of a small black sailboat drifting off into an orange sunset. There are lots of them, maybe 400. About a quarter of them are ones he scrounged from various free sites, the rest are from some Russian site and from lindaloveslace.com—it's that last one he's after. He clicks randomly on one of the icons and sees the Russian girl sitting on a sofa with her legs spread. He feels a vague thrill well up, an echo of the familiar horniness, the horniness of a moth-eaten old ape.

Come on, where are they? He decides a slide show is more efficient, clicking through the pictures for speed. First he races like a madman through the forest of free pictures, then the Russian girl whizzes by, kneeling, bending, lying, squatting, fingering—yes, there she is, he recoils at the first photo he sees. She is standing with one foot on a curly-backed chair, elbow on her knee, lips pursed, breasts in a soft pink bra. Gasping with shock, he shoves the computer off his lap. The resemblance is more insidious than he thought. He goes over to the minibar and takes out a can of Budweiser. You already knew there was a resemblance. He paces across the soft wall-to-wall carpeting. The beer is so cold that his eyes water. You have to look at it analytically. Like a scientist. Like a detective. How well does he know Joni's figure? Slender, healthy girls under twenty-five are hard to tell apart. But that face . . .

He sits back down. Analyze. Luckily he is already familiar with the pictures; he can therefore examine them coolly. The first series is shot in a hotel room. He has to find that recurring room, he seems to remember one location that keeps coming back. A boat? Yes, there's a ship's cabin too . . . A series of thirteen photos taken in the same room, clearly not a hotel room, in the background a computer, a full bookcase, houseplants, a poster of two kittens in a beach chair, Celine Dion, a skylight . . .

Linda. Linda from Tennessee, or Kentucky, or Utah, or who knows which obscure state. The session starts in a Roaring Twenties outfit, a short, straight-cut green dress and one of those floppy round hats pulled down over her ears, white satin elbow-length gloves, bright red lips—God, she does look like Joni. Then off comes the dress, she's standing in the middle of the room in black pumps with a ribbon on the toe, white garters, caramel-colored nylons. In the next picture she's sitting on a chair, hands covering her bare breasts, hat off, the jet-black hair hanging loosely, it looks dyed, so black it's nearly blue. Could be a wig. Certainly. Next photo, the panties have come off, she sits on that chair with her legs spread, she . . .

Again he shoves the laptop away from him and flops back onto the mattress. Why in God's name does he even want to know the truth? Monday, when he's back in Enschede, he'll unsubscribe from the site and never give it another thought. Unfortunately, that is just not how he is. For a while he stares up at the wooden blades of the ceiling fan. Your mind's in a muddle. Maybe Tineke was right. It's that business about Wilbert, it's paranoia. Be realistic. The chance that Joni resembles that girl is thousands of times greater than that it's actually her. Everybody has a double, there might be 100 of his own walking around. Smooth-skinned girls are a dime a dozen. He sits up and brings the computer back to his lap. The plastic underside is hot. Turn it around—you owe it to her to turn it around. Look for evidence to the contrary.

He enlarges the photo, zooming in at its edge, focuses on the bookcase. He can read the spines. English-language paperbacks and hardcovers: Mary Higgins Clark, Harold Robbins, Barbara Taylor Bradford, Tom Clancy, Danielle Steel, John Grisham, Sue Grafton. Pulp. On the next shelf down there are larger books, also in English, books about gardening (*The Practical Rock & Water Garden*), cookbooks (*Eating by the Book: What the Bible Says About Food, Fat, Fitness & Faith*), self-help junk (*Narcissism: Denial of the True Self*). Come on, this is a genuine American bookcase! This half-baked little library is somewhere in Utah. Belongs to a completely different girl. Who is this Linda, anyway? She still lives at home, no, she's being raised by her deaf great-aunt and this is the long-forgotten attic room. He drags the photo upward with the cursor, bringing the bottom shelf into view. Behind the slender zoomed-in ankle and chair leg he sees four books in familiar yellow and black. *Beekeeping for Dummies, BBQ Sauces, Rubs & Marinades for Dummies, Jazz for Dummies . . .*

Jazz for Dummies. A brand-new thought comes bulldozing through his head: who does this babe make her coquettish crap *with*? He zooms back out, studies the entire picture again, clicks ahead a couple of photos: they are professionally done, they're almost . . . slick. She can't do it alone, of course she's not doing this alone. Just say—just say this girl *is* Joni, then it would have to be . . . that makes . . . the guy whom he meets twice a week on the judo mat responsible for . . . Stop it, stop right now. Joni *and* Aaron?

He clicks further, pausing at a photo taken in what looks like a boat. She is naked, except for a green bikini top (does he know Joni's bikinis?—no, of course not), lying on a round bed with a red coverlet. In the background he sees arching wooden cabinets, a transparent door that probably leads to the shower cubicle and, higher up, rose-colored portholes. Her black hair has now been put up (can you put up a wig?), she holds the tip of her tongue against her upper lip and looks into the lens with blasé nonchalance. In the next photo she is kneeling in front of the bed, left cheek on the beige carpet, her back hollow, breasts on the floor. Knees spread, the pink soles of her feet closest to the camera, she thrusts her butt backward, still looking at the camera, to the left, next to her face, a pair of silver heels. The sharpness of the face: he can make out the grains of mascara on her eyelashes. The brazen litheness with which she offers her ass and gazes at him with that open, stunning, indifferent look. In the next shot she's holding her smooth-shaven netherlips open with her index and middle finger, after that one, there's a dildo; suddenly this huge black thing penetrates her, deeply at first, and since she is pulling apart her butt cheeks with both hands, with each successive photo it's slightly less deep, until the plastic penis is lying on the rug. The last photo is a close-up of her face.

Those eyes, he sees in slow motion, are blue. The eyes are *steel-blue.* A wave of euphoria flows through his body. Joni's eyes are dark brown! He pushes the laptop aside, gets up and walks back and forth between the curtains and the bed. He goes into the bathroom, splashes cold water on his face. *It isn't her. Of course it isn't her.* He walks back to the bed, closes Windows, turns off the computer. Turn it off, all of it.

He takes his trousers from the chair, fishes around for his cell phone. Call Joni, say something nice to her. It's half-past eleven, making it . . . four-thirty in Holland. He scrolls through his contacts until he finds her name, presses the green telephone icon. A Chinese voice says something, and then the line goes dead. No connection? He finds the number of her student house and dials. Rustling silence, ever deepening, then a busy signal.

Still relieved, he throws off his robe and walks naked to the minibar. He takes out a second Budweiser, sits on the high bed, pillows propped behind his back. He turns on the television and takes long swigs of beer. He surfs along a Chinese opera, a film with Kevin Costner and Whitncy Houston, a kick-boxing match. He gets caught up in a news broadcast, a Chinese female newscaster is talking about President Jiang Zemin, he sees Madeleine Albright getting off an airplane somewhere. Then there's an item about an accident in some foreign country. He sees a European-looking residential neighborhood with fireworks exploding above the houses in broad daylight. The crackle and claps on the TV get louder, the picture becomes choppy—his eyes fall shut. Only now that the catastrophe has been averted does he realize how exhausted he is. He lets the remote control slip out of his hand and rolls over onto his side.

3

Until this morning, my sister was the only one from Enschede I'd heard anything from, more than five years ago already. It must have been late summer 2003, just before I moved to Los Angeles and disappeared off the face of the earth, and the first time since Siem's death that anyone from the family had contacted me. I was still leading my cushy bourgeois existence with Boudewijn and Mike in San Francisco. Janis was traveling along the West Coast for a month with a guy named Timo. They stayed with us for one night up on the hill.

Janis had already been in California for two weeks when she phoned. Maybe it was the migraine, but I didn't recognize her voice right away. She was calling from a pay phone in Monterey, disturbingly nearby, en route to San Francisco—*you do live there, don't you?—that is where you live, right?* They'd spent more than thirty dollars tracking down my number, a complicated phone marathon that started with McKinsey Amsterdam. I was touched that she'd taken the trouble.

The next morning, a blue rental Ford crunched up the driveway and out stepped a sunburned Janis, followed by a pallid fellow who wore his lustreless black hair in a long braid. Despite the heat he was dressed from head to toe in heavy black clothes. By way of contrast, Boudewijn ambled over to them in his espadrilles, a hot-pink polo shirt and minuscule bathing suit, and led them, chatting cheerfully, around the side of our typical Russian Hill house to the secluded backyard. There I stood, at the edge of the kidney-shaped swimming pool, and found myself in an awkward hug with Janis. She had got heavy; she had our mother's figure. "So you're Joni," Timo mumbled, without taking off his sunglasses.

I showed them the New York-designed living room and felt an odd apprehension as they walked over to the panoramic glass wall and looked out silently over the Marina District. No one had ever stood there without oohing and aahing. The glass curved around the corner and into the kitchen, it made you want to hang glide down to the ocean. "To the left, in the distance, you can see the Golden Gate Bridge," I said, "and Alcatraz off to the right," but they didn't say a word.

I led them downstairs, where I had made up a double bed in the garden room. Timo traced his finger through the dust on Boudewijn's Seeburg V200 and asked if we had a room *without* a jukebox. So I showed them their bathroom, after which I threw open the doors to the sloping lawn. Janis walked across the grass with a choppy gait, inspected the flower beds and the pruned palm trees, and squeezed her broad backside into the Toys "R" Us swing set bought with Mike's future toddler years in mind. "Do you guys have a gardener?" she asked.

When we went back up a while later, we were met by a muted whining: Mike, who had woken up from the unfamiliar bonk of Timo's boots on the stairs. A brief but intense splash of surprise across Janis's red face. A child? Without a word she bent over Mike's crib in his baby-blue room and lightly ran a finger over his stomach.

"I didn't know Janis was an aunt," Timo said to break the silence.

"I didn't know Mike had an uncle," I answered.

After a taciturn lunch at the Japanese Tea House, which Timo paid for with an edgy snicker, we walked in pairs through Golden

Gate Park, Janis and I side by side, Boudewijn pushing the stroller and conversing with the pasty-white "commie," as he called Janis's boyfriend in the blissful privacy of our own car. I could tell that Boudewijn stepped up their tempo to give Janis and me some time to ourselves. As the men turned into little dolls, Timo a squaw with that braid of his, my sister and I sauntered through the decor of blossoming willows and ancient oaks. It was hot and humid, and sweat beaded up under Janis's cropped henna-hair. Our parents used to bring us here when we lived in Berkeley, twenty eons ago; we would pile into the pickup and drive from Bonita Avenue over the Bay Bridge, Janis and me on the sticky front seat, wedged between my parents, my father at the wheel. I asked her if she remembered that.

"I hardly remember anything about California."

The path sloped slightly. Our footsteps crunched precisely in time. How old was Janis back in 1982: five?

"Tineke used to fill that red wicker basket with food," I said to refresh her memory, "you know, the one out on the front porch of the farmhouse in Enschede."

"You're calling your mother by her first name? What's the deal?"

I took a deep breath and said: "Janis—why do you think Siem killed himself?"

Her pace faltered for a moment. She took her sunglasses off her spiked hair and set them on her nose, which by now had taken on the color of a grilled sausage.

"Do you and . . . Mom think *I* had anything to do with it?"

She stopped and placed a sweaty hand on my shoulder. "There's something in my shoe," she said, wobbling, as she wriggled a swollen foot out of her All Star. Someone, maybe Pocahontas over there, had drawn a peace sign on the green canvas with a blue ballpoint pen. She shook a pebble out of the sneaker and got down on one knee to put it back on. "Joni," she said to my thigh, "Mom and

I haven't heard from you in three years. You weren't at the funeral. We don't think about you much. And if we do think about you, we're more inclined to think you have nothing to do with anything at all."

After we had put Mike to bed, with those two almost palpably killing time in the living room, Bo installed himself in the open kitchen as a man who is out to impress his twenty-years-younger in-laws and whipped up some pasta with fresh Bay crab. I sat upright on the sofa across from Timo and Janis and listened to a peevish account of their tours of those "ludicrously commercial" Hollywood film studios and endured a report of the financial details concerning their recently acquired row house in Deventer. There was some to-do about a permit regarding a tree in their neighbor's yard, or maybe the tree was in their own yard, and the tree needed to be chopped down or not chopped down, and Timo was taking or not taking legal action. He was clearly a good match for my sister; I could tell he detested me on ideological grounds. I was too rich, I was too pretty, I had a despicable boyfriend, McKinsey was despicable. The deliberate way he nodded when I said anything, or just sat there fiddling with his black cuffs, indifferently picking at a loose cuticle—his entire demeanor announced how pleased he was with the 9,000 kilometers between San Francisco and Deventer.

The evening sun nudged our shadows across the floor tiles; below us, the illuminated houses of the Marina twinkled like a thousand tea lights. We talked awkwardly about nothing. I was already longing for my bed when Janis suddenly launched into an account of the terrible ordeal our mother had been through, the heartbreaking sale of the farmhouse six months after Siem's death, and how she phoned her every day in her rental flat in Hengelo, for a chat, but in fact to make sure she was still alive.

"She hates me because I left my mother in the lurch," I said to Boudewijn later in bed. "And because I didn't tell them about Mike." Now that those two were downstairs soiling our sheets, I felt the anger well up.

"Sisters don't think that kind of thing," Boudewijn said from his half. "This just takes some getting used to. She didn't just show up for no reason. You're obsessing. I didn't think it was so bad. Tomorrow, after breakfast, we'll take a walk through Chinatown, let Timo loose among the comrades. They'll thaw, you'll see."

My irritation had subsided by the time I got up at 4 a.m. to soothe a crying Mike. As I calmed the little guy down I realized that Bo was right: Janis was the one who'd taken the first step, not me, even though that step hadn't really amounted to much yet. Even in the old days, when we were just starting to think for ourselves, we argued about fundamental issues, had furious arguments about nuclear weapons, about money, about music, capitalism—anything, as long as it was principled and painful—in each other's face like a pair of bickering fishwives, after which, as if by magic, a contrite peace came over us, probably thanks to the fact that we were in the same genetic boat.

Come morning, I fetched Mike and laid him in bed next to Boudewijn while I padded downstairs in a cotton dress. I had a strange urge to really splash out, flaunt our bourgeois American Dream. So on Friday, just after Janis's phone call, I had left Silicone Valley, throbbing migraine and all, and interrupted an already long drive home to stock up at Safeway and even went all the way to a Holland Deli in Palo Alto, a ridiculous little shop with a ridiculously oversized wooden clog as big as a small car at the front entrance. I bought Gouda cheese, Dutch gingerbread, currant buns, and *speculaas*. Already at the checkout counter I hated myself for going the whole hog, but now I was glad I did. Whatever Janis reported about me back in that chickenshit country, it wasn't going to be my fault.

The morning sun warmed the varnished hardwood floor and mint-green cabinets, sparkled on the espresso machine and the dish racks. The potted basil, marjoram, and bay plants on the windowsill above the counter sucked in the light. I laid my favorite tablecloth on the recycled wood table, was of two minds about which dishes—modern or traditional—and opted for Boudewijn's grandmother's German porcelain. It was almost nine o'clock. I prewarmed the oven for the ciabattas and bagels, beat some eggs for the French toast, arranged blueberry and pear-honey muffins on an oval platter. Fresh fruit, salami, three kinds of ham wrapped in cellophane, little dishes of marmalade, cereal and muesli, milk, yogurt, honey. I constructed a little Dutch island on a side table, with the currant buns, cheese, and packets of chocolate sprinkles and flakes. I squatted down next to the stereo, but reconsidered: I wanted to be able to hear the downstairs shower. I poached four eggs and made an espresso, for myself as well as for the aroma. She could take her pick.

Boudewijn came downstairs with Mike just before nine-thirty. I could just gobble them up, they looked so cozy and too, too domestic: Mike, already dressed, laughing and jabbering on his play rug, Bo squatting down alongside him, aglow from his shave, his wavy gray hair combed back with gel. He was wearing his felt Church slippers with the "BS" monogram on the toe, which usually irritated me. Things hadn't been so great between us, but he now was scoring points big-time. "And? The guests of honor up yet?" he asked with a smile.

Janis, I recalled, was a late sleeper who didn't do well with short nights, so we drank tea and thumbed through the *San Francisco Chronicle* as a matter of form. Just after ten Boudewijn gave me a wink. "Why don't you go wake them up," he said. "They'll appreciate that. I never like oversleeping at friends'."

I went downstairs and tapped gently on the garden-room door. I thought I heard movement, so I waited, then knocked again.

"Sleepyheads."

Since there was no answer I cracked open the door. Daylight and fresh air streamed in. I stuck my head into the deep, low-ceilinged room. The beds were empty, the covers crumpled in a heap, one of the doors to the yard stood wide open. I went in, picked up a wet towel from thc pinewood floor. The bathroom was deserted as well, the halogen spots above the washbasin were still on and tepid water trickled from the showerhead. While I scanned the wet floor for Timo and my sister, as though they had shrunk to the size of Q-tips, I realized they had been gone for hours.

Although morning rush-hour traffic on Sunset Boulevard was lighter than usual, I still managed to nearly rear-end the Chevrolet in front of me a couple of times. The memories of Janis threw me off—but not as much as those of *Aaron Bever.* During breakfast I happened to check an old Hotmail address, an account I used to buy and sell shoes and dresses on eBay, and was flabbergasted to stumble on a three-week-old e-mail from Aaron. It gave me a real shock. There are certain people who are out of the picture for so long that it's like they no longer exist. Aaron? *Uh-oh.* My first reaction was: trash it, so I sent the message straight to the wastebasket unread. I was never one for maintaining old contacts, but since that weird visit from my sister I had written off Enschede and all its ghosts once and for all. I left Holland in 2000, I didn't follow the news, had no contact with Dutch people, and after leaving Boudewijn and Mike didn't even speak the language anymore. My links to the mother country had been severed. And I wanted to keep it that way.

So in that sense it was a good thing there was big news waiting for me on Coldwater Canyon Avenue. Even before I closed my office door behind me, reception put me through to Víctor Sotomayor's assistant. What I was hoping for, what we all had been hoping for the past week, happened: the sale went through, there was a deal, for $16.3 million we could call ourselves the owners of the Los Angeles Barracks. Woohoo, party time.

Rusty stormed in and kissed me like it was New Year's Eve, and five minutes later we were standing there in the old lobby, all fifty of us, drinking a toast to our new premises. Rusty, who had nudged me up the staircase a couple of steps, reached over to refill my glass at least three times from one of the gold bottles of champagne we'd been keeping chilled all week. "Here," he roared in his nasal West Coast Irish accent, "in return for all the sleepless nights you've cost me." Then he drew everyone's attention to me. "Friends," he declared nervously, "a toast to *us*. A toast to the success of the Barracks. A toast to future colleagues. But first and foremost, a toast to Joy. This amazing woman here"—he shook my hip with his free hand, so that I had to grab the wobbly wooden banister for support—"has put us, shall I say, on the cutting edge."

He then nearly pulled me off the stairs and, in addition to two kisses, gave me the floor. Speeches still made him panicky, even after all his years as company director. It really was something, all those faces looking up at me. Cameramen, directors, make-up artists, the IT folks, a few actors in white bathrobes with half-made-up faces. Dedicated, loyal, eager, often decently educated loners, packed together into the wood-paneled lobby of our creaking Victorian manor house in the middle of Studio City (which Rusty, ever since I wanted to leave and he didn't, insisted on calling "Hollywood"). I explained to them one last time why the L.A. Barracks was going to make the difference. I repeated my promise that a year from now we would be the world's biggest player. And I have to admit: it felt like a personal triumph, I had pulled this off single-handedly, and for a whole hour I didn't give Aaron's live grenade a moment's thought. I was tickled pink that I had managed to get not one, but *two* pig-headed men—Rusty himself, and then Sotomayor on top of it—to listen to me.

Of course, the whole thing still gave Rusty pause; $16.3 million was, even for Rusty Wells, a shitload of money, tenfold his biggest investment ever. "Joy," he would sigh when, at the end of a workday, I launched into my umpteenth sales pitch for the Barracks, "do you realize how much I love Hollywood? And do you have any idea what it means for a boy from Belfast to earn his living a stone's throw from MGM?" "You want a tissue?" I would answer, knowing full well we were not hurting for money. This old pile, built in the late nineteenth century by British immigrants who for decades had run it as a family hotel, had charm; its twenty-four irregularly shaped rooms were spread over three uneven, staggered, moldy-smelling floors. Jade-green lampshades hung in the hallways like floppy turbans, the reception desk shone like a Steinway, the lobby gave you the impression that Paul Newman and Robert Redford were somewhere upstairs smoking cigars in a clawfoot bathtub. Rusty had shelled out a million bucks for it back in 2001 and brought in a motley nine-man crew who sort of knew how to put a film together. But that was then. Nowadays the gray-slate roofs and blue-painted bay windows nearly caved in when all fifty of us turned on our PCs at once. It was time to move on, and Rusty knew it.

"But why a feckin' 200,000-square-foot fortress?" he asked. "And why for twice our feckin' 2007 profit? Last year we earned just under eight million—eight, Joy, not eigh*teen.* And why in feckin' Compton, of all places? You want us all dead? Why a *historical landmark*? Why a *listed* monument? You want to spend your time squabbling with sixteen amateur historians? You want to start a fight with half of the goddamn *city council*?"

When we decided to become business partners back in 2003, we made a deal: we can fight, we *should* fight, but with a twenty-four-hour limit. After that we'd get out and earn money again. About three weeks ago we rented a squash court out on Irving Drive, we do that now and again, with the agreement that for forty-five minutes we wouldn't talk business. But this time we were at each other's throats about the Old Barracks before the ball even got warm. The same old argument. Our CEO and founder stood there in his faded Guinness T-shirt, milk-bottle legs spread, clutching his racket like a dagger in his freckled fist, hollering: and I'm *damned* if I'm gonna shell out twenty million for a cinder block spook house, and I *don't* need my face in the *L.A. Times,* and I *didn't* sell you shares only for you to turn around and bankrupt me. It was the first time since we'd teamed up that we were on totally opposite sides of the fence.

Although I had seen the eruption coming, I was still taken aback. The often costly changes I'd been allowed to make over the past few years attested to Rusty's confidence in my business sense. I had taken the initiative to shift us from one large to six more specific websites, gradually of course, but with resounding success. I was the one who insisted on buying better cameras and investing in faster connections, so our film sets were now technically on a par with the big Hollywood and Burbank studios. He had given me carte blanche in recruiting personnel. And not only the creatives: when I suggested hiring marketing people, a controller, and even a personnel manager to draw up pension and health care plans, he didn't flinch. Since then our profits had risen from a piddly under three million to last year's eight.

Squash courts are ingeniously designed kill traps: you can't get out, no one hears you, the light is merciless. I needed to find his weak spot, and in his case that was Europe. "Wells," I said, no longer as restrained as during the past month of arranging my arguments like a floral bouquet, "you are *so* conservative, you are *so* slow, you have no guts—what are you, a European?" Rusty enjoyed taking the occasional fifteen minutes to lambaste the big multinationals from what he called the "olde worlde economy": Shell, Barclays, Renault, Total, the same old list from his days at Goldman Sachs, and the same old pseudo-intellectual explanation that probably was based on some or other rule of thumb and that he presented with such aplomb that you didn't know if he was serious or pulling your leg. Rusty, sitting on the edge of his desk like a guru as he raked the European business world over the coals.

"The classic CEO just doesn't get it, Joy. A wimp like him thinks: I have to be innovative, I have to be sustainable, I have to go green, I have to do this, that, and the other. He opens up a can of managers and realizes a year later that those feckin' morons thought up something totally different than what he meant. So he says: whoa, let's wait it out a bit. *Stupid*."

"What do you want," I asked him that day on the squash court: "to go back to Belfast, or tack an extra zero onto your year-end profits? In two years we'll either be making fifty million, Wells, or we'll be broke. What we're doing now, anyone can do. It's got to be better. It's got to be bigger. *Different*. And you know it."

"That's pure ballax," he retorted. On the rare occasion that he lost his velvety patience, his English turned thick Irish. Rusty

Wells: if there was anyone who wanted to obscure his background but couldn't, it was Rusty. He was raised in Belfast in a moderate Catholic family that spent the whole of the 1980s scared to death of the IRA; not because the terror in any way touched the family itself, but because the terror appeared to be carried out in their name. He once mentioned the nervous loathing and misplaced guilt that had colored his youth. From then on I thought I had that incessant smile of his figured out. At rest, his face betrayed subtle wrinkles that encircled his lipless mouth, folded around the corners of his mouse-gray eyes—wrinkles that, strangely enough, vanished when he laughed, which he did effortlessly and at random, so often that the smile was in fact his face's default mode.

"I can't do it," he said with the pinched voice of some B actor trying to emote. He let his spine slide down the wall until his little Irish tush hit the floor, the back of his head resting against the whitewashed cement under the red stripe.

"Rusty, am I hearing you right?"

"I. Can't. Do. It."

"What can't you do?"

"Take such a big risk."

I couldn't believe my ears. "And what about your real estate larks?" For years he'd been playing the big shot with his gangster house in Bel Air, alongside a handful of other properties he'd picked up on spec, all of them in Beverly Hills or on Sunset. Thanks to a sweet bonus deal I was able to buy a fabulous house from him at the beginning of Sunset Boulevard—a Frank Lloyd Wright clone sticking halfway out of the cliff and supported by tall pillars—that Rusty wanted to "keep in the family." "And your pet Rembrandt?" He like poking around art auctions. In the Dutch Masters section of the Getty there is a tiny painting, a bathroom tile, no more than that, but it *was* a Rembrandt, a *gen-u-ine* Rembrandt, and that genuine Rembrandt was the property of Rusty Wells. A risk-taker? Rusty *burned* dollars.

"That's different," he said. "It's private."

Around 2000 he got rich overnight by selling off a dating site just before the dot-com crash. He likes to tell the story of how, right after signing the papers, he walked out of his poky two-bedroom apartment in Redondo Beach, got into a taxi and told the driver to take him to Mulholland Drive, and step on it, man, let's see some trees, but slow down at For Sale signs. When he saw the villa he wanted, he got out and offered the owners fifty percent above their asking price—you'll have your money tonight—on the condition that they clear out on the spot. He never set foot in that dump in Redondo Beach again, hadn't even taken the trouble to sell it, the sink was probably still full of dirty dishes. Probably all bullshit, just like what he was telling me now.

I squatted down in front of him and looked hard into his pale irises. "Where's the daredevil who only needed five minutes to wheedle me away from McKinsey?" I whispered seductively. "What happened to Wells the go-getter?"

He blinked nervously. His blond eyelashes made his eyelids look too short.

"How do you think they got so big at eBay? At Amazon? By shitting in their pants?"

Instead of chewing me out, which maybe I deserved, he fed me that story about his father. "If you must bring up Belfast," he said, "my old man . . ."

I remember thinking: if there's one thing I do not need to hear, Rusty Wells, it is some sob story about your father. In San Fernando Valley people don't have parents. Forget them, I wanted to say, that's what I did—but I restrained myself.

"My pa," he mumbled, and I still thought it was all an act,

"worked on the payroll for twenty years, he was a traveling linoleum salesman. Iceland. New Zealand. Indonesia. Linoleum roller-skating rinks—it's what he said to anybody who would listen. When he was home, that is."

I have to say that I wouldn't have missed this story for the world. Until that moment Rusty was like an ancient Egyptian on a roll of papyrus: a total badass, the whole package, but two-dimensional. He stepped off the page by telling me that his father had one great "passion," and that was *magic*. Magic—the word said it all. For half of Rusty's youth, his father sits up in his attic fiddling with marked cards and pulling rabbits out of a hat, spends the spare hours of his business trips scouring hole-in-the-wall magic stores on the outskirts of town. At age fifty-two, a coronary bypass already behind him, he makes a decision. The man who, according to Rusty, has spent his entire life vexed, no, *infuriated* that he has a boss, turns his back on linoleum. He borrows 400,000 pounds from the Bank of Ireland and falls for a small theatre just outside downtown Belfast. A small but pricey theatre.

"So you've got showbiz in your blood," I said. "What was it called?"

"Wellington's Magic Venue."

I attempted a smile, tapped my racket against his pointy knee, but he did not react.

"The place was a dump. And *expensive.* I had just started working in the City, my job was to evaluate investment plans, and so I flew my dad over to London to go through the whole enterprise with him. Buy or rent, he asked—buy, I advised. What could possibly go wrong?"

"Don't tell me," I sighed. A chill started coming up through the floor. But Rusty, never at a loss for words (particularly during meetings), kept on going. He told me his father spent two solid months polishing his act, had double-sided color pamphlets printed that he and his wife distributed all over Belfast. The act opened four months after he'd turned in his notice. I didn't dare ask how it ended. "Three years later, my mother sat on a hard plastic garden chair in that stripped-down barn, still shuddering from the public auction. They even ripped out the velvet theatre chairs. My folks tried everything, but they couldn't get it off the ground. Not far enough, anyway. Magic is a tricky business."

"Whew," I said. "And your father?"

"Dead. Heart attack. Mortgage stress. Millstone cancer of the heart. You get my drift?"

I didn't get his drift, none of it. I had never heard such rubbish, the Barracks had little to do with Rusty's late father's Magic Venue, absolutely zilch, to be precise. It started to dawn on me that my business partner had more of a sensitive side to him than I suspected. Under Rusty's tough, jovial, rebellious exterior he was all white meat, squishy and irrational. What he did not know, not in detail at least, was that I had been working on Sotomayor for some weeks already—according to the *L.A. Business Journal,* the most powerful real estate baron in the South. He owned the L.A. Barracks and was itching to get rid of it, this was common knowledge. Everyone knew that for four years Sotomayor had been trying to peddle the former National Guard Barracks to a whole parade of real estate developers, up to and including a pair of Hungarians. Everyone also knew that it was first supposed to become luxury apartments, then a social housing project, after that a rehab clinic, then a parking garage—but neighborhood committees managed to scuttle one plan after another. The highest bid he'd been offered was fourteen—everybody knew that too. We'll top that, I promised him, and quietly arranged a preliminary and non-binding tour of the premises, just me and one of Víctor Sotomayor's little helpers in that enormous brick fortress; it was terrific.

"I understand, Rusty," I said. "But you could at least go have a look."

I finally got around to taking him over to the Barracks the week after that squash game; until then all he'd seen were site plans and photos. Accompanied by yet another of Sotomayor's girl Fridays, we drove for nearly an hour straight through Los Angeles, heading for what not only looked like a medieval fort, but also *was* a medieval fort. The Barracks, built in 1916, mimicked, in a grim, evil way, a Moorish fortress. For some sixty years the National Guard insignia fluttered above the thirty-four-meter-high corner towers; Sotomayor flew the Stars and Stripes as well as a single Cuban flag. Behind the battlements, cadets were trained and the lead-reinforced vaults had stored ammunition and matériel. The façade had a rough, unpettable brick skin: for every five normally laid bricks was one that stuck out from the wall, sometimes at an angle, sometimes half broken off. The drill court, covered by a large arched roof, used to be the place, in the '30s and '40s, where boxers faced off: "Joe Louis and Max Schmeling," I told Rusty, who promptly broke into shadow boxing. The Army pulled out in '78, leaving behind 160 empty rooms—cinder block dormitories, walnut-paneled dining rooms, oak ballrooms, massive staircases, an industrial kitchen, swimming pool, indoor shooting range, bathrooms, engine rooms, basements, dungeons. All for Rusty.

It paid off. I noticed his transformation as we rambled through the labyrinth, an hour-long hike through the Barracks' filthy corridors, offices where half-disintegrated files lay stacked on sagging shelves, officers' quarters with forgotten regimental tunics draped over dusty chairs; his footsteps began to echo, his expression turned greedy, he became more and more chatty with Sotomayor's bimbo. When we got back to the covered drill court, the size of four ice hockey rinks, she said: "This is where George Lucas shot the outer-space scenes in *Star Wars*"—and at that moment, on the ceiling of Rusty's head, a fluorescent lamp sprang on.

But after that Thursday afternoon in Compton, Sotomayor suddenly started playing hard to get. Phone calls and e-mails went unanswered. Only after sending three faxes to his head office in Dallas did I get a roundabout reply from some secretary or other, what it boiled down to was that the Barracks was suddenly no longer for sale. Fuck you, Víctor. I assume he had got wind of our plans, he'll have envisioned flack from the neighborhood, negative press, God knows what. So in my next fax I suggested executing the sale quietly. After that, the Compton shopkeepers and hoi polloi were *our* problem. "Everything's for sale," read the fax, "I don't think I need to explain that to Víctor Sotomayor—and not everything has to get into the papers." And even if it did get into the papers, there were advantages to that too. I reminded him that since Villaraigosa became mayor of L.A., it had escaped no one's attention that he and Sotomayor were buddies. A few years earlier, the real estate baron grudgingly admitted to the *Los Angeles Times* that he—a fellow Latino—had contributed generously to Villaraigosa's election campaign. Since then the allocation of public works contracts seemed to tip quite blatantly his way. "Víctor, my friend," I wrote, "maybe this is your chance to do something the mayor is *not* keen on. Think about it. We're offering you fifteen. I can be in Dallas next Monday at four o'clock."

No reply. Of course not. Sotomayor didn't care for my upfront tone. He was a more-luck-than-talent Cuban with a sweaty boxer's nose, not accustomed to negotiating with women. His corpulent, pear-shaped body was clad in shoddy pastel-colored suits on which he wiped his beringed fingers before giving me a tepid, flabby handshake.

"So I take it that's a yes," I said to Rusty. Last Monday I boarded a flight to Texas, and at five to four in the afternoon I stepped out of the fingerprint-smudged mirrored elevator on the eleventh floor of Stone Tower in downtown Dallas and knocked, without an appointment, on the matt-glass door to Sotomayor's office.

I disappeared back up the stairs earlier than my celebrating colleagues, under the pretext of getting back to work, setting an example—but in actual fact, with an unexpected knot in my gut. That e-mail. With every step, the bustle downstairs ebbed and the mystery swelled. Was it wise to have deleted his e-mail unread? What was Aaron after? Back in my office—formerly a bridal suite—with the door closed, the only sound was the soft hum of the PC. What did he want? Reading it couldn't hurt, I thought, whether or not to respond was the next choice, and that was more the point. I retrieved the message from the trash folder. The rush of success and the relaxing effect of three glasses of Armand de Brignac Ace of Spades apparently allowed me to overcome my reluctance. Without giving it any more thought, I opened Aaron's e-mail.

(No subject)
From: Aaron Bever (a.bever@hetnet.be)
Sent: Thursday, April 17th, 2008, 04:49
To: Joni Sigerius (jonisigerius74@hotmail.com)

i'll bet you were surprised when your mother told you we spoke at brussels central what an amazing coincidence without realizing it we sat across from each other all the way from maastricht, we only recognized each other at the last minute, i hadn't seen her in so long either. i'm doing fine, i hope she told you that too, boy did she look good, so thin, so cheerful, so feminine, i was pretty surprised to see her in brussels, but that was mutual, because how could she have known i live in linkebeek now, i'm not going to say exactly where, because i value my privacy. actually that's why i'm writing to you, because you know better than anyone how badly that mess back in 2000 shook me up, you helped me an awful lot then, I heard that from dr. haitink, was i a little bit nice to you? when i saw your mother with your husband i could hardly believe you'd settled in brussels too, now there's a coincidence for you, funny how these things go, i spotted you just a couple of days later at the playground of the klimOP, I HAPPENED TO BE TAKING CLASS PICTURES THAT DAY, ALTHOUGH WHAT'S COINCIDENCE, WHAT *IS* COINCIDENCE, JONI? AND I SAW YOU WALK ACROSS THE PLAYGROUND PUSHING A STROLLER, YOU WERE WITH YOUR HUSBAND, THE SAME GUY WHO CAME TO PICK YOur mother up at the station in his bmw, it was kind of comical, we looked at each other right away and knew we were rivals, i wish you two all the happiness in the world. it was easy to pick out your daughter on the photos, i spotted juliette in a jiffy, third grade, miss jeanne, front row second from the left, the spitting image of you as a kid, two little blond braids, and what an enviable last name, jalabert, juliette jalabert, it sure sounds a lot better than bever, maybe even better than sigerius, but what's in a name? i'm sure that rich boyfriend of yours is awfully kind to juliette, but that's not why i'm writing, the reason i'm writing is that i've had a bit of a setback the last few days, i just wanted to warn you, in fact it's not going well at all, i'm sleeping so badly again, darling. tineke told me that terrible news about your father, siem has been dead for years, she said, i only half believed her, i believe it, i have to believe it. i had no idea, i didn't know, really i didn't, i swear, i'm so sorry, i could cry about it all over again. everything came flooding back, it's washing over me from all sides, the past few nights it's been gnawing at me constantly, i had to go through it again in my mind, everything that happened, whose fault it is, the fights we had, etc. etc., and it's LOGICAL. DON'T YOU ALSO THink it all started with the fireworks disaster? that ruined everything. after that it all went so goddamn FASt, everything fucked up, fuck, fuck, fuck. what i want to ask you is if you'll tell me whereabout you live and work, then i know where there's a chance i might bump into you, because that one time at the klimop i nearly freaked, i followed you all the way through sint-jansmolenbeek, through scheutbospark, all the way to anderlecht, but then i lost you, until i saw you in a green bus heading for koekelberg. well it took me hours to get home, i was up to my waist in mud. that's it. i hope everything is ok with you, you've got a nice husband and a pretty daughter, what a goddamn shame that her wonderful grandpa

Her wonderful grandpa? A haze hung over the Valley, a blend of mist and smog. Below, on the broad sidewalk along Coldwater Canyon Avenue, an Asian kid in a Dodgers jersey gingerly opened the wrought-iron gate that separated our front yard from the street and climbed up the sandstone steps with a newspaper he'd taken out of a shoulder bag.

Her wonderful grandpa. I went out into the corridor. Danny and Deke were hanging in the Recruiting doorway, glass in hand. I greeted them, silently went down two flights of carpeted stairs and in the kitchenette I found a tray of used champagne glasses. I took the cleanest of them and filled it to the brim from one of the open bottles on top of the fridge. Sipping, I walked back upstairs and sat down at the computer. I opened Microsoft Office and sent an official reply to Sotomayor in which I indicated I wasn't prepared to fly to Dallas a second time. He could just organize a lawyer in L.A.

I pulled the elastic band from my hair, shook it loose, and stared out over Coldwater. The paperboy opened a gate across the street. The cuffs of his formless jeans were squashed under the soles of his sneakers.

So Aaron was still off his rocker. I opened the letter again and as I reread his garbled missive an unpleasant mix of pity, relief, and disgust settled over me. For the time being I was relieved; it seemed to me to be a completely harmless e-mail from someone with no plan or ulterior motive. The guy had just sat down and let himself go, apparently in one confused spurt. I'd forgotten he had this e-mail address, I had opened the account during my McKinsey internship. The last time I saw Aaron was at the end of December 2000, when he went off the deep end. It seemed like half a lifetime ago, an old-time newsreel, it genuinely hurt me to think that he still . . .

Or *again*, of course. As I read his little epistle for the third time I realized that the line between fact and fiction wasn't so easy to trace, if there was even anything factual about it at all. Much of it was grotesquely nonsensical: to start with, I was single, mother of a little boy, and hadn't been in Brussels in thirty years. My heart skipped a beat when he started in on that child. Juliette—where the hell did he get that from? What did it say about the rest? Had he really spoken to my mother? Of course not. Tineke *thin*? That seemed to me confirmation that he was imagining things, for some reason confusing a perfect stranger with my mother, just like he thought he saw me at a school playground. I did not know much about psychiatry, but this seemed to me completely delusional.

On the other hand, he was using a Belgian provider, but what did that prove except that maybe he did live in Brussels, he was quite detailed about that, although it was beyond me what he'd be doing there. A malicious image welled up in me, I envisaged a busload of crazies from Enschede on a day trip to Brussels, and Aaron wandering the streets for a few hours while the orderlies searched for him.

I brought the empty champagne glass to my lips and looked past its slender outline at the moisture stains on the ceiling. What I didn't get is why he would make contact now, after eight years of silence. There must be a reason. Could he really not have known about Siem? Was that possible? Could he have missed it? Maybe he just read it now somewhere, or saw it on television, and the news had set him off. It was bizarre, utterly ironic, that Aaron of all people—chairman of the Siem fan club himself—wouldn't know. I reread the part where he mentioned my father. I let his question about whether it all started with the fireworks disaster sink in. Not so crazy after all. If you thought about what had happened to the three of us after May 13, 2000, then the answer could well be: yes.

All three of us were out of town the day SE Fireworks exploded. Siem, if I'm not mistaken, was in Shanghai on university business, Aaron and I were at a wedding in Zaltbommel. We were safe.

None of us was left homeless (although in Aaron's case it was a close call, a matter of just fifteen meters), nobody lost an arm or a leg. Still, I too was inclined to believe that the merciless blast had a disruptive effect on us all. Maybe it's a law of nature that a blowup of those proportions sets unforeseen mechanisms in action, produces shock waves that in turn bring about bizarre developments, create misunderstandings, compel decisions. It seems like disasters of this scale act as miniature Big Bangs that expand into spaces buzzing with consequences, intrigues, possibilities, and impossibilities. A physical disaster like a fireworks accident is a maternity ward where new disasters are born.

Not that we had any inkling that day—on the contrary. On the day itself, no clue. That Saturday, May 13, 2000, Aaron and I were safe and sound, digging into the marzipan wedding cake of a certain Etienne, the only high school friend Aaron still saw, and down there in Zaltbommel we found it difficult to really take in what had happened in our city, 150 kilometers away. Being among the all-day guests, we decided to spend an hour back in our hotel room while the bridal couple prepared for the photo session. On the steps of the town hall, Aaron gave Etienne Vaessen a squeeze round his creamy waist and said we were nipping out for a quick break.

Not long before good manners pressed us to drive out to the estate where the dinner was held, I switched on the television. It was about five o'clock, I had just showered, Aaron was still in the bathroom fussing with his cuff links. Channel-surfing from the bed, I noticed that three stations were broadcasting the same images of a city, the view of a city you see when you approach it in a Boeing, and from that city rose an immense black column of smoke, *that* I saw, and the city was called Enschede, I registered that too. When Aaron came and sat down next to me, we watched footage from the ground, burning cars under a pitch-black sky, policemen shoving bewildered people in short pants out of a rubble-strewn street. If he'd looked a bit closer he would have seen that the street was the Lasondersingel, 150 meters from his house. "We've got to get back," he said, "and ransack the Grolsch brewery," a little joke I had to laugh at, simply because I just could not for the life of me imagine that the well-worn stoops that led to that little joke, the cobbled streets along which on other Saturdays we would stroll up to the Roomweg to buy fried rice at the tiny Chinese take-out, or a little farther on, order RAS French fries with herb salt at De Roombeker cafeteria, let's just call it the road map of Aaron's daily life—because it was utterly inconceivable to me that that inert, inviolable, unalterable reality had *ceased to exist.*

I hadn't recharged my cell phone, and Aaron didn't own one back then. There was a pseudo-classical bakelite telephone in the hotel room, a matt-black stagecoach with a dial and coiled cord. I tried to reach my parents, but soon concluded that the network around Enschede was overloaded. Aaron didn't think it was necessary to phone Venlo. Afterward we found out how many friends, family, and acquaintances had a very different opinion on the matter. His parents had been phoned by an uncle, a friend of his mother, his grandfather, his brother Sebastian, a classmate, his ex-judo instructor, the mother of an ex-girlfriend, an editor from *Tubantia Weekly*: understandably and genuinely concerned people who all asked, in a variety of ways, the same question: was Aaron still alive? His mother reached us the next day at my student house in a terrible state—she had spent the entire night in the living room, poring over teletext updates and sitting through reruns of *Nova* and the evening news, hoping for a sign of life. His dad, Aaron told me almost derisively, had exhibited less patience. "I'm going there," he said at nine-thirty—and I could just imagine how Aaron's tawny, bearded father grabbed his car keys and a pack of shag from the dining room table, and without further commentary drove off in the froggy-green Toyota Corolla he used to fetch us with when we took the train down to Venlo. To no avail, of course. His father, a pastry baker whose forearms carried the scars of 100,000 red-hot baking sheets, spent an hour wandering up and down police barriers and caution tape, accosting firemen and emergency personnel until they finally shooed him away.

"Your father is livid," his mother said.

"Who takes off to Enschede on a gamble in the middle of the night?"

"You watch your mouth. That you didn't think to phone us is bad enough. You could've been *dead.*"

From the booze, anyway. While the father was scouring the burning streets of Enschede, the missing son was whooping it up in Zaltbommel, partying like there's no tomorrow, swigging glasses of pink champagne that don't make you pee but do make you dance. While ambulances rode in and out of his neighborhood, Aaron joked to anyone who would listen that Roombeek was just like meat fried in Croma margarine—"it doesn't spatter on its way to the platter." When he lay down among the balloons and plastic beer glasses to do an imitation of Chinese firecrackers, I dragged him off the dance floor by his collar.

The next morning in the car, the radio stations were full of the news of the war zone we were heading toward, and once we got to Enschede we felt strangely apprehensive as we approached the edge of Roombeek. Like his father twelve hours earlier, we parked alongside the fence in the median of the Lasondersingel, there was no getting any closer. We smelled the sulfury odor of spent fireworks and gawked at the shingleless roofs and wrecked chimneys on houses that had only just survived the shock wave and blocked our view of the real crater. A twisted metal shipping container had bored into the grassy median; the only way it could have got there was in an arc *over* the houses. Across from the damaged Rijksmuseum, a man sat staring through the fencing from a folding fisherman's stool. He told us that the fire had spared the Vluchtestraat. On the ground next to him was a thermos of coffee, but he wasn't a rubbernecker: his own house, on the H.B. Blijdensteinlaan, was on the verge of collapse, according to the experts. We drove in silence to my student house in the city center. In the kitchen we listened to my housemates' reports; one of them was driving our shared minivan through the Deurningerstraat at the time of the explosion and watched a block of cement crash through the roof of the car in front of her.

"Pity we weren't home," Aaron said with genuine regret in his voice. "This was not to be missed."

They had flown Ennio by trauma helicopter to the Groningen Academic Hospital with severe burns and lacerations. It was my mother who mentioned it to me in passing a week after the fireworks disaster. We were standing in my parents' laundry room, Aaron and I had already been staying there for a few days. She jammed the drum full of bedding, but in fact she was spin-drying *me*. The news sent me whirling, the blood draining from my veins.

Ennio Aaltink, a full-blooded Italian from the town of Forlì, ran, curiously enough, a British bodega in the Havenstraat passage, a long, narrow shop where as a first-year student I tended the cash register on Wednesday afternoons. The two of us helped German day trippers and the closest thing to Twents landed gentry negotiate the pots of Colman's English Mustard and Haywards Pickled Onions, packs of Shredded Wheat, Honey Nut Cheerios, tins of baked beans and sausage, mushy peas, black peas, parched peas, and chutneys in a whole range of baby-poop colors. But most of the time my boss and I were alone.

From age sixteen to thirty Ennio had sailed around the world, his last stint as a ship's cook, and he wholesaled in exotic stories. Intentionally or not, the things he told me always posed a dilemma, touched on issues about how a person *could* live. About what it's like to be stuck on a tanker off the coast of Sakhalin when you're depressed. What it's like to very nearly marry an Angolese. Or if your captain orders you to smuggle thirty Filipino women. "Tell me, Joni, what would *you* have done?" He was forty-something, dark and handsome, with a nose as long as your finger and shining brown eyes that in fact were fingers too, with which he spent those Wednesdays poking at my unsullied little soul.

In charming Twents-Italian, where the words would unexpectedly pile up onto one another, he told me about his youth, about his crackpot parents who had drummed the magnificence of Benito Mussolini into Ennio and his brothers. Since Il Duce's death, everything in Italy had gone to the corrupt, half-assed, democratic dogs, according to Ennio's father, a tormented windbag who confused a difference of opinion with a blood vendetta and sold newspapers at Forlì Station from a sun-bleached kiosk that gradually became silted up with fascist diatribes, Duce hagiographies, and cardboard devotional cards depicting the intrepid leader on horseback. Every Sunday the family piled into their tomato-red Fiat and drove, fresh roses on the rear shelf, to Mussolini's birthplace, not coincidentally a stone's throw from Forlì, their excursion culminating at the family tomb where Ennio's father, chin jutting forward, would recite one of Il Duce's orations.

Some two years into his *scuola media* a history teacher laid the hard truth about Mussolini on Ennio. It took him a couple of weeks, but he finally realized, for good, that his parents worshipped a depraved, destructive, clownish megalomaniac, and that his father was not only stupid but probably evil himself. So he left. One night, while his younger brother lay sleeping behind him, he wrote a farewell note—I could just see it, a twenty-five-year-younger Ennio writing the letter, his letter of resignation, by candlelight. The next morning he hitchhiked to the harbor in Ravenna and boarded a cargo ship bound for India.

In exchange for such open-heartedness I told him, amid the jars of marmalade and stacks of felt-lined picnic baskets, about my own background, a story that paled next to his—back then, at least. Like everyone else, he asked if I still saw my real father, and when I told him I felt no need to, he reacted differently than I had expected. He told me I was stupid, slack, even heartless. That's what he said. Cold. He, of all people! The man who for years had given Italy a wide berth, who had fathered, with a gym teacher from Boekelo, a spidery little daughter who didn't even know she *had* Italian grandparents, a man who had even gone so far as to take his wife's last name. "My father, he play fascist in Italian parliament," he said. "That is because of the reason, Joni. Iffa you don' have good reason to abandon family, then don' do it."

I liked him. For a year we chatted, we slid past each other, until one afternoon I threw my arms around that skinny torso of his. I pressed my breasts against his body, a body corseted by self-determination, by obstinacy, by wanderlust and the yearning for authenticity and independence (or so I thought in my love-smitten, puerile teenage head), by a principled unfetteredness, I thought too, because I assumed impermanence and itchy feet made that hard, sinewy exterior all syrupy on the inside. A man without roots. He lifted me up and kissed me. He wants me, I thought, all I need to do is ask and he'll put this lousy little shop up for sale and whisk me away to New York or Rio de Janeiro.

He just laughed at me. No way! Didn't I understand how much he loved that gym coach of his? And his daughter? "But," he said, "if you promise not getting in love, we close-a the shop on Wednesday afternoons." It was after six, I was already tallying up the cash register. "You think about it." Well, thinking was the last thing I needed to do: the following Wednesday I raced to the bodega like a burning fuse. For a good two years we spent the weekly afternoon break on his black-velvet IKEA love seat back in the storeroom, a red-hot hour right in the middle of the week that rose like a bead of oil in a glass of water, and even once I hitched up with Aaron it floated there like a bubble on the surface of my daily existence. I still filled in there a few times a year, and every time he locked the front door at twelve o'clock sharp.

In the laundry room, eye to eye with my mother, I had no idea how badly hurt Ennio was, but the thought that his smooth, caramel-colored skin, his slightly sunken chest, his fine legs, even, God help me, his stern face, might be damaged by brute force, by flying shrapnel, by extreme heat, was unbearable. "But how?" I sobbed to my mother. "What in God's name was he doing in Roombeek?"

"I know a lot of things, darling," she said, "but I don't know everything."

The rest of the day at Coldwater passed in a haze that darkened by the hour. I lost myself in memories of Enschede, of Aaron, Ennio, my father, of all those Twents bridges I'd burned behind me. And although I had my hands full with organizing the closing—phone calls to the lawyer, to Sotomayor's people, whether or not in L.A. (for a moment it looked like Dallas again after all), with or without Sotomayor in person, and especially: *when*—Enschede kept rearing its ugly head, wove its way through the lunchtime conversations with colleagues out in the crumbling gazebo. After lunch I made two attempts at answering Aaron's e-mail, immediately trashing both. What was the point? My hesitation may have been tangible on the other side of the Atlantic Ocean, because at eleven minutes past three I received a second message.

4

"If you must know," Aaron said gruffly, "my father passed away. Quite suddenly."

The woman, who announced herself as the headmistress of De Klimop and nothing more, so that he spent the entire telephone conversation trying to remember her name, was taken aback by his lie. For a moment the line hummed with her awareness of mortality. Death, now that scared people. Aaron had been confronted by her abrasive voice on his answering machine three times, each message sharper and chillier than the last, and although he acknowledged she was entirely within her rights—of course he had not held up his end of the bargain, the photos should have been delivered long ago—he dreaded that righteous anger.

"I'm terribly sorry for you, Mr. Bever," she said, suddenly calm. "My condolences." Again she fell silent, a grudging respect that he milked for as long as possible. She cleared her throat. "Why didn't you inform the school? You should have phoned me."

She sounded about his age, even a bit younger. She was the head of a good-sized primary school with mostly immigrant pupils, a typical ghetto school in a run-down part of Sint-Jansmolenbeek. Right from their first meeting, on picture day itself, he tagged her as one of those no-nonsense idealistic types, he'd seen enough of those. As the classes of somber, raucous, and unruly African schoolchildren passed in front of his camera, his admiration for her courage and sense of responsibility grew. Everyone he spoke to at the smaller village schools had an opinion about the Brussels ghetto schools, but this woman, he had to hand it to her, she stood with both feet firmly in the muck. Still, who she was irked him no end. Her milk-white pageboy haircut, her large asexual face, footwear with Velcro fasteners, a sign she was slipping away from the adult world. She e-nun-ci-a-ted exaggeratedly, repeated everything she knew better at least three times, to him and undoubtedly at parent-teacher evenings as well.

He said: "The past two weeks have been extremely painful and hectic. My father was my business partner. I had to close shop temporarily."

He'd rather not think about the impression he made of himself. He had photographed the children the morning after his chance encounter with Tineke, and even then his mind had already begun to unravel. At least, he guessed as much from a disturbing panic–e-mail he'd discovered in his Sent box that he'd apparently written to Joni Sigerius. If he understood his own message correctly, upon finishing the photo session at De Klimop he'd gone on a mad ramble through Brussels, a story Joni fortunately hadn't responded to—if she'd even received it. Just to be sure, yesterday evening he plunged a brief apology e-mail into the black hole, and consequently had been sitting at his computer the entire afternoon waiting for a reply that might never come.

"But yes, you're right. I should have phoned."

She audibly drew a breath. Her principal's office smelled like crayons and was full of children's books. She *read* children's books, only children's books, which is why her jaw and skull kept growing. She ruined her mind with kiddie books, like you could ruin your eyes by reading with too little light, or your ears with the volume too soft.

"Why'd you phone Juliette Jalabert's parents?"

"Excuse me?" Her question surprised him. That little girl, he recalled, had featured in his e-mail to Joni. Had he been pestering strangers? What was she talking about?

"You heard me. Juliette's father came by. He says you've called three times to pester them with bizarre questions."

He began to dig through his memory, like a police dog searching for something dead. Juliette Jalabert's father . . . He drew a blank. He suspected that he'd been out of it for at least a few days, not so unusual after an attack. Since the BMW carrying Tineke Sigerius drove out of his life, his brain was like a war zone.

"I'm sorry," he said. "I have no idea what you're talking about."

"Well, think about it then," she said. "And forget the order. Consider it canceled."

"But—"

"And I'm only going to say this once: no photos of our pupils on your website."

He set the receiver down with a groan and kicked himself away from his desk. His chair rolled backward into the room. He lit a cigarette. On the screen of his iMac was one of the class photos from that damn Klimop he'd started working on this morning. At the bottom of each group photo he had spelt out, in gold block letters, the name of the school, class number, and year; on the individual portraits, the child's name in florid italics. No sign yet of a Juliette Jalabert. He shut the program without saving his changes and bit his lower lip.

Feeling numb after his extraordinary encounter with Joni's mother, he had transferred to a local train to Linkebeek, where he fell prey to a mixture of anguish and indignation. The news of Sigerius's death, as stale as it was, hit him hard; the entire way home his legs felt heavy and his chest strangely empty. What had happened? God damn it, why didn't anybody tell him?

As he led a relatively anger-free life, he did not immediately associate the swelling irritation with his disease; instead of running upstairs and grabbing a strip of Seroquel from the medicine chest, he went into the kitchen and warmed up a can of Chinese tomato soup on the induction stove. Big mistake. After that he climbed the two sets of spiral stairs, his teeth chattering in rage, up to the attic and flopped onto his unmade bed. How could the guy be dead for seven years without him knowing about it? He tossed and turned the whole night, in the darkest hours gazing into the mitre of trusses above his overheated head. Sigerius had been cold in his grave since the start of 2001, Tineke had said. Ah, now he got it: Sigerius must have died during those three weeks when he himself was off in outer space. From the end of December 2000 until sometime in June 2001 he had been locked up in the secure unit of the Twentse Tulip, a psychiatric hospital on the outskirts of Enschede—more than six months in all, the first three weeks in solitary confinement. So just then, at the absolute nadir of his own life, the news of Sigerius's demise must have spread through the Netherlands.

As soon as he was admitted to the Tulip, they let him cool down in a concrete "separette," as they dared to call those hayless stalls. It was furnished with a bare gray plastic mattress and a stainless-steel toilet. On one of the cold, soundproofed walls was a blackboard with white chalk. Nothing came in and nothing went out. Dressed in a burlap shirt and paper underpants, he'd screamed his lungs out—and meanwhile they had buried Sigerius?

The irony of it all was that there in his cell, deprived of news, of weather forecasts, of *himself*, he saw himself as a clairvoyant. The myriad air bubbles in the cinder blocks of his cell enveloped him like a cosmic mist. When he lay on his plastic slab and breathed deeply, the space constricted and the stars jabbed his skin like needles. The universe was his lung, he commanded space and time, he fathomed everything, in every dimension and on every scale. He knew, down to the picosecond, exactly when and at which latitude and longitude his parents had conceived him, and he also understood the precise causality of that evil deed, the billion-plus-year chain of events that were inextricably riveted to the Big Bang. He knew *everything*.

And yet, nothing. Even after he was released from his cube of insanity, they left him in the dark. Why?

The late-afternoon sun fell across the American pine flooring that spanned his workroom like an unswept ice rink. The window above his desk was open; a puff of breeze lifted an envelope from the tax office. It was sunny but brisk. He tried to read a book, lay on the floor listening to a Monk record but dozed off. When he woke up, broken and dopey, he went to his computer and checked his e-mail for the umpteenth time. A pair of snow-white doves fluttered through his room: *she had written back.* Her name in bold black letters on the monitor—it was an electrifying sensation. His fingers trembling, he opened the message.

> Yes, Aaron, it sure has been a while. I hope you don't remember me as someone who's easily shocked. But I have to admit I was pretty surprised by your first e-mail. You can imagine that sometimes I still worry about your health. Hopefully it was a temporary setback?
>
> You'll also appreciate that it's hard for me to be sure whether or not you really did bump into my mother. All I can say is, I haven't had any contact with her in years. And no, I don't live in Brussels; I've been in Los Angeles

for about five years now. I work for a company that makes Frisbees and surfboards. And I'm not married either (although I did live in San Francisco with Boudewijn Stol for a while, maybe you still remember him).

Yeah, if you look at it like that, the fireworks accident did set all kinds of things in motion. For you, for me, *and* for my father. But Aaron, because I know how sensitive you are: don't forget that to commit suicide—the term says it all—is a conscious choice. Don't ask me why, but Siem wanted it that way.

I hardly ever think about it. Preferably never.

Take care,

Joni

He smoked two cigarettes. Stiff from all that sitting, he walked to the middle of the living room, looked up at the rosettes and ornamental borders on the ceiling—not a single dove to be seen. *Suicide?* The overwhelming joy he had felt had completely evaporated. He reached into the top drawer of the dresser, pulled out a box of oxazepam, and took it to the bathroom. He popped three pills in his mouth and swallowed them with half a glass of chalky water. *Whaddya know.*

Evening fell. Behind the drawn curtains he worked feverishly on fresh reconstructions, brief variations on the idea that he didn't miss just Sigerius's death, but a major tragedy. A disaster. A conspiratorial "they"—individuals, organizations, parties, syndicates, secret services?—had pulled the wool over his eyes, lied to him, deceived him. The bastards had held back pertinent information. Siem Sigerius, at that time the brand-new Minister of Education, his ex-girlfriend's goddamn father, commits suicide, and nobody tells him? He wondered all sorts of things, too much, too quickly, too deeply. Was the Twentse Tulip in on it? Who had gagged the few visitors he had? Was it even legal, ethical? Secret meetings where psychiatrists connived to keep the truth from patient Bever? Weren't they being paid to help him *come to terms* with it? He could just hear them, the white coats, colluding: mum's the word around mad old Aaron, keep newspapers out of sight, no TV for the cue ball.

For a few hours he sat motionless in one of the red-leather armchairs in his living room and succumbed, eyes closed, to the new reality into which Joni's e-mail had plunged him, trying with all his might to fend off all-too-inflamed reasoning, anything to keep him from being swallowed up again by the Psychotic Ocean. As the hours passed, he calmed down slightly, the self-centered conspiracy theories stabilized, the whirlpool of thoughts widened and slowed. Just try to be realistic for once, he told himself. An entire loony bin putting on a masquerade just to protect Aaron Bever from some bad news? There must be more plausible scenarios.

What to make of Elisabeth Haitink. His confidante, the conductress of his convalescence, the therapist who had piloted him through his insanity. From the very first session he had put her on a pedestal. Pretty tight-lipped, she was. In the Twentse Tulip she was the only one he completely trusted, maybe because she unfailingly treated him like the perfectly normal, intelligent young man he—against all evidence to the contrary—thought he was, unlike the dim-witted orderlies who drew his blood or brought him his food, and in whose eyes he saw himself reflected as Vasalis's idiot in his bath.

Spring 2001—Haitink was pushing sixty, he figured. She'd

probably quit working by now; the image of a retired Elisabeth Haitink, finally liberated from the Tulip and its nutcases and invalids, gave him a sense of sympathetic relief. Trim, fragile, femininely accentuated in virgin-wool *deux-pièces* and respectable chiffon and satin dresses. She deserved something more cheery than specimens like himself—directorship of a glossy fashion mag on an Amsterdam canal, for example—but she wouldn't hear of it. She enjoyed and was dedicated to her work.

Every Tuesday and Thursday morning she fetched him from his bedroom that looked out onto the static acacias and elms on the institution's grounds—cultivated, phony, demonstrative nature, there to highlight the chaos in his head, to encourage him to be more like the garden, although he knew full well that nature was, in fact, a termite mound gone berserk, with the snout of an anteater sticking out of it—and he tagged after her like a poodle, trotting along the gallery behind her delicate figure, past the communal living room painted with enormous tulips, to the kitchenette, where she poured them each a mug of decaf and, stirring in the powdered creamer, followed him up the stairs to the staff rooms, where at the end of a bare corridor they arrived at her tidy treatment room. For some fifty intensive hours she grilled him under an immobile copper ceiling fan; she managed to raise precarious questions as though she were helping him through ice-cold breakers, and in retrospect, most of their conversations centered on Sigerius. With the one not insignificant difference that *he* was talking about a living person and she about a dead one.

At the time he thought nothing of it, they appeared to be no more than a protocolar psycho quiz. She wanted to know how he perceived Sigerius, she wanted to know what they did together, she wanted to know precisely how often they judoed, and what went on in a training session, she wanted to know what Joni thought of their friendship, whether he and Sigerius discussed his relationship with her, whether he ever made comparisons with his own father, not consciously but maybe unconsciously? If they ever had words, if he had friends his own age, if he considered their friendship a balanced one, and so on and so forth. Haitink never tired of his fascination for the man, no detail bored her, and he in turn never tired of answering her questions. Only now did he appreciate how consummately she pinpointed her target. From day one Haitink had suspected that under the polished enamel of his Sigerius adoration lay a soft core of dry rot. Something was not right. Whenever her questions got difficult, he used his hero-worship for Sigerius to divert her attention.

"Tell me, Aaron," she said one morning not long before the breakthrough, "where does it come from, your boundless ability to look up to people? You talk about Sigerius as though he's the Dalai Lama. Do you look up to me?" You? he thought, offended—*you* I find hot, but he did not respond. "Who were you actually in love with?" she continued—a taunting, even hurtful question that he eventually, after an abashed silence, answered with a command: go buy *Who's Who in the Netherlands* at Broekhuis bookstore and read for yourself about your Dalai Lama.

That *Who's Who* was a *Volkskrant* pamphlet that had been on sale for a year now. Haitink nodded, she knew the title, it was a booklet listing the achievements of the 100 most influential Dutch figures of the twentieth century. Sure enough, the next week she had it with her, still in its brown Broekhuis wrapping paper, and he watched as she pored over the pages that extolled Siem Sigerius and his mathematics, an entry bookended by laudations to the somewhat older Ruud Lubbers and the somewhat younger Freek de Jonge. The article was written in layman's language; the book's science editor portrayed Sigerius as a colorful late bloomer with a curious start as a world-class judoka, and thereafter zoomed in on his brilliant scientific career. It mentioned the often spectacular proofs the "mature student" Sigerius produced for various decades-old theories in all corners of mathematics, and how he managed to transform his initial reputation as a Houdini-like "problem solver" into one of a major mathematical theorist. Of course, the article cited, albeit superficially, the "knot theory" breakthrough that had earned Sigerius his Fields Medal.

While Haitink perched on the tiny seat of her severe stainless-steel chair to read the pamphlet, Aaron kept a close eye on the minute movements of her mouth, how it pursed and then relaxed, little grains of lipstick stuck in the wrinkles of her lips. She sat upright and rotated her ankle, and with it a sleek Parisian pump. This'll teach her, he thought. In the atypical quiet of the therapy room he let his mind wander back to when he asked Sigerius to explain the deal with those knots.

"What do you want to know?" Sigerius had asked.

"Y'know—everything."

"But it doesn't interest you."

"Sure it does," he insisted.

"It's either bafflingly complicated or childishly simple."

"Give me simple."

"OK. For years I've locked myself up with circles randomly scattered in a three-dimensional space. Still interested?"

"Now more than ever."

"All right. Imagine tying a knot in a shoelace and stitching the ends together so you've got a closed circle. Only then do you have a mathematical knot. Got it? Two apparently different knots are identical if you can change the one into the other without having to cut the shoelace. The number of unique knots might be limitless, we don't know. On the other hand, half the time, outwardly different knots are secretly identical. How do you tell one from the other? For sixty years, research kept hitting a brick wall. And then someone came up with a polynomial, an algebraic formula you can use to give each knot its own identity. That someone was me. Can't make it any simpler than that." And then, as though the knowledge had been successfully transferred, he scribbled the formula in the margin of a newspaper, as fluently as a medium, a braid of digits, letters, brackets, and Masonic symbols.

As things tend to go with revolutionary mathematics, the Sigerius Polynomial (as the strand was officially called) turned out not only to be indispensable right down to the hair follicles of mathematics, but also for unraveling the structure of plastic polymers, for DNA research, for the string theory, in other words: the theory of the universe.

"So you're a kind of Einstein," he said.

"Yeah, if Liberace is a kind of Beethoven."

When Haitink was finished reading, she clapped *Who's Who in the Netherlands* shut and ran her hand pensively over the cover. "I *hate* math," she said. Sigerius used to blow his top when someone with a good set of brains uttered this kind of nonsense, and was proud of it to boot. "What they meant to say is that they're *warm-blooded*," he'd growl, fidgeting furiously with his ears, "artistic, spi-ri-tu-al, more a 'people person' than a 'number cruncher.' Meanwhile, Aaron, they fall for all sorts of pseudo-scientific, semi-religious bullshit because they can't make heads or tails of simple numerical relationships. They are stupid, Aaron. *Stupid.* They *want* to be stupid. They hate math but looooove Uri Geller. I'll show you how you can beat the pants off that Uri Geller with a simple probability calculation."

He looked at Haitink. "And Sigerius hates me," he said.

She eyed him, frowning. "I know you think so. But why?"

• • •

Why did he confide in her? Because she spoke the language of the civilized world, the language of the campus that had chucked him out? Because in that godawful Tulip there wasn't another normal woman to be found? (The women in his section had forearms as gouged as the cutting board his grandfather used to slice salami, they claimed to be Saddam Hussein's mistress, but then on CIA directives, of course, and with orders to abscond with the regime's laser-powered weapons, so don't get worked up—but still.) Or did he realize that it was simply her professional confidentiality, that in fact he sat here talking to *no one*, to a kind of ball-shooter, to a mercenary who would ignore him entirely if they ran into each other later in the supermarket?

No, he trusted her because she laughed at his jokes; when he said something witty a smile would pass across her bony, wrinkled face, not out of indulgence, or worse, out of pity, but because her clinical poker face was simply not wisecrack-proof. If on a good day he'd refound something of his old frivolity, he could crack her up, which made her sixteen instead of sixty-one. And for him, a complete and utter wreck whose self-respect lay like a deflated soccer ball on the clinic lawn, her giggly abandon had a greater healing power than her entire arsenal of psychotherapeutic gimmicks. Although only his nostrils quivered when she asked him that question—why do you think Sigerius hates you?—internally he sprinted as fast as he could to the edge of the long-kept secret, pushed off from the dusty sand and leapt, limbs flailing, over the cliff of profound silence he had managed to maintain for four long years.

"Because I am his daughter's pimp," he said. "That's why."

Haitink, as he recalled, did not bat an eye. She never batted an eye, she was trained not to bat an eye. With her thumb and index finger she pinched a piece of fluff from her woolen leggings. "Tell me about it," she said.

He told her, very concisely, about how he and Joni had run an amateur sex site from the end of 1996 until their unmasking in 2000, a paid website for which he had taken the photos, week in week out, photos exposing every square centimeter of Joni's body, in the most titillating settings possible: to put it bluntly, porn. And sometimes a little bit of himself. "A little bit of yourself?" asked Haitink, pulling a quasi-alarmed face.

Yeah, well, whatever. He made his confession without going into the gory details, after a four-year vow of silence it was all he could do to force out the basic facts. She had questions, and as always she played the certified question mark, she wanted to know exactly what they were talking about; he saw she forgot to take notes.

"Was it your idea?" she asked.

"Yes. No, both of us," he answered, not even stopping to realize that it had been *her* idea.

"Did this, um . . ."

"Joni."

"Did Joni use her real name on the website?"

"No, of course not."

"Then what?"

"She was supposed to be a girl from the American Midwest. That was the website's look."

"Just pictures?"

"The Internet is too slow for videos."

"And how racy were these pictures?"

"You do know what porn is?"

"Eh . . . I've an idea."

"Well, that. They used to call them erotic images."

"And you had to be a member to view these . . . erotic images?"

"If you wanted to see all of them, yeah, of course."

"OK. And what was the site called?"

"Lindaloveslace."

"And this Linda, that was Joni?"

"No, me."

"Just asking."

"This is the first time I've told anyone."

"That's very brave of you, Aaron. But? Did it work out?"

"Are you kidding? We hit the jackpot. It was an unbelievable success. We couldn't believe it."

"So Joni is that pretty, is she?"

"She's breathtaking."

"According to you."

"According to thousands of men."

He told Haitink that one day they woke up and realized "it" had become bigger, bigger than their relationship. "We went to bed as a couple and woke up as business partners. We realized that we were a pair of managers, managers with a secret. Managers *of* a secret."

"And all that time you were scared witless that her big-shot father would find out."

"Uh-huh. Pretty much, yeah." He attempted to explain to her how incredibly complicated it was to keep it quiet, to create a vacuum around something that was so all-consuming and so successful, and at the same time so totally inappropriate; it was not just a sleight of hand, it required constant vigilance. "We led double lives. And at the same time I was getting chummier with Sigerius. On a first-name basis with her caring, loving *father.* An impossible juggling act. To be honest, it was awful."

"What were you so afraid of?"

He could not suppress a groan. Did she really not get it? The question annoyed him as much as her hardhanded debunking of his admiration for Sigerius. Did she learn this 100 years ago in psych class? It occurred to him that he shouldn't have made her read *Who's Who in the Netherlands,* but an entirely different book altogether, a handbook for the novice judoka that Sigerius had written for the youngsters in his dojo and had printed and bound at Tubantia's print center. Since the late 1980s Sigerius gave free hour-long judo lessons on Thursday evenings for children from Twekkelerveld, a grim housing project across from the campus's main entrance. His handbook explained, in terms thc kids would understand and accompanied by clumsy illustrations he drew himself, the technical fundamentals of judo as well as the philosophy behind it, but what Aaron mostly remembered was the three-page code of conduct for the "sportsmanlike judoka." Sigerius had probably drawn up this edifying list because he saw it as his duty to inform the often immigrant youngsters, boys he rightly categorized as underprivileged, of a set of values different from the ones they picked up around their piss-stinking apartment blocks. "If I have my judo partner in a hold, I will not cause him unnecessary pain." "I promise to engage in fair play." "If I win a match I will not boast about it." "I will not lie on the mat, but will sit up straight while listening to the sensei's instructions." "I will remember to brush my teeth before going to the judo lesson."

Haitink was still looking at him. Her expression was mildly mocking, the look of someone who, because of her '60s upbringing, was obliged to play the enlightened woman of the world. Fine. Instead of lecturing her on the degree of betrayal they were talking about here, on the devious measures you had to take before you had a secret, well-organized sex site up and running, he asked her if she had children herself.

"A son," she said.

"That's a pity," he said. "Married?"

"Ingmar has a boyfriend."

"Terrific. Even better. I'll just assume Ingmar and his friend are nice, decent guys, sociable, good at their work. I'll bet he's good-looking."

She frowned at him. "Ye-e-s-s . . . ," she said.

"OK. So one day you get a tip. Go to this or that Internet site, and you do, and you discover a meticulously designed website, a site your son updates every week with new pictures of himself. Crisp photos of Ingmar and his hard cock. I'm just putting it in clear English for you. And if you type in your credit card number you can have access to thousands of photos showing the vast assortment of meat and plastic that gets rammed up Ingmar's spit-lubed anus—as long as it takes for that handsome face of his to contort into a grimace and his smooth-shaven dick to ejaculate. The following Sunday you see them again, your son and his boyfriend, but this time in the flesh. They're coming over for dinner."

For a split second she sat there frozen, maybe because of the imagery, maybe because of his rough language, and he intensely enjoyed seeing her brick-red mouth hang open, a filament of saliva stretching between her smallish, aged teeth. Her wise, pistachio-green eyes stared straight ahead, aghast—but then she regained her composure. "I wouldn't exactly break out the champagne, no," she said. "But—"

"Sigerius would go apeshit," he interrupted, more rudely than he had intended. "He'd blow a fuse. Siem Sigerius discovers that the apple of his eye is an Internet whore?" He bit his upper lip and cringed. "I'd be first," he said. "First he'd slit my throat, and then his own. You know, if I wasn't safely locked up here I'd be lying at the bottom of Rutbeek Lake right now. And Siem next to me."

She eyed him pensively. She was thinking. And now, seven years later, he finally knew what about: the dead Sigerius. But instead of telling him there was nobody alive anymore who wanted to slit his throat, she asked: "So why didn't you just stop?"

It had started to rain. Cold droplets spattered on the back of his monitor and the photographic paper on his desk. With a shiver he reached over and slammed the window shut.

The key question, of course. Why didn't he quit? He didn't know himself, not exactly at least, it was a medley of motives, some of them clearer than others, something muddy that had kept him, despite intense attacks of guilt and doubt, from stopping. On and on, week after week. He could have given Haitink *five* different honest reasons, motivations he could classify from light to dark, from logical to completely off the wall, from courageous to cowardly and back again.

Just to be done with it, he pulled out the most superficial. An incentive for all ages: the dough. Moolah. Big bucks. The incredible mountain of dollars the website raked in. From day one, men from all corners of the globe signed up—at least he'd assumed it was men—and the filthy lucre started pouring in, thousands of dollars at first, pretty soon tens of thousands, month in month out, for four years—more money than they knew what to do with. Money they sank into a brand-new Alfa Romeo in which they floored it to a bank in Luxembourg, money with which they secretly bought a luxury yacht that never left the Mediterranean, money no one else knew they had. For Joni it was a dream come true, years ahead of schedule. He didn't know anyone else with a subscription to the *Financial Times.* When they started she was twenty and already the owner of a portfolio of shares and stock options. She did her trading at the beginning of each trimester. "Hey Miss Frumpy," he said when he first found her up in her student attic room sitting cross-legged with the telephone in one hand and the stock market pages in the other, four in the afternoon in her nightie, window shades shut, plates caked with yesterday's spinach pasta on the floor, "don't you need to shower?" She still smelled deliciously like nighttime. "I earned 6,000 guilders today," she said without looking up, "how about you?" On their first date, when he asked her why she was studying Technical Management Science, she did not give the typical freshman-girl answer—"to be involved with people in an organization"—but, simply, "to get rich quick." He had burst out laughing, she wasn't serious, but she *was* serious. "In home economics class you learn home economics, at the dance academy you learn to dance, and in Technical Get-Rich-Quick Science," she said, smiling, "you learn to get rich quick." And that is precisely what she was planning to do: Joni Sigerius envisioned herself starting her own business, taking it to the stock market, and selling it before she turned forty.

"I don't know how you were doing at twenty-six," he said to Haitink, "but I sure didn't mind earning as much as Dennis Bergkamp."

"That's a football player, isn't it? I *hate* football."

"With a weekly evening photo session we earned as much as a pro footballer. At our peak in 1998 we had 11,000 subscribers . . ."

"Subscribers?"

"Paying members. Men willing to shell out twenty bucks a month. *Eleven thousand*. Tally that up, why don't you."

Haitink draped one slender leg over the other and flicked at an imaginary abacus on the wall behind him. "Yes," she said after a few seconds, too short to have really worked it out, "that's quite a bundle. Amazing. So it was all about the money?"

"Yeah. Well, that too. Mostly it was—"

"Hang on a second," she interrupted. She leaned over to her desk and reached for a large calculator. Several ticks later she looked up with girlish excitement. "Eleven thousand subscribers at twenty dollars a month," she said, "and that for a year, that comes to . . . $2.6 million, that's almost, no, *more than* five million guilders . . . Aaron, are you pulling my leg?"

"No. I'm dead serious. Sigerius—it's *his* leg I was pulling."

"But that's . . . I mean . . ."

"It *was* insane and incredible and awesome, that's what I'm trying to tell you. Even keeping it a secret was fantastic . . . Addictive. Nobody knew, but meanwhile 11,000 guys *did* know, they knew *everything* . . . It was unbelievably exhilarating. A source of continuous conspiratorial . . . um . . ."

She looked at him musingly. "Sexual arousal?"

"Horniness, yeah. That's the word I was looking for."

He phoned the Thai take-out on the edge of town, ordered a green curry with rice, and showered in the half hour before the delivery scooter drove up the hill to his house.

It made you inhumanly horny. Naturally. Every week they almost floated out of his attic room, or wherever they did the shoot, in five-star hotels, on the *Barbara Ann*, at bed-and-breakfasts in Zeeland or East Groningen with museum flyers next to the electric kettle. It was always good. For years, their week was a cycle of horniness that started with provocative preparations, scouting out locations, buying new lingerie for Joni in chic or downmarket shops, with the ecstatic event taking place on Tuesday or Wednesday evening. They spent hours making the 100 to 150 photos they owed their clients, and the days that followed were consumed by an exhausted, satisfied after-session that consisted of examining what was being simultaneously examined on 11,000 other computers—by 1998 standards, a mind-blowing concept—and once they'd had enough of themselves they checked their bank balance, withdrew 1,000 guilders and drove to Paris, or to Berlin, or to Ameland for a new session. Their arousal seemed insatiable and its source inexhaustible. Sometimes it was like living in a dream, he imagined himself the rector of his own paradisiacal campus—until the high wore off. When the thrill passed, the real campus reappeared, a grassy campus with a damned real farmhouse, and in that farmhouse lived a real-life rector, Joni's father, whom he stood next to in the university sport center's showers twice a week.

He turned off the water. There was, he considered, also a reckless aspect to it, something masochistic. Constantly pushing his luck by gravitating ever closer to Sigerius. As though he were deliberately trying to get caught.

He paid for his food and ate it in his workroom. When the plate was empty he went back to the iMac and reread Joni's e-mail. He noticed that he kept getting stuck at a remark that had, of course, stung him right from the start, but that he hadn't yet found the time to get worked up about.

"I did live in San Francisco with Boudewijn Stol for a while," she wrote, "maybe you still remember him."

Boudewijn Stol—so she'd been with that goon after all. Behind the shock of Sigerius's suicide, something else started to itch. Maybe it was just an old reflex, but he could not let go of the idea that Joni was taunting him with that "maybe you still remember him." Of course he remembered him. So those two had shacked up. The minute he tried to imagine it, Joni under the same roof as that arrogant greaseball, he just about burst a blood vessel. The poison associated with that time! He was surprised how easily he fell back into his old love spasm, an echo, certainly, but still: neuralgia he hadn't felt in years. His and Joni's story was also a story of four years of pathological jealousy. One-sided jealousy, mind you: *his.* The constant fear she would leave him. The fear of being dumped. Of being supplanted. At her parents' house. Behind his camera. (He: "You know, I also kept it up because I knew I was expendable." Haitink: "You mean you were afraid she'd carry on with someone else if you called it quits?" He: "Yes." Haitink: "Was that realistic, do you think?" He: "It seemed to me a foregone conclusion.")

The memories of Etienne Vaessen's wedding came crashing over him, that intense exhaustion once again poured into his legs, his obnoxious recklessness, the humiliation—it all came rushing back. How he was wrung through the mangle of jealousy during the dinner that had kept them away from Roombeek on May 13, 2000.

They had been sitting glued to the hotel-room television for too long, and suddenly they had to rush. So while the horsemen of the apocalypse were galloping through their neighborhood in Enschede, they careered at 140 kph toward the Groeneweide estate. Joni fussed with his crookedly knotted bow tie; he mused sourly on the garish bash that awaited them. Arriving late, they parked the Alfa next to an enormous pond stocked with swans. "Don't panic," he exhorted her as they trotted up the broad marble stairs. They were courteously greeted by young men in livery, one of whom hurried ahead through the cool foyer decorated with gilded friezes and life-size oil paintings. Rooms off to each side were being prepared for the festivities later on in the evening, and somewhere in the depths of the estate a klezmerish ensemble could be heard rehearsing. They stopped before a pair of velvet-clad doors, which the lackey carefully opened, revealing a banquet hall so vast that from a distance the company resembled a kindergarten class at their cookie break. The decor was even more over-the-top than he had expected. Amphoras with long-stemmed sunflowers; here, too, oil portraits and hunting tableaux; an ornamental plaster ceiling, blue and gold regimental-striped wallpaper, the parquet floor a geometric mosaic of various kinds of wood over which waiters skated back and forth.

Their Louis Seize chairs must have been empty, disturbingly empty, for a good twenty minutes, and as though she wanted to make up for lost time, Joni strode ahead of him, ticking across the slick floor, and sat down, smiling, at one of the empty places. His soles slipping out from under him, he creaked around the grid of lavishly set tables, his gaze focused above the alternately black and bare backs of the guests, his destination being the bridegroom's reddened ear, into which he whispered their alibi, concise, euphemistic: there was some problem in Enschede, nothing to be alarmed about, carry on eating. When he walked via the other side of the dining room to his seat, he saw to his satisfaction that the news of the fireworks factory caused no more of a ripple than a pebble tossed into the surf. Vaessen was already laughing again.

Meanwhile Joni had struck up a conversation with an older man in a white dinner jacket. Something he was saying made her laugh, ". . . and when I got home that evening," he caught, "she'd bought *another* thing with an electrical cord." Next to the man sat a much younger woman with gathered-up brown hair who said something back that he didn't catch. "Long story short, something had to be done," the man said, exclusively to Joni. "Eventually she was bathing the garden gnome twice a day." Aaron cleared his throat and pulled in his chair. It took the man a fraction too long to notice him; he cut himself short as though Aaron was meddling in some way.

"Boudewijn Stol," he said, and a tanned hand shot across the table. Aaron shook it, a sturdy, dry grip. He noticed Stol's improbably tight curls, which were combed back with something greasy, Brylcreem maybe; after a few inches the graying coif turned wavy, distinguished, classic, exposing his high forehead. The man sat straight up in his white dinner jacket with his stumpy Carthaginian chin thrust forward: at once, all the black tuxedos in the banquet hall fell flat. Even before Aaron realized who this Boudewijn Stol was, he already hated him.

"I'm a colleague of Etienne's," Stol said to Joni, apparently in response to a just-asked question. "His boss, actually. At McKinsey Netherlands."

Aaron nearly choked when he heard those words, Joni shifted in her chair, her heels scraped across the parquet floor. He glanced around and noticed that everything in this fairy-tale gala hall zoomed into sharper focus: the fifty-plus place settings, the clatter of countless knives and forks, the glistening platters, the shimmering dresses and glittering jewelry, the chatter emitting from dozens of mouths, the swirl of moving eyebrows, cheekbones, corsages—all at once. "His team leader?" he heard Joni ask. Quit showing off, he thought, and stared at his plate. Next to him sat a man with a mustacheless beard, whose sultry B.O. prickled his nose and whose whiskers scraped over the collar of his shirt like a dish-scrubber.

"Aha," said Stol, "so the young lady is in the know. No, I'm not his team leader. I'm the managing partner in Amsterdam. Or franchise holder, whatever you want to call it."

"How about 'head honcho,' " Joni suggested. "Head Honcho of McKinsey Netherlands."

"Don't spread it around," said Stol.

An hour ago when they sat watching Enschede burn, nothing had happened to him. Now suddenly *everything* was happening to him: bad things. Liters of blood were pumped with elephantine force into his head; his back, his hands, buttocks, face, and feet spontaneously ignited like matches. Heat radiated off him, even the lace-collared pursed and powdered mugs of the oil portraits in their gilded frames began to perspire. Head Honcho McKinsey, he thought, Jesus H. Christ, and as though someone were now *un*focusing the lens, the whole damn Sissi palace faded into a blotchy blur. He focused on Stol's powerful neck, where a muscle twitched; the guy had a neck like an oak, a centuries-old trunk whose roots burrowed into virile, rounded shoulders under the white fabric of his dinner jacket. There was undoubtedly a fitness room in the head-office basement where he pumped his daily iron; this was the kind of guy who lifted sixty kilos but left the bench press at 120, just to knock the next monkey's morale down a notch. Aaron rubbed his eyes with both hands. "My contacts," he mumbled. A ropy bite of veal that had absorbed all his saliva had lodged itself under his tongue. He removed a contact lens from his eye and studied the plastic disc as though seeing it for the first time.

"So how many consultants do you manage, Mr. Stol?" he heard Joni ask.

"Mr. Stol doesn't manage anything," he said. "*Boudewijn* manages an office of about 150."

Her laugh was full of excited admiration.

"But," continued the smug voice, "as I'm sure you know, consultants are independent-minded. We feel quite confident, for instance, sending our little friend Vaessen here out to play. Once a week I read him the riot act, that's more than enough."

And again that crystalline laugh Joni reserved for special

occasions, a laugh that began deep in her chest and lacked gracefulness. What he heard was unconditional surrender. Not that this guy was in any way a comic genius, his jokes were lazy, simplistic—it was *power* that exerted, via an unmarked detour, an influence on Joni's humor. The full-fat power on which he gorged himself stretched the button of the white dinner jacket Stol had pulled out of his walk-in closet this morning. He had chosen this white jacket to quash any misunderstandings, just like a dominant chimpanzee wastes no time in pushing his ass into your face. An alpha male, Aaron had read in the career brochures that he summarily chucked in the wastebasket, the type who makes his subordinates sniff his feet because he thinks they smell like raspberry pie. He placed the lens back in his eye. If Joni saw that he was already starting to lose it, this dinner would be his Waterloo. She was not to find out that he was scared to death of this guy.

Well, if *this* wasn't poetic justice. He and his spiteful swagger about this kind of man. Consultants are charlatans, stupid and greedy, he would sermonize whenever Joni mentioned a possible future in consultancy—a future, by the way, she was being trained for as a Technical Management student, a future she had in fact already opted for and which she would undoubtedly take by storm. Instead of supporting her, as soon as she said anything positive about a company like McKinsey he scrunched his forehead into horns, perfidious drivel dripping from his cloven hooves. The "consultancy sector" was a decadent indulgence, he would say, "bullshit" in plain English, a perverse luxury that would evaporate the minute the stock markets crashed. His idle contempt was always ready. And whenever Joni let him goad her into contradicting his clichés, he would snort something snide about the untalented boys and girls these days who turned up their noses at a proper professional training and instead ate away at their college education like aphids. Unhindered by any decent form of ambition, they coasted into law or economics or communication or some other Styrofoam discipline, after which, at age twenty-two, off they went to peddle spurious advice.

To illustrate this constructive criticism he would drag his own friends through the mud. Etienne was a classic example of this breed: the former biology student who egoistically jettisoned that old radio-show slogan "Keen for Green" once he realized that it did not apply to his biologist's salary. And now? Now Etienne wrote reports full of corporate gobbledegook acknowledging the inevitability of layoffs, or mergers, or this or that sort of white-collar crime, summarized on a single corrupt PowerPoint page, which some hoity-toity board chairman could wave as he sashayed into the workplace, announcing: I regret, dear employees, to have to fire you, it's all here, read it for yourselves. She wanted to waste her talent on *that*? A master's in Lame Excuses? "Aaron," she would sigh (implicitly forgiving him, because his argument was no more than subversive claptrap, and they both knew it), "I'm going to be an engineer."

He swigged back his glass of Corton-Pougets and stared at the plaster grapevines on the ceiling. What now? One way or another, the conversation had to be steered away from McKinsey. In answer to another of Joni's questions he had missed, Stol replied that his consultants were today's mineworkers: every company had value, if you dug deep enough. The conversation turned to the quickest, most efficient methods of digging. For the first time, Aaron got a good look at the woman next to Stol. She was a damn sight younger than her husband, translucently pale, slightly over-muscular and slightly over-perfumed: he realized that the smell coming from across the table, penetrating his veal cheeks with sautéed escargot, must be her scent.

"So what does your daughter do?" he heard himself ask with a pinched voice.

Now all three of them were looking at the woman. She was weighed down by rather a lot of gold: rectangular earrings, four chunky rings, a necklace kept at body temperature by her decidedly trashy cleavage; the upper part of her dark-blue dress consisted of a loosely draped flap of velvet that covered her large breasts like a black bar across a criminal's eyes. Her intelligent, subtly made-up face was at odds with this rampant eroticism. Her long, pale hands were covered in freckles.

"Brigitte is my wife," said Stol. "I was just saying to your charming sister here that a few years ago I bought a stable for Brigitte. It was on the verge of bankruptcy, and dilapidated, you'd hardly recognize it now, she has—"

"—her own mouth," Brigitte interrupted. She looked at Aaron with warm, dark-brown eyes; he couldn't distinguish the iris from the pupil. "But he's right, it was a dream come true. I'm mad keen on horses." She had a thick Hague accent.

Stol said: "You mean you love horses."

"When we bought it, the stable had just one star, now we've got three. Like I said, I'm mad keen." Or was it a Leiden twang? As common as dirt, anyway. The point was, though, he had struck a chord with her, the equine chord, because she shifted her chair, as though to reposition herself for her moment of glory. She was hot to trot. "How many horses do you have?" he asked, interested, "or, no, sorry, what I meant to ask was, where's the stable?" Joni shot him a surprised, questioning glance.

"Between Scheveningen and Wassenaar," she answered, "right on the beach. You couldn't ask for a better location, smack in the middle of the dunes. *Black Beauty Manège*, do you remember that TV series? We thought it was a neat name. It was his idea." She gestured at Stol; her index finger sported a golden ring with a ludicrous little watch on it.

"I always watched *Black Beauty* as a kid," said Joni. "I'm crazy about horses."

"What's also interesting," said Brigitte, steeped in her own story, "is that when Máxima and Alexander go riding along the beach they always stop in for a cup of coffee, once a week at least"—she paused for a moment to gauge the effect of her hobnobbing with the royal couple. "Then I'm like, we're not doing so bad after all. Hey, hon?" She snuggled her shoulder against Stol's.

"Not bad indeed," he said. "But Willem-Alexander has to drink coffee somewhere, doesn't he, babycakes?" He stared listlessly at a distant point beyond Aaron's shoulder. The mist of boredom between these two was too thick and clammy to ever burn off; Joni thought so too, he saw from the brazen twinkle with which she caught his eye. "I rode until I was sixteen," she said. "Do you ride too?"—that's right, Aaron thought, shift the attention to the person who *does* interest you. In fact, he and babycakes were completely irrelevant, they were just along for the ride. "A little," replied Stol, "but I'm sure you ride better. I can definitely picture you astride a galloping horse."

Aaron's molars crackled. "Naked and bareback, I suppose?" he quipped. It was meant as a joke, but it came out sounding like he had a throbbing pain somewhere. Stol and Brigitte exchanged glances. Joni laid down her silverware, wiped her mouth, and gave him a look of feigned fondness. "We've been together for four years now," she said, "but Aaron's fantasy is as vivid as always."

Stol chuckled quietly. "Say," he asked in a theatrical attempt to rescue the conversation, "what does the young lady actually study, to know so much about McKinsey?"

Aaron butted in before Joni could answer. "She has a computer," he said, again with that strange pinched voice, "and what d'you know, it's got Internet on it. And on that Internet she surfed all on her own to the McKinsey website. That's how."

A new silence, a few shades deeper than the previous one. Regret filled Aaron's sinuses. What he had just done, what he had just done *twice*, was the verbal equivalent of punching someone in the face; he was trigger happy tonight, suffering from a serious loss of self-control. With the least provocation he lashed out like a brute. Stol looked at him with a devious, slightly amused expression. Hard-blue eyes that scorched the peeling paint of his inner self. Aaron knew exactly what Stol saw: if anyone could tell how morbidly jealous he was, then he could. He was a calamity. How would Stol react if he told him about the night before Joni's interview for an internship at Bain & Co., maybe a year ago, how after a few hours of agitated tossing and turning, he snuck out of bed, took the stack of clothes Joni had laid out into the bathroom and subtly spattered tangerine juice over her blue skirt and white blouse, tore tiny runs in strategic places in her stockings? He couldn't stop himself. He was convinced that Joni would dump her freelance photoboy the minute she set foot in one of those mirrored-glass office towers. Somewhere in the world was a skyscraper that would steal her from him. London, New York, Tokyo: he was going to lose her to consultancy.

Of course he often wondered where this fear came from. At first he presumed it was just a stubborn offshoot of garden-variety jealousy; the first few euphoric months of all his relationships were coupled with the disproportionate fear that a rival would put paid to his happiness. But with other girlfriends his paranoia waned after a month or two, along with his affection. In Joni's case, nothing waned. Naturally, anyone who wanted to go out with Joni Sigerius had to deal with it, she was exceptionally beautiful, she was *intolerably* beautiful. Intentionally or not, she bombarded the nuclei of masculine propriety with beta particles, men would lose all sense of decorum as soon as Joni Sigerius came anywhere near them, and that nuclear reaction created aggressive hunters, he'd seen it happen so many times. She allowed a teacher from her own art school to body-paint her a couple of times a year, and twice she had won the campus wet T-shirt contest. Portrait photographers plucked her from the sidewalk for so-called artistic sittings. Who was it that he heard texting her in the middle of the night? And the unfamiliar first names and phone numbers in her diary? In clubs, men growled hoarsely in his ear that his turn was up. For years she was woken up in the morning by a heavy breather—turned out to be the dean of her department. What'd she mean, the masseur insisted it was "on the house"? Every few months she'd get antsy and go to Amsterdam with a gay friend for a night in the iT, in a T-shirt so flimsy Ray Charles could see through it. And him? He sat at home in front of the TV with a slice of apple strudel. Drove him up the *wall*.

"Anything exciting happen?" he would ask when she returned at six in the morning.

"Nothing much. Getting in was kind of a hassle."

"Oh? How come?"

"I had to turn in my bra."

"*Wha-huh?*"

"My bra. Turn it in."

"What kind of nonsense is that?"

"The bouncer said so."

"The bouncer? What kind of bouncer is that? And then?"

"And then I turned in my bra."

He was a calamity—but so was she.

Calamity Joni smiled at Stol. "If I want to know anything about McKinsey," she said, ostensibly unperturbed, "I can always turn to

Aaron. He knows *everything* about consultants." Exactly how Joni was going to carry out his execution, he wasn't sure, but that it was going to happen—that was inevitable. His disastrous jealousy had a parallel effect on her. *If only he could get out of here.* "As far as this one here is concerned," Joni continued, "McKinsey is not a free agent. You people are corrupt. According to Aaron, McKinsey shits reports on demand." He felt her hand on his shoulder, she was about to say something else, but off to one side a voice called out his surname.

All four of them looked to the right and saw the towering bridegroom approach, weaving his way through his chattering dinner guests. A telephone was pressed against Vaessen's ear, not a sleek cell phone but a house telephone with a rubber antenna; he nodded his blond head at Aaron, a smug little lift of that self-satisfied chin. Twit, he thought, inviting your boss to your wedding, sleazeball, brownnoser. "Yeah, he's here . . . just a sec," said Vaessen. "Bever, for you." He passed him the telephone across the table, and then squatted down between Stol and Brigitte for a chat.

"Hello?"

"Aaron, you are one hard-to-reach dude."

He had to think a moment before realizing it was Thijmen Akkerman on the line. Thijmen, his personal physician, had studied medicine in Utrecht, but was working as sales manager for a high-tech prosthetics firm, computer-driven limbs, hips made from Playmobil plastic. Thijmen had been supplying him with sleeping pills via scrips pinched from his father, who *was* in fact a bona fide GP. It sounded like he was hanging on a Delta kite.

"Speak up, Thijmen," he said, "I can barely hear you. I'm at a wedding. How did you find me?"

"I phoned your home number," Thijmen yelled, "but there was no answer. So I went looking for you. I'm right near your house. I only just remembered you two were at Groeneweide." That's right, Aaron did tell him about the wedding; apparently as a student Thijmen had had a job there as a dishwasher. "Your whole neighborhood's on fire," Thijmen continued. "It's unreal what's happening here."

"What about my house?" Vaessen, he saw, had already buggered off. Stol and Brigitte looked attentively at him; Joni, unruffled, carried on eating. Just that irritating way she sat there stuffing her face made him know exactly how he had to handle this. He knew it.

"There's a blaze," Thijmen shouted, "right across from your house. An inferno, I'm not kidding you. But they say it won't spread to the other side of the street. The fire department says the wind's blowing the other way. I'm just calling to set your mind at ease. I'll bet you two are shitting yourselves."

"An inferno, you say?" he said. "Jesus Christ. And my house?" He heard sirens in the background, and a roar. "Thijmen, you still there?"

"Yeah, yeah. Sorry, a couple of fire engines just passed by. Hang on. Your house is still OK, but the glass wall is busted, you know, that . . ."

"The sliding doors?"

"Yeah, those. They're gone. Wait. They're shooing me away. All the windows have been blown out. Everywhere. Unbe*fucking*lievable."

He turned to Joni and pointed his thumb downward. He covered the mouthpiece with his hand and said: "I think we have to go back," after which he stuck a finger in his ear and reassured his friend at the other end. "Thijmen, calm down. Take it easy. Joni and I are here, in Zaltbommel. We are fine. We're eating veal. But I'm really glad you called. Yeah, it's terrible. Yes. Yeah—it's not far. We can be there in an hour."

Thijmen had listened in silence. "Aaron?" There was bewilderment in his voice. "There's nothing you can do, man. Just stay where you are. Be glad you're *there*. You go party. I've got to hang up now, kid, I'm out of here."

"Got it, Thijmen, understood. You're absolutely right. We'll do that. You just get out of there safely. See you, dude."

With a little crackle Thijmen hung up.

"What's that?" Aaron asked the dial tone. For a brief moment he looked straight into Boudewijn Stol's eyes. "OK, Thijmen, hang in there, buddy. Sure thing. We're on our way. Bye."

He pressed the end-call button and set the telephone down next to his plate.

"Well?" asked Brigitte. "Doesn't sound too good."

"No," he said. "There's something awful going on in Enschede. A fireworks factory has exploded. We saw it on the TV back in our hotel room just now. That's where we're from, you know, Enschede. I live right near that factory. It's much worse than they thought. Being broadcast on all three stations."

"Huh," said Stol.

Impressive analysis, he thought—*huh*. "The sliding glass doors of my house have been blown out," he said, "and . . ."

"If that's everything," Joni interrupted. She did not look at him, but sliced off a piece of veal and dragged the tender meat through the gravy. She stabbed a snow pea along with it and stuck the assemblage into her mouth.

"For the time being, yes, that's everything," he said. "But the whole street is on fire. If the wind shifts my house will be toast. We've got to get there. Now." He wiped his mouth with his napkin and demonstratively shoved his chair back. Joni kept looking at her plate and continued chewing. He watched anxiously as she ate. Damn, you know, this was *his* house they were talking about, nobody else here could claim *their* house was about to go up in flames. She swallowed. A golden-blond wisp slipped over her cheek; she gently, calmly, slid it back behind her ear. Then, as though deciding she had been watched for long enough, she laid down her cutlery and looked at him. "Aaron," she said, "don't be so unbelievably childish. We're at the wedding of one of your best friends. We can't just take off. Calm down a bit, honey." She winked at Stol. "Good thing *he* doesn't have a stable."

He took a deep breath and exhaled slowly. "No, Joni," he said, palpitating with a surging rage, "I don't have horses, but I do have two house pets, remember?"

"Guinea pigs," said Joni.

Brigitte hid a snicker behind her hand.

"And forty original jazz LPs belonging to your father next to my turntable," he added quickly. "And a laptop. And a fortune in photographic equipment. And 2,000 books. Maybe we can salvage some of it? Just a suggestion?"

"Go get the car," said Joni, "while I fill a bucket with pond water."

Stol intervened. "I understand where your boyfriend's coming from," he said soothingly. During their brief squabble he occupied himself with his handkerchief: leaning back casually, he produced, magician-like, the crimson silk hanky from his breast pocket, spread it out over his left hand and picked it up from the middle, as though it were soiled. A little shake and he took hold of the underside with his free hand, carefully folded the cloth in half and grasped it like a marmot. Prising open his breast pocket with thumb and index finger, he released the little silk beast into his pocket, appraising Aaron all the while. "His instinct tells him he has to rush to the fire-storm. It's happening there, and he's stuck here. His most cherished possession, a house containing all that defines him, is in danger—this is clearly no trifling matter."

Aaron blinked. Why did the Oracle not address him directly? Had he even asked for his opinion?

"If you ask me," said Stol, as though he could read his mind, "you should put your emotions aside for a moment and consider the nature of the situation in Enschede. And Arend's likely role in its solution."

"My name is Aaron."

"That is what you should be thinking. Now rather than later. Better to realize here, instead of *there,* that by going there you'll probably do more harm than good."

"Who said anything about doing harm?"

"I did," said Stol. "There's a fire, there's the danger of collapsing buildings. Poisonous fumes. The whole ball of wax. The only thing the professionals want from the general public is that they keep out of their way."

"And what makes you the expert?"

Stol, smiling, sized him up.

"What's so funny?"

"You are. You are a really funny guy." With a couple of quick tugs he pulled his cuffs out from under the sleeves of his jacket. He turned to Joni. "But say your boyfriend goes anyway. What then? Then there's Arend wandering around a disaster area with nowhere to sleep. He's in the way. And say the wind *does* shift, then all he can do is stand there, drunk and helpless, and watch his house burn to the ground. You have to be able to handle that. And if I judge him right, I'll bet he can't handle that too well. He's already freaking out." Stol picked up his fork, skewered a bite-sized hunk of veal and put it into his small mouth. "In other words, if you go there," he said, chewing and jabbing his empty fork in Aaron's direction, "you're risking a trauma."

Joni sat with her elbows on the table, she looked back at her plate and held her hand like a visor in front of her eyes. Aaron inhaled slowly. All right then. Go on, shit on my head, thanks for the hat. Make a monkey out of me. And no, they weren't going anymore. He had lost. So what were they staring at now, the three of them? He looked at his plate, his food gone cold, and rubbed his right eye. "My contact," he said, "there's something stuck to it." He tried to whisk the plastic disc out of his eye but realized his hands were shaking violently. Stol's eyes burned through the skin on his head.

"Listen here," he shouted as he got up, "I want all of you to know I'm pro-family and anti-drugs." Without looking at anyone he marched off, cupping the contact lens in his hand, in the direction of the double doors where they had entered. His face burned. The banquet hall pitched like the hold of a galleon, cannons yanked on their chains, chandeliers waltzed back and forth across the ceiling. He felt the exhaustion of having slept badly for weeks. As he staggered along the gold-leafed floorboards and the eating backs he accidentally kicked over a handbag. He shuffled over the parquet floor, mumbled "sorry," and when he flicked it back up with his foot he saw in the distance that Stol, Brigitte, and Joni had gone back to chatting. They were laughing heartily.

The coolness of the marble cell, rose fragrance from a spray can. He locked himself in the first stall he found and slumped onto the matt-black seat without dropping his trousers. The tank gurgled softly, he laid his churning head in his hands, closed his eyes, and listened to the murmur. The water mocked him, he could hear it snickering above his head . . .

When he returned to the banquet hall, it appeared smaller than before: the ceiling was lower and was charred around the edges by candle flames. As he hurried toward their side of the table grid he could already see that Stol had removed his white jacket. He did a double take. What the? . . . Stol had taken off his shirt too, he sat bare-chested at the table and was smiling at him. In his hand, or rather in the crook of his arm, he held a dirty plate against his hirsute chest like a Frisbee. A slab of calf's cheek, drenched in gravy, slid off it and landed with an audible thwack on the table. As if on command, the entire hall fell silent and stopped eating. Everyone turned and looked at Aaron.

"No!" he screamed. "What are you doing?"

With a bitter grimace Stol flung the plate at him. He ducked and fell forward off the toilet seat, *bonk*, his head banging squarely against the white stall door.

"Ow-ow-ow-ow," he whispered. The crown of his head throbbed. He felt blood.

5

Sigerius stands stock-still in the hall. He has just picked up the mail from the doormat. He had planned to walk through to the living room, but now he stands in the doorway, looking anxiously at his daughter's profile. She is sitting on the padded armrest of the large sofa, she's wearing denim hot pants, it's hot out, one of her bare legs is crossed on her lap, she picks intently at her toenail polish. She is arguing with Aaron, but he can't see him. "Come on, just go with me," he hears him say. "I think it'll do you good."

"Why on earth will it do me good?" She glances up briefly from her foot. "Just tell me that."

"Because then you'll get a realistic picture. Instead of letting your imagination run wild."

They are talking about tomorrow afternoon. Aaron, as a resident of the disaster area as well as a professional photographer, has a double invitation to ride through the remains of Roombeek in a minibus laid on by the city council. Without first checking with Joni, he has arranged for her to have that second seat.

"My boyfriend's idea of victim assistance," she says. "Go stand in front of the burned-out, caved-in ruin where your half-dead ex-boss used to live. It'll do you good."

The scowl on her self-assured forehead, the full lips that she squeezes tight, either out of irritation or simply from focusing on her nail polish. He has a lot of nerve, actually, watching her like this all week.

When he got back from Shanghai and, half in shock, surfed through all the news programs, Tineke suggested they invite Joni and Aaron to stay with them. The kid can't get into his house, and now they're sleeping in Joni's stuffy attic room. Of course they're welcome, he had said, the door's always open, but haven't they been sleeping in that attic for years now? He believed Joni would turn down the offer, maybe they shouldn't put her on the spot. Upon which an uncharacteristic quarrel ensued. Tineke said that *she* would like it, it seemed nice to *her*. Nice, he repeated, nice?—what he thought was nice was that they raised their daughters to be independent. He shouldn't be so silly, she said, she just felt like having Joni at home. And since reasonableness is one trait of Tineke's that he admires, and to "just feel like something" is so out of character, he asked if there was some special reason.

"No," she said.

"Tell me anyway."

With a sigh she sank heavily into the swivel armchair across from him. "You won't believe it," she said, "but he phoned yesterday."

Every day he had 110 different *he*s after him, but he knew at once it had to do with Menno. So was this crap about to start all over again? Wijn's Utrecht drawl echoed in his head. "You're kidding," he said. "What'd he want? And why are you only telling me now?"

"Honey, Sunday wasn't really the right moment. I mean: I thought the fireworks accident was enough for one day. I haven't forgotten how upset you were at that reception. You do understand, don't you?"

"Tien, you should have phoned me in Shanghai. Immediately. What'd he want?"

"He wanted . . . he wanted to know if Joni had survived it."

"Menno Wijn?"

"Menno Wijn? *Wilbert.* Wilbert phoned."

"Oh fuck."

"Now do you understand? I got the fright of my life. He called while I was having dinner, alone."

"How did he sound? Where'd he call from?"

"He sounded calm. But unfriendly. Curt."

"Where's he live?"

"Darling, you don't think I asked him all that, do you? It all went so fast. It's been ten years since I've talked to the boy."

So he agreed to it, of course he agreed to it; now that he knew the whole story it wasn't such a bad idea for Joni to stay with them for a while. He insisted they not tell her about the phone call. As far as Tineke could remember, Wilbert didn't specifically say to, so technically speaking they weren't keeping anything from her.

"That's for us to decide," he said.

And so on Tuesday evening the evacuees appeared on their doorstep, themselves apparently not displeased with the idea of a clean bed and their own shower. For his part, he spent the next two days hotfooting it from TV station to TV station, ran himself ragged organizing Portakabins for students made homeless by the explosion. It was all quite hectic. Since learning of the fireworks accident he hadn't given Linda and her website a second thought—until the moment those two dropped their bags in his living room. They greeted him and sat down on the sofa across from him, after which the Roombeek routine unfolded: he listened to their fireworks stories, they to his—and all the while it throbbed through his head: *or maybe it is her . . .*

"Even if it's worse than you thought," he hears Aaron say, "then at least you know what you're agonizing about. But really, you'll be OK with it. *I* was OK with it."

"*OK* with it?" Joni shook her head and went back to picking at her toes. "Weren't you going to go buy a judo outfit? Go buy it then. Instead of playing Mr. Psychologist."

Sigerius urges himself into action. Quit this observing. For five days he's been observing his daughter. He studies her like an anthropologist, no, like an inquisitor. Often, now for instance, he notices nothing out of the ordinary: there she sits, Joni, upset by that awful story about Ennio, looking only like her own vulnerable self. But still. If he bumps into her in the hallway or on the path around the side of the house, or just a few minutes ago, when he happened to catch sight of her—each fresh meeting is a body blow. With each fresh sighting he sees what he first saw during the reception: an unnerving resemblance. He pushes open the living room door, catches Aaron's eye and says: "You don't need to buy a new judo outfit. Come with me."

The irony of it is that he turned to the Internet because it seemed like a safe alternative. Until recently he thought: anything's better than that debacle of a year and a half ago.

It all began at Jaap Visser's farewell reception. Visser, head of Communications since the early '80s, who had been at his post for about ten years too long, and whom he should have dealt with as soon as he became rector. Siem gave a concise, warm speech. The reception was held in the Bastille club, a grand, dark bowel of brick and burnished copper, where he stood at the end of the massive bar talking to Vlaar, his spokesman, and four of his policy assistants. And the same waitress kept coming by with a tray of drinks, a delicate Asian girl with an open, attractive face who looked him briefly but intensely in the eye every time she handed him a glass of white wine or mineral water. She looked at him as though she was waiting for his reaction to a witty comment.

By around seven, just before it had begun to thin out, he'd had enough. He went over to the far corner of the club, where Visser and his wife were surrounded by three timid sons and some ex-colleagues. He offered a round of handshakes, wished the man all the best, and tried to make it to the exit without getting buttonholed. The girl stood rinsing glasses at the end of the bar. As he put on his scarf and stuck his arm into the sleeve of his overcoat, he could feel her looking at him. "Wait a second," she said when he made eye contact.

Later, when they couldn't get enough of analyzing that first encounter, he told her that in his recollection she didn't walk around the bar, but leapt over it like in a cartoon, to which she responded that she didn't take kindly to being compared to a comic strip character.

"Don't you remember me?" Dark-brown eyes streaked with slivers of bright copper looked up at him, she wasn't that tall, but slender, and now that she was standing under his nose and he could smell her jet-black, put-up hair, she looked nothing at all like a comic strip character. It was a long time since he had stood so close to a young, unfamiliar woman.

"Give me a hint?" he said.

"No, that's too easy. Put on your thinking cap."

"Let me guess, you're a Student Union officer." He knew she wasn't, but it seemed to him a complimentary remark.

"No, but give me a couple of years. Think."

He looked at his watch and said he ought to be getting home. She said she thought a *rector magnificus* could decide for himself what time he got home. "I'll help you out. It was . . . let's see . . . six years ago."

He acted as though he thought six years was an awful lot and surprised himself with a wisecrack: "Six years ago you were clapping out the erasers for your teacher."

She poked him in the belly with her index finger. "Just for that you owe me a glass of wine." With supple agility she slid behind the bar, uncorked a bottle in a flash and filled two glasses without spilling a drop. "Does the name Marij Star Busman ring a bell?" she asked without looking up.

No way, he thought. Are you Marij Star Busman's daughter? He needn't have felt terribly guilty that he didn't see it: Marij Star Busman was a stout, strawberry-blond prototype Dutch woman whose heavy-set figure appeared more fertile than it actually was. In the early '80s she and her husband had adopted this little Thai girl, and later a boy from Burma; the information arranged itself in his head. He'd got to know the family later, during his first year as rector, when he made it a priority to hire female professors. At that time Tubantia had just one, an embarrassing track record surpassed even by universities in the Islamic world. There had been a young female lecturer at Chemical Technology who published non-stop, even in *Nature*, and whom the students had elected teacher of the year. I must have her, he thought straightaway, and after an informal lunch he was even more convinced. Marij Star Busman was an ambitious, intelligent, extremely capable scientist who, he felt, had to be given a full professorship, and fast.

Hardly a week after he'd put his case to the university administration, he had received news of a pile-up on the misty A1 near Zwolle involving his new protégée, two hard, opposing but by no means self-canceling metallic jolts. At first, Marij Star Busman appeared to have escaped with just a broken nose, but after a few weeks she was nearly immobilized with back and neck pain. She ended up at home on the sofa with a neck brace, mood swings, and a memory like a soggy punchcard. Sigerius visited her every few weeks during her six-month recuperation, once or twice together with Tineke, and gradually a polite friendship took root. In addition to an extremely amiable husband and that Burmese toddler, a shy, skinny, slanty-eyed little girl fluttered around their Schothorst duplex; and the instant that same little girl, now a fully blossomed young woman, handed him a glass of wine, he remembered her name.

"Isabelle," he said. "Welcome back to Enschede."

To his chagrin, the family had moved to the west of the country after the dean of Chemical Technology started to quibble with Star Busman's appointment (too young, too inexperienced, too difficult), tensions that, to make matters worse, the university newspaper got wind of. Predictably, the Delft University of Technology snapped her up with the offer of a department chair. Three years later Star Busman received the Spinoza Prize for the construction of complex molecules and hyperselective catalyzators. He felt justified in rubbing it in over at the stodgy chemists' clique.

"Cheers," her adopted daughter said. Isabelle showed an unbridled interest in his doings, subjecting him to a barrage of questions alternated with coquettish asides and charming titters, all of which contrived to make him increasingly shy. How he liked Enschede, why he didn't take that Cabinet post (how did she know that?), how many of these dos did he have to "schlep" through, whether he still practiced judo. Did he remember that her little brother asked him what happened to his ears? No, he said, smiling, not mentioning that he also remembered precious little of the thirteen-year-old Isabelle. She told him that her mother was still grateful to him, even though things had taken such a weird turn. She told him she was

studying management, lived in a "pretty OK" dorm and "s
tized" with Joni, who by the way had hazed her. She didn't t
her eyes off him, not even once. When he left the Bastille a ha
hour later and walked past the gym and the minimart on his way home, he felt a strange . . . lightness.

Two days later his secretary forwarded him an e-mail from a certain Isabelle Orthel. Isabelle Orthel? Only after reading the message—"Hi Siem, did the wine floor you too? Rotgut. Café De Appel in Hengelo has a really good red"—did he realize that Star Busman was her mother's maiden name. But Isabelle Orthel wasn't any name for a Thai girl, it was a name for a seventeenth-century French lyrical philosopher. Should he respond? It was a busy Wednesday, and he let his reluctant curiosity simmer for the rest of the day. In fact, he'd decided to drop it when, out of the blue, he sent off a reply just before heading home. "No hangover. Better to mail me at Sigerius@xs4all.nl from now on. Bye Isabelle."

Only at half-past seven the next morning, as he walked through the ice-cold administration wing, did he think of her again, and instead of making coffee he first checked his private e-mail account. She had sent him two messages. The first was a full-length paragraph about how "inspiring" their conversation was, about her participation in the D66 youth council and how his name was mentioned there often. This alarmed him. In the old days, before he was married, he had had difficulty recognizing flirtatious females; in the meantime he'd got good at it, but these days he couldn't tell genuine interest, erotic or not, from what one now benignly called "networking."

The second message was short and to the point. "So *do* you like red wine?"

He was at a complete loss. For twenty-five years he'd reacted to female advances in the same way, namely by *not* reacting, and yet

...oticed that all weekend his thoughts were funneled toward this ...n. At night, lying next to the unconscious Tineke, he imagined ...hem sitting across from each other at that cafe of hers; stretched out on his back he tried to recall certain parts of her body. On Monday morning in his office, in an unguarded moment, he typed: "Isabelle, I'm dying for a good glass of wine."

Their e-mail correspondence snowballed, eventually it hit thirty in a single day. That ever-flattering attention: she buried him in cheerful, energetic, infinitely interested paragraphs and sentences, questions about his work, about his daughters, his opinion about this and that, about films and books he knew, or maybe didn't know, about his past, about his youth—for days on end, until he couldn't stand it any longer and started to tweak the tone of their exchange. Yes: *he* was the one who started openly lusting. Loosening up the attitude. After a fortnight, even periods and commas carried a double entendre. If she mentioned having gone swimming he asked her to describe her bathing suit; when she described her bathing suit, he asked what kind of underwear she had on, right now for instance.

"None," she replied.

"None?!"

"My God, Siem, of course I'm wearing underwear."

"Isabelle, what *kind* of underwear?"

"What kind of underwear would you like me to be wearing?"

He was surprised by his own randiness. He was not the sort of man to slack off at work while chasing erotic thrills, let alone allow a nineteen-year-old teenybopper to undermine his stable, entirely becalmed private life. Not that he never took any risks in life—he felt that he was constantly taking risks, but these were dangers that presented themselves to him in broad daylight and were far removed from adulterous urges. He was a man without e secrets. Maybe even without erotic desires.

Nevertheless he spent those first few weeks scouring the campus in the anxious hope of catching a glimpse of Isabelle Orthel. He pored over her sorority yearbook (on his office bookshelf: he had penned the preface) and found two photos—God, that's her all right. And still he was gobsmacked when, at the official opening of a new hockey canteen, he saw her standing right up in front. Was she *that* beautiful? Her pale face seemed illuminated, like a landmark town house. He'd forgotten how nonchalantly she put her straight, black hair up. Forgotten how she stuck her thumbs into the waistband of her jeans when she listened to someone, and how attentively her glistening mouth pursed, eager to reply.

Fortunately she waited an hour before approaching him, apparently the time she herself needed to summon her courage. It was absurdly wonderful. Only later did he worry about how it looked, the hotshot and the hockey babe: broad gestures, nonchalant touches to the shoulders and forearms, whispering in each other's ears, unrestrained bursts of laughter—at one point she even gave him a little rap on the cheek, "Rascal!" she laughed at something, he had forgotten what.

Among his injudicious resolutions for 1999 was a date in a bistro in Almelo, the nearest place he dared to meet her in public. He hadn't laid a hand on anyone other than Tineke since 1974, and all evening he felt like he was in heaven. They talked about his bleak youth in Delft, about her scintillating plans for the future, the difference between jazz and classical (she had once toyed with the idea of studying voice at a music conservatory), about neckties and the benefits of being a girl, about her curious aversion to Thailand, about fidelity and infidelity, and he realized: I am in love. On their way back to the station in the dark (he traveled first class as

.caution—"chicken," she called him) she shoved him into an .eyway and started to kiss him. He rested his ice-cold hands on .ıer shoulders, and was aware of her own hands as they explored his body under his clothes, ended at his buttocks and, after a few minutes, undid his trousers. She removed her deerskin gloves, but he pushed her fingers away. With a "quit fussing" gesture that took him rather by surprise, she released his penis and pulled at it. He was a head taller than she, so that he could avoid her coppery fox-look. He felt discreetly uncomfortable.

The train journey through the evening landscape made him tender and reflective. From his otherwise empty first-class compartment, his startled, half-erect member pressing against his inner thigh, he stared out at a nearly full moon, knowing that somewhere else in the same train an unruffled, gentle, improbably attractive girl was staring at that same scoop of ice cream, thinking of *him*. He was amazed by her audacity, by her vivacity, her strength. No trace of the kowtowing he was accustomed to, because he was thirty-five years older, because he was the boss of the university where she still had to pass her qualifying exams. Isabelle Orthel was brimming with confidence. He involuntarily compared her to Margriet Wijn, the only other nineteen-year-old girl who had ever shoved him into an alley. The differences were *so* great that he suspected he was in love with the contrast itself.

He had spent enough time at the Star Busman home to know that any member of the exemplary family where, by a twist of fate, Isabelle had found refuge, had standards to live up to. Her adopted grandfather sat on the Supreme Court and in his free time wrote biographies of the Dutch maritime heroes Maarten and Cornelis Tromp. He was a man who fathered professors rather than children. Like her mother, the impressive clutch of aunts and uncles

Isabelle mentioned were Ph.D.s in one thing or another—collectively, it seemed, serious people with serious positions at universities, law courts, or human rights organizations; if not, they painted or sculpted something that merited exhibiting. The old oak tree had branched out sufficiently over two generations to provide Isabelle with a cousin or two in pretty much every college fraternity in the country—the Star Busman clan was, to put it bluntly, a potent entity that convened at least twice a year in Isabelle's grandparents' villa in The Hague to report on its advancement in society. Isabelle rose to the occasion. Like her adopted family, this privileged girl, who waltzed through her exams, who earned her pocket money as a singing waitress in a piano bar, who organized a student trip to Prague (including a visit to Theresienstadt), who had the choice of three women's debating societies, knew exactly what she wanted out of life.

And Margriet? What did Margriet think about when she was nineteen? Not about booze yet, at least not the whole goddamn day anyway. What went on in that foggy head of hers was a mystery to him; in any case, it had nothing whatsoever to do with the future. Bugaboos, worries, complexes—his first wife had been stuck in an emotional morass that would have swallowed up *anyone* in postwar Holland, no matter what their background: rich or poor, clever or stupid, privileged or not.

He got up and followed the moon through the train carriages, first class, second class, until he found Isabelle reading a newspaper. Finger to his lips, he slid into the seat next to her and kissed her wondrous softness until they had to get off in Drienerlo. "Ladies first," he simpered. He gave her a 100-meter head start, then followed her through the darkened campus, never once taking his eyes off the green leather jacket and the moonlit bluish hair above

.. She did not look back when she turned right onto the Calslaan and he continued on toward the farmhouse. He would never have believed that the high point of their affair was already behind them.

He goes first, Aaron follows. The wedding shoes he is still wearing click across the flagstones. He's been listening to him talk about buying a new judo suit for the past two days, and kept postponing his generosity. *Just wait.* As long as he doesn't know for sure, he finds it difficult to be cordial. He finds it difficult not to look at that bald head with the watery-blue eyes and think: who the hell are you anyway? Supposing it's true—what's your role in it? He notices a conspicuous but perhaps logical division in his frame of mind: what for Joni arouses concern, for Aaron elicits aggression. Premature aggression, he's aware of that. He forces himself to suspend judgment. Supposing, supposing, supposing . . . You need *proof.* Certainty. And then: *think*, stay calm, be analytical. Avoid knee-jerk reactions.

"Nice of you, Siem," the kid says, "but it's really no problem to buy my own."

"Don't complicate things, man."

For two days he's been wandering aimlessly and awkwardly through his own house; he's been caught unawares by the unexpected invasion of his home, Joni's weeping about her injured friend, that phone call from Wilbert, the sooty smell emanating from the lacerated, smoldering city—everything permeates his farmhouse. Fate has turned it into a country estate from a second-rate Agatha Christie. Crammed together *now*, of all times. His protectiveness means he is forced to keep an eye on the telephone, fearful of another call from Wilbert; right now he is anxious, because the phone is out of reach. Without speaking or looking back, they enter the master bedroom. Tineke has made the bed and opened the terracotta-colored curtains. The mustard-yellow carpeting turns Aaron's shoes into soundless slippers. "Come on," he says, and opens the door to the dressing room.

Last night, wide awake at half-past two, he got up and fished his wallet out of his trouser pocket, with one ear tuned in to Tineke and the other to the restless city. He crept upstairs by the light of the summer night. Windows open throughout the house, the pregnant summer air pervading the rooms. He tiptoed past the guest room and along the hallway, opened the door to his study, closed the windows above his desk, shoved a stack of documents to a corner of the cool desktop and, in the light of his desk lamp, switched on his laptop. He hadn't looked at the website in months. It took some courage. A seven-centimeter plastered wall, and behind it, that pair in the guest bed. The modem dial-up resounded like the pealing of a carillon. He knew this would accomplish nothing, and even if it did: what then? Crash through the wall and drag the two of them out of bed? Beat the living daylights out of them? Throw himself at them, weeping? He was appalled anew by the home page, a sensation incompatible with the complacent lust that he could recall from the two or three months in which he had been no more than a casual consumer, a satisfied, unscrupulous dirty old man. The sight of the stylized opening photo of the girl (resemblance, of course, is not a matter of eye or hair color, he understood that, but of form, the angles of the face, the unmistakable triangle between the corners of the mouth and the rounding of the chin, the way the broadish jaw catches the light, the thin arch of the eyebrows) plunged him into a panicky sorrow. He took out his credit card and began entering it on the billing page, precision work requiring the exact input of random characters that failed three times in a row, he'd punched in the wrong number or skipped a letter, and then the modem cut him off. His bare thighs stuck to the leather seat of his desk chair.

During his fourth attempt he heard, through the merciless screech of the modem, a door being opened. There was someone in the hallway. Joni or Aaron. His heart stopped beating, he posthumously switched off the desk lamp, clumsily attempted to close the browser, his clammy fingers fumbling with the mouse—in vain: the page froze—and as a last resort he slammed the laptop closed.

He pricked up his ears in the suddenly humless darkness. After a few terrified moments in which he had repeated visions of the door flying open he heard a distant squeak, the squeak of the bottom tread of the staircase. But why, they had their own bathroom here at the end of the hall? In his left hand he held a hole punch that he squeezed gently until he lost his grip and it fell to the carpeted floor with a thud. He bent down to pick it up, felt that its clear plastic bottom was still attached to the reservoir. He waited and waited, until he began to suspect he missed whoever it was returning to their room. He waited even longer, and then snuck like a thief back to his bedroom, where he was slightly alarmed to find an empty bed. He was already lying on his side, pretending to sleep, when Tineke returned and proceeded to brush her teeth in the darkened bathroom.

"Where were you?" she asked when she came back in. He did not answer. As she lowered the heavy freight of her body into the bed, puffing and panting, she said: "I know you're awake."

"Had to pee."

"Not true," she said.

"Is too—upstairs. Downstairs was occupied. And you? Have you been eating?"

• • •

He had returned from his Almelo adventure to a slumbering farmhouse. He undressed in the laundry room and put his clothes in the hamper, regretfully showered off Isabelle's perfume, and climbed into bed next to Tineke. But the evening's events were too exhilarating for him to fall asleep. What was now sizzling through his body was far more blissful than the pleasure that other, legal, ostensibly more important events had brought him—so that for the first time in his life he doubted the point of it all. What good was half a lifetime of cerebral discipline? All that solitary perseverance! He thought of Isabelle, at this very moment sleeping somewhere on campus, and felt like smacking himself on the head for all his dutiful sublimation. In a surge of guilt he laid a hand on the comatose mountain next to him. Compared to that delicate figure in the alley, Tineke's back and hips were like the still-warm cadaver of a rhinoceros. He tossed and turned for hours, imagining Isabelle's slender body against his own, and each time he rolled over he became even more aroused.

And that night, too, he got out of bed and went upstairs to his study, this time wearing a bathrobe and heavy woolen socks. Sitting at his ice-cold desk, he did something that went against his nature: he texted Isabelle in the middle of the night. He told her how wonderful it was, and that he wanted more. Texting a college freshman at 3:30 in the morning—had he lost his mind?

To his amazement, he received an answer almost immediately: she also thought the food was great. Wha—? "Wiseacre," he texted back, grinning. "Did I wake you?" After twenty minutes that felt like a week at the North Pole she replied that she was "letting her hair down" at the beauty parlor. Letting her hair down at the beauty parlor? It took him a few seconds to solve the cryptogram: the Beauty Parlor was a disco in downtown Enschede. The jolt of jealousy that shot through his body was not generated by that nightclub, nor by the vivid image of Isabelle on a sweaty dance floor, but by the realization that his Asian lover had followed up their intimate candlelight dinner by hitting the town. He imagined how she touched up her make-up, changed into a slinky dress, and cycled into Enschede. Jesus.

He gathered his composure and texted back that she must be a pretty good dancer. He waited in vain for another half hour, but the cold drove him down to the living room for a glass of whiskey. Back in bed he switched his cell phone to silent mode and set it on the floor next to him. Every two minutes he checked to see whether she had come through. After a miserable hour and a half he fell asleep.

The next afternoon he received a formal rejection letter on his office computer. She had thought about it long and hard, but she "couldn't handle it anymore." Until now she had managed to block out all thoughts of his wife, but the fact remained that he was a "cheat," a "rat," an "adulterer," an "unreliable man." Now that they had become "more intimate," she considered it an "insoluble problem." She regretted it. "Don't e-mail or text me anymore."

He gave computers a wide berth for the next few days, like a lifelong smoker determined to kick the habit. Every fiber in his body, every one of his brain cells, screamed out for contact. In the evening at home he heard his cell phone chirp with phantom texts. Three days after receiving her Dear John letter, just before four in the afternoon, he typed out a message, his heart pounding: "consider this message unsent" and nothing else. Once he'd clicked "send" he despised himself for it, but at the same time hoped it would make her laugh and break her silence. He spent the last hours of his workday gazing at his in-box like a fisherman waiting for a nibble, refreshing the page every few seconds, until he was engulfed in darkness. The low-rise administrative wing, with his spacious office at the end of it, stuck like a foot out of the tower adjacent to the campus's main entrance. He gazed out of the picture window across the empty parking lot. If I turn on the light, he thought, there'll be a madman on display.

And for days on end, nothing. At night, he hardly closed his eyes; usually between three and four in the morning he took to his study with a glass of whiskey and a packet of tissues, and sat in his leather reading chair jerking off to her yearbook photo. Twice he wrote her lengthy, pathetic letters on his laptop and then deleted them, not out of common sense, but out of fear. Isabelle's principled tone unnerved him. When, after the weekend, he returned to his office at 11 a.m. from a meeting and, against his better judgment, opened his private e-mail account, the name Isabelle Orthel appeared like a burning bush on his computer screen. He touched his left ear and opened the message.

"Is it such cold turkey for you too?"

He wonders how she's doing. Is she still living on campus? Maybe she was in Roombeek at the time of the accident. He and Aaron walk deeper into the dressing room, an illogically L-shaped space. Around the corner, along the base of the L, his wife has built shallow, made-to-measure shelves for their shoes; on the rear wall is a walnut cupboard with steel modular shelves, a hanging section on the left for his academic robes and dress tails. It smells of the dried lavender Tineke has placed in sachets among his clothes. He squats down, his joints make a snapping sound, and like a forklift he pulls two judo suits from the lowest shelf.

"The jacket to this one," he says to Aaron, his chin on the top suit, "probably won't fit you. The bottom one is my old competition suit. Take that jacket."

Aaron takes the stack from him. "Try it on here?" he says.

"You sleeping all right?" He can see that Aaron does not like the question. "You look knackered."

"Reasonably. It gets pretty warm at night."

Sigerius turns, reaches up and pulls an old black belt from the uppermost shelf, a supple, time-worn thing; the spot where the button dug itself in, year after year, has been scuffed white. Aaron wriggles out of his shoes. Sigerius waits until his new jeans have dropped to his ankles and he wobbles on one leg while removing the other. "Here," he says at precisely that moment, "my lucky belt," and tosses it too hard—flings it—at his shoulder, it is a ridiculous gesture. But Aaron does not notice, or pretends not to.

"Thanks," says Aaron, and bends down to pick up the belt. "Your competition belt?"

"That too. Just my old belt."

He watches as Aaron pulls the bleached-white judo trousers up over his long, suntanned legs and bony hips, ties the string of the waistband in a bow. His torso is lanky and has the form of a question mark. Aaron wouldn't do something like that. It is unkind of him to take out his paranoia on this kid. Isn't it the same old tune? he suddenly wonders. Him and sex. Isn't he always projecting his guilt onto others when it's about sex? Did he conjure up his idiotic, paranoid ideas because the moralizer in him feels he should be punished for all that Internet cruising? Isabelle would say: *Yes*.

After they picked up where they had left off, she told him during one of their battery-guzzling telephone conversations that he owed it all to her mother. Owe all what to your mother? Well, she said excitedly, her mother watched her pine for the past four days and said: just e-mail the guy.

"Your mother?" he exclaimed, "does your *mother* know about this?"

"Of course she does," she said, "what d'you think?"

"You're kidding, this isn't something you go and tell your *mother.* What we have going here is strictly confidential, Isabelle."

She burst out laughing. "Get used to it, big guy, in our family we tell one another *everything.*"

He did not get used to it. Worse: now, eighteen months later, he still cringes at the thought of Marij Star Busman knowing about his escapade with her adopted daughter. When he sent her a tentative e-mail a few weeks after Isabelle had spilt the beans—"I just wanted to say, Marij, what a nice, spontaneous daughter you have"—her reply was not moralistic, but dead serious: "I have complete faith in your intentions, Siem, but I don't like seeing my daughter hurt."

Hurt? He had no idea what she was getting at. Her daughter did not make a hurt impression, at most she acted piqued, moody. Ever since what they continued to call "cold turkey," their phone calls and e-mails increasingly focused on what she saw as his spineless gift for committing adultery. And when the conversation—all post-Almelo communication was carried out by phone or e-mail—came anywhere near sex she would text him: isn't this difficult for you? Or: what would your daughters make of all this? Or: don't you think of yourself as a bad person? Although it might have been better to explain to her that judging him was not exactly the job of a *maîtresse,* he wore himself out setting straight what she in turn would bend back out of shape for him. When he asked her if she thought Bill Clinton was a bad person, she answered that he mustn't hide behind other people. When he tried to explain what it was like to wake up next to the same woman for twenty years ("that's for as long as you've been alive, Isabelle"), she replied: "You're not even halfway there, man." She was Monica Lewinsky and Kenneth Starr wrapped into one.

So now Monica and Kenneth were hurt. Instead of wondering about his own failings, he left the administrative building in the middle of the day, his eyes bleary with concern, and called her up. Why didn't she tell him she was hurt? And what from, honeybunch? She answered that she was not his honeybunch and that he apparently did not appreciate what she was going through. *She* was always alone, she *slept* alone, she went to her parents' alone, to parties alone—and the whole time, all she could think of was Siem Sigerius.

"And what about me then?" he said. "All I think about is you, Isa. And what goes through *my* mind is that *you're* free, *you're* the one who's constantly running off. *You* and that Beauty Parlor of yours, *you* hanging out in one of your bars until four in the morning, three times a week. *You* going on one blind date after the other." (This was true: she kept him fully abreast of the fratboys who accompanied her to galas and house parties all across the Netherlands.)

"Siem," she sighed, "they're pimply little creeps."

"Maybe, but you go to bed with them. The pimply creeps get to have sex with you."

Be-e-e-ep.

He heaved a sigh, crossed the rain-soaked asphalt of the main road, and called her back. "I'm right, though, aren't I?"

"Yeah, *my* turn, OK? You sleep every *night* with that wife of yours."

"And I'm still happy. With us! Come on, Isa, just this once pretend to be an adult. When can we meet? De Appel is waiting."

"You are *such* a coward."

"Coward? I *crave* you. We can do whatever we want!" He stood with one arm outstretched, like a Shakespearean actor on the phone. It was cold, he blinked back the half-soft tears, trying to focus on the bare branches of the oaks and elms. "As long as you keep it quiet."

She did not thaw, she exploded. She exploded just like SE Fireworks would explode a year later. *This* was precisely what pissed her off, every time, she shrieked. Did he *really* not get it? She was not someone for *on the side*. She was *disgusted* by his underhanded approach, she was disgusted by his asking her to keep it from her parents.

"Coward," she snorted, "don't you ever, and I mean *ever*, forbid me to be honest with the people who saved my life, you got that?"

"Isa sweetheart, just listen . . ."

"No, I will *not* listen, I've got our house bible in front of me, I know exactly what kind of manipulative little man you are, this book never lies. Listen is the last thing a person should do with cheats like you!"

Book? To his astonishment, a housemate of hers, a girl who sat on the corner of her bed drinking camomile tea during their conversation, had handed her a book entitled *Never Satisfied: How & Why Men Cheat*. The sorority's "house bible" in which she'd spent an entire evening underlining passages with a ballpoint "because it was all just so familiar."

"But Isa," he moped, "at least tell me what I have to do."

She went silent, a loaded pause like a piano being dropped from the tenth story, but instead of crashing to smithereens she answered with saccharine sweetness: "You've got a month to leave your wife."

• • •

Put an end to it. A man in his position, a man who shoulders considerable ceremonial and administrative responsibilities, a man at the head of a family that would unanimously agree that they'd put up with enough already—a man like this, you would expect to put an end to it. But no. The only thing he can think of is Isabelle's hand, that petite Asian hand that had so startled him that evening in Almelo; day and night he felt that phantom hand, tugging gently on his nervous system, driving him crazy, crazy with desire. There were moments when he was prepared to die for that hand. During that topsy-turvy month of March 1999 he tried to imagine himself inhabiting a future even more topsy-turvy, but because he was so turned around himself it hardly fazed him at all.

Often, at night, an hour or so after he had watched, from his half of the nuptial bed, Tineke remove her acres of textile and dig herself in, panting, next to him, he saw everything as clear as day: he would leave her, the woman who understood him so well, who for years had put herself second for his sake, the woman for whom he felt a massive, inert, deeply satisfied love—she had to go. Since Isabelle had issued her ultimatum he had difficulty falling asleep; tossing and turning, he abandoned himself to what began as practical, rational musings: he imagined short-term rentals in downtown Enschede he could move into until the divorce, he projected himself into Isabelle's daily routine, saw himself sitting in her student kitchen on weekday mornings, his suit as crumpled as himself, drinking coffee from an oversized mug missing its handle. He pictured them driving off to Delft on misty Sunday mornings to visit his fifteen-year-younger mother-in-law-to-be, he pictured them at the procession into the Grote Kerk, arm in arm, for the opening of the academic year, Isabelle in a handmade hat intended for menopausal women—the idea of a middle-aged man with, *nota bene*, a Thai girl, would this go over well?—problematic scenarios he eventually allowed, unresolved, to swirl around in the eddy of increasingly carefree fantasies: city trips to Barcelona and Paris, romantic evening strolls through Europe's finest parks, hotels, or B&Bs for which he would foot the bill; and only when he had worked through *those* visions, only after that endless, chaste foreplay, did he give in to her slender hand. Sweaty and curved like a jumbo shrimp, he lay on his half of their Auping mattress, as close to the edge as possible, a suit of armor around his erection. He barely touched himself, afraid that his mechanical shaking would waken Tineke, meditating on the passionate maneuvers Isabelle would perform on him, maneuvers that by now he was painfully aware he dreaded. How was he going to get through this? In some things in life, Siem Sigerius was extremely talented, a champion, even, he'd proved himself over and over—but he was downright lousy in bed.

He'd never been much good as a lover. The only period of his life when he could lay claim to that qualification was in the mid-1970s, after Tineke's conquest. For a year or year and a half they were bewitched by sex, and had sex the way sex was probably supposed to be had. For him it was utterly confusing, a drizzly no-man's-land where he, without knowing it at the time, was busy replacing his one sacred goal—to become the world's greatest judoka—with something else, something more uncertain, something completely absurd, that private dream world of formulas and graph paper. Aimless, vexed, a failure—that is how he felt at the climax of his sexual career, hopelessly out of condition too, but at the same time wound-up, and tense, and charged. In fact, it was the only phase of his life when he felt like sex.

Before that, when alongside his jobs he trained three, sometimes four hours a day (judo, running, wrestling, jujitsu, weightlifting—a man with muscles like a gorilla but the protein levels of a hunger striker—the pockets of his duffel bag stuffed with raisins and bananas and dark chocolate, so that he didn't keel over from exhaustion, and then fasting for days before weighing in, jogging in a rain suit, waking up in a pension next door to a tournament stadium with eyes glued in their sockets and a tongue of ox leather)—in those years his libido dangled on his consciousness like a sad, frayed shred, a strand of desire that tickled his loins maybe twice a month, nocturnal moments when he shook Margriet out of her drunken stupor and mounted her like a komodo dragon.

So he could pride himself on a sex life of a year and a half, slightly less than his military service, and then it was over; his physical interest in Tineke faded with alarming speed. Mathematics took hold of him, grabbed him by the scruff of his neck, and poof, it was over. In retrospect he thinks—a thought that under no circumstances should be allowed to leave his mind—that his sexual surge was a form of de-training, the result of the pent-up physical energy accumulated on his camp bed in the little upstairs kitchen, the conversion of physical labor into mental gymnastics and wrestling. He used to lie on top of Kiknadze and Ruska and Snijders; later, he released himself onto Tineke?

It was humiliating how quickly he had reverted to his old obsessive, solitary self. Before he knew it they were in America, where everything went well for them, everything thrived and flourished in California: guavas, tangerines, lemons, his new daughters, his and Tineke's love for each other—everything except their *moyenne*, a word that still makes him nervous if he comes across it in one of those adult-lifestyle magazines. In Berkeley and Boston he lived for numbers. Men of his ilk were now named Quillen and Wiles and Erdős, skeletal digi-poets made of translucent rice paper who had retreated into the furthest reaches of their own cranium. When visiting Berkeley, Paul Erdős occasionally stayed with them in their clapboard house on Bonita Avenue, and then he and the maestro explored barren wastelands, penned an article the minute they had cracked a hypothesis, put in eighteen-, sometimes twenty-hour days, and once, when they sat talking in the grass in the backyard after one of those tabletop marathons, Tineke said jokingly to Erdős—but, oh yes, in effect to *him:* "Mathematicians, Paul, are little more than machines that convert coffee into hypotheses, don't you think? Always those hypotheses of yours, I can't bear to *hear* the word anymore," at which Erdős guffawed in agreement and clapped his trembling hands.

In those days, as they lay in the bed she had hammered together herself out of pure love, Tineke sometimes slid her hand under the elastic of his pajama bottoms—his signal to launch into a soliloquy on algebra, on the glass wall separating him from the proof he was after, and how he was going to smash through that wall, tomorrow, once he was at his desk at Evans Hall. And yes, he felt guilty and inadequate. But Tineke appeared to accept his escape route, she followed his achievements closely, she seemed to believe that the cultivation of genius entails certain sacrifices, maybe she was simply happy that between seven and nine in the evening he did his damnedest to be a good father to Joni and Janis. By the time they had moved to Boston and he honed in on his breakthrough, sometimes sleeping on an air mattress in his office at MIT, sex was something they talked about like it was an overgrown lawn that needed mowing. And for the past ten years or so they talked about nothing at all. The erotic scenario was put off and, eventually, called off. They respected each other's privacy. They kissed on the cheek when leaving or returning home.

Returning home was something, incidentally, he never did unannounced or noiselessly or as a surprise anymore, not since that time he inadvertently saw Tineke in the possession of an apparatus made of gray East Bloc plastic, the color of an old-fashioned dial phone, out of which stuck an iron rod with a hard rubber knob on the end, and which, when you plugged it in, pounded violently up and down, a brutal, hammering rattle. A noisesome machine one might use to crack walnuts, but which his wife used after a hard day's work in her studio, he discovered one afternoon when the sound drew him to the bedroom, to pleasure herself.

His memory tells him that he spent the month following Isabelle's ultimatum in his study, half naked and at night. That was when he discovered the websites. His study is cube-shaped, but the slight curvature of the roof and the stacks of yellowed periodicals and dusty books in the corners and along the walls make it resemble the inside of a bird's nest. It is the only room in the farmhouse to have evaded Tineke's woodworker's hand. It is his man cave. Daddy's jerk-off den.

Isabelle had opened the faucet all the way, and rusty water, confined to the pipes for decades, gushed out. Their routine consisted of texting each other after Tineke fell asleep—Isabelle never went to bed before three, did she actually ever sleep?—and as soon as he received an answer, the jumbo shrimp slipped out of bed, swam up the stairs to his study and switched on his laptop. He excitedly sent her e-mails laying out the future he had been dreaming up for them. That it was mutual, he gathered from the visions she herself sent back: she wanted to take a long trip with him, she would like to live in a real house with him, she asked whether he was in fact sterilized, and more such talk that, coming from someone else's mouth, sounded rather big.

Now that they were being so explicit, he sometimes succeeded in texting her away from her sorority house, luring her to her dorm room, where she disrobed and, like him, sat naked at her computer. "Tell me exactly what you are going to do to me, soon, when we're on that trip." How literally Isabelle took that "soon" was evident the following afternoon. "Baby," she texted him, "how did T react?" *How did T react?* Hang on, she'd given him a month. "I'm waiting for the right moment," he texted back.

The days and nights passed, and again something changed in Isabelle's attitude. He had previously seen her switch from admiring and uninhibited to preachy and moralistic—and now she turned harsh. Her e-mails became shorter, more time elapsed between them. "When are you going to tell her?" she answered when he asked if she was turned on. Sometimes she would get him aroused, and then give him the silent treatment for a quarter of an hour, an hour, the whole night. And because it was, in the end, always a let-down, because she never really cooperated—but also because he never gave up, addicted as he was to those little digital envelopes—he began, out of desperation, scouring the Internet. Driven insane by deferred fulfilment, he found photos where he could actually see what Isabelle was withholding from him. He was shocked to discover how many girls, Asian or otherwise, he could conjure up on his screen with just a few simple search terms. But it worked—and how. By the time Isabelle went to bed—always suddenly and unannounced—his laptop nearly melted from the tabbed sex sites, downloaded pictures of floozies in all manner of positions, pop-ups and weird, virusy dial-up programs. Sometimes it took him a good fifteen minutes to clean his hard drive, after which he would do the same in the upstairs bathroom to the raw chipolata between his legs. The release was followed by a peaceful gloom that got him restfully through the remainder of the night.

• • •

"Who knows if I'll even get to see the inside of the house again," says Aaron. He puts on the judo jacket, his hands and forearms shoot out of the sleeves like broomsticks, he overlaps the front flaps.

"Don't be so pessimistic."

They hear the soft thwap of flip-flops from down the hall. "Guys?" Joni. "Dad, Aaron, you guys ready to eat? The table's set."

Aaron squats down and picks the belt up off the floor from between his bare feet.

"Where are you?" Her footsteps echo as she walks through the gently ventilated bathroom into the dressing room. "Am I disturbing?" Her face does not express irony, but irritation.

"You never disturb, honey," he mumbles, with exaggerated sweetness.

"Coming," Aaron says.

She sniffs and walks off without a word. The last time Joni disturbed him was at the end of the month Isabelle had given him; after a sleepless night he sat in the administrative wing like a prepped corpse. Something that seldom happens, happened: his secretary announced Joni. What was she doing there? He still remembers how optimistic she looked: spring was still pondering its next move but Joni was already wearing a summer frock. Her appearance cheered him up, they kissed on both cheeks, sat down at the corner of the conference table. He looked tired, she said; I have a busy job, he answered.

She said: "When you're in love, anything's possible."

He asked: "How do you mean?"

"Dad," she said, "I don't want to butt in. I'm just here to warn you."

"Oh? And what about?"

She leaned over and pulled a folded-up newspaper page out of her bag. She opened it, flattened it out, and slid it toward him. He recognized the photo in the middle all too well: him naked on the riverbank. He'd never shake it.

"You know Aaron took this picture, right?" he asked, just to ask something.

"I took it off the toilet door at our house. Look a little closer."

He'd seen it already. But to buy time to pull himself together he made a point of scrutinizing the handwritten comments her housemates had scribbled next to his naked body over the past few years. Someone had drawn an enormous balloon in felt-tip pen from his gaping mouth with the text: "Ladies, is Joni behaving herself?" And lower down, under his bare feet in the grass, in large block letters: ERECTOR MAGNIFICUS. "Good one," he mumbled, "except I don't get this one." He tapped the red circle around his shivery penis. "Property of Isabelle Orthel," read the caption.

"It's all over campus, Dad. If they write something like this about my father in *my* house, in *my* WC, then you can assume everyone knows you're doing it with a freshman."

"And what if it's true? What then?" It occurred to him that she was four years older than Isabelle.

"I don't begrudge you anything, Dad. But—"

"But what? What're you here for, Joni, to chew me out?"

"No. I'm here for Mom—"

"She's not here."

"I don't want Mom reading about your escapades on my bathroom door."

Aaron has tied the belt around his waist, a tidy, flat knot, and examines the inside of the jacket. "I've heard that here and there in the Vluchtestraat interior walls have caved in," he says. "They want to inspect the houses one by one to assess the danger of collapse. It'll take another week or two. That's what they say at the information post."

Sigerius swallows and tries to think of something that sounds friendly. Before he can come up with an obligatory assurance that Aaron is welcome for as long as necessary, they hear the ringtone of a cell phone.

6

"That's me," Sigerius said. He pulled out his Nokia from the pocket of his khakis and checked the number on the display. He frowned. "Sigerius," he said, allowing his eyes to wander around the dressing room. "Hello, Thom. No, no bother. (. . .) Terrible, never seen anything like it. But Enschede is resilient. (. . .) Yes, yes, we're OK, Thom, we're all fine. And you? Yes. (. . .) Go ahead, I'm listening."

But Aaron wasn't, at first. He looked around the narrow space. On either side, meters of aluminum racks were stuffed with clothing: to the left, suits and sport jackets arranged by color; to the right, twice as long, Tineke's dresses and caftans. He was used to this—it was nearly impossible to talk to Sigerius for more than ten minutes at a stretch. What did take some getting used to was what he called the everyday Sigerius: they'd never been at such close quarters before. He noticed that Sigerius preferred to keep to himself, more often than not retreating to the living room while the rest of them were out on the terrace. During meals he could be downright grumpy. Maybe the fireworks disaster brought on extra stress at Tubantia, maybe he sensed the tension between him and Joni, although Aaron could hardly imagine that something so banal would affect his mood. Just to have something to do, he sniffed at the sleeves of the judo suit, the white cotton smelled fresh, old-fashionedly fresh, as though it had come straight from the prehistoric '60s. Ruska and maybe even Geesink had clutched it, or pulled the collar over Sigerius's head during a sparring match.

"... sounds very interesting," he heard Sigerius say. He stood a quarter of a turn from him, with his free hand he gently nudged the toes of a pair of running shoes in the rack. "You folks are really on the ball (...) Yes. (...) I understand, yes. (...) Of course I'll consider it." Sigerius wheeled around, his dark, hard gaze locking into Aaron's eyes. He smiled sheepishly, but Sigerius did not see it. Aaron's head was reeling. They had been staying at the farmhouse for a week now, and still he hadn't got a decent night's sleep. He and Joni were condemned to each other in a narrow guest bed that creaked as though it were slowly contracting; every night he lay there, a nervous wreck, until five in the morning, lest he make it creak or crack, it creaked every time he swallowed, and by dawn he himself was a stiff, groaning plank.

At first he thought it a nifty idea, a few weeks at his in-laws. He was curious about the day-to-day routine on the Langenkampweg—but now he realized how uncomfortable it was. Even more wearing, if possible, than his insomnia was this strife with Joni—it was terrible timing, now that they were living with her parents they were at each other's throats, they had never bickered so easily before, about everything and nothing. She still seemed pissed off about that wedding. And he in turn was being driven crazy by all her speculating about Boudewijn Stol and his wonderful internships.

And then there was that Ennio. Like hundreds of other Enschede residents, the poor guy lay crumpled in the hospital, bruised, beaten, and burned, not a pretty sight, and he could well imagine that for Joni the accident had "hit close to home," but what he couldn't take—Jesus, there wasn't much he *could* take, that endless sniveling and blubbering was the least of it—was that he felt excluded; wherever he went, whether into the living room or out onto the terrace for a smoke, there she was, usually in the company of her mother, red-eyed, weeping, in an apparent heart-to-heart that was cut short the minute he appeared. If he asked whether she was all right, the answer was invariably "yeah, fine." Apparently he was not the one to come crying to about other men. Sigerius had told him yesterday, not to his displeasure, that Ennio had moved to the Kievitstraat after his wife had kicked him out of the house. Apparently on account of messing around with a young female employee.

"When do you want to know?" Sigerius asked. "Fine. (. . .) Strictly confidential. Understood. I'll get back to you within two weeks. It's a deal. Talk to you soon. Bye. Bye, Thom." Sigerius held his telephone at eye level, stared briefly at the display, and then slowly dropped his hand. He looked at Aaron and said: "Well, just look at you."

"Like it's tailor-made," he replied.

"Two weeks," Sigerius said.

"Two weeks?"

"If he hasn't fallen before then." Sigerius eyed him thoughtfully. "Aaron, listen, can you keep a secret? Yes, of course you can. You've already heard half of it anyway."

Without waiting for an answer Sigerius confided in him (his deep, calm voice sounded charged) that it was D66 chief Thom de Graaf who called to say that Kruidenier, the current Minister of Education, was expected to be sacked within a month, or would resign, which in itself wasn't earthshaking news: it had been the talk of the town in The Hague for the past few weeks. "And would I make myself available." Normally his father-in-law spoke deliberately, placing a full stop after just about every word, but now the sentences gurgled forth like a brook, his small nostrils flared with triumph. "Could be as early as next week. Or six months from now."

Sigerius looked at him expectantly. Aaron racked his brains

for something appropriate to say, but drew a blank. He was overwhelmed by the news, more forcefully than Sigerius could have been, it had a physical effect on him, as though he'd been given a kick in the backside. Sigerius a Cabinet minister—somewhere in his exhausted body a sprinkler started spouting adrenaline. He had to say something about Kruidenier and his squabbling with parliament, he'd read about it, the guy had misinformed the MPs regarding alleged fraud in public colleges. But his mouth was too dry to get a word out. He stared at the shoe racks alongside Sigerius's face, a dark blotch on which no doubt surprise or even disbelief was starting to take form. He focused on a pair of waltzed-out, matt-black pumps.

"If I say yes, that is," he heard Sigerius say. "Anyway, the party's fed up with Kruidenier. Maybe he'll just pack his bags himself. That's what they're hoping."

Aaron was overheating, his jaw was clenched. Those pumps had suffered under Tineke's weight, they were ruined. Sigerius sniffed. From the hallway came a loud, life-saving shout. Tineke. "*Boys!* We're about to start!"

"We're coming," Sigerius called back. He laid a hand on Aaron's cotton shoulder and squeezed past him. From the doorpost he said: "I'll tell them you're getting changed. Mum's the word for now."

Blissfully alone, Aaron let the judo jacket glide off his clammy torso. He stepped out of the white cotton trousers, pulled on his stiff new jeans. He walked into the bedroom. Between the two copper-colored bedside tables, each with a tidy stack of books, was an unusually high double bed, with old-fashioned sheets and blankets. No clothes strewn about. He wriggled into the polo shirt Sigerius had lent him and stood at the full-length mirror mounted on the closet door. He examined his hot head. At the very crown of his skull there was still a small scab, a souvenir of his tumble against the men's room door.

As he walked through the living room—heavy blue velour curtains kept out the evening sun, Joni's *Financial Times* lay quartered on the sofa—he could already hear the clatter of cutlery. And like an ostinato, Sigerius's bass voice.

". . . so I know him a bit, once I had him work something out for the Socio-Economic Council, it was maybe . . . six years ago? He was still a partner at McKinsey. He came to give a presentation, and I have to say . . ."

Aaron halted in the middle of the room, long before he could be seen from the sunroom, and grabbed hold of the back of the swivel armchair. Were they talking about Boudewijn Stol?

There was a lull in the conversation, Sigerius did not finish his sentence, maybe they had heard him coming. With a sigh he propelled himself into motion, circumvented the two enormous ferns that guarded Tineke's open kitchen, and stepped into the sunroom. "Bon appétit," he said. Tineke smiled at him, Sigerius dished himself up some salad, Janis and Joni carried on eating without looking up. He sat down next to Joni, directly across from her father. She swallowed a mouthful and said: "Hey, guess what."

"I give up," he said stiffly. The sliding door was open, clumps of poplar fluff hesitated on the threshold, he heard the old chestnut tree rustle in the May breeze.

"While you were in the shower Boudewijn phoned, he asked if I would do my internship with him in Amsterdam." She said it coolly, but her voice curled at the edges. He felt himself getting all hot and bothered again, this time with impotent rage.

"Amsterdam?" he asked hoarsely. "I thought you were all gung-ho about going abroad. Why would you want to go sit in an office in Amsterdam? Seems to me a . . . a complete waste of time."

She smiled at her parents across the whiteness of the table. "Aaron and Boudewijn Stol didn't hit it off."

"We hit it off just fine," he said.

"Really?" Sigerius asked with a mouthful of food, ignoring his comeback, "I was just saying that I know Boudewijn a little . . ." He took a sip of wine, swallowed and continued: "He's a decent guy, and extremely good at what he does nowadays. Sounds to me a golden opportunity, Joni."

"Me too," Aaron said weakly. "Naturally. But my point is that Joni shouldn't sacrifice her foreign adventure for something like this." This was a disadvantage of Sigerius: he was a friend you want to keep as a friend, and sometimes a little voice deep down wondered if that kind of friend really was a friend after all.

Sigerius nodded thoughtfully, but was startled by the loud metallic clink of Joni's fork. She turned to Aaron, leaned back, and eyed him mockingly. "Oh, *now* listen to him," she said, "that's a good one. When I told you I wanted to spend a few months in America you were nearly in tears. You were practically clinging to my leg. And now this."

There was a painful silence. He noticed that Janis, who never did pay him much notice, sat there smirking at him. In an attempt to regain his composure, he picked up the porcelain dish of potato croquettes and, with a trembling hand, scooped a few of them onto his plate.

"But I do have a funny story about that Stol," said Sigerius, breaking the impasse. Although he was still keeping it to himself, the news from The Hague seemed to have perked him up. "After that SEC meeting he gave me a lift to Utrecht Station, and that was a memorable ride, I can tell you. My heart still races when I think about it."

"What kind of car did he have?" Joni asked.

"Some sporty thing. A BMW, I think."

"So what happened?" asked Janis.

Sigerius rested his broad, hairy forearms on the table and started telling them, in a relaxed tone of voice, that he and Stol were on the A12 just outside The Hague when they were ruthlessly overtaken by a Golf with an ostensibly normal-looking couple inside. He, in the passenger seat, got the fright of his life, and Stol even more so: he not only slammed on the brakes, but also sat on the horn. That was not entirely to the Golf's liking. It slowed down alongside Stol's BMW, the passenger window rolled down, a bleached-blond woman squirmed out, just about to her waist, and flung a paper sack of *patates frites* against Stol's windshield. "Can you believe it!" said Sigerius. "We pulled onto the shoulder and spent the next fifteen minutes cleaning globs of mayonnaise and curry sauce and onions off the windshield. What's the deal with those idiots in the west?"

Janis laughed. Joni said: "That Bo seems like just the type for an hour-long car chase."

"Bo?" Tineke asked.

"Boudewijn," she explained. "He said to call him Bo."

Aaron thought he was losing his mind. For the second time in a week he was on the ropes thanks to that asshole Stol, and aside from being just plain fed up, he saw it coming: Joni was dying to give her parents a blow-by-blow account of his behavior during that dinner of Vaessen's. She could hardly hold it in. She thought he had made a fool of himself, that he was a boorish exhibitionist, and while he himself had a different opinion on the matter, he estimated his chances of winning this contest here at the dinner table as fairly slim. When he heard Sigerius say that, in his opinion, "this kind of punk" deserved to be dealt with mercilessly, another tall tale occurred to him, a comparable situation involving his brother, and before he knew it he had commandeered the conversation. Enough of that Bo. Finito. End of story.

"Well, I've got another one," he began, and waited until all four of them looked at him. "Back when I was still studying Dutch I was sitting in my taxi one weekend in Venlo . . ."

"You never drove a taxi, did you?" Joni asked.

"Briefly," he lied, with more confidence in his voice than just now. "A year or so."

In truth, it was his elder brother Sebastian who for years drove a provincial shuttle bus in Venlo every Saturday. But in his version it was he who, one Saturday afternoon, was heading toward Tegelen, just south of Venlo, on a two-lane road, and just before the hospital exit was nearly sideswiped by a red Ford Escort with black spoilers. The other driver swerved into his lane just before the red light, the car rocketing, tires squealing, in front of his taxi-van and up the entrance ramp to Sint-Maartens Hospital. "He missed ramming my front bumper by a hair," he said, "so I honked and flipped him the bird."

Just there, his anecdote brushed Sigerius's, and he saw he at least had their attention, even Joni's. Tineke asked Janis to pass her the bowl of cauliflower. "And so as I'm sitting there at the red light," he continued, "the Escort, instead of driving into the hospital parking lot, pulls a U-turn, plows over the shoulder and stops. The door flies open and out gets this guy, about thirty. He tosses away a cigarette butt and marches over to my car. I can see right away he's scum. He had to walk about twenty meters, his head tilted back the whole time so his chin stuck way out. He glowered at me over his jawbones, tongue pushed between his bottom teeth and lower lip. I could see that thick tongue of his, a nasty, blotchy slab. Greasy, jet-black hair, suede jacket, shiny red polyester training pants, Kappa, y'know, those Milan ones Gullit and Van Basten used to wear."

"And Rijkaard," Janis said.

"And Rijkaard," he said. The anecdote was etched in his memory; he'd heard it from Sebastian at least three times, go on, tell it again, and he had retold it himself so many times he could recite it in his sleep. "So this guy," he continued, suddenly more self-confident than he had felt until now, "was wearing black leather clogs with white socks. That's how Venlo trailer trash goes out in public. I knew right away this guy was trouble. That sort of trash is easy to spot." He told them that because of the balmy late-summer temperatures his passenger window was wide open. It seemed wise to raise the window: storm a-brewing. "So I hold down the button. But it goes slowly. Just before the window's shut, the guy grabs the top edge of window with his fingers and deposits a great big green gob of spit onto the glass. He hangs there on it with his full weight. Our eyes are glued on each other as I keep my finger on the button. He screams: "Oh yeah? Oh yeah?" For a second his fingers are caught, but then he pulls the window down with one long, slow tug." Aaron demonstrated this with both hands, his face contorted into a malicious grimace. "*Snap* went the little motor. The guy leans halfway into the car and grabs me by my work tie."

"What a creep," Tineke said, still busy loading up her plate and otherwise uninterested. Sigerius was paying close attention, that's what mattered. "A creep?" he grinned. "But nothing happened."

"Drop the tough-guy act, Dad," said Janis, "you'd be peeing in your pants."

"I'd be peeing in *his* pants," her father answered. Aaron looked over at Sigerius, inwardly satisfied. He had not seen him like this all week, momentarily relieved from his irritable earnestness. He had shifted into fighter mode: don't vacillate, take quick action—entirely atypical for a man of his age and position. Janis scornfully shook her close-cropped head.

"So then what does this guy do, he gives my tie a tight twist and winds up with his free arm," he continued. "Now I'm going to get a fat lip, I thought. I pictured myself staggering off to the emergency room. But he doesn't hit me. He yells something pretty vulgar and pushes off with his fist in my throat. He slides back out the window, sidles back to his car, and drives into the hospital parking lot." He was impressed by his uninhibited word choice, he felt a million times better than ten minutes ago.

"So what did he yell at you?" Sigerius held the porcelain gravy boat in the air, five centimeters above the damask like a ghost galleon. He stared at Aaron, and traced circles with his tongue on the inside of his gray-stubbled cheeks.

"Drop it," Joni said. "I don't think I want to know."

Aaron glanced at her; her face was glazed with disdain. Maybe the others figured her scowl was meant for her father. No siree. The family bitch was ashamed of *him*, ashamed of her other half, she was worried about the show he was planning to put on this time. In theory, a week like this was a perfect opportunity to show her parents what a refreshingly nice couple they were. Usually this was something she excelled in: play nice for Mommy and Daddy, pretend they had nothing to hide. Usually she reveled in pretense, theatre, flashy falsehoods. Not now. Now she was entrenched in the homeyness of her family, she observed him through her parents' eyes, and what she saw was a jealous dork who prowled around her childhood home in the middle of the night.

"Go on, tell us anyway," Sigerius said.

In a strange, hyperconscious way, Aaron knew he had landed on the right side of his fatigue: the temazepams he took last night had worn off; he felt lucid. "First he spat at me, another great big wad, this time at my ear. He yells: 'BALD TWAT!' at the top of his lungs. The cyclists at the stoplight turned and gawked. And then turned straight ahead again."

"See what I mean," said Joni. Sigerius shook his head and sniffed.

"And suddenly, with three cars honking behind me, I'm *pissed.* Furious. Not because of that twat, or because of that green spit-wad on my head, no, not—well, yeah, that too. But mostly because of my window. That lowlife busted my window." His lack of sleep allowed him to *become* Sebastian. "I pictured myself having to face De Zwart, my boss. Not the most easygoing. I can kiss my overtime goodbye, that's De Zwart. 'It's coming out of your paycheck, Bever.' De Zwart doesn't ask if you're OK, De Zwart withholds your salary. God damn it, I think. So I park my minivan next to that Escort and walk over to the hospital."

Sigerius's face breaks into a conspiratorial smile, the gravy boat makes a safe landing, finally, and with his now-free hand he strokes his deformed zero-tolerance ear. "So you go after the guy," he says. "Way to go."

The setting sun warmed the glass sunroom where they were eating, made their faces glow, reflected orange-red in the table-ware, and Aaron described, also to himself, how in that hospital you had a long, low reception desk to the right and, to the left, a busy self-service cafeteria. "I couldn't see the guy anywhere. Not at reception, maybe he'd walked through into the central hall. Just as I was about to ask where they'd sent the gentleman in the red training trousers, I spotted the asshole."

"Is that what you said: red training trousers?" Sigerius asked.

"Of course not." Joni.

Without looking at her, Aaron tut-tutted her with his left hand. "There he was in those clogs, his anabolic back to me, wedged in between the rest of the grazers, shuffling past the window displays with a tray in his hands. I walk over to him, on his plastic tray are two sweaty half-liter bottles of Heineken. Three sausage rolls hang over the edge of a too-small plate. But I smell sweat and piss. I tap him on the shoulder, he turns to me, he's a head shorter than I am, and from down there he looks up as though he's never laid eyes on me before. I say to him: 'Sir, you just broke my car window. How are we going to resolve this?' Even the blackheads on his forehead look startled. 'Me?' he says, 'whatcha talkin about?' 'Outside, just now,' I say, 'you were in that red Ford Escort.' 'You got the wrong guy,' he says, 'I don't know you, I just come from my sick mama.' "

"Did he say 'sick mama'?" Sigerius's mouth flew wide open, his brown eyes squinted into two little slits—he laughed noiselessly.

"Weren't you scared?" Janis asked. "You could've just gone back to work and called the insurance company." Which is more or less what Aaron had suggested to his brother at the time. He felt fascination, but also apprehension, a vicarious fear.

Sigerius: "He could have gone sniveling back to his minivan. He could have shouted 'He-e-e-e-lp!' But some people take action when action is called for." Behind his dark, stubbly face, a face that did not suit a *rector magnificus* because it had nothing solemn about it, that did not suit a Fields laureate because there was no unworldly genius radiating from it, and that least of all suited a Minister of Education, a transformation took place—you saw Sigerius change into the man for whom, in some distant past, that sensual, folksy head had been intended. A man who himself was capable of impulsive, quick-tempered action, who had once recalled, with great relish, an incident that took place in the canteen of an American swimming pool where he sat waiting while Joni and Janis had their swimming lesson on the other side of the plate-glass wall. He wanted a cup of coffee and made three grown-up attempts at getting the attention of the canteen kid at the far end of the counter, who stood shooting the breeze with two swim-moms. Sigerius was a swim-dad who, in such circumstances, didn't try a fourth time, but reached over the bar, fished a soggy yellow dishrag out of the sink and hurled it in a perfect parabola against the young layabout's ear: coffee, please.

"A little scared," he said to Janis. "But anyway I say to this trailer trash, because that's what he was, of course, trailer trash, I say: 'Oh yes, just now you stood out there alongside my taxi. You demolished my window.' The guy glances around and says: 'I'm gonna eat. So quit talkin crap. I'm going to sit down and have a peaceful bite to eat,' and he slides his tray a little farther. All this in coarse, Venlo trailer trash lingo."

"Now that's a fact," Joni said drily. "Trailer trash, there's a lingo for you."

Aaron had arrived at the heroic portion of the story. Not only had he appropriated his brother's heroism, but he also jazzed it up a bit. "I bend over that sweaty neck of his," he said, "and whisper into his ear: 'You're gonna pay.' The guy whirls around. 'You know who you're talking to, asshole?' he screams. Like a banshee. The whole cafeteria goes dead quiet. 'Manus Pitte'—again at megaphone volume. OK, I got the picture. The Pittes are a notorious Venlo family, and not because of the smell of their cooking. A whole clan of hooligans. Half of them are behind bars—violence, drugs, prostitution, the works."

"We know just what you mean." Sigerius.

"Speak for yourself." Joni.

"Joni also knows exactly what you mean."

Tineke's chair squeaked. Aaron looked at her. She leaned back and observed him with distant, chilly eyes.

"Before I could respond, this Pitte guy shoves his tray aside, one of the half-liter beers crashes to the floor, *bang*, glass everywhere."

"Beer in a hospital?" Joni.

"Take it up with Customer Service. Pitte leans over sixty degrees, not forward, but sideways, from his waist—despite all those deep-fried meat snacks and satay hot dogs, the guy's nothing but muscle—and while he stands there like a gymnast (he only stood like that for a second, but it's a pose I'll never forget) he grabs my pant leg with one hand, just above the knee, and my chauffeur's jacket with the other hand. He starts dragging me toward the door. 'Ousside,' he yells, 'ousside. Gonna bust on ya.' He kept yelling it, all the way through the dead-quiet foyer. 'Ousside. Bust on ya.' "

"Outside. Beat you up." Joni Sigerius, interpreter, twenty-five years old, unmarried.

"You just said you can spot a scumbag a mile off," Sigerius said. "I can too, whether it's Rotterdam or Shanghai. Always could. Africans, Russians, Asians, doesn't matter—I could always tell. But how? Even if a guy is stark naked, I can still see it on him. You?"

"I don't think I've ever seen riffraff naked."

Sigerius grinned. "I have. For nearly a year, every day."

"Siem." Tineke. She seldom called him by his first name. Sigerius clapped the air with his right hand as though it were someone's back. "Don't interfere," he said.

Joni got up from the table. "I think I need to pee. I can't take this."

Retrospectively, in light of the scene's disastrous ending, he would identify this moment as the turning point. He recalled clearly that Sigerius paid no attention, he completely ignored his elder daughter. Instead he picked up his napkin, slid off its copper-colored ring, and then slammed it onto the table between him and Aaron. His mouth had an imperative look, his eyes were dark and fanatical. "Imagine this Pitte naked," he said. "Would you see it then?"

He answered that he thought so, it seemed to him something innate. "Yeah. In his look. They have a look that's stupid and aggressive at the same time. No . . . smart and stupid. Is that possible?"

"A person's look is a matter of breeding," Sigerius said. "Right, Aaron? We've come that far a century after Lombroso. It's all about the nature-nurture ratio. You can nudge a born criminal in the right direction."

Joni was back surprisingly soon; it was hard to believe she'd actually been to the toilet. It seemed more likely that she had been eavesdropping from behind one of the ferns. "But *you* can't," she said as she glided past Aaron's back on the way to her chair.

Huh? Had he heard that right? This was a frontal assault, although he wasn't sure whose front was hit or what with, or why. But such a rebuke. Why now? Was he missing something? Yet more astonishing than Joni's sneer was Sigerius's reaction, namely *none*. His concentrated face rippled ever so slightly, a barely noticeable twitch. He set down his knife and fork, silver with heavy handgrips, and wiped his mouth with the back of his hairy hand.

"Aaron, I want you to tell Joni as precisely as possible what happened. Don't skip a single detail. I want you to tell us how you taught that punk a lesson."

No. Of course Aaron Bever had not taught Manus Pitte a lesson. He had never seen this Manus Pitte guy, never smelled him—he'd almost forgotten this himself. And *if* Pitte *had* parked his Escort on the side of the road in order to sock Aaron Bever in the kisser, then Aaron Bever would not have hesitated for a second before tearing out of there—beat it, burn rubber, before that pleb, that roughneck, that lout, even came anywhere near his minivan. Get out and start swinging? He wouldn't stand a chance, just like his brother didn't stand a chance. If Pitte had dragged Sebastian through the revolving door, then he'd have knocked out all his teeth and flattened him like a tube of toothpaste in no time. Back at the trailer park, Pitte would have stuffed him with horsehair and old newspapers, propping him up in the back of the trailer between the karaoke set and Grandpa's stuffed sheepdog.

"Luckily it didn't come to that," he said. "He dragged me as far as the revolving door; I went to grab the doorframe, but suddenly he let go. We both fell over backward. Pitte had seen something that gave him a real shock. And when I saw it, I got a shock too. But Pitte was more shocked, Pitte nearly shat himself. Out of the revolving door came a man, probably for the outpatient clinic, or maybe he came to have himself euthanized. It was a terrible sight. Pitte and I, sprawled on the floor tugging at each other, look at him at the same time, we see him at the same time. Together we see a monster. The Elephant Man. They weren't burn wounds, it was something else, an alien landscape, the dark side of the moon; a single eye looked at us from that mass of flesh, the other one was overgrown with some gross protuberance, an orgy of pulpy flesh, a riot of warts and boils . . ."

Joni spat a piece of beef onto her plate. Cud. "Aaron, give me a *break*."

"You give *me* a break." Sigerius. "Go on."

Aaron took a gulp of wine. "Well, OK, our hero scrambles up and starts shuffling backward into the hospital. Funnily enough, he picks up his tray and goes into the foyer without paying for the sausage rolls, looking back a couple of times."

"And you?"

"Followed him, naturally."

Aaron's description of his pursuit, stairs up, stairs down, elevator in, elevator out, released an avalanche of pleasure. With his cell phone to his ear (that bit about the cell phone was a sudden brainwave, no one at the table was alert enough to realize cell phones didn't exist back then, in reality his brother had asked the hospital personnel to call the police), he trailed his suspect: a manhunt! "Pitte abandoned his tray in front of the elevator." Sigerius's face went purple and his head fell back in hilarity when Aaron told him he helped himself to the sausage rolls.

"And what, you bite into his sausage roll?"—the final words dissolving into a guffaw that bellowed forth from deep within Sigerius's throat, like an eruption of magma. But the women at the table did not laugh with him. Joni's irate face swung from Aaron to her wet-eyed father, and Janis dragged a cooled-off potato croquette through the gravy with her fork.

"Jesus Christ," Tineke muttered. She got up and went into the kitchen with the empty Wedgwood platter. They could hear her give the deep-frier basket a hardhanded shake. Sigerius shoved back his chair, still har-harring, both hands on his belly, which filled his polo shirt like a strong nor'wester.

"Dad," said Joni. "Just cut it out." Her neck was covered with red splotches, all the way into the graceful V-neck of her blouse. But Sigerius appeared not to hear, he just kept on braying, and Aaron noticed that his sensation of triumph was beginning to evaporate. There was something going on here that he had no part in.

Tineke returned to the sunroom with the platter of sizzling potato croquettes and looked at her husband. Her puffy face, framed by ash-blond curls, seemed expressionless, as fat people's faces often do. Maybe that is why the bang of the platter on the table came as such a shock. "Siem—*stop it.*"

Silence.

Sigerius looked at her, silently and sadly. His face was instantly transformed into an abandoned warehouse.

"Tell them the truth then, damn it, instead of that juvenile giggling."

"What truth?"

"Come on. Don't play the fool. Go on and tell them, if you know so much about it."

"Guys," Janis hushed.

Her mother did not hear her. "If you're a real man, Siem Sigerius, then you'll tell them who called last Saturday. Which piece of scum."

"Tien, spare me this. Spare us this. What does Saturday have to do with this? For God's sake."

"Plenty. Everything. And you damn well know it. Tell them. Or I will."

Sigerius did not move a muscle. Although on his rector's skull, under that cropped, slightly graying hair, one little one did. An unseen, uneasy muscle. "You're ruining everyone's evening," he said, "and you damn well know *that*."

"Then *I'll* tell them." She looked across the table at Joni and Janis. "Sweethearts," she said, "don't be alarmed. Wilbert called. Our very own scumbag rang up. Saturday night, especially for you two. Wilbert Sigerius. Wondering if you survived the explosion."

He was cold. He was so caught up with himself—with his own mendacity, with Sigerius's response, with his revenge on Joni and her beaus—that he didn't understand what had just happened. He couldn't make rhyme or reason of it. Apparently he was not the focus of his own act, but had hammed his way through a one-man show while the main performance was taking place not onstage but in the stalls. There were so many things he didn't get: he didn't get why no one was relieved at Sigerius's spectacular mood boost, he didn't get why Tineke started in on that telephone call while her husband was dead set against it, he didn't get the antipathy between Joni and Sigerius. And worst of all: how could he not have realized it was not about Manus Pitte at all, but in fact about Wilbert Sigerius?

He of all people, who thought he knew something about the IJmuiden Basher and the family over which he cast his ragged shadow. Ever since that evening long ago in the canteen of the campus gym, when Sigerius acquainted him with the résumé of the family's very own lowlife, it had become a research project. It fascinated him. He had started with Joni, using all the tact he could muster up, and barraged her with questions: what did *she* know about Wilbert, aside from the shreds of information she'd already given him? Not much, apparently. Even less than her father had already confided in him. Yes, he was doing time, that much she knew, but no details. She clearly didn't like talking about it; in fact, no one else in that family did either, they'd sooner bite off their tongue than mention that goddamn jailbird. Figuring he understood that, he undertook to find things out for himself. One morning he cycled to the public library and delved into the newspaper archives for court reports of Wilbert's case. The conviction was handed down in 1993, Sigerius had said so, at the Haarlem courthouse. That was all he had to go on. But he had time. Since the Enschede library did not save past copies of the *Haarlemse Dagblad* he installed himself at the oval reading table across from the coffee automats and perused, without success, every copy of the Amsterdam *Parool* from 1993, after which he had them bring up a stack of *Telegraafs* from the depot, and what do you know: just as he was about to lose hope, his eye fell upon a dry little item.

Further in the section he found an extensive article, its blocks of text in boldface, containing details that would occupy his thoughts for the rest of the day.

Wilbert S. appeared before the court on November 16, 1993, for beating to death one Barry Harselaar, fifty-two, process manager at the Hoogovens steelworks, in a blind rage with a four-kilo sledgehammer. Thanks to prior mediation by North Holland Probation Services, Aaron read, the "revolving-door criminal S." worked the morning shift as an odd-job man in the factory complex of hot rolling mill 2. Things went well for a few weeks, until his foreman—Harselaar—noticed that Wilbert S., who had done time earlier for sexual intimidation, had been making unwelcome advances to a forty-one-year-old canteen employee. After the woman had complained to Harselaar about "boob-grabbing," he decided to teach the newbie a "sympathetic" lesson. According to two eyewitnesses, Harselaar was leaning against a sledgehammer next to an empty iron barrel, about a meter high, when he called Wilbert S. over. "Listen, pal, my pack of shag's lying at the bottom. You should be able to reach it with those sticky fingers of yours." When Wilbert S. leaned into the barrel, his waist folded over the iron rim, Harselaar picked up the sledgehammer and gave the side of the barrel a massive wallop. That'll teach him and his filthy paws. What Harselaar did not know is that Wilbert S. had already taken lessons: Aggression Management Training, offered by the National Parole Board for easily inflamed individuals. "Have a short fuse," Aaron read the blurb on the Parole Board's website, "but not sure where it comes from? Aggression maintenance begins by finding the causes. Self-control ultimately leads to inner calm."

"S." clambered out of the barrel, his ears ringing, and screamed as he set upon his foreman, taking him by the throat. According to bystanders, after a short skirmish he grabbed the sledgehammer, promptly raised it above his head and brought it down with a splitting smack between Harselaar's neck and left shoulder. The foreman collapsed. Intervention was impossible: one of the two witnesses, twenty-one-year-old Ronald de H., attempted to intercede, which earned him a broken pelvis from a well-placed backswing. What they saw happen under their very noses in the next thirty seconds must have been traumatic. Wilbert S. beat Barry Harselaar with the hammer, shouting "fucking prick" at least fifteen times, until the man had been turned into a mangled, bleeding bale of flesh and bone. The autopsy determined that Harselaar's body suffered no fewer than twenty-six broken bones. The only thing that was still intact was his organ donor card.

Having spent his aggression, Wilbert S. flung the sledgehammer against a wall and fled through the 600-meter-long rolling mill, out an emergency exit and into the steelworks complex. An hour and a half later he was arrested in a storage depot behind one of the coke plants.

Because S. was a recidivist (twice earlier convicted of assault and battery), because it was not a matter of self-defense or undue provocation by the victim, and considering the brutality of the crime, the Haarlem District Attorney demanded ten years' imprisonment plus mandatory psychiatric treatment. Although the judge shared the DA's revulsion at "S.'s uncontrolled rage," his verdict was eight years in prison minus four months' prior detention on remand. Mandatory psychiatric treatment was out of the question, because S., according to the psychiatrists at the Pieter Baan clinic, was entirely *compos mentis*.

The evening after his visit to the library, Joni joined him for dinner at his house on the Vluchtestraat, and when he shared his findings with her during the washing-up she began to cry. It was the first time he had seen her in tears, and while he felt an innate tenderness he still found it difficult to understand her reaction. He asked questions, the wrong questions.

"Are you crying because of the foreman he murdered?"

"No, I didn't know him."

"Are you crying because you're ashamed?"

"No, of course not. Why would I be ashamed?"

"Because of the gruesome details, for instance."

"No!" she blubbered, "yeah, that *too*, I'm crying about everything, you know? And it wasn't murder, it was manslaughter. I'm just sad for the guy himself, for his bad luck. In spite of everything I really feel sorry for him. Is that so crazy?"

Yes, he thought, that is crazy. Crying for a boy who dumped a bootful of sand on your face and twenty years later bashes a full-grown man to a pulp. Strange indeed.

Things got even weirder at the dinner table. This is what happened. Janis was the first who could get a word in after Tineke told her daughters that Wilbert had inquired about their well-being. She cleared her throat and asked, with an atypically small voice, if Wilbert had phoned from prison. No, Tineke answered, he was free.

"Is that what Wijn was doing at the reception?" Joni demanded, harshly, distrustfully.

Those honorary doctorates—Aaron knew immediately what she was talking about. ("Oh. My. God," she had said when a tall, badly dressed man with a battered face walked into the foyer. "That over-dressed construction worker over there," she'd whispered to him, "the one with the gray Schwarzenegger hair? That's Menno Wijn." She left it at that. So you're Wilbert's guardian angel, he thought to himself.)

"To tell us about Wilbert's release," Tineke said.

"And I only find out *now*?" asked Joni. It sounded unbelievably rude.

"The city has exploded, in case you haven't noticed," Sigerius said. He sat half-turned, staring outside, only his right hand lay on the table, his thumb and index finger fidgeted with a napkin ring.

"Mom," said Joni, "repeat to me exactly what Wilbert said." She grasped the tabletop with both hands. Either to provoke her husband, or because she was afraid Joni would flip the table over, Tineke did what was asked of her. It was a brief, bone-dry conversation. "Those two still alive?"—"Yes, they're alive"—and that was about it.

"Where does he live?" Joni asked.

"America," Sigerius said without turning around.

"How do you know?" asked Tineke. All four of them looked at the back of his sullen head; Sigerius's ears resembled amputated fireworks fists.

"I don't know anything," he said. "I'm only wishing out loud."

"How is he?" asked Joni.

Tineke told him that she had asked Wilbert just that, at the last minute, they were already finished—and he had brought the receiver back to his mouth and answered rather sarcastically that he was still alive too—and that was that. Just then Sigerius turned to them. "What a pity," he said, his face still flushed from laughing. "It would've saved us a lot of trouble. Wilbert calling up to let us know he's dead."

Aaron was the only one who laughed, out of awkwardness. Janis and her mother were silent. Joni looked at her father for an entire second, her mouth trembling. She got up, picked up the Wedgwood platter of potato croquettes with both hands, turned her upper body a quarter of a turn (Tineke: "*Joni, what are you doing!*") and flung it to the floor with a shrill roar, smashing it to pieces. It was an unbelievable crash. Janis shrieked. They heard the shards skitter across the floor; the croquettes tumbled against the skirting boards, spun in little circles. Sigerius sat motionless like a deaf-mute.

"What a shitty thing to say," she screamed, and yet it sounded restrained. She began to cry, short little gasps, they were more like angry sobs. They looked at her, the four of them, the way she stood there, her shoulders trembling, her furious eyes directed at her father.

"Malicious *coward*."

That Sigerius did not make short shrift of this exhibition—Aaron did not understand that either. The man who just heard he was about to become a Cabinet minister, the man who steered a management team of twelve intolerable deans. It was as though he'd been crying all evening instead of laughing.

"Fuck it!" Joni shouted. She turned and rushed out of the sunroom, now sobbing at full throttle. They listened to the sound of her flip-flops as she crossed the living room into the wide entrance hall and stormed up the steps. Upstairs a door slammed.

The sounds from the garden, the rustling of the poplars, permeated the sunroom. Sigerius rubbed his hand over his stubbly jaw. "Well." And then, when no one answered, casually, much too casually: "We should have stayed in America ourselves. We should never have come back. Never. I wish we were still in Berkeley. Don't you, Tien?"

7

So back to feckin' Dallas after all. Víctor Sotomayor got all persnickety about the bank guarantee, vetoed the notary Rusty and I had suggested, and a portion of those millions had to be funneled through a bank in Havana to a private company in Amsterdam. To make a long story short: endless niggling and hair-splitting that we just swallowed for fear the Barracks might elude us yet. So Dallas it was, there was no getting out of it. Just before leaving Sunset Boulevard for LAX I checked my various in-boxes and was slightly unnerved to see that Aaron had sent me seven messages in the past few days. I really wasn't in the market for a pen pal. I skimmed the first e-mail, the longest one; the rest were brief PSs. "Why haven't I heard anything?" he mailed the day before yesterday. "You aren't sick, are you? Maybe you're on vacation."

Mulling over his letters in the plane, I decided not to answer for the time being. He'd kind of started off on the wrong foot by inviting himself out to Los Angeles, which he subsequently took back, saying that his "health" would "probably" prevent long-distance travel. In the third or fourth e-mail he backtracked again, that it would still be "really and truly special" to see me and go to Berkeley together; now that bygones were bygones he thought it would be "cathartic" for us both, he was "dying" to see where I'd spent my youth, having heard so much about it. I was extremely happy there, he knew, couldn't we . . . etc. etc.

No, we couldn't.

I eventually managed to iron things out with Sotomayor up in his Stone Tower penthouse. I couldn't help thinking that I'd been summoned back to that mahogany-polish-stinking office of his just as a reminder of who was boss. After an interminable prelude on his part, the business details were worked out in a matter of minutes; he then led me through two heavy doors to an adjacent space. Valued business partners, he said with satisfaction, should have the opportunity to see this. What's up, you Cuban porker, I thought. For the moment I was afraid Víctor had got wind of our plans for his Barracks, that Rusty had shot off that flounder-mouth of his. He led me into an ominously old-fashioned-looking office: large, dusty succulents in brown gravel, yellowy-brown Venetian blinds I hadn't seen in any of the other offices. The spherical feet of a heavy oak desk rested on a faded Persian carpet. On the desktop with inlaid green leather stood an ancient, bulky computer in the same mashed-potato color as the rest of the room. Lots of photos in gilded frames. Right in front of the high-backed, cracked leather desk chair was a pile of yellowed documents, a pair of horn-rimmed reading glasses, and, on a flattened-out gentleman's handkerchief, a small steel-nosed instrument whose tongs clutched tiny curls of black hair. I eventually realized it was a nose-hair trimmer.

Behind the desk was an open cupboard holding about 100 black cardboard dossiers, with the year—ranging from the mid-'60s until 1991—handwritten on the spine. It smelled like death in here. I wasn't completely comfortable with this setup, I expected a hairy paw at any moment to grab my neck and force me to bend over that desk. So I asked the asthmatic Sotomayor, who stood panting behind me, if his secretary had the day off. "Here, Miss Sigerius"—his high-pitched voice took on an emotional warble—"in this very room, this cherished chamber, my dear father once worked. My late father was the founder and first director of our company." But even with this holdup I finished with Sotomayor surprisingly quickly, and after reporting back to Rusty I treated myself to a London broil in the steak house next to my hotel. It was so quiet all I could hear was the grinding of my own molars. I got the uneasy suspicion that Aaron was already on his way. Could be, of course. That he got it into his head to book a flight. When I flew back to L.A. the next morning I seriously considered the possibility that I'd find him standing on my doorstep with outstretched arms. But I found my house as quiet as I'd left it.

I had to be off again straightaway. For the past year or so I had been Rollerblading with a group of about forty people every Tuesday evening through Santa Monica, often into West Hollywood or downtown L.A. Relaxing outings which required just enough concentration that for the entire evening I felt completely at one with the warm air flowing through my hair and the purring asphalt under my wheels. The ever-growing club met at the Pacific Coast Highway, just beyond the pier across from Seaside Terrace, a little more than half a mile from my house.

I buttered a bagel and carried my Rollerblades to the elevator that would take me down to street level. I skated the first few meters between the imposing pillars that supported most of my house, hummed around Sunset's curves toward Ocean Drive, but instead of liberation I felt a nervous kind of melancholy. Aaron was troubling me. Twice I was passed by oncoming taxis, and twice I saw him sitting in the passenger's seat. I turned onto the coastal road, crossed a busy line of traffic, and skated with measured glides toward the pier.

But I had second thoughts once I got a glimpse of the raucous group off in the distance. I just couldn't face it. With a sharp turn I skated up onto the pier, took off my Rollerblades and socks and strolled among the throngs of tourists. My gaze focused on the warm, knotty planks; I walked past the seafood stalls and Pacific Park's neon-lit Ferris wheel. The slamming of the waves against the piles under my feet. At the end of the pier, a couple of hundred yards into the ocean, I spent the next half hour staring out onto the glistening expanse, and then headed home.

I had to laugh at my own paranoia: a new message from Aaron. His tone was agitated. "I won't be coming any time soon," he wrote. "Berkeley is probably a bad idea anyway. You probably went there with Stol. Am I right?"

Bo and I had been living in San Francisco for a while when, one Saturday morning, we strapped Mike into the backseat of the Land Rover and drove across the Bay Bridge over to Berkeley. Mike was screaming blue murder so we made a short stop on Treasure Island, a man-made island halfway across the bay, and wondered over a cup of coffee whether we should just turn around. "Is this a good idea?" Boudewijn asked. "All those memories." "No," I answered, "but it's also stupid not to go. It's a stone's throw. It would be ridiculous not to."

We continued along I-80 through Oakland, through *run-down* Oakland, I noticed, and drove down University Avenue to the entrance gate at the west edge of the UC Berkeley campus. We parked the Land Rover and Bo put the drowsing Mike in the baby sling. We walked onto the campus past drumming students in Bears sweatshirts. Boudewijn asked what was going on: didn't we know?—in a couple of hours the Berkeley football team was playing UCLA, you guys need some tickets?—but our goal was farther along. Evans Hall, the cube-shaped Mathematics Department where my father had cooped himself up with his knots for those two eternal years. I recognized the gravel paths, the white neoclassical academic buildings that had survived twenty years of seismic stir. Students sat under enormous oak and willow trees, chatting and laughing like actors in a campus soap. Bo, who in his red-velour hip pants and herringbone jacket looked like a well-heeled alumnus, seemed impressed by the pastoral beauty. We crossed a six-sided court planted with a matrix of pollard willows, on which he figured Nobel Prizes grew, walked around a trimmed lawn and suddenly found ourselves in front of the hideous Evans Hall. As though it were yesterday, I pushed open the brown steel and reinforced-glass door and led Boudewijn and Mike to a wood-paneled elevator that took us up to the tenth and top floor. I automatically turned left and walked down the oatmeal-colored linoleum to the small office where my father worked.

"Go ahead and knock," Boudewijn said when he saw me hesitate in front of the door. The next room, a classroom, was open; you could see whiteboards and lecterns and the open air. "Or we could just have a look in here," I suggested, but Boudewijn said: "Knock."

No one answered. I turned the door handle downward and pushed, but the room once inhabited by Dr. S. Sigerius was locked up tight.

"And now?" Boudewijn had strapped Mike in and started the car.

"Just drive."

I directed him to Telegraph Avenue, after which we followed Bancroft back toward the bay, so we could swing by Berkwood Hedge, the small elementary school with the waxed floors where Janis and I walked, hand in hand, every weekday morning for two years. Here, too, typical Californian streets, every house different from the others, Cedar Street undulating like a gray belt toward the bay, the glistening vanishing point of every perspective here. The intersections we crossed, with their just-for-show traffic lights, brought me inexorably back to 1982, and suddenly I saw the school building, damn, there it was, a stuccoed thing with a blacktop playground out in front.

"You want me to stop?" Boudewijn asked.

A classroom full of American know-it-alls, sharp as tacks and not particularly nice. Back in Utrecht, six months before I parachuted into their midst, I knelt in front of the record player as it cranked out the red Beatles double LP and looked up "Love Me Do" word for word in an English dictionary. That was the extent of my English. But I just pretended I understood. A yes here, a no there, mustn't let them get me down, and if they managed to get Janis down I cheered her up all the way back to Bonita Avenue. Buck up. Don't cry. What will Mom and Dad think?

"Turn left here," I said to Boudewijn, "we're getting close to our old house."

A few blocks northward on the busy Martin Luther King Way, a jog right and left, and we drove onto Bonita Avenue, a quiet street with telephone poles and neatly parked family cars and lush, full trees. Siem said he'd picked this street especially because I thought "Bonita" was such a nifty word. I wrote the address at the front of the Enid Blyton book I'd brought with me from Utrecht. Joni Sigerius, 1908 Bonita Ave., Oakland, CA, USA, World, Universe. Maybe because the trees in the yards and along the sidewalks had grown since then, greener, fuller—but after a short delay I realized that everything else seemed smaller. What a crummy little street. The Land Rover crept along the spotty asphalt. With my hand resting on the warm roof I peered at the passing wooden houses.

God, there it was. The shingled house appeared from behind an overgrown hedge and an olive tree, the two small dormer windows peeking like eyes out of the pitched roof. As a kid I always thought the front of the clapboard house resembled a surprised face, and now I saw it again. That foolish expression was partly because of the front door, a gaping mouth exactly centered under a tar-paper-covered overhang. The soft bang of the wood as the door closed behind him when he got back from the university at night, suddenly standing there in the living room, boom, his leather briefcase hitting the floor, two firm kisses on my mother's mouth. "Hello girls, I'm home!"

To the left of the house, separated by a gravel path, the McCoys' pharmacy, now an abandoned brick building with a side extension. A "For Rent" sign on the front, stacks of waterlogged and then dried-out moving boxes on the front porch, two bright-blue garbage cans on wheels. The bedridden Mrs. McCoy, long dead for sure. Cancer in her voice, the neighborhood boys said. She talked through a kind of tube in her stalky neck, a raspy, unamplified croak that would startle me awake at night, in a cold sweat. Voice cancer. A brownish hole in her throat, you could see it. Didn't really tally with running a pharmacy, the only brick house in the neighborhood, stacked to the rafters with pills and potions. Comes from smoking, my mother said, so for a while when I was home alone I'd flush her open pouches of shag down the toilet. That yammering of Mrs. McCoy, that raspy grumbling. A croak that carried across our yard, across the oil stains on the driveway, drowned out the rooster somewhere behind the houses across the road. "Got a frog in her throat," our new father said, which our mother didn't approve of, making fun like that, but I could see she also had to try not to laugh. The McCoys had a Great Dane, one of those bareback horses that the pharmacist, a friendly man with horn-rimmed glasses, took for walks in Live Oak Park.

And he always had his arm around a diminutive black lady. The dog all to and fro with a stick, he laughing with the woman snuggled up against him. "Did you know," I apparently said, "that Mr. McCoy's sister is black?"

"Stop—here it is."

Boudewijn pulled over to the curb and shut off the engine. He tugged his polo shirt loose from his belly. The chirping of crickets, somewhere a bus pulling out.

"I'll be right back. You stay with Mike."

Curdled air. I'd lived in California for more than a year and a half now, every day I felt the mugginess, saw palm trees, and smelled the sea—and still the atmosphere on this street was different. An older America. Incongruous Luxaflex, half shut, hung in the windows. We had light-brown curtains with orange circles, my mother sewed them, suddenly having entire days to herself. I only learned later that she couldn't get a work permit. At the end she used to go to the shipyard in the morning, on the sly.

Mike started crying. I slid between gleaming car bumpers, onto the wide sidewalk, and laid my hand on the wooden fence, still splintery. On the bare grass a plastic kiddie playhouse with peeling Bugs Bunny decals, a bike with a child's seat leaning against one of the pillars supporting the overhang—still, the yard looked better than when we lived there. It was a mess back then. A mother with a Black & Decker workmate. Old cabinets in the yard, particle board, sawdust, tools, work gloves. It didn't take the neighborhood kids long to figure out that this was the place to be, you could do *anything* at Janis and Joni's. In the back of the living room my mother had a candy jar full of Dutch licorice drops sent over by Grandma and Grandpa. All day long, even if no one was home, children would walk in and help themselves to a handful. My mother knew how to spoil an American brat.

Boudewijn quieted Mike down; his voice sounded surprisingly close by. "Why not ring the bell?" he called through the open window. "Maybe they'll let you look around inside."

The Luxaflex in the left-hand dormer window went up. A sturdy, middle-aged Latina threw open the window, stuck her arm out and shook a dustcloth. She saw me, I withdrew my hand from the fence and smiled. She gave a barely discernible nod, peered down the street, and pulled the window closed.

A Spanish-speaking woman, it came back to me, was a fixture at Scotty's parents' house. A bitter, peevish poltergeist who did the washing and ironing. I looked across an overgrown driveway toward their front yard. Scotty, the chubby blond son of Wyoming natives who had come to work in the Oakland harbor. "Billy Bunter," Siem called him. Always came over to play, usually just as we were sitting down to lunch. His fat little sausage-fingers on the fence: "Joni!" Shrill and persistent, until my mother would eventually lay down her cutlery and get up from the table with a sigh.

"Can Joni come out and play?"

"Joni's eating right now, Scott."

"Only one sandwich, tell her."

"I'm going to have a look farther up," I said to Boudewijn, gave the Land Rover a little slap on the roof and walked over toward Scotty's house.

It was still there, of course, just as I left it. The prettified, high-gloss, prim little palace. Two-storey bay window and classical veranda with—just like back then—a porch swing. Pristine white paint, the trim in what they call Delft blue back in Holland. Inside, brass bowls, brass lampshades, a wall-mounted antique rifle with brass fittings. I recalled a pried-open violin with dried flowers sticking out. I spent remarkably little time inside that house. Shoes off, don't break anything. Scott and his younger sister had to play outdoors; the warden who so closely guarded the house was a talkative housewife who, every other day at a fixed time, appeared on the porch with pink rubber gloves and a bucket of suds to give the front of the house a thorough going-over. Scotty had a mountain bike, and when we weren't cycling together through the neighborhood he'd pull me on my roller skates by a rope tied around his waist, up and down the hilly streets, up north behind the Berkeley campus where the students had their sandwich shops and bars and coffee houses. Sometimes he would stop abruptly, lay down his BMX, and sit cross-legged in his short pants on the blacktop.

"What're you doing?"

"I'll be done in a minute."

"But what are you *doing*?"

"Waiting until I don't need to anymore."

"Need to what?"

"Poop. I push it back, then I don't need to anymore."

Poop-sitting, that's what the little stinker called it. Once, one afternoon in this dream landscape, I explained to Scott with a piece of chalk on the sidewalk how you spelled his name. *Skot*, I wrote, S-k-o-t, with a *k*, and certainly not with two "t"s. But that bossy little poop-pusher, a grade behind me, kept insisting that you wrote Scott with a *c*; a half hour later we were still at it and tears streamed down his pudgy cheeks. I let him dry up and said: OK, let's go ask your mother. I was mistaken, and Scott's mother made sure I knew it; she called me uppity, sassy, and ill-bred. "And take your hand off that chair." "That's not a chair," I answered in perfect English, "it's a sofa"—and although I was right, it *was* a sofa, a flowery love seat, this exchange did not exactly endear me to Scotty's mother.

Scott loved us. During our second summer in that house he used to drop by at about seven in the evening. He'd walk around to the backyard and greet us collectively with "hi Joni," upon which we'd respond in chorus with "hey Scotty," and then I'd laugh and my mother would sigh, and even Janis, five years old, got the joke—everyone except Scott himself. His eyes scanned the overgrown grass until he spotted the leather soccer ball we'd brought with us from Holland, holding it clumsily above his head, trampling my mother's plants, calling out "excuse me" while my father, exhausted from a day of advanced mathematics, did the washing-up with the elder of his brand-new daughters like a machine of flesh and blood, singing or joking all the while, or inquiring after my day at school. Sometimes I would go out back with a wet plate to join in my mother and Scotty's chit-chat, and hear him whisper in my ear to ask my father if we could go play soccer. Because that's what he came for: football with Siem. What he felt for that friendly, funny, interested, strong, athletic man back there in the kitchen, I felt too. The energetic pace of his dish-washing routine, his handling of the platters and pans and glasses and lids, told me that we had lucked out, that Mom, my sister, and I should be mighty pleased with this new dad.

Nine times out of ten, we *did* play soccer. Once the dishes were done we'd all walk over to Live Oak Park or to Berkeley campus, where we could always find a vacant field. My mother sat on the grass and watched as Scott and I teamed up against Dad and my little sister. Within a few minutes Janis would end up behind the goalposts we'd made with Siem's leather sandals and sweatshirt, plucking flowers, while my barefoot father, laughing and sweating, had his work cut out for him with me and the ebullient Scott.

• • •

They did not resemble each other in the least, the light-blond Scotty with his fructose body and the athletic gypsy boy we had left behind in Culemborg. And yet, or maybe for that very reason, those soccer evenings always made me think of Wilbert. I could picture him back in Holland: angry and alone. He wanted to go to Berkeley with us, he said so himself. "You're going to America?" he asked while we dug out a sewer pipe in Grift Park in Utrecht. "Me too then. Tell my father I'm going with you." I promised to tell him, but when I saw Siem I kept it to myself.

It was the only time I saw Wilbert after the divorce, a few months before we moved to California, and shortly after the sober wedding of his father and my mother. Siem had already been living with us for a while, and what started out feeling weird—the upstairs neighbor who ate with us and stayed on, week after week—had meanwhile become normal, and fun too. (He was a new addition to the family, like Janis had once been a new addition. But what do you tape to the window when you get a new *father*? Surely not a cardboard stork.)

In fact, I had almost forgotten that Siem had a son who lived with Margriet in Culemborg—until Wilbert showed up on the doorstep one Friday afternoon. His little fist, rings on his fingers, grasped a plastic Edah supermarket bag containing a frayed toothbrush and a wadded-up sweater. He'd come to stay with his father. Unannounced. The first drawback was that Siem was out of town—which he hardly ever was, but now he was in Berlin or Munich or somewhere, working on his dissertation—so my mother and I awkwardly drank a soda with our guest, who cracked jokes, but also had a good look around the living room, and summed up in a matter-of-fact tone which objects we had stolen from his mother: the green cuckoo clock, the rattan chair he was sitting in, the two camel saddles he said his mother had bought herself in Egypt, which struck even me as far-fetched.

"How was your trip, Wilbert?" inquired my mother. "Fine, fine," he answered, "my uncle brought me in the car," and with the completion of the official portion of his visit, he and I got down to playing—come on, Joni, let's go out and have some adventures, and as though *he*, not *I*, had been living in the Antonius Matthaeuslaan for the past two years he led me on a ramble through Utrecht neighborhoods I'd never seen before. We ran over apartment-house galleries in Overvecht, he made a small fire in an elevator that blazed alarmingly well, we followed a man pulling a roller suitcase for an hour to the end of the Blauwkapelseweg, where the man got into a car that Wilbert, tongue between his teeth, pelted with a wad of dirt. In a suburban shopping center I had to wait for him outside a tobacconist, and after running like mad after him for a kilometer he handed me three packs of chewing gum and a handful of lotto tickets.

That evening my mother brought Janis to Grandma and Grandpa and took us to the movies; she'd reserved tickets for *Herbie*, but Wilbert thought a talking Volkswagen was for babies, so instead we went to *Grease*, which Siem had spent the past six months saying I was too young for. He sat next to me smelling of fire and sweat, he breathed like a strange animal. You only saw boys like Wilbert at the carnival, they parked the bumper cars, steering nonchalantly with their butts resting on the side. "Don't mention the movie," my mother said afterward, which was easy, because before long I was up to my ears in things I knew instinctively were better kept quiet.

His black hair styled into a grease quiff with sugar water, Wilbert told us during the croquettes and fries that he often stood at the

Culemborg bus stop with his gym bag, planning to visit, he missed Siem, but his mother wouldn't let him, and his uncle had stashed the bag for him in a locker at the sport school. "Maybe it would be cool if I went to America with you, Aunt Tineke," he said. We'd have to wait for his father my mother said, and when the doorbell rang Wilbert clamped his mayonnaise-covered fingers over his full lips in anticipation, but it wasn't his father, it was two uniformed policemen. The party was over. The policemen established, with the aid of a form my mother had to sign, that Wilbert was Wilbert Sigerius, nine years old, reported missing by Menno Wijn that morning. They chatted a bit with my mother in the kitchen, and when they were done they took Wilbert away with them.

Later that evening, when Siem arrived home, travel-weary, he—and I, positioned within earshot—was treated to the full story. The police had traced Wilbert via a handicap vehicle stolen in Culemborg, one of those mini-cars that can only go 45 kph and was discovered with an empty tank in the Vaartse Rijn. A gas station attendant had spotted him in it on Friday afternoon putt-putting his way from Culemborg to Utrecht.

That Sunday night I lay stiff as a board in bed. My mother and new father were having their first argument; his voice was loud and carried far. In the weeks that followed, weeks marked by preparations for our great crossing, no one uttered a word about Wilbert. And once we lived here, in this new country, in this new house on Bonita Avenue, and everything about Holland seemed amazingly far away and long ago, we behaved as though that horrible boy had never existed. Certainly in retrospect, in America we enjoyed the best, happiest, and most carefree time the four of us ever had. By far.

But I had my own thoughts on the matter. And aside from

Janis we probably all did. When I sat on my swing that Siem had hung on the leek-green veranda and thought back on the bottom half of the duplex on the Antonius Matthaeuslaan, with that weird, threatening, charged house upstairs, and what went on there, then I not only became miserable with happiness, or the other way around, but also a reverse reasoning took shape in my head: I began to believe that we hadn't left Margriet and Wilbert and that creepy uncle of his behind in Holland, but that we had run away from them. We had to start anew. And we did that here, in this cozy little neighborhood, where Siem had a job at the university.

I also heard my parents fight in America now and then, our wooden house was a soundboard, and then I sprang out of bed and stood at the top of the stairs, my heart pounding. Sometimes I could make out that it had to do with Wilbert; Menno Wijn had phoned and their conversation would turn Siem gruff and surly for the next couple of days. After each angry outburst I was scared stiff that Wilbert would come over anyway, or, what's worse, that Siem would have to return to Holland, that the four of us being a family just wasn't meant to be, and that we'd all have to fly back there tomorrow and go back to living in that awful house on the Antonius Matthaeuslaan.

What could I do? *Keep the secret.* I made a solemn pledge. Now that I called Siem "Dad" and myself "Sigerius," now that we had embarked on a new beginning in this faraway country, and I noticed that my mother could laugh again, no one would be allowed to find out the truth. We were a *regular* family. Tineke and Siem had made me together, and after that they made my sister. That's how it was. Stick to the story.

• • •

Someone tapped against the middle pane of the bay window. I was on the concrete sidewalk, still halfway in front of the next-door neighbors. The lace curtain moved, a hand slid the sheer fabric aside. I looked into the eyes of Scotty's mother, unmistakable—how in fact did memory work? She seemed to recognize me too: the overly made-up, skeletal face emanated delight and dismay at the same time, the pink-glossed lips moved, formed a word. I looked back: Boudewijn had Mike on his lap in the passenger's seat. I walked across the neatly mown grass to the window, the wrinkled lips mouthed something. "Tineke." The woman released the curtain, gestured for me not to leave. As I waited I realized that twenty years ago my mother was *thin.*

"Joni, dear, is that you? Good heavens . . . I thought for sure it was your mother. Come in, come in, what a sur*prise*." Her left foot was stuck in a Stop & Shop bag fastened around her ankle with a rubber band, the right foot in a gray furry slipper. She led me into the living room, dragging that plastic foot. A sour smell took my breath away, a mix of old wallpaper, Brasso, cigarettes, fried bacon, the body odor of a nursing home. "Sit down, dear—God in heaven, you *are* the spitting image of your mother." She showed me to a chair with a view of the Land Rover, Boudewijn still had Mike on his lap, his arm hung lazily out of the window. They were asleep. "Don't mind my foot," she said, "I broke my toe, *snap*, just like that, I stubbed it against that chest there, I was doing the floor. Infected and all. Something to drink, dear? What do you want to drink. Just say what."

She was nervous, that's for sure. A skittish woman, who called everything that wasn't going to rob or murder her "dear." Her long face twitched like an anthill that I'd poked with a stick. Her hair had thinned, was gray at the roots, but she dyed it . . . what shade was it? Purply red.

She disappeared into the kitchen. The living room had changed as little as she had, the flowered sofa was still there, on either side the same curly armchairs, greenish velvet, nappa leather with brass tacks. In the middle of that well-worn sitting area was the mahogany coffee table, onto which she set a glass of Coke Light with a trembling hand when she returned.

Chug this Coke and I'm out of here.

"My gosh, Joni, tell me, how are you? What brings you here? Let's start with that. You've got a minute, haven't you? Maybe you're just passing through . . ."

That last comment was undoubtedly her most fervent wish: to see the back of me. What was her name again? She sat down across from me in a snot-green armchair and slid her crinkling, bagged foot under the coffee table. Her eyes shot from my hands to my flip-flops, to my knees, to the bay window, to my nose.

"We're on vacation," I lied.

"Oh, how wonderful. You're having the best luck with the weather. It's always hot as blazes here. Dear. How *mar*velous. With your parents?"

"With my boyfriend. He's waiting in the car."

"Wouldn't your fiancé like to come in? Call the boy in, dear."

She half got up, her wrinkled, ringed hands resting on scrawny thighs covered by a dark-blue skirt. For a minute I thought it would be fun to invite a fifty-year-old guy inside, just for the effect. How old would she be now? Early sixties? She wore a pearl necklace with a gold medallion, and matching clips on her sagging earlobes. Once, Scott and I were playing up in their attic and there was this steamer trunk full of fur coats, necklaces, bracelets, boots, shoes. I could tell him what to put on. I'll bet the jewelry hanging on her wrinkled neck, on her wispy wrist, came from that trunk.

"No, please don't bother. He'll wait for a bit. We're in San

Francisco for a couple of days. I thought, let's go check out the old neighborhood. It hasn't changed much."

"So you still live in Amsterdam . . . You were such a nice, spontaneous family. You so enjoyed doing your own thing."

She was lying. We were a thorn in her side. She confused the Netherlands with Amsterdam, of course she did, Sodom or Gomorrah, what difference did it make.

"And how are things here?" I asked. "Your husband? Is he still such a keen sailor?" Scott's diminutive father. A hard worker with a droopy blond mustache who cheerfully climbed into his convertible every morning wearing steel-toed shoes and drove off somewhere, a factory or shipyard or God knows where, but come weekends he made a distant, irritable impression in that little showroom of theirs. One Sunday morning Scott and I gave his walrusy father a hand. A little elbow grease, he said, will earn you both five dollars. With the top down, so that we had difficulty hearing each other and it wasn't so obvious that Scott's father was a walrus of few words, we drove to the bay, past a marina and a container company, and stopped in front of a dented shed made of corrugated metal that turned out to be stacked to the rafters with long iron strips. Alongside the storeroom, the skeleton of a ship's hull rested on wooden blocks, so rusty and pathetic that even my nine-year-old eyes welled up with tears. Was he trying to build a boat himself? The obvious failure of this enterprise sent blood rushing to my cheeks. Without further explanation he disappeared into the shed and, cursing under his breath, worked several strips free and slid them outside. Scott and I took turns dragging his father's heavy, dangling metal slats to the other end of the hull. The sharp iron cut into the palms of my hands. Scott let go of one, the rusty edge scraped off his skin as it swished over his left knee. "Aaaaaah," he screamed, and started to cry, guilt-ridden and afraid, a red apple leaking juice. "Who's the little girl here?" Scott's father asked. "Well?"

"Malcolm," said the woman. Her jittery gray-blue eyes suddenly came to rest, at least they stopped flitting. "Mal died six years ago. I've been alone since 1996. He was forty-nine."

"I'm sorry . . ."

"His heart. Never ate a vegetable, only mayonnaise. He even scraped the tomato sauce off his pizza. But what am I nattering on about?"

We both stared at the glossy tabletop, as if to reflect on this brief in memoriam. The coffee table was improbably small and low. Hard to imagine that we sat at it that afternoon, all seven or eight of us. And still everything fitted, including little dessert plates and soda glasses, and in the middle, where a brass fruit bowl with bruised apples and spotty bananas now stood, a half-eaten birthday cake. Scotty's birthday party. We knelt around the little table. Seven or eight suntanned playmates—half of them I didn't know, because Scott went to an Evangelical school just outside Berkeley. And in two of these bordello chairs sat his father and his mother. Malcolm and . . . *Betty*. That's her name. I knew for sure that Betty was also thinking back on that afternoon.

"But I have a lot of support from Scotty and Jennifer, they're such sweet children." She tried to smile, but her painted lips went through one position after another.

"What's Scott up to these days?"

"Just a second." She got up, smoothed out her skirt and dragged her Stop & Shop foot over to a chest of drawers in the front room. "Scott's an appliance repairman," she shrieked. I heard a spraying sound. A cap on a bottle. "Dryers, dishwashers. Everything. That boy is so good with his hands."

"Married?"

"Scotty? No. No, not Scott. Jennifer is. Jennifer's a mother of two. Two little boys."

With a sharp perfume now wafting off her, Betty pushed an oval picture frame into my hands. In front of a caramel-brown photographer's backdrop sat two adults, a seated woman and, half behind her, with a long, slender hand on her shoulder, a man. Jenny and Scott. The tall, slim fellow that Scott had become—his apple-ish roundness was apparently a sleight of hand, the Malcolm genes had lost the battle—so dominated my attention that Jennifer was no more than a blotch, a woman so ordinary that cones and rods just don't react to her. Scott wore a leather singlet, a black metal hole had been punched in each of his large ears. If his mother talked Scott's ears off, at least she could hang them up neatly on the coat rack. Despite the bourgeois photo studio, the conventional pose of the children, it was plain as day that Scotty was gay. I set the frame on the coffee table, alongside my glass of prematurely deceased Coke.

"Nice," I said.

At first all the kids at that birthday party were shy, at least that's the way I remembered it. This house was so tidy that it left you speechless. How the birthday boy came up with it was unclear, but even before we each had a slice of birthday cake on our plates, he said it. We were sitting across this eye-shaped table from one another, each on a pointy bit. He didn't really come up with it, he just said it, for no reason. "Joni, Siem's not your real father." A triumphant, judgmental expression formed on his round face.

"They're wonderful children," Scott's mother said. She sat down, but got right up again, as though an electric current were running through her chair. She picked up the frame and brought it back into the front room. "And dear, how are your parents? Your mother was so happy here. I was so sorry when you left."

"We were too," I said.

"Joni," Scott said, "Siem is your stepfather." Maybe because everyone else froze and didn't say anything, he added: "Why do you always lie?" I opened my eyes as far as they would go, and they slowly filled with tears. "He is too my real father," I stammered. The other children looked at me, and I could see that they were on Scott's side.

"Is not," he said.

"Is too!" They started flowing, slow, heavy tears. My voice sounded strange, canned.

Betty tilted her head like a bird and asked: "And your father? Still a professor, Joni? What a clever one, isn't he, dear. A remarkable man. A genius—Mal and I said so all the time. Scotty once told us that just after you left your father had won the . . ." she hesitated for a moment, like she was embarrassed about something, "the Nobel Prize. We only found out *years* after you'd moved away. The . . . Nobel Prize for mathematics, wasn't it?"

"Something like that, yeah. That's right."

"How is your father, dear?"

Dead, that's how. *He hanged himself.* The genius pulled the plug. Not angry, just disappointed.

"Fine. He's emeritus now . . . professor-in-retirement. He and my mother live in the Dordogne."

"Italy . . . how *lovely*."

"They run a bed-and-breakfast. Siem has started taking saxophone lessons."

"My goodness, yes . . ." Betty said, purring contentedly, "I remember your father was always listening to jazz. Nervous music. According to Malcolm."

There was a sadistic expression on Scotty's rosy face. "Siem is your *step*father," he said. "Your mother said so to my mother."

They must have been tears of rage, blood of vengeance flowing through my muscles, because I leapt onto the table, on my knees. It was over this very coffee table that I crawled toward that rotten kid, straight through the marzipan birthday cake, knocking over soda glasses, and jumped on him with all my weight. My whipped-cream knees on his fat shoulders, Scotty fell over backward, I was on top of him, clawing and beating him, and screamed, half in English, half in Dutch: "He is *too* my father! Take it back, you stinking pig! He is *too* my father. You're just jealous! You *wish* you had a father like him!"

Ten seconds, it didn't take her longer than that, Scott's mother, this woman, this timid Betty, to intervene, and with a vengeance. She dragged me off her son by my ear.

"God damn it, have you gone crazy?" she screamed, "hateful little brat," and in front of all those children she dragged me in one tug through to the kitchen, unlatched the back door, and shoved me down the steps, onto the grass.

"Out of my yard," she said, "and fast. Go tell your parents what you've done. Little witch."

8

After Tineke had run out of the room behind her elder daughter, up to the bedrooms, and he and Janis had scooped up the cooled-off potato croquettes and Sigerius, tight-lipped, had swept the shards of porcelain into a dustpan, loaded the dishwasher, and drawn all the curtains, after the only human sounds to be heard were their footsteps, their occasional sniffs, the awkward little coughs when they got in each other's way, and when the sunroom was once again the sunroom and Sigerius had settled into a recliner, headphones over his ears and a whiskey in his hand, and he shuffled upstairs, miserable and suddenly dead tired, when he had undressed in the guest room, swallowed his temazepams in the bathroom at the end of the landing and finally crawled into the wooden three-quarter bed behind the curled-up Joni, the long night of May 20, 2000 began.

"How about you tell me what happened down there," Aaron said a quarter of an hour later, during which he had been guardedly caressing her shoulders and hips.

She was asleep, or pretended to be. He turned onto his back, the window was an aquarium filled with floating May stars. A few minutes later he got out of bed, tripped over the clothes she had thrown off in her fury, and pushed the window farther open. The outside air was warm and thick; he drew the curtain. He heard her sniffle. "Come on," he said.

"All right," she said when he lay down next to her again. "For starters, you should know that Wilbert lived here for a while. About a year."

"Excuse me?" he asked. "*Where*. Here?"

"Here. In the farmhouse. For nearly all of 1989 he lived here. With us."

It was as though she were informing him that the garbage had to be put out on Thursdays from now on. He switched on the bedside lamp, his hands clammy, and gaped wide-eyed at the back of her blond head. Did he really know *nothing* about her life? "You're shitting me," he said.

"Wish I was."

He was speechless. After a while he asked: "But why? What was he doing here?"

"Living. You live here now too, right? Sometimes people just need a place to live."

With the same restrained, infuriating aplomb, in complete contrast to her temper tantrum just now, she started to explain what happened when she and Janis and her parents returned from America. During their first years living on the Tubantia campus they picked up signals that things were going badly, *seriously* badly, with Wilbert's mother. She drank. She *binge*-drank. Gone were the years when Margriet Wijn lived up to her name by putting away a liter of wine a day, no more but no less; she'd moved onto hard liquor, whiskey, jenever, cheap vodka, which she also drank by the liter, lending her surname an optimistic, even nostalgic quality. Margriet's brother told them she occasionally spent a few months on Texel, locked up in a rehab clinic. "So one day," said Joni, still with her back to him, "she was dead."

Not twenty-four hours after Wilbert's mother had drunk herself to death, by unlucky coincidence on her son's seventeenth birthday,

Menno Wijn had informed his nephew that living together under one roof was getting tiresome. You can say that again, said Wilbert. A few days later, Sigerius watched them lay Margriet's booze-ravaged body to rest at a Utrecht cemetery. Only at the very end of the coffee reception did he walk over to his son—without any plan, he confessed to Joni years later; in fact he was motivated by the evil looks from his ex-in-laws. In a fit of guilt-ridden fatherliness he assured Wilbert that his door in Enschede was always open, and he should keep it in mind.

That offer did not fall on deaf ears. Two weeks after his mother's funeral, Wilbert turned up at their farmhouse. Unannounced. Seventeen and vagrant. He didn't park his motorbike on the road, like a normal person would, but roared around the back with it. He planted the thing in the middle of the clover-grass lawn and himself in front of it, waiting for his new family to step into the April sunshine. Aaron could just see it: the idling off-roader and, in front of it, the future murderer, sprouting, pimply, petulant, in a sleeveless T-shirt from which, he imagined, hung two sinewy limbs—suntanned arms made for unloading Rhine barges, throwing punches, wedging girls against brick walls.

He asked numbly: "Did you recognize him?"

"Sure did," she said. "He looked just like I had pictured him." Eleven years on, Wilbert's saddle-like face was still gypsyish, except that the oil-paint teardrop had made way for a highly flammable sneer, untrustworthy and mistrustful at the same time. His hair was still jet-black, almost blue, but longer and greasier.

According to Joni, 1989 was the craziest year of her life, but Aaron was only half listening. He was stunned by the news itself. So the IJmuiden Basher had lived here. For four years Joni had not uttered a word about it, not Sigerius, nobody. Sigerius must have assumed he knew—a perfectly normal assumption, because how could he *not* know something like this after four years together with Joni. Aaron was so dumbfounded that he forgot to get angry, too preoccupied with the insane idea that Wilbert Sigerius had stretched out in his gym socks on the old-rose three-seater downstairs, had filed out the cylinders of his Honda on the terrace in the garden, had rinsed off his greasy mitts in the same shower he was expected to use the next morning.

"So where'd he sleep?" An idiotic, all-important question.

"Next door," said Joni, "in my father's study. The day he arrived the two of them dragged out the desk, and brought in this bed. He slept in this bed."

"No way."

She sighed. "The first few weeks were the worst. The guy was just suddenly *there.* At breakfast, in the bathtub, his big fingers all over the remote control in the evening. At the beginning I used to burn candles in the hope that he'd just go away."

"Candles?" He was angry, but curious.

"Here," she said, "on the windowsill. Tea lights. Sat here praying he'd bundle up all his junk back onto his motorbike. A real bigmouth, all of a sudden. He was shy for precisely ten minutes. If they asked me at school who he was, I lied, said Wilbert was an exchange student from Hungary."

He heaved a deep sigh. "Why does nobody ever tell me anything? What was it like?"

"At first everybody did their absolute best," she continued. "Dad, Mom, Janis, me—even him. He showed up with the weirdest presents. We're out in the garden, for instance, and my mother mentions in passing that her hairdryer conked out that morning, and the next day he gives her a brand-new one. Out of gratitude."

"Stolen?"

"Not even. Wilbert had money coming out of his ears, he

bought the most expensive hairdryer. My parents didn't know how to react. So there's my mother on an ordinary Tuesday evening, unpacking this gift-wrapped hairdryer. Gosh, um, why thank you, Wilbert. My father was suspicious, he went to the V&D and to the Blokker and to Scheer & Foppen, until he got to the Kijkshop and they told him that yes, a young fellow with a motorcycle helmet and a West Coast accent had bought the hairdryer. You see? he'd say. The first few months my father was the driving force. Still so optimistic. He was going to get Wilbert back on the rails."

"Big mistake."

"You know how it turned out," she said. "We were clueless. For instance, I wasn't even aware that he'd already done time. More and more, he and Dad would go at it. God, could those two clash, unbelievable. And then it wasn't even about the real shit, I mean: the incidents, the fights downtown, the break-ins, the cocaine. No, it was, like, normal day-to-day stuff. Forever arguing about everything and nothing. Those endless arguments about his musical taste, when I think back on it . . ." The drone of an ambulance siren wafted in from outside.

When she carried on with her story, she sounded more upbeat. "Wilbert liked rap and hip hop. Public Enemy, especially. I actually found it kind of interesting. Chuck D, Flavor Flav, Terminator X, I know all those names by heart. *Yo! Bum Rush the Show, It Takes a Nation of Millions to Hold Us Back*, blaring the whole day long from four huge speakers he'd managed, within no time, to pick up somewhere. *Turn it down!* I can still hear my father screaming. The anger and desperation in that shouting from the bottom of the stairs. When I biked home from school via the campus, I'd ride up the Langenkampweg and even before our house appeared between the trees you could already hear the pounding. 'Louder than a Bomb.' All from that little cubbyhole next door."

“I also used to get into rows about music. That’s normal.”

“Believe me,” she said, “it was *not* normal. They were at each other’s throats over the most trivial things. Over nothing, over . . . over *cola*. We were never allowed cola at home. Wilbert shows up, turns out he’s hooked on cola. All his life Wilbert is used to drinking two liters of cola a day, not just any old cola, but *Coca*-Cola. Any other brand he pours down the drain, except Pepsi: Pepsi he flushes down the toilet, I saw him do it. Come Sunday evening, if there was no bottle of Coke in the fridge, he’d ride off in a sweat to the nearest snack bar.”

“Perfect,” said Aaron. “Cola kills you. Eventually.”

She pretended not to hear him. “So, OK, fine, Janis and I can have cola too. One day we’re sitting at the table talking about my sister’s fillings. Janis had just come back from the dentist, eleven years old and two cavities. So we’re discussing brushing, sweets, and so on, the usual routine. Wilbert says: ‘I’ve got zero cavities.’ Gosh, Wilbert, says my mother, that’s terrific. ‘Zero cavities,’ he says, ‘*therefore*, cola is good for your teeth.’ A normal person gets a laugh out of that kind of claptrap, is amused by that ‘therefore,’ or maybe not amused, but anyhow doesn’t take it seriously. Siem, he takes it *dead* serious. Reacts way over the top. For months he’s been convinced Wilbert has the same toxic effect on his daughters as two liters of cola a day has on your teeth. He goes ballistic over that ‘therefore.’ A normal kid backs off, says: ‘Just kidding, take it easy,’ but Wilbert is not a normal kid, Wilbert is itching for a fight, constantly. He’s adamant about it, keeps insisting that cola is good for your teeth. That he has *scientifically* proven that cola is good for your teeth.”

“Was he serious?”

“He was needling him. And you know Siem, he’s reasonable, he’s intelligent, but humor: *nada*. You know what a short fuse he’s got. He goes berserk. But Wilbert doesn't budge an inch, he says: vodka, now that's bad for you, just look at my mother, but not cola, oh no, cola's got fluoride in it, and he taps his teeth with his knife, tick, tick, tick. That's how it went, about the most trivial things. And my father just kept taking the bait."

She gave Sigerius less than his due, he thought. Maybe in her anger she forgot how alien to her father's nature Wilbert's fooling must have been. Cola good for your teeth, for fuck's sake. Once, Aaron was talking to a doctoral student, a hefty Korean who was allowed to study Sigerius's writings, where one could follow the bumpy road of his argumentation. "So krool," the fellow said a couple of times, before Aaron realized he was saying *so cruel*, referring to how mercilessly Sigerius threw his own work overboard as soon as his theories could be disproved. Months of work, sometimes years.

"I only heard later that there was a lot more to it, more than they told me and Janis about." She sniffed and rolled onto her back. "They fought like cats and dogs about Coca-Cola, but in the meantime there were hassles about cocaine, about dentist bills for having knocked out somebody's teeth. There was some flap about a job my father had wangled for him at the university's Technical Services. He'd pinched two grinding machines and sold them."

As he listened, Aaron wondered how he would have reacted to a similar invasion himself. What would he have done when he was fourteen if some out-of-control hooligan had moved into their house? Someone like . . . Piet Suiker, he thought of Piet, an incredibly tough and brash kid from his youth, a creep who hadn't crossed his mind for some fifteen years. Piet Suiker, "Suik" to his sidekicks—the most explosive maniac of them all, who called it quits after his fifth year of primary school, he didn't go on to sixth grade, what good was that. A lunatic from the early Middle

Ages of his life, whose nerve-racking presence seemed certain to last an eternity, but who suddenly, like a plantar wart, shriveled and vanished. Suik, from whom you could order the sport shoes of your choice for just a fiver, which he would then shoplift from Sijbers' Sporting Goods across the bridge in Venlo; who in the shower room after swimming lessons would grab the nearest pair of glasses and put them on his dick. When he was eleven he'd take you back behind the rose bushes and for a guilder show you how he could, from that same, now shockingly distended noodle, yank out "jism": still, to this day, by far the most disgusting word Aaron knew. When his Zündapp motorbike was stolen, Suik marched into Genooi, the Bronx of Venlo, armed with a baseball bat, and sure enough, he returned with that bike. While Aaron was doing his high school finals, Piet was roaring down the streets in a souped-up Opel Manta. That kind of kid. What if one night Suik had parked that Manta in front of their house and his overpriced Adidas on the shoe rack next to the kitchen door? That's what it came down to. Suik at their kitchen table. Suik in his pajamas on his dad's Commodore. "Boys," his mother would call from the TV room, "*Run the Gauntlet* is about to start," at which point not only he and Sebastian, but also that brawny nutcase would come barreling down the stairs. *That* is what happened to Joni.

She loosened up, her warm side touching his. "And even with these kinds of things going on—horrible things, really, I thought so too—I started to take a liking to Wilbert."

Now he held his breath. With the subtlest possible movement he shifted himself loose from her skin.

"It was a dilemma: of course I didn't *want* to like him. But he was nice to me. Protective. He brought me to the station on his motorbike. He insisted on picking me up if I was out late."

"Great guy," he said. She didn't answer. He thought he heard her grind her teeth.

"He introduced me to his music. LL Cool J, Run DMC, NWA—got them all from him. Listen to this, listen to that. He bought me a Walkman . . ."

"Stole you a Walkman."

". . . a really expensive Sony. He took me to Amsterdam on the sly, to Paradiso: just the two of us, to Public Enemy—my first concert, my father still doesn't know. We got the earliest train back. And I taught him to ride a horse. What's now the workshop used to be Peggy Sue's stall. He couldn't get enough of it. When he wasn't on his motorbike or bumming around Enschede he was with my horse. He was determined to learn to ride. I used to go with him to the Horstlinde stables, ride circles in the ring."

"Drienerlo Probation Service." He was trying to sound blithe.

"But the worst part was, he was so damn funny. Janis and I, and Mom too, got such a charge out of him. He turned everything into an act. If my father asked him to refill the gravy bowl, he didn't get up, no, he'd take a dishcloth from the table and lay it across his lap just so, and pretend he was ninety years old and his chair was a wheelchair, squeaking, squawking, turning, and twisting, and shuffle over to the counter. 'Wankin' around, nothing to do but pound, randy days and Mondays always crank me down,' he hollowed all through the house in his best Muzak voice after my mother had been given a Carpenters CD."

Aaron did not laugh. He wriggled his shoulder out from under her head. "Guess you just had to be there."

He stared silently across the room, toward the pale-pink curtains with white horses woven into them. Her mother had covered the seat cushions of two wooden desk chairs in the same material.

ith new eyes, apprehensive eyes, he examined the stuffed animals on the pink-painted bookshelf that also housed her literature list titles. He imagined the adolescent Joni, curled up on her bed with these books, blinking, startled, when Wilbert came roaring up the drive. Or did she perk up? Inside the white wardrobe, its sliding door open, he saw shoeboxes that undoubtedly contained her old school datebooks, her exam papers and notebooks full of "a"s and "o"s drawn like Bubblicious bubbles. He felt the urge to sift through them for signs of Wilbert: his name, a Public Enemy emblem, anything. On top of a stool lay a stack of *Elle*s, precisely one year's worth, the subscription they'd given her, after incessant begging, for her fifteenth birthday, but having found it so "irritating" she was allowed to cancel it after just three months. This kind of trivia, *this* was what she'd inundated him with. Jesus H. Christ. No matter how hilarious she thought that prick was, 1989 must have come to a sorry end.

He asked: "What went wrong?"

No answer. Then: "We've got to get some sleep." She reached under her pillow and brought out a sleeping mask.

"What went wrong. Come on."

"Did something go wrong? Yeah, it went wrong." She put the mask back under the pillow and exhaled slowly. "At home, actually. It all happened too close by, more or less in Dad's face, and then enough was enough. After eleven months Siem had totally had it with him. Wilbert had to go, the rotten apple had to be chucked out, and soon, before they hurt each other. That mood hung in the house for weeks. They needed a scapegoat."

"A scapegoat is someone who's innocent." He slid his hand between the covers and her belly, he felt her pull back. With a sigh he switched off the bedside lamp.

"I was getting tutored in French at the time," she said. "And those tutorials were given by a woman—an adult, or so I thought at the time, but in fact she was still a girl, about as old as I am now—who had just graduated cum laude from Utrecht specializing in, um . . . whatshername, Sartre's battleaxe."

"De Beauvoir."

"Yeah. Her. But shit, what was that girl's name again . . ." She was concentrating hard, it was something with an F, she said.

"Does her name matter?"

"She was a prig, but a pretty prig. Well groomed, chic, uppity, like one of those governesses in a film. Lily-white, beauty spots."

"You were being tutored," he pressed. Stick to the subject—but she launched into an exposé of the educational regime in their home. The minute she or Janis were faced with a C-minus, her parents would rustle up a private tutor. "Achievement is the secret code word in this family, although they'll never admit it. Just graduate? Come on. I didn't *have* to be valedictorian, but it would be nice. In Berkeley they didn't send me to just any private school. Berkwood Hedge: small classes, emphasis on culture, tuition in the thousands. Later, in Boston, Kids Are People Middle School—American Montessori education, a Shakespeare play a year. A 'C' was way below par for a Sigerius."

"And meanwhile a juvenile delinquent sat in the garden revving his motorbike," he said.

". . . Vivianne! Vivianne Hiddink. My parents doted on her. She had lived in Strasbourg, studied for a year at the Sorbonne, had started organizing programs for Studium Generale here in Twente. We'd hardly started the lessons and already my father had to invite her round. In America they used to have Richard Feynman over, if the name means anything to you, but anyway Mademoiselle Hiddink was interesting too, so why not."

"Sure, why not?" He felt himself getting angry, all that elitist hot air, in that respect Joni was a bit soft in the head too. But he held back, for fear of stalling her.

"This boyfriend of hers, Maurice was his name, had a doctorate in theoretical physics. Early thirties, squeaky-clean black hair, British tweed jacket, Van Bommel dress shoes. Spent the whole evening squinting drily through his little Schubert specs, one witticism after the other. Never met anybody since then who was so completely different from Wilbert. It hurt your eyes to see those two at the same table. But you couldn't very well send Wilbert to the kitchen to eat his steak, although that would have suited Dad fine. I remember that Wilbert, who had otherwise kept unusually quiet, asked Maurice what he actually did all day at that 'research institute' of his. 'I've got a room there,' he answered, polishing his Schubert specs with a soft cloth, 'with just a sofa, that's it, and I lie on it all day, thinking.' That must have sounded familiar to Wilbert: your own room with nothing but a bed to lie on and think."

She chuckled softly, probably pleased with herself. She was a good talker and she knew it.

"So Vivianne always came to the house on Saturday mornings, from half-past nine to half-past eleven, for me it was torture, and on top of it I had to get dressed in a big hurry. We used this room, sat there at Grandpa Sigerius's desk, which she so smartly called a *bureau ministre*, and from then on so did we."

"And me too, now."

"Except Wilbert," said Joni. "He had another kind of French on his mind. We all noticed how he hung around downstairs early Saturday morning, way too early for him, and stole every glimpse of Vivianne he could. If he got the chance he'd take her coat, hang it neatly on the hallway coatrack—we teased him for being such a show-off, gently of course. What the heck, I thought it was sweet and understandable. Vivianne was quite a . . . sight in her *ensembles*. The house smelled like Chanel until dinner time."

He pressed his nose into Joni's neck.

"And then one Sunday afternoon Maurice was on the line for Dad. A nonplussed conversation, not the least bit witty or clever, from the sound of it—within two minutes he went to take it upstairs, asked if I would hang up the receiver below. Fifteen minutes later he came into the living room. He said: 'Vivianne won't be coming anymore.' And that was it."

"Oh?"

"Later that afternoon, when Wilbert was off to who knows where on his motorbike, Dad said she was considering filing a police report." She cleared her throat and swallowed. "It all started with her scarf, which should have been tucked in the sleeve of her coat but wasn't. Maybe she'd left it somewhere, lost it. These things happen. The next week, this Maurice guy tells my father, on her way home Vivianne reaches into her coat pocket for a handkerchief, Irish linen, one of those perfumed ladies' hankies. I'd seen those *accessoires* of hers. Well, that hankie had been transformed into a clammy wad. It no longer smelled of Chanel, but of lukewarm sperm. Although it was 'horrid,' she said, 'horrid,' she kept her mouth shut about it, even to Maurice. Of course she could guess whose glue douche that was."

Joni paused for a moment, turned her shoulders. The bed creaked.

"Let's be adults about this, Vivianne resolved, the kid's a teenager, a bit of a lout, she had already caught on to that. And besides, she really *liked* coming to our place, it *clicked*. Maybe she was even flattered, who knows. A wad of spunk is a compliment in a way, isn't it?"

A pleasantry, at least."

"Two weeks after that hankie incident, which no one except she and Wilbert knew about, Vivianne and I were sitting up here and as usual, sometime during the second hour, after my mother had brought us coffee and *krentenwegge*, she went off to use the toilet, here in the upstairs bathroom. So she's sitting there, door locked, and soon enough she hears something behind the shower curtain, she hears a noise. She hears someone breathing—that's how she put it in court—"

"In *court*?"

"In court, yeah. She hears breathing, and freezes. For a moment she thinks she's just heard herself, her own panting. Then she braces herself and yanks open the curtain. There he is: stark naked, his jogging pants around his ankles, holding that Scottish scarf she's been missing for the past three weeks. He's standing there jerking off, sniffing that fucking scarf, just a few feet from Vivianne—"

"Fucking hell."

"But what does she do? She doesn't scream. She spares him, not deliberately, mind you, no motivation behind it whatsoever, she says later—she saves his ass by *not* screaming. 'What do think you're doing?' she whispers, and he comes. She just sits there. He takes a step toward her, so he's almost hanging over her, and sheds . . ."

"Spurts."

"OK, *spurts* cum all over her wrist and thigh. 'You're out of your mind,' she hisses, and still manages to contain herself, maybe paralyzed by the shock, at least that's her take on it. She tugs the curtain closed again, wipes the muck from her legs with some toilet paper, pulls up her pantyhose and skirt, forgets to flush, does think to wash her wrist and walks back to my room."

"What a scumbag," said Aaron.

"Yeh . . . ," she said with a shrug. She went quiet for a mom "But," she continued, "that Vivianne was a strange one too. S walks back into my room, goes over to the mirror, smoothes out that Laura Ashley blouse of hers, and sits down. '*Bon*,' she says, 'where were we. *Future du passé*, always a tricky one . . .' Nothing! Not a word about Wilbert. I swear, until that phone call I didn't even know anything had happened. That woman just finished off our French lesson, I walked her downstairs as usual, we even stood chatting with my mother in the hall, and then she gets into her little Renault and drives off to Maurice."

Outside, beyond the campus, probably from the tracks leading to Drienerlo Station, an intercity train blew its horn. The drawn-out sound penetrated the guest room and brought him to himself. He couldn't gauge the atmosphere. What kind of mood was she in? She seemed to be criticizing the woman. Or not? For days he'd been misreading everything and everyone.

"Sounds like Vivianne wanted to think things over first," he said. "She wasn't stupid, of course. She didn't scream blue murder straightaway, you could call that self-control."

"True," said Joni. "But at the same time it's weird. It's weird not to utter a peep about something like that. As if nothing happened in that bathroom, that's how she acted. And who says anything did happen?"

Rather than letting the suggestion sink in and pretend to at least consider the possibility, he barked: "You can't be serious! Nobody makes up something like that. Of course it happened."

"Hang on a minute," she said, "he never admitted it . . ."

"Yeah, right. Why would he?"

You say nobody makes up something like that, but you could also say: nobody does something like that. You'd sooner make it up than actually do it."

He felt himself getting angry. "Beating a guy to a pulp with a sledgehammer, Joni, that's something I've also considered on occasion. And I still didn't do it. That Wilbert of yours, he does whatever pops into his head. That's where it all goes wrong. I take it the judge agreed with me?"

She turned away from him, thumped her backside into his pelvis like a boxing glove. "It was his word against hers," she said. "There was no proof. No one saw or heard anything."

He sprang upright and looked at the dark outline of her shoulder blades against the sheets. Was she serious? Did she really doubt what had happened in that bathroom? "Joni," he said, "don't be so incredibly naïve. And what about that jizz-hankie? Made up too? Come on, be reasonable."

"Look who's talking," she snarled. "You're going to tell me what's reasonable and what's not?"

"I'm just expressing an opinion, and yes, I think you're being highly unreasonable. What was the upshot of the case?"

"Highly unreasonable . . ." She sighed theatrically. "Goddammit, Aaron," she exploded, "I can't really take this right now. You've been acting like an imbecile all week, just now too, at the table, with your tales of heroism, and you're calling *me* unreasonable? Go take another sleeping pill. Good night." She jerked the sheet farther to her side and buried her head in her pillow. He was glad the light was out, because he could feel himself blushing. "Tales of heroism?" he said as calmly as possible. "What are you talking about?"

She did not answer.

"Well?"

"Aaron. You don't really think I bought that crap abou
do you?"

"Then don't buy it."

"I don't believe a stinking word of it."

Silence. Five minutes. Ten minutes? He gazed at the gently billowing curtains. He started to believe she was sleeping, and that infuriated him. She knew he couldn't sleep after an argument. You don't sleep *without* an argument either, she'd say tomorrow. In the silence he suddenly sensed that she was keeping something from him. She fobbed him off with a sanitized, Aaron-friendly version of the story. She knew better than to be honest about anyone with a pecker. In the four years of their relationship, jealousy had become such a powerful mechanism that it was impossible to guess what she actually thought of the guy. Even if she'd had twins with that Wilbert she wouldn't tell him.

"Another one of your crushes, I'll bet," he snapped.

"Whatever," she snapped back.

He swallowed his anger. "And you still haven't answered my question. Why the tantrum? Why smash a dish of potato croquettes to smithereens?"

She did not answer. For several minutes he looked at her back. Until he could hear from her breathing that she was asleep.

In the days that followed, Sigerius avoided his elder daughter; for Aaron, at least, it was hardly a coincidence that they never once sat down to eat at the same time. Sigerius mostly ate out. Joni seemed to have forgotten their nighttime conversation and avoided *him*. Her behavior annoyed him; one minute she was like a toddler in happy anticipation of America, the next minute she sat there blubbering about Ennio.

..s part, he was busy at *Tubantia Weekly*. Thank God. The ..ks disaster had undeniably brought out the best in him, and ..ite his sleepless nights he had outdone himself these past few ..eeks. Blaauwbroek was impressed. His boss was the first person they had heard on Joni's answering machine, far ahead of the platoon of concerned friends and family, and he sounded like an eleven-year-old watching the circus ride into town. "Bever, good afternoon to you, Henk Blaauwbroek here on the machine. I assume you're alive. Did you also hear a blast? Hibernation's over, kid. Have you got photos? We're putting out an extra edition, you get the picture."

He and his boss had a love-hate relationship. During staff outings and over drinks they were boisterously brotherly, but at the workplace it was a constant battle. Since Aaron had studied at the Art Academy and not at journalism school, Blaauwbroek accused him of having artistic aspirations, a card he never tired of playing. "It ain't gonna hang in a museum, kid," or "why not try a shorter shutter speed," or "there's our still-life fetishist"—how often had he put up with remarks like that. And he *was* a lousy news photographer, he was the first one to admit it. Too slow for the real work, too hesitant, not passionate about hard news, but that's why, he'd reply snidely, he worked for Blaauwbroek and not for Reuters.

But now he strode through media-clogged Enschede as though dispatched by *Time* magazine itself. For once, he'd come up with ideas all on his own: at a Chinese wholesaler in Liège he took before-during-and-after photos of 1.1-class fireworks, the ammonium chloride kind stored in the Enschede storage bunkers. Together with two ex-residents and the local police chief he crisscrossed the disaster area in a space suit. He shot a series of portraits of now-homeless Roombeekers whom he talked into posing in the torn and blood-stained clothes they were wearing that Saturday,

May 13th (his photo of the man wearing one flip-flop ar barbecue tongs, who had wandered for hours half naked the burning streets, made it into a Victim Assistance broc From atop the dilapidated roof of the Grolsch brewery he pho graphed the scorched neighborhood—a shocking war-zone photo a national newspaper bought from him.

The air on his calamity-planetoid was, to put it otherwise, rarefied, and it made him light-headed. He maintained that every Enschede resident who was alive and still had all his limbs had no business grousing, and to suit his actions to his words he returned, as the first and only "victim," the 1,500 guilders cash the city council had distributed to all those affected by the accident. Joni thought his gesture pompous, even tactless. "It's time you drop the stunts," she said.

On their last day at the farmhouse he went to the university library to update their website on a public computer, a shit job that made him wonder why *he* was the one doing it; this whole website thing was Joni's idea, but *he* took the Dreamweaver course; *she* talked about clean prostitution, but *he* sat here shitting himself every time a student walked into the room. These were the last photos from the series they had shot at the Golden Tulip, they had to hurry up and post something new.

When he left the library the atmosphere hung like a crystal ball over the campus. Satisfaction with what he had just accomplished temporarily blocked out the visions he'd had while dozing at the library table; he'd dreamt he saw himself lying on the mossy tiles of the central square. The first stars wove through the uppermost blue, elongated wisps of orange hung above the treetops to the west. While he unlocked his bike the Bastille spat out a women's ub, garrulous girls who had just gobbled up their weekly sausage with fries and limp-boiled vegetables and were usily searching for their bicycles.

He decided to take the inside route. A leafy cycle path led him to the broad dirt jogging track. Three runners scuffed with a muted crunch over the gravel, two female students sat in the middle oval with a bottle of wine. The sun sank behind the ivy-covered wall that hid the outdoor pool from view. Warm air caressed his scalp. He shut his eyes for a swarm of bugs and was wondering if the pool contained enough water to extinguish that orange ball when, with a whack, his camera bag was knocked off his shoulder. It dangled on his forearm and rattled against the spokes of the front wheel. A girl on an upright bike passed him, muttering a barely audible "sorry."

"Fucking bimbo!" he shouted, surprised at how readily his contentment turned into rage. Breathing hard, he coasted to a standstill and stood with his legs spread. Jealousy, the fear of losing her, was always the root of everything.

It was snowing when he arrived at the farmhouse. The poplars on the northern edge of the garden blossomed so furiously that the twilight sky was saturated with flakes and the grass was covered with a translucent layer of fluff. Cuddly clumps of white danced around Joni's bare ankles as she sat on the mossy terrace alongside the former stalls, like a . . . yes, like a what? Like a melting snowman.

Tineke sat across from her at the scrapwood table, between them their emptied plates and a carafe of water. As he approached them he was overcome by revulsion. He could guess what was up. "Hello," he said and sat down next to Tineke. Joni answered his greeting with a gurgling, drawn-out snort into a piece of paper towel. Her eyes were puffy. Her mother sighed and looked at him. "Hungry?" she asked.

"Hungry *and* thirsty," he said. Instead of asking Joni why she

had been crying, he took her glass an
gulped it back and wiped his mouth. "Mmm,

After an awkward silence Tineke made a mo
go," Joni mumbled. She stood up, pulled the spagh
her shoulder and shuffled across the fluffy backyard. Onc
in the kitchen Tineke laid a hand on his wrist and said qu
"She's just back from visiting Ennio. Try to be nice to her."

He nodded. "What actually happened?"

Tineke glanced toward the house, from the pantry they could hear the hum of the microwave. "It's a terrible story," she said. "Just awful." Keeping her eye on the door, she said: "The guy was on fire. From what I understand he was napping on the sofa when the living room window imploded. His entire back and legs full of glass. Then the rug under the coffee table caught fire, and then the sofa too, everything completely synthetic, of course. He rolled outside through the broken window and only then realized his trousers were on fire." She shook her head. "And while he's trying to put out the fire—it's too terrible for words—he's hit full-on, right by the front gate, by the chimney of his own—"

She cut herself off when Joni opened the screen door. Nifty physics problem, he heard himself thinking as Joni approached. Givens: rolling velocity of the man and the height of the chimney. Assignment: calculate the depth of the yard. Joni looked like she was in pain, and she was: with a moan she slammed a steaming plate of tandoori chicken under his nose. She blew on her fingers as she rounded the table. She looked pretty bad.

"I've had a hell of a day . . . ," he said before she even sat down. "I photographed these three Evangelical students. In their emergency shelter. They lived in a dorm right across from the fireworks factory. Blown to kingdom come with biblical ferocity. Photos, term papers, a brand-new practice piano, two rented tuxedos: everything

t you know it, they still believe. Well-
the Lord they weren't home. Evangelists or
derstood that humor is the best way to deal with

en to see Ennio," Joni said.

ithin just two days," he continued, "they had a whole reper-
ire of May 13th jokes. They're stuck in that makeshift apartment all day long. 'What did the firecracker say to the roman candle?'—that kind of thing, the whole time." He smiled, popped a piece of tandoori in his mouth and looked at Joni while he chewed. "I heard," he said with his mouth full. "But now he's able to have visitors. So he's on the mend."

With a strange motion, a kind of spasm, she knocked the roll of paper towels from the table. "On the *mend*?" She inhaled like a sponge diver and disappeared under the table. "He's in the ICU, Aaron," came the voice from underwater. When she resurfaced with the paper towels she banged her shoulder against the edge of the table, hard enough to bring on new tears.

"It's not easy, honey," said Tineke. "Have a good cry."

(Bawl, doctor. *Bawl.* No, that's not how he said it; months later he would express himself more euphemistically: he felt that Joni, for his taste, overreacted to what she had seen in that ICU. As though she'd had her tear ducts surgically shortened. Those two little geysers, he observed, made her curiously ugly, in contrast to what tears had done with his earlier, less attractive girlfriends: crying made them prettier, their tears *softened* them. He compared Joni's sob-gob with her usual Scandinavian freshness. The broad face with its smooth, taut skin; I really should get some fresh air, you thought when you looked at her. The upper half radiated well-being, at least under normal circumstances, strength, genetic gold. Joni's shrewdness, the sexiness, her flammable femininity—these were lower, they gathered around her mouth, now a pale, quivering stripe, but usually a deep-red anemone with an ever so slightly forward-jutting lower lip that always looked moist. The tiniest pout and all that wellness became overripe, decadent. Although she was aware of her external weapons, she sometimes pushed down the tip of her modest little nose with her index finger: she felt that it swung upward. It didn't. Amazing how much snot could come out of it.)

And how was Ennio faring? He must have asked something of the sort, because in barely intelligible stages he learned that the guy had third-degree burns all over his body, five broken ribs, a perforated spleen, and countless open flesh wounds. The doctors had covered Ennio's legs, chest, and a good bit of his back with donor skin—like a dish of lasagna, he imagined. Every morning the wounds had to be disinfected, smeared with salve, and dressed, a painful affair for which they gave him painkillers and tranquilizers. Meanwhile Ennio lost liters of fluids into the jungle of tubes and apparatus, and all sorts of organs refused to function, the reason why he was permanently hooked to an IV that made him swell up in unexpected places.

Joni paused to catch her breath, nestling her rounded chin on her arms, which lay crossed on the table.

"So he's still alive," he summarized, and made a feeble attempt at reaching across and laying a hand on her shoulder. As she felt him she sprang up, furious. "Yeah, he's still alive," she screamed. She kicked her chair back and got up.

"Joni . . . ," Tineke said.

"Alive, but they've given him pretty slim odds, you prick. He's got blood poisoning and pneumonia. He's at death's door. And everybody's distraught—everyone in that family is totally devastated. You always make out like things are just hunky-dory!"

"Aaron doesn't think that," Tineke said soothingly. She shook her head. "It's just awful luck, so soon after his divorce. Kicked out of his house, and then this." She looked worriedly across the yard, her chin dragging the fat of her neck with it, she stopped only when her gaze met his—questioningly, it seemed.

"Wasn't Ennio screwing his salesgirls?" he said. A heavy silence. "That's what they say, anyway."

Joni blew her nose in a paper towel, threw the wad onto the table, and stared into the yard.

"There are people," he added, "who, in a case like this, would say: God punishes mercilessly and without delay. But you won't hear me say that." His comment hit them like seagull shit, he realized as much, but at the same time he was pleased with it, his lack of sleep cleared his head; wonderful how sleep deprivation made you more alert. That Ennio was nothing but a dirty bugger. Each season new first-year chick between his chutneys.

"If you were my son," said Tineke, "I'd slap your face right now."

But I'm not your son, he thought. He scooped together the last bits of rice and sauce, shoveled it all in his mouth and said: "Gotta go. Judo."

When he and Sigerius returned back home around midnight, dead beat, Joni was already lying in the guest bed. Her sleeping figure radiated anger.

He cautiously slid alongside her, fully prepared for another sleepless night. It was the first time since the dinner table incident that he had been alone with Sigerius, and was quick to notice that his father-in-law was harboring a whopper of a grudge. They were sitting on the edge of the mat, next to the large sketchbook, discussing *katas*, when Sigerius asked if Joni had said anything about "the fuss." You mean Ennio, he had answered quasi-nonchalantly, or California? No, no—Sigerius meant that to-do about Wilbert, you know, at the table, the commotion over my son. He replied that they'd spoken about it briefly, Joni told him bits and pieces about when they were young, but that they hadn't spoken much the past few days. It was a father-daughter thing, Sigerius assured him, nothing to worry himself about, but still there was this nagging question: did Aaron know if Joni had been in contact with Wilbert? Phone calls? Did he pick up anything along those lines?

No, he didn't know a thing.

OK, good—say no more, water under the bridge, let's get to work, case closed, it seemed—but for Aaron it was case *open*, water over the bridge, certainly now he lay there, once again, wide awake alongside Joni. For now at least, no tormenting fantasies about her escapades with the chutney-hawker, for now no agonizing about Stol and McKinsey, but you could hardly call it a solace. What had happened? What was Sigerius so worried about? Why did she keep him in the dark? The night stretched itself out like a torture rack of time. Sigerius's fear had become his own, now *he* suddenly had to know if she'd talked to that jailbird, and more to the point: *why*. What was going on here?

While she lay in a deep slumber next to him, as far away as possible on her side of the bed it seemed, he worked his way through the worst possible scenarios. Wilbert had molested her. No, they had had an affair. Bonnie and Clyde. Year after year she visited Wilbert in his cell for a weekly hour of hanky-panky in a cube of tempered glass. There was a child of theirs out there somewhere, she'd given birth, or at the very least had an abortion—and his morbid fantasies whirled around in this vein, picked up speed, flung themselves about, ever faster, ever wilder, until the electric field was enough to rouse Joni: she woke with a start. She lay there panting and smacking her lips to dreams whose content he could only guess. She flipped on the bedside lamp, groped for her watch. "Damn," she said. Only then did she look beside her. He was sitting upright, his back against the textured wallpaper. The glance she shot him was . . . indescribable. What was in it? Ice. Disdain, disapproval. Contempt? Her anger had fermented, and what he tasted was . . . *loathing.*

And yet he managed to produce a complete sentence. "Joni," he choked, "has Wilbert phoned you?"

She sat up, wrestled with the bedsheet, looked at him mockingly. She let out a contemptuous little chuckle, for a moment he expected an answer, but she turned away, shaking her head, burrowed her blond hair deep into the pillow and said: "G'night, dickhead."

He was allowed back in his house. "Goin' home," he chirped after their last breakfast at the farmhouse, and without another word to each other, but as though it was perfectly normal that Joni should join him, they loaded their bags into the Alfa and drove off, he at the wheel, Joni in the passenger seat with the guinea pig cage on her lap. The sky above the campus was bright blue. They drove in silence down the Langenkampweg and the Hengelosestraat; he was familiar with these arguments and knew exactly how long they would last.

They didn't go for outright bickering, and both considered drawn-out arguments a royal pain in the ass. Of course they'd had plenty of rows, clashes that shook the doors off their hinges, but these were incidents that diminished in frequency the better they came to assess each other's weaknesses and flashpoints. Joni hated arguments because she was too efficient, because she was focused on the shortest route to success, which for her was not the same as being right or winning an argument (as it was for him) but about arriving at a situation that offered her an *advantage*. As far as she was concerned, arguing was, she once screamed at him during, ironically enough, a grueling, entirely out-of-hand dispute, "un-pro-duc-tive!"

As they approached his street their attention drifted along the wooden partitions, the eye-level piss-yellow fencework that ran the length of the Lasondersingel and turned the corner at the Blijdensteinlaan. "Just like Asterix and Obelix's village," he said to Joni, "only less invincible." She did not laugh.

He himself was a coward. He avoided confrontations whenever possible; an argument with Joni was more than anything a risk. For the past four years he'd been telling his friends that Joni would be the mother of his children, and to avoid anything that might jeopardize that, he had, until recently, tiptoed around her.

They toddled uneasily up the path to the front door, the key he'd been given by the town council slipped effortlessly into the brand-new lock. "Leave the animals in the hall for now."

Glass. He'd heard endless accounts of the shock wave, an invisible Hun that swept relentlessly through the streets of Roombeek without skipping a single address—and still he was awestruck. The entire ground floor, which felt small after two weeks *chez* Sigerius, was littered with splinters, shards, and rubble. On the table, on the armchair seat cushions, on every uncovered centimeter of his bookshelves, between the buttons on the remote control, on the windowsills of opposing windows, one of which had been blown out, in the kitchen sink, on the cabinets—there was glass *everywhere*. The city council had boarded up the shattered sliding doors with wood panels.

"Double glazing," he said, "gotta get double glazing."

They drifted about the sparkling living room for a quarter of an hour at a loss for what to do; and still Joni was silent. He handed her the only pair of rubber gloves he could find under the sink, and put on his own winter gloves. The thaw would set in within an hour, he estimated. He vacuumed the windowsills with his Nilfisk. They scooped the broken glass into garbage bags, in silence. He picked up the two breakfast plates they had left standing on the coffee table the morning of the wedding, and on the way to the kitchen he held a half-eaten slice of bread now sprinkled with glass under her nose. "Wanna bite?" he asked.

"Cut it *out*!" she screamed. With a furious swipe she knocked his arm away, the plate arced through the air and broke noisily. He exploded, grabbed her by the chin, squeezed it hard, and hissed through his teeth: "*What* went on between *you* and that *fuck*ing Wilbert?"

"Let *go* of me," she said.

He squeezed harder, spit trickled onto his hand. "Tell me," he bellowed, but instead of answering him, she growled with rage. He pushed her away. "I'm *sick* of it!" he screamed. "*Sick and tired!* Always these half-truths. Just fucking tell me what's going on!"

Her eyes grew to unnatural dimensions. She was taken aback by his outburst, he could tell, the conceit drained from her face. She slumped into the armchair nearest the demolished sliding door, realized the seat was strewn with shattered glass and jumped back up. She cursed.

"Turn around," he said. To his surprise, she obeyed. He slapped off bits of glass from her buttocks with the flat of his hand, and had to squat down to pick the splinters out of her skirt. This operation released the tension, apparently for both of them, because before he was finished she said: "All right then. Listen." She sighed deeply, but remained silent.

"I'm listening," he said.

Again it was a few moments before she spoke. "This isn't to get any farther than this room. What I'm about to say is . . . let's just say I'm not proud of it."

"OK," he said, worried but eager. "*Talk.* You'd got to the court case." As she was now glass-free, he placed his hands on her hips, his thumbs resting against the flanks of her buttocks. She allowed it.

"Siem insisted I testify," she said, suddenly businesslike. "He wanted me to say I heard what had gone on in the bathroom. That I was in the hallway and overheard the whole shebang. The sounds. What was said. You follow me now?"

He did not respond, but pressed his thumbs softly into her buttocks.

"Siem demanded that I blow the whistle on his son, my step-brother. The kid I'd gone horseback riding with the week before. That I . . . *shaft* him. That I *lie* in court."

The word "shaft" did not sit well with him. He gave her ass a shove, she took a step forward. "Excellent," he said. "The gloves are off."

"Asshole!" she cried. She gave the armchair a kick.

"Why? He had to go. Your father was completely in the right."

To his surprise, she stayed calm. She grabbed the vacuum, turned it on and cleaned the seat of the armchair. When she had finished she mumbled: "The bag's full." She dropped the hose wand and looked at him. "Aaron, try to relate. Just this once. I perjured myself. Against my will. I was put under pressure to betray a kid I liked. In a court of law. To his face. I committed perjury in front of him. He heard it, and he *knew* it."

"And then?"

"And then?" she barked. "And then? What do you think 'and then'? They gave him ten months. Thanks to me lying. Thanks to Siem's manipulation. *That's* what 'and then.' "

He nodded. "Did Wilbert phone you?"

She wanted to say something, again something irate, but just at that moment her cell phone rang. While fumbling to retrieve it from her skirt pocket she cooled off and said: "I called him. We met up."

She answered the phone. After announcing her name she listened attentively, stuck out her hand to him like a traffic cop, and disappeared into the kitchen. She pulled the door shut behind her with a bang. Who did she have on the line? He hurried after her and saw through the window that she'd gone all the way to the end of the overgrown backyard. She was talking indistinctly. With that criminal?

It was strangely quiet in the street; it took him a while to realize he heard no birds. The fauna had abandoned Roombeek. He had fled his house in order to simmer down. He left a note on the table saying that he'd gone to buy more vacuum cleaner bags and get something for them both to eat.

He wanted to cycle up to the Roomweg, to a small housewares shop across from the French fry joint, but once he saw the wooden fence he realized the shop now only existed in his memory. So— she *did* go to see Wilbert. He rode past the museum and into the neighborhood beyond it. Should he be jealous, or worried? Past the primary school he turned left and arrived at the "flower monument," a public garden on the Deurningerstraat that overflowed with cellophane-wrapped flowers in memory of the victims. Why was he unable to show any empathy?

With a vaguely uneasy feeling he rode through Blaauwbroek's street, glanced in the living room window, but no one was home. He crossed the railroad tracks and biked into the city center, following the Langestraat until he reached the Hema. Had his capacity for compassion completely evaporated? Was he overlooking a sort of fundamental jealousy, a blind spot that determined his view of even the most serious matters?

He paid for the vacuum cleaner bags, as well as a hunk of cheese and six muesli rolls, and walked his bike to the lingerie shop in the Havenstraat. Not entirely by coincidence, he passed Ennio's delicatessen, on whose dark-red door hung a note saying "Closed until further notice"; he stood in front of the busily decorated shop window and examined a small tower of jars: Colman's Original Mustard, miniature jars of Wilkin & Sons No Peel Orange Marmalade, tall jars of Mrs. Ball's Peach Chutney, all stacked in the shape of a little man. On top, attached with barely visible nylon thread, was a bowler hat, and alongside it, on two threads, a diagonal walking stick. He imagined Ennio fussing with his wares behind that cramped window display, and concluded that Joni couldn't possibly have had sex with the sort of person who thought up and constructed this kind of nonsense.

Was he too jealous? Should he back off? Could he be imagining things? Stol, Ennio, Wilbert, fuck, fucking, fucked—three guys who robbed him of a good night's sleep; did their number say something about Joni, or about him?

He walked farther and went into the lingerie shop. One way or another, today or tomorrow, they had to shoot a new photo series. Maybe he could buy something usable here, something to demonstrate his goodwill. The older saleslady nodded at him. From an overfull rack he chose a brassiere made of black see-through tulle, with red stitching on the half-cups, and in a plastic bin he found some black net stockings that—said the saleslady—would suit madam perfectly. Back to work, call a truce. He cycled back to the crater, pondered his wording of the suggestion to go up to the attic and get changed. For the first time in weeks he felt something that resembled sexual desire.

For the second time that day, again almost as if it was a perfectly normal thing to do, he entered his house, this time conciliatory. "Hello!" he called out as he went into the living room. No reply; maybe she was still on the phone. He walked through the empty room, looked through the kitchen window into the backyard, but she wasn't there either. He went back into the hallway and knocked, against his better judgment, on the WC door.

He smiled: would she have had the same idea, the eternal peace-making elixir, and be up in the attic already? Who knows, maybe their telepathic signals had survived the storm. He bounded up the stairs and scanned the landing—the folding stairs had not been pulled down, he saw at once—but still looked, his mouth half open, up at the attic hatch. Shut tight. Of course. The copper-colored padlock glowered frostily at him. The house was empty. Through the bathroom window he could see that her bike, which had waited for her alongside the conifers since the wedding in Zaltbommel, was gone.

His arousal long dissipated, he crashed down the stairs. Since the vacuum cleaner bags lay on top, it took him a few minutes to find his note on the dining room table. Her handwriting under his own.

His reaction to what he read was atypical for him, for the situation, for his deeply rooted fear of losing her, but apparently not at all atypical in a pathological sense, because when he recalled his behavior to Haitink some months later, she nodded furiously, a pumpjack on the fields of his psyche. He described to her how his consciousness did not shrink into a small, hard ball of regret, as one might hope and assume, but expanded into a universe of rage and resentment. "*Fuck*!" he screamed, "Fucking hell! You *bitch*! You sick, snivelling little *bitch*!" He then spent several minutes tearing the cardboard packaging of the vacuum cleaner bags to shreds, slammed the bags against the corner of his dining room table, and then tore each of the bags individually to shreds. With sweat dripping from his skull, he seized the note from among the scraps of paper, wadded it up, and took it to the toilet. He pissed on it. Before he flushed he fished it back out of his urine ("Aaron," said Haitink, "try to ascertain for yourself just why you did that") and reread what she had written.

> *Aaron, I've got good news for you: I've just heard that Ennio is dead. Also, I'm glad you can get back in your house, because for the time being I have no intention of seeing you. Don't call. Joni.*

9

Now that it's finally a bit calmer on campus—the last exams of the academic year have been wrapped up, most of the staff have gone abroad, either in campers or airplanes; as he cycles to the administrative wing in the morning he finds Tubantia as in his nightmares: ready to be disbanded—Sigerius goes to The Hague to test the waters. He likes traveling first class. Seated at an out-of-the-way table in Café Dudok's back garden, he lunches with Frederik Olde Kannegieter, who has been at the Finance Department for the better part of the morning. They have managed to squeeze in an hour to discuss which way the wind blows, in Kannegieter's opinion, in the Cabinet deliberating Sigerius's appointment. They've known each other since Boston, where he had arranged for Kannegieter to teach a course on decision science. Many an afternoon was spent in his MIT office working together on an article on the "traveling salesman problem," a piece that, for reasons that now escape him, never came to fruition. Later, Kannegieter was rector in Groningen, board member at KPN, and was now in his fifth year as chairman of the Central Planning Office.

"Do it," he said a week ago over the telephone, when Sigerius told him he was in the running. "*Do it.*" And then the flattery: "They'd give their eye-teeth over at Education for a strong, competent minister, someone with a well-grounded vision, and at the same time a guy with balls, a leader." Sigerius was worried about the short-term nature of the post, two years, not even that: "What's a year and a half, Frederik?" But Kannegieter was having none of it, all politics was short-term, he said, there was no such thing as certainty. And the location: "Zoetermeer, Frederik, who the hell builds a ministry in Zoetermeer, of all places?" "Grab it," Kannegieter said. *You* always grab it, you old vulture, he thought. If Olde Kannegieter doesn't advise you to grab it, a week later he'll grab it himself.

Of course he has made himself available. He weighed up both scenarios: a hectic government life in the public eye, or in the shadows of a farmhouse on the fringe of a provincial university where his role would shortly be played out. Back to his own institute, or worse yet, a faculty post—he can't picture that. He considered America, he always considers America. Princeton's itching to have him, he could be a full professor, but he doesn't want to mess around with them: his mathematical acuity has dulled over the past ten years or so. Besides, he has to admit he's hooked on the idea of public office, and maybe on power itself.

Kruidenier, meanwhile, is tenacious, surviving one no-confidence vote after the other. Sigerius's intuition tells him that time is not on his side, which is why he pushed for this meeting with Kannegieter. Between bites of club sandwich they ask after each other's families, he fields questions about the situation in Enschede, and then gets to the point. "The problem is," Sigerius says slowly, "that the Prime Minister's got a candidate of his own. He never wanted Kruidenier in the first place, D66 shoved Kruidenier down his throat. The more time the PM gets, the more likely he'll make his own choice. Unless, perhaps . . . I was thinking . . . and that's why lunch is on me, Frederik—unless you exert a bit of your influence."

"And you think Wim will listen to me?" His friend has taken off his imposing glasses and polishes them with a jagged-edged yellow cloth.

"I do, in fact." Kannegieter is not only the Cabinet's official comptroller, the man who supplies the PM's office with facts and figures, but he is also a prominent PvdA member, a Labour Party ideologue who contributed to the recent manifesto and the guy who whispers in PM Wim Kok's ear when the masses need to be addressed with a worker's heart. If the PM is forced to backpedal on an issue, the party's thinktank is for Kannegieter only a bike ride away.

He inspects his glasses in the sunlight. "So do I," he says, "so do I." Mock vanity, sarcastic irony, even back in Boston it was his forte. Sigerius recalls a reception for a chemist who had won the Nobel Prize, they stood chatting with an American woman who could only talk about whether or not to dump some or other click fund; you guys are mathematicians, what do you think? I have advice, said Kannegieter, dead serious, but it would only apply to complex dollars in an infinite-dimensional Hilbert space.

They both looked in silence for a moment at a waiter whose orange apron was emblazoned with a flag of the Dutch lion sticking out of Dudok's façade.

"What time does the inquisition start tonight?" Kannegieter asks.

"Quarter to nine."

"Siem," he says, "let me put it another way. I spoke to Wim a few days ago, we talked a lot about you, he brought it up himself—and yes, doubts, doubts . . . he respects you as a scientist, believe me, and as an administrator too, only he's not sure where you stand politically. It's a gamble, of course." A bit of bacon flies out of Kannegieter's mouth, arcs across the table and lands on the edge of Sigerius's plate. "He asked, so I told him about our time in Boston, about our working relationship, about mathematics, naturally—but also about our friendship, Siem, the family outings, the kids' sleepovers. What it boils down to for him is: can he trust you? Don't worry about it too much."

The skies suddenly darken in Sigerius's head, as they have done so often the last few weeks. Kannegieter's sweet talk neither reassures nor gratifies him; rather, it makes him somber, latently aggressive; it doesn't interest him, inside him the little speech forms a syrupy pool of indifference, he has to actively resist his neurotransmitters to prevent himself from exploding. Friendship? He is infuriated by the largesse with which the word passes over Kannegieter's lips. They glance at each other. What's left of their "friendship"? Of their once so familiar and frequent association? How tight *were* they? Oh sure, they were like two peas in a pod when it came to the rarefied abstractions of their work; twice, three times a day they perched on each other's desks to discuss unital C*-algebras with a predual—What do you think, Fred, are they unique? Like a Banach space, I mean, or maybe always? Isomorphics excepted, etc. etc., for hours on end—and yes, *that* was good. But friendship? How often do we still talk, Kannegieter? *What do we know about each other?*

The man seated across from him expected a different response, he holds the right lens of his glasses between thumb and index finger, keeps rubbing just to hold a pose. What if he were to ask a *real* question. Just spit it out, boom, his real concern, his worst fear. What if he said: "Listen, Frederik, I'm worried that my daughter is prostituting herself on the Internet." His hands go clammy with the thought. Can't do it. Somewhere behind the hedge that separates them from the Binnenhof a car honks, they both look momentarily at the leafy wall.

"Thanks, Fred," he says distractedly. "I appreciate your putting in a good word for me."

After he's paid, they walk around the pond to the square where Kannegieter's chauffeur is eating an omelette at an outdoor café. The atmosphere has become awkward. They say goodbye.

• • •

He strolls through the windy Korte Houtstraat, kills a quarter of an hour flipping through bins of jazz albums in the Plaatboef. Does he even know what friendship is? The contacts he maintains: are these what you could call friendships? While he walks as slowly as possible to the Health Ministry, his mind pages through his address book. He might look like a collegial kind of guy, his contacts handed to him on a silver platter, but in fact he chooses sparring partners, competitors. The other as yardstick, a whetting stone.

He walks through an architecturally correct archway, crosses the ministry courtyard. "I'm an egotist," Menno once said en route to a tournament in Düsseldorf, "and you are too, Siem. We're loners, our kind, friendless in a way."

At the reception desk of the enormous redbrick building he's given a badge. He takes the elevator to the fifth floor and steps out into a corridor paneled in light veneer. He attends some ten hours of meetings a week. But talk? Who with, for God's sake? He stands in front of one of the tall windows and stares at the steep gables of the main towers until it is two o'clock on the dot.

The vice-premier's bright office has the same wood paneling, her glass-topped desk is half the size of his own in Twente. She receives him cordially, with a trace of inattentiveness he regards as typical for those at the top. They know each other from the obligatory hand-shaking at party congresses; her job is to massage the Cabinet, and Kok in particular, into accepting his nomination. The interview goes well, they talk for nearly two hours, she is "delighted" with his motivation and compliments him on his articles on higher education. "We can't afford any more inopportune appointments," she says. They discuss the tricky dossiers, he mentions his own views, her intelligent female voice lists the potential stumbling blocks. Every so often he sticks his left hand into his pants pocket and rasps his thumb over the sharp teeth of the key.

Groups of singing football supporters swarm The Hague Central Station; he has to run to catch the 4:06 train. When he alights in Enschede two and a half hours later, he goes to a phone booth and dials the number of Aaron's house. He lets it ring until he hears a busy signal. Then he calls Tineke on his cell phone. "Still at The Hague Station," he says. "I'll just come and watch the match at home."

"Great," she says with her dependable, pleasant voice, "Janis'll like that. How'd it go?"

"Useful. Frederik sends his regards. He's really done his best."

"Shall I save you some dinner?"

"Please. OK, got to board now."

"Have a good trip, dear."

He leaves the station, in front of the Bruna newsstand a kid with curly wet hair and an overnight bag nods at him, he smiles back, always smile back, and decides to take a taxi.

He clears his throat. "Vluchtestraat."

The Mercedes glides through the orange-bedecked streets like a stingray. Children have painted the wooden partitions. Dark red-brick row houses that retain the day's heat, open windows with screens. Nightfall is hours away. The street Joni and Aaron drove off from five days ago, the car fully packed, is festooned with orange banners, flags, balloons—as though the explosion never happened. Enschede is a salamander that's lost its tail.

He has the driver stop at the end of the street, pays him, and removes the key from his pocket before he gets out. He takes a deep breath and, without lingering, walks along the quiet Vluchtestraat, past a sort of nurses' residence, then crosses diagonally and cuts into the short path leading to Aaron's front door. If he rings the bell, just for show, the neighbors might hear. No, this needs to be done like a Band-Aid: rip it off in one quick jerk. Holding his breath, he inserts the virgin steel into the lock. It refuses. He jiggles it back and forth, softly, his fingers become moist.

During their last week at the farmhouse Aaron showed up with a brand-new key, and while Sigerius listened to his story—the city had replaced the locks on all the doors they'd had to force open—he registered precisely where Aaron put it: on the key ring in the pocket of his summer jacket, a corduroy blazer he hung neatly on a hanger in the front hall closet. He was the last one in the living room that night. While the rest of the house slept, he smuggled the keys out of Aaron's pocket and took them to the bathroom, where he wrestled the only one that looked like an unused house key off the ring. The next day his secretary had it copied at a Mister Minit.

The wrong one? A superstitious person would see the hand of Fate at work. (*You're making a mistake, go home, forget everything.*) He wipes his hands on his trousers and looks around. *Never look around.* On the second attempt the lock glides open.

He steps inside and closes the door softly behind him. It is a full minute before he can hear the silence above his own heart. A vague animal smell penetrates his nostrils. He exhales and considers locking the door. A neighbor who waltzes in and starts filling a watering can. He rehearses his reaction: insurance papers, my son-in-law phoned from his vacation address, a fender-bender, I'm just busy upstairs.

A small stack of dish towels lies on the white-painted steps, a pair of running shoes on the next step up. That is where he must go, upstairs, but first, just to be sure, he opens the door to the living room.

It is cramped and dusty, he feels clumsy, as though he'll knock things over. On the coffee table, around which they congregate once a year for a slice of birthday *vlaai*, lies a pair of badminton rackets and a container of birdies. Opposite the TV, a stylish sofa with soft purple upholstery, matching armchairs, two pillar-shaped speakers he and Aaron bought together in Münster, an old Dual turntable and next to it a stack of jazz LPs he recognizes as his. The fascinating wall of books coaxes a smile out of him, but it is a nervous smile. Out of the corner of his eye, to the left, he notices a large, dark rectangle with glowing edges: the curtains to the backyard are drawn. Something starts humming resonantly. The fridge? The curtains on the street side are open, unfortunately; a Moroccan woman pushing a baby stroller along the sidewalk glances at him as she passes. Always smile and wave. Behind her, a low apartment block; beyond that, the provisional fence around Roombeek. His heart bulges: someone comes crashing down a flight of stairs, thud, a door clicks shut—the next-door neighbor? Stay calm. France is a long way away. You whisked them neatly out of the country.

Here, take 1,500 guilders and beat it. Relax, enjoy. Talk things out. He walks into the kitchenette and picks up a glass from the counter, fills it from the tap, and drains it sloppily. It was an emergency measure, he would rather have bided his time. An opportunity to use the key would present itself sooner or later, those two were always jaunting off on some vacation or another, it made you wonder where they got the money. But then Tineke told him the relationship was on the rocks. Serious trouble. Hanging by a thread. Tineke had gone to Ennio's funeral, a depressing, poorly attended affair; she had expected to see Joni and Aaron together, but their daughter was there alone. Afterward, in the chapel, she told her mother about the argument with Aaron, and expressed her misgivings about their future.

That made everything a sight more complicated. They wouldn't be going on vacation anytime soon, maybe never. And he couldn't very well break into the house of his daughter's ex . . . The previous week, their last training in the dusty gym: five minutes before they were to start it occurred to him that Aaron might not show up. But he did, after all. Let him bring it up, he thought. They laid out the mats, thwap, chatted about the upcoming European Cup, warmed up in silence, practiced groundwork, and went through *katas*—and all that time, not a word. "Aaron"—he eventually got the ball rolling himself—"what do you think, will you and Joni patch things up?"

"Have you spoken to her then?" They stood there arranging their suits, the bald beanpole with his black belt between his chin and chest.

"Have *you* spoken to her?"

"No. I'm not allowed to phone. And you know Joni." *I know Joni? Don't make me laugh.* "It's awful, Siem."

Another silence. Aaron seemed to hesitate, and then told him she was going to see Wilbert. He had dragged that out of her during their last argument. "But Siem, please," he said with a voice like an old dishrag, "you didn't hear it from me." While recovering from this piece of news Sigerius noticed how emaciated Aaron looked, instead of flushed from exertion he was as gray as an egg carton. His skin could peel off his skull any minute and crumple to the mat like a burlap bag. "I really hope we can work it out, Siem. I've never told anyone, but from day one I've seen Joni as the mother of my children."

He nodded. Let's kill two birds with one stone. With a bit of luck he could derail that meeting. Start by putting it off, and work your way toward *call*ing it off. "Aw geez, Aaron," he smarmed with the kind of duplicity he usually reserved for his deans, "I wish there was something I could do. What I'm going to say to you now, I'll say to Joni too, I promise. You two belong together. What you've just told me, it's serious stuff. I don't want you both chucking it all away. Everything's been thrown off-kilter these last few weeks, for everyone in Enschede and for you and Joni too. I think you two should take a vacation. Together. On me. And as soon as possible."

"Wow, Siem, you mean that?" he said, his lower lip trembling. "That means a lot to me."

The kid almost cracked, and he noticed that he enjoyed it. He accepted Aaron's gratitude with a fatherly smile, but in their last bout he totally smoked him up. They always were fanatical, sparring seriously at the end of each training session—but this time he smelled blood. Grab him, reverse, grappling from the left to confuse him, high on his collar, his rigid wrist against Aaron's hot, resistant neck. When they first started training, Sigerius could beat him literally single-handedly, he swept the mat with that gangly body, the empty gym echoed deliciously with the thuds. But as Aaron got used to his style, caught on to his tricks, his weaponry, he began to lose his edge; Aaron became fitter, started moving better, the twenty-five-year age difference started to show. (He recalled that time Joni came to watch them train. Up until their final match she stretched out, smiling and making faces, on the long, low bench under the wall racks, but by the time he and Aaron let go of each other a quarter of an hour later, she had bolted. She was already up in the gym's canteen, beaming pompously and sipping a Diet Coke through a straw. "What a stupid sport," she pronounced from her bar stool. "I had to either leave, or jump in and separate you two." You haven't seen *anything*, he thought.)

He was unleashed. Something from long ago had been roused, his killer instinct. Aaron kindled his bloodthirstiness. A hostility flowed through him that he had seldom felt since 1972. The mat was larger than the competition mats in the Nippon Budokan; he dragged the kid back and forth across the endless canvas, pulled him down, swept his legs out from under him, middling results, the bastard fought back hard, but he cornered him, tried to tear him down. They wrestled with their free arms, the kicks to the inside of Aaron's ankles were mean and hard, several times he pulled the jacket up over the sweaty head. *I'll nail you, you little pimp.* Grab, shake loose, grab again, drag—and *now* move in, *uchi mata,* he flung his leg between Aaron's legs, tense it, the kid lay on his hip, skip, pull through, hard—no, back, and now, again. Yeah, now. The short-long floating, for a moment only his big toe touched the mat, Aaron flew, weighed nothing, *there, bam,* smack against the ground. *Ippon.* The smell of the dust that he'd beat out of the mat with his prey. That's how he had floored Kiknadze, that's how he made mincemeat of Maejima. Sigerius skipped farther on one leg, his good leg, the longer one, looking up at the ceiling he traced a celebratory semicircle.

"Come on, man, get up."

He goes back into the hall. Taking large, careful steps, he climbs the stairs; the air gets thinner with each step. He is serving the truth. The landing presents four gray doors. Dull secondhand daylight seeps through the frosted glass at the top of the doorframes. He was up here once before, years ago, for the obligatory house tour. One of the doors is ajar, a green laundry rack hangs over its top edge; at the front, T-shirts, boxers, two pairs of jeans—nothing of Joni's. Way at the back, a judo suit, *his* judo suit, the one he'd lent him. An unexpected wave of warmth flows through him, a reservoir of familial compassion. What the hell is he doing here? He wants that feeling back, he wants at least to revert to how it felt *before* all this mess.

Don't go all soft, not now. The bedroom. He hastily inspects the stripped double mattress; underneath, curls of dust, a wadded-up T-shirt, an earplug. Behind the cupboard doors: men's clothes straight from the spin cycle, complete chaos, he reaches around behind the piles. Nothing. On the bedside table, books, more earplugs and a nearly empty strip of pills: temazepam, he reads. When he turns around he stands face-to-face with himself in a full-length mirror; the light-gray linen of his summer suit is wrinkled from the train trip, his mustache is brushy, like a third eyebrow. Does he always look so . . . deathly? A nobody disguised as someone with a paying job, his persistent five o'clock shadow, the black, deep-set eyes milky and bloodshot from stress. Who does he look like? With a shock he realizes: like Wilbert, he's got the same look Wilbert had after three weeks in jail. What would his son look like now, after six years in the slammer?

He goes back out onto the landing, glances into the bathroom at the back; mold is growing on the ceiling above the shower cubicle, the washing machine door is open, he roots around in the plastic laundry basket behind the door: towels, washcloths, and again: men's clothes. On the plastic shelf above the yellowish washbasin is a square bottle of aftershave; without thinking he walks over, pulls off the cap and sprays some on his neck, a heavy, vaguely familiar scent.

Only now does it occur to him that most of the photos were taken in an attic, under a sloping roof. Back on the landing, he looks up at the ceiling for the first time: a brown hatch, secured with a copper-colored padlock. A short cord is attached to a metal ring in the wood, he can just reach it. Two rectangular indentations in the carpeting betray the footprints of a folding stair. You shove the stairs upward, and hey presto, no one thinks twice about a little old attic.

And now?

He searches agitatedly for the key. First he rummages through the bedside table drawers. Stacks of train tickets, business cards, magazines, ballpoint pens, yellowed newspaper supplements, pill strips, pill boxes, half-chewed loose pills, an open bottle of Bokma jenever in the one drawer; in the other, nothing but a hot-water bottle and two Singapore Airlines sleeping masks he'd kept for Joni. He picks up the books, reinspects all the cupboard shelves, in vain; walks downstairs, fishes out anything that feels hard from the jackets on the hallway coatrack, sifts through four chaotic kitchen drawers under the garlicky-smelling metal countertop, opens all the cabinets, feels, gropes, looks—and discovers, between a tin of cinnamon and a two-pound bag of salt, a key.

His heart bounces ahead of him up the stairs. He drags a wooden chair from a small utility room with an ironing board and a mountain of wrinkled washing and stands on it. A stab of pain shoots through his shorter leg. The key is too big. "Goddamn." He climbs down off the chair, picks it up by one of the armrests, and slams it against the floor. One of the legs breaks off in splinters. Panting with rage, he pushes his face into the washing on the rack. The fresh scent of laundry soap flows into his nose. *Calm down.* He grabs his judo suit and bites into the washed-out collar.

That aggression. The situation makes him angrier and more unrestrained than he considers acceptable. All his life he's been proud of his ability to channel his anger—and now he smashes an innocent, defenseless piece of furniture? Control over your inner current—he'd learned that from Geesink. Exploding at just the right moment is just as tricky as *not* exploding. Deciding for yourself when you call upon that intoxicating mixture of concentration and volatility, and *when* you decide to call upon it, you attach the battery cables to your muscles at once, you feed the day-in-day-out judo mentality with pure aggression, no more reflection, no neocortex: volt and ampere, let the flow of electrons do the work. He preserves crystal-clear memories of the first time he detonated at just the right moment—it must have been in '62—and, like it or not, he's transported back to that smallish gym above an automotive garage on the Jansveld in downtown Utrecht. Geesink was already world champion, he was still doing military service, nineteen and green; green and gullible, just like now.

He'd only been practicing judo in Utrecht for six months when one evening three guys from Tun-Yen, a club from Amsterdam, showed up. He knew they were a strong bunch, but what made this unannounced visit spectacular was that Jon Bluming was a Tun-Yen member. That Bluming, nowhere to be seen, but you heard about him all the more: ever since Geesink had turned the judo world upside down in Paris, Bluming strutted around openly challenging the brand-new world champ. Every chance he got, he ranted that he would chew Geesink up and spit him out: "I'll fold him up like a lawn chair." He was quoted in *Panorama* as saying that Geesink wasn't the best in the world, in Japan he knew plenty of judokas who turned up their nose at tournaments where Europeans took part, and Bluming claimed to have taught every last one of them a lesson. Geesink just let Bluming shoot off his mouth. It didn't faze him.

But he, Sigerius—*he* was burned up. It insulted him. He took Bluming's bluster personally. For him it was an honor to stand on Geesink's straw mats; for him and for the rest of humanity Geesink was a judo god, a hero, a leader. When he lay mangled on his cot in the Kromhout barracks after an evening at the Jansveld gym, he thanked the good Lord he could train with Anton

Geesink. It was *awesome*—the most fantastic judokas inhabited that upstairs gym, every one of them technical and explosive. You had Pierre Zenden, you had Joop Mackaay, and of course Menno Wijn. The Snijders brothers, identical twins from his battalion, they had to move heaven and earth to be given leave four times a week to go to that dojo together. It was amazing. He had recently watched Geesink capture the world title in Paris, from the bleachers; he still lived at his father's place in Delft. He and a few of the guys from the club drove to Paris in a Renault Dauphine, bought tickets like everybody else for the Stade de Coubertin and cheered the towering Hollander as he beat one Jap after another; and now, hardly a year later, this same ace stood there advising him on how to improve his shoulder throw, gave pointers on honing his left-handed techniques, said it was time he became a real man and bought some barbells. "So you're from Delft?" Geesink asked with that deep, sluggish voice of his. "Good. Next time you're on leave you can come by bike, Simon, not by train. For years I cycled to Antwerp every month. Trained with Strulens. Cycling is good."

Sometimes, as he drifted off to sleep at night, his head resting on a straw-filled pillow, he let Geesink loose on that animal Bluming, and of course in his fantasy Geesink beat the bejesus out of Bluming four out of five times, but the last round was often a painfully different story, then he saw how Bluming chastened his hero, mercilessly dragged the world champion across the mat, for he still wasn't entirely sure; Bluming, as the story goes, was no sissy, he carried bullet wounds from the Korean war, he claimed to be not only fifth dan in judo but also a black belt in Asian martial arts they can't even pronounce here without stuttering.

But here they were in their locker room, three burly Amsterdammers, Rinus Elzer, somebody named Hoek, and a grinning blond bear with a torso they'd dug up in Rome with a shovel—was that Bluming? Smaller but more muscular than he had imagined, younger too. No one spoke. They were more than welcome, of course, Geesink was gentlemanly and hospitable, he received them like a real champ; he was visibly delighted, Geesink was always thrilled about strangers' muscles, that's the only way you got better, *that's* why he went to Japan so often, to sink his teeth into all that unfamiliar meat.

The Amsterdammers took part in the *randori* (Geesink skipped the free practice), balcony doors open, sparring in the fresh air, rotating every five minutes, and they weren't bad at all, that was clear. Menno had taken a moderate beating from that Elzer, and even before Geesink had laid a hand on any of those guys, Sigerius found himself face-to-face with that canary-yellow statue. "Teach that Bluming a lesson, will you?" Menno whispered in one ear.

It was strange, of course he knew all along that the blond guy was the enemy, you just know, but now that he was certain he was no longer scared, but something else, something in his heartbeat and muscle tension changed, and in his head too. So you think you can go around badmouthing Geesink? His arms, his chest, his calves filled themselves with sympathetic rage, and on behalf of his sensei, on behalf of the world champion who tolerated his presence and took the trouble to improve him, he took hold of Bluming. Square and compact, grounded like a dolmen, that's the sign of a real judoka, a real judoka weighs 400 kilos, his feet take root in the mat and grow outward for meters—and this was one of them. At once stiff and supple, Bluming conducted him around the room, and the first flash was a low shoulder throw, he landed hard on his shoulder, but he responded to Bluming's second attempt with a throaty yell—he'd been practicing it the past few months, a series of takeovers, the timing of his throws—and the power with which he threw his rival backward and dragged him a couple of meters across the straw-filled mat attracted the other men's attention. They watched. The subsequent points were his, a raw Siem Sigerius emerged, he tore into Bluming, he attacked with a venom that would become the foundation of his judo career, and perhaps his entire *life.* For minute upon minute he flung the hollow braggart every which way, *osotogari, tai otoshi,* to take hold of him; there lay the great martial arts king, and once on the ground he squeezed Bluming's slanderous throat shut.

Only later that evening—after the three visitors had hotfooted it home, after Geesink had repeated his punishment drill for good measure, but only the light version—when he cycled back to the barracks with Jan and Peter Snijders, glowing with satisfaction, did he hear that the Amsterdammer with the straw-colored hair wasn't Jon Bluming at all. Say what? "Don't let Wijn kid you, Sigerius," said Jan Snijders. "The blond guy you're talking about is much younger than Bluming, name's Ruska. Willem Ruska."

It's a quarter to eight, he's got to get back to campus before eight-thirty. He returns the ruined chair to the utility room, pushing the leg a bit into the splintery wound. The only place left is the study, the room facing the street, maybe he'll find that key after all. The poorly laid wood floor glows pale brown in the sunlight, it looks to him like a simple floor base, it's not tiled or carpeted. The room is a sauna, sweat oozes from his pores, he feels the heat in his shoes. On the wall opposite the window, his family looks at him through non-reflective glass: the portraits Aaron took for their twentieth anniversary. In the middle of the room is a mattress with rumpled bedclothes, there are two cheap bookshelves filled with academic books: *Sentence Analysis, Child Language Development,* a poetry handbook. He sees binders of *Tubantia Weeklys*, a meter of *Willy & Wanda* comics. In the right-hand corner, halfway under the window, a desk, bare wood on aluminum legs. There's a PC on it. He keeps looking outside, the street is empty. He sits down on the gray plastic desk chair and pulls open drawers, one of them is locked, the others are stuffed with bank statements, business correspondence, old birthday cards. He takes a few random samples. Uninteresting. No key.

A bulletin board above the desktop is thumbtacked full of newspaper clippings, cartoons, postcards, baby announcements, and photographs: Aaron with his parents and a formal-looking boy that vaguely resembles him, a strip of passport photos of Joni. He then digs doggedly in the plastic stacking boxes on the corner of the desk. Warranty receipts, a phone company contract, bills to the *Weekly*, a magazine missing its cover. A glossy blue cardboard folder, a brochure, in the middle bin catches his eye. He takes it out, "Palmer Johnson," it announces, "the most desirable luxury high-performance yachts in the world." The aerial photo on the cover shows a streamlined yacht cutting through the dark ocean, the metallic blue bow trailing a train of snow-white foam; the lounge sofas on the roof and rear decks are antique pink. Only when he realizes that the little pink postage stamp on the aerodynamic foredeck—the ship seems to be nothing but bow—is in fact a swimming pool, do the proportions fall into place.

He leans back and thumbs through the folder. On top are two loose photos on regular photographic paper, one of them is apparently the same ship as on the cover, anchored among similarly macho yachts in a sunny harbor, the other probably taken from the deck, out at sea, a coastline in the distance, no people. In the brochure itself: horizontal and vertical cross-sections, technical specifications, pictures of the innards: a living room bigger than the one downstairs; glossy, curved, built-in amenities; recessed lighting; a bedroom with the looks of a five-star hotel suite. At the back he finds a receipt from Port Privé de Sainte-Maxime. In barely legible handwriting there are two dates and a name. "Barbara . . . ," and something short after it, a brusque "A" and two "w"s. And a "Monsieur Bever"—does it really say that?—who agrees to the sum of 12,779.75 French francs.

He stares at the boat on the cover for a moment, then takes a pen from a holder full of pencils and shavings and paper clips, and jots down the name of the manufacturer and the model number on the back of the receipt, which he then folds up and slides into his wallet.

Why would Aaron rent a thing like that? It's one of the questions that plagues him at home while he watches the soccer game, pillows propped behind his back. Holland is slaughtering the Danes, and he cheers each goal right on time along with his daughter, but he's not really there, he needs to know about that boat. After the match Janis decides at the last minute to return to her room in Deventer, Tineke offers to take her to the station, and, as soon as he sees the Audi drive past the living-room picture window, he goes upstairs to his study and switches on his laptop. It's too late to phone that marina in Sainte-Maxime, so he goes to the manufacturer's website, and what he sees only fuels his anxiety. He is no boat expert, but he doesn't need to be, even a Swiss bumpkin could see that this is the top of the line. Palmer Johnson's website oozes exclusivity. His heartbeat accelerating, he looks over the boats, the interiors, specifications. The "sport yacht" in the brochure is relatively small, just twenty meters long, and apparently there were only three of them made, the last one in 1997. His eyes nearly devour the monitor, but nowhere does he see how much the yacht costs, apparently Palmer Johnson considers itself too classy for a price list. He opens Google and types in the model number and "price" in the search field. He lands on a website in North Miami Beach that doesn't sell yachts, but rents them. During low season you can sail along the Florida coast for $110,000 in a PJ 115 Sport Yacht, in peak season you'll shell out $130,000. Per week.

10

Your child is your most precious possession. And a focused, expert touch can ensure memorable class photos. Aaron Bever School Photography has been successfully serving the Brussels area since 2002.

A well-organized approach is the key to making "picture day" a happy experience for your child. Aaron Bever identifies with the world of children and creates a child-friendly atmosphere, capturing them at their most natural and relaxed. He always finds a suitable location for group photos.

Today's school pictures are tomorrow's cherished memories!

The site sagged under children seated at classroom desks, children clasping toys, children in steel pedal cars that brought back memories of my own primary school days. The kiddies' pal himself was nowhere to be seen. On a separate page he offered his services as a restorer of antique black-and-white pictures. ("Aaron Bever employs the most up-to-date apparatus and techniques in photographic restoration. The difference is in the details!") In the sample photograph I recognized the half-disintegrated wedding portrait of his grandparents, a time-worn, warped, and water-pocked piece of paper that he kept propped on his bookshelf and with the slightest puff of breeze fluttered to the floor like an autumn leaf. Alongside it the spruced-up, spotless version. I looked at his grandmother's awkwardly fitting wartime dress. The hairline of the young man who had been his grandfather was already receding, but even in his Venlo nursing home he wasn't as bald as his grandson.

My own head was still heavy from yesterday. After work about thirty of us boarded three Chrysler vans that took us from Coldwater to the Gold Digger, Rusty's favorite hotel bar in downtown L.A. He treated, said we had to celebrate the Barracks deal. Earlier that day Rusty, Debra from Personnel, and I had already been to see a renowned interior architect on South Hope Street, offices on every continent. This was just the ticket, Rusty said, these guys (who turned out to be two women and one man) had done Amazon.com, Deutsche Bank, a complete make-over of the Sheraton, they're the tops, he guaranteed they'll be purring once they saw the Barracks. If we're gonna go bankrupt, Joy, then let's do it in style. But he'd rather end up in *Fortune*'s 100 Best Companies to Work For, did I get his drift? That list was an obsession from his Goldman Sachs days, and although I cautiously prepared him for a letdown—I couldn't imagine a firm like this wanting to take us on—they actually warmed to our proposal, and after that Rusty was unstoppable. That evening, in the Japanese restaurant where we all sat around one of those teppanyaki tables, he launched into a slightly boozy State of the Union address, a discourse on corporate identity, the revolutionary "open plan" office interiors, the "cool" titanium scooters we would glide up and down the long hallways on. He managed to get all of us into the Digger before midnight, where we stood on the hip rooftop bar until the wee hours catching cold. It was already light when the van dropped me off on Sunset Boulevard.

I washed down two Tylenol with a gulp of coffee and reflected on Aaron. What kind of life did he lead in that Belgian hick town? The thought of him at those primary schools pained me in a complicated way. I wondered if I had any right to feel like that. Looking at the goofy website, I realized that someone who didn't know better would think he had found his niche. But this wasn't the Aaron I knew; if I had predicted this future to the old Aaron—putzing around primary schools, *Belgian* primary schools, in a minivan—then he wouldn't have even scoffed at me, he'd have begged me to put him out of his misery then and there.

I straightened my shoulders. This meticulously maintained website aroused latent feelings of guilt in me, even more than those creepy e-mails of his. The suspicion that I had tricked him into starting that sex site (like the accusations against Colin Powell and Tony Blair) reared its head again. The same old reflex: it was all my fault. I inhaled hard through my nose. I had sealed our fate just at the moment I wanted to be rid of him—that kind of agonizing. For a brief moment I was back on the Vluchtestraat, sitting across the breakfast table from him, that morning long ago when I put his head on the chopping block. We had been taking pictures for months, just for the fun of it—so I said, and so he believed—and it was then that I laid my plan on him. We'd had a degrading night; in the middle of it I woke with a shock to a terrible scream, a curse, and saw Aaron cowering on the chair in the corner where I had draped my clothes a few hours earlier. He was crying. On the floor all around him: a notebook, ripped to shreds, that I immediately recognized as a school notebook we'd already argued about interminably. Since I was thirteen I had kept a kiss list on the two glossy inside covers, a chronological inventory of all the boys I had at least made out with, date, age, first name, location, eye color, hair color, hair *length*, God knows what else. In all there were more than 100 names, a number Aaron called "astronomical," and he accused me of being an "astronomical slut," he kept going on about that stupid list, and why were there two girls' names on it? ("Why do you think?")

I had long since stopped being amused by his jealous whining, and actually I had decided to dump him weeks earlier—just beat it, go jump in the lake—but when I saw him sitting there surrounded by shreds and wads of paper, I was struck by the powerful emotions I had released in him. I knew I had a certain sexual clout, I was aware of my effect on men, but this? He was in my power. This guy would not only never leave me, but he would also do anything necessary to *keep* me. That's why I didn't break up with him that morning, but instead, between two bites of toast, said there was something I had to tell him. "I'm going to start a sex site," I said. "You know, on the Internet." I still remember his jaw dropping open, I could see the glop of half-chewed bread and aged cheese on his tongue. "Preferably with you, of course," I said to reassure him.

There were voices in the hallway; Rusty was showing his guests out, I heard them talking as they clattered down the stairs. Once it was totally quiet again I clicked on a button called "Backgrounds," half expecting to read about how Aaron had ended up in the exciting and fulfilling world of school photography, but I was wrong, it was a page of background patterns for behind the portraits: solid light blue, soft pink roses, speckled pastel tints, "or why not try something completely different: linen! For that special effect, Aaron Bever will print your son's or daughter's portrait on a genuine linen canvas, so your school picture will resemble a freshly made oil painting."

• • •

The *children* . . . A thought so painful that I clapped my hand over my mouth, it slid into my consciousness, filled it—of course he hadn't just randomly chosen this profession, these kids were the whole point. Going through his e-mails in my head, I knew for sure he was childless. For a man in his late thirties this was not earthshaking, but I knew that Aaron had a deep-seated and lifelong yearning for children. With his illness, the schizophrenia from which he surely suffered, it seemed unlikely to me that he'd ever find a woman who would dare get pregnant by him. It wasn't rheumatism or allergies—as far as I could tell he was halfway to hell. I knew something of the progressive misery that plagued him. (Rusty, of all people, had told me the story of a schizophrenic man in the apartment below his, back in his start-up days in Redondo Beach. Rusty called him "The Voice," and he wasn't referring to Frank Sinatra either, although the downstairs neighbor was famous for his timing and phrasing: for two years the guy opened his throat, at random times [but always at night], bellowing surreal texts at the top of his lungs; sometimes it was a song, "Black Betty" by Ram Jam, or an AC/DC number, but mostly he yelled the same mantra over and over at stadium-filling volume, something Rusty would perform with a grin, relieved that this period of his life was over: "BIIIIIIILLLL!!! You hear me, *BILLLLL?!* You owe me one point two FUCKIN!!! BILLION!!! DOLLARS!!!, *BIIIILLLLL!!!!*" For hours on end, half the night, without a break, without Clinton ever coughing up the dough. Rusty called 911 a few times and pointed the receiver at the floor, to which the dispatcher asked why he had invited the man—a regular at the Redondo Beach mental health services—into his apartment. It was not a disease to snag girls with. Nor to start a family with.)

"I want children." It was one of the first things Aaron confided in me. If I'm not mistaken it was the first time we met, a curious conversation we had in the snow in front of the Technical Management Studies building; a camera hung around his neck, a flat woolen cap on his head—I knew about his ambitions to have a large family before I even knew he was bald. Still, I only grasped how serious he was when I dumped him four years later. "Do you know what Aaron told me?" my father asked just before we left on that last vacation. "That he wants you to be the mother of his children."

That was sneaky of him—I still remember thinking that. Sly old fox. We had hardly spoken to each other for two weeks, and there he was, Siem the couples counselor, armed with an excuse to break the silence. Brooding over life without Aaron, I walked into our big student-house kitchen, and two pancake-frying housemates pointed upstairs: "Your dad's up in your room." And what do you know, there sat Mr. University President in his shirtsleeves, his silk tie draped over the back of my desk chair, drinking green tea from a plastic milk cup. "I thought I'd just wait here for you, hope you don't mind?"

He started by being nice about Ennio, was I able to sleep, he'd heard from Mom how upset I was, he was proud of me, so much empathy. Pause. Here comes Wilbert, I thought. Go on, lemme have it. I resolved to say absolutely nothing about the nerve-racking telephone conversation I'd had with Wilbert. (He came across as completely uninterested, his mutinous voice lower than usual, but no less malicious, and still as hard as nails. "If I ask if you guys are still alive," he said, "it doesn't mean actually I hope so." "You living somewhere now?" I asked, tongue-tied. "How about you?" he shot back, "you living somewhere? Why don't you come around, you can see where I live." In between sentences he made strange slurping noises. By the time I hung up I was exhausted, done in, drenched in sweat.)

But my father didn't start in about Wilbert. "Joni," he said, "do you want to tell me what's going on with you and Aaron?" He had heard the "awful news" from my mother as well, and he wasn't really surprised, he'd seen us together close-up, and he was the last one to underestimate the effects of a disaster like the fireworks accident, everything was intertwined, but, he said in closing: you couldn't, under these circumstances, make decisions about a relationship. He wanted us to take a vacation together. "I'll pay."

"Get lost, Dad," I said. "Butt out, will you. Leave me alone. You don't know what you're saying. I'm finished with that guy."

He got up, shook his head, picked up his tie. "Come with me," he said. "Let's go grab a bite at De Beijaard."

We got up early because of the heat, and left our rented Corsica villa at eight in the morning. Crossing the maquis via narrow, jagged paths we hiked inland, picking lemons and kiwis along the way. As the coast retreated we started getting sunburned, the heat was merciless on that island, and although we trudged mostly in silence, sometimes we suddenly had a serious talk, as often happens on vacation. My father's intervention seemed to work. We talked a lot about him, and we realized full well that without him we wouldn't be on Corsica right now, without Siem we'd probably have called it quits. We agreed that he deserved credit for putting out the fire.

But then, in those Corsican woods, we smelled *real* fire. Aaron had read somewhere that in the summer the *libeccio*, a sultry southwesterly wind, was at its most persistent, more treacherous than the mistral. Among the tall pine trees and cork oaks we heard the brief thunder of galloping swine, the weightless rustle of mountain goats—animals you otherwise never saw—and before long we could see the fire, an orange fury that sucked away our oxygen, and we heard the sizzling and crackling. Making a dash back to the coast, laughing and looking over our shoulders, at times skidding to the ground, abandoning the bag with lemons and kiwis on the way—a waste, I thought as we clambered up the hill alongside the villa. So there I stood in my bikini, peering into the distance at the black ring of smoke surrounding the wooded hills, hand in hand with the guy who, on the way here, I had hated with a passion.

He had picked me up on Saturday morning, after more than a week of no contact. God, how I hated him then. Aaron being "dry" as usual, our first stop was the Central Pharmacy on the Beltstraat. He ran inside with one of the refill prescriptions a doctor friend of his had artfully photocopied; meanwhile, I scooted over to the driver's side of the double-parked Alfa. When he slid into the passenger seat, a satisfied grin on his face, I snarled at him that he was a junkie, always upping his intake of sleeping pills, and then always *bigger* pills, a pill like a Christmas tree with a drip-tube next to Aaron's bed, and after that a pill like a church steeple that stuck out above Aaron's street. I charged out of Enschede toward Maastricht, intentionally reckless and belligerent, hanging over the wheel like a jaw surgeon, I braked late and aggressively, tailgated every car I could. If Aaron turned the air conditioning up a notch, I turned it back down a notch. We hobbled over the potholed Belgian roads in silence, my rancor filling the car like mustard gas. Outside, industrial parks coughed noxious rubber clouds into the June skies, the asphalt cracked under our wheels. We loathed each other. Just to punish him I avoided the toll roads, lurched at 90 kph over the parched provincial asphalt—the result being that we ended up in some shitty little pitch-black town and slept in separate shitty hotel beds in a shitty fleabag hotel. The next day we drove the rest of the way to Sainte-Maxime in one surly sigh; the *Barbara Ann* lay in the gleaming marina, wagging its tail like a dog that knows full well something is up with its owners. We navigated out of the harbor, followed the coastline along Cannes, Antibes, Monaco, and brusquely cast anchor at San Remo, where we ate pizza with long faces and refueled.

Once we reached the open sea things relaxed a bit. Aaron realized it was up to him to start. I eyed him through my sunglasses from the foredeck's Jacuzzi, he stood holding the cherrywood rudder that was actually meant for a sailboat, but that I had instructed the Palmer Johnson builders to put in anyway. "How was Ennio's funeral?" he shouted; I pretended not to hear. Five minutes later I got out of the tub, balanced my way around the helm and through the sloping salon, changed into another bikini in the bedroom and climbed back up on deck. "It sucked, of course," I shouted in his ear.

When he offered his condolences an hour later, I let rip. I raged about how much he pissed me off, his jealousy, his oafishness, his inane behavior—yeah, yeah, he understood that. And just to test whether he really meant it I told him I could start at McKinsey in Silicon Valley in August. "Did that Stol call you?" Aaron asked. I answered that just before we left I'd gone horseback riding with Boudewijn, and Brigitte of course, I quickly added, and because he reacted to that piece of news more maturely than I had expected, I went to the salon and brought out a bottle of white wine.

"So how'd it go with good old Bo?"

"That rhymes."

"Yup."

To spare him the details I made a point of the strange atmosphere in the dunes. It was weird. I'd caught an early train and taken a taxi to Black Beauty stables. After a mozzarella and tomato bread roll at the bar, the three of us rode to the coast. Boudewijn proved to be a far worse rider than Brigitte and myself: we lost him during a vigorous, spontaneous gallop along Scheveningen beach, and after ten minutes' wait, still no Boudewijn. "He'll be OK," Brigitte said. When we got back to the stable in the early evening, we heard that he'd returned his mare hours earlier. The man who hosed down our horses said that "Mister Boudewijn" was thrown off his horse while scaling the dunes and had twisted his ankle, if not worse.

Aaron laughed for the first time all week. "But instead of jumping straight into her Aston Martin," I said, "or at least calling home, Brigitte offered me a complete tour of the stables." More than an hour later, in the car, she suddenly gave me a worried look. "I wonder how he got home?" The couple lived in a gray cement villa that was like a jukebox museum on the inside. "Haven't you started dinner yet?" Brigitte asked when we entered the sparse, low-ceilinged living room and found Boudewijn with an ice pack on his ankle. He was watching the Tour de France on a flat-screen TV, a crate of 45-rpm singles next to him. "What do you think?" he barked. Out of politeness I disappeared to the bathroom, where I pretended to pee by spitting tap water into the toilet, and took my time putting on lipstick. When I got back, Brigitte was in the kitchen stir-frying spring onions and Boudewijn was setting the long glass-topped table. A tense hospitality hung over the dinner table. Boudewijn followed a sulky account of a recent renovation project on the house with a few obligatory tips for if I were to get that internship in Silicon Valley.

"So it's not sure yet?"

"It is now."

"Did they say anything about me?"

"About you? Yeah of course, Aaron, you're all we talked about."

I chose not to say that Brigitte did in fact ask after Aaron, and rather eagerly agreed with me that I had some thinking to do about "that, um . . . boy," and that we all couldn't help thinking back on Etienne Vaessen's wedding dinner. For my part at least, I recalled Aaron's return from the bathroom, where he'd been hiding out for an idiotically long time, ten minutes, twenty, a half hour, in fact I'd already written him off. We gaped at him, the three of us, he looked terrible, as gray as papier-mâché, with a white tuft on the crown of his head—toilet paper, he told me later, to stop the bleeding—which made him look like a burst hard-boiled egg.

"So America it is," he said now.

I nodded and looked out over the endless blue surrounding us. Boudewijn insisted on taking me to the station despite his bad ankle. The seclusion of his car seemed to perk him up. "She's forgotten you the minute she's sitting on a horse's back," he said. The leather steering wheel sliding in his hands, the easiness of his driving manner: alert and ironic instead of on the defensive. That's how I remembered him from the wedding. As we glided over the highway he thanked me for sending my résumé, he thought I would make an excellent "Academy Fellow," he would send a recommendation to his colleague in Silicon Valley on Monday.

"Nice guy?"

"Woman. Really nice woman. That is, as long as you turn in your ovaries at HR and save up your vacation days off until after you're gone."

"Funny term, 'vacation days off.' "

"Perfectly normal one. Only not at McKinsey."

"Funny word, 'ovary.' "

Then, at last, he laughed, and just about the moment he took a slightly wild swing around the mini-roundabout, we both lost our balance and he grabbed hold of my leg, high and warm, his fingers between my thighs.

Aaron and I made a toast to the Ligurian Sea. And to the *Barbara Ann,* our ridiculously luxurious yacht that we whored up together and bought on a reckless whim—why, we weren't really sure, maybe because two secret millionaires have to splash out on *something.* But it did the trick. This was ours. Who else could I sail across the open sea with except Aaron Bever? That very night, I think, we finally resumed our photo sessions. We sailed around Cap Corse and down the east coast of Corsica, past Bastia, and moored at Santa Lucia di Moriani, the small seaside resort where we had the rental house. We chatted freely about the immediate future, about America, we laughed about the number of pictures we'd have to take in advance. He said he was planning to come visit me in California, he'd like to join me there.

"Are you still going to go see Wilbert?" he asked a few days later.

"No," I reassured him. "The day I was supposed to go see him, we'll still be here. It's better this way. Dad brought it up again when we went out to eat. He was afraid I was up to something. I didn't tell him I'd already talked to him."

"How'd you get his number?" Suspicion had crept back into his voice.

"Easy, from my parents' phone."

I didn't tell Siem that either. I had a war president of a father who had dragged his son into court, just like that. Since then, our household was well and truly devoid of nuance: you're either with us, or against us. Wilbert's name hadn't been mentioned at the farmhouse since 1990. You didn't dare. Let alone phone him up. Let alone go *see* him.

"Did you cancel?"

"Not yet."

The afternoon of the bushfire Aaron asked how I'd feel if he didn't return to the Vluchtestraat and I gave up my student house: "We'll just ship all our junk," he said, "you know, emigrate. And not come back for the time being. Ship our stuff? Heck, we'll just ditch it. What do you think?" And although living together had never really occurred to me before, and was, more to the point, exactly the opposite of my conclusions over the previous weeks, I shared his audacity: Yes! Let's do it! The more we philosophized about it, the more gung-ho we became about moving to California—*together*—after just six days on vacation, six days away from screwed-up Enschede, six days after our deepest ever relationship crisis, we were, to our amazement, talking about *living together*, we fantasized excitedly about a new start in the USA. Recovering from a crisis like this one, we told each other, requires more than patchwork, and as we stood there on our hill watching that bushfire, I wondered whether the prickly smell of millions of popping pine needles had cleansed our muddled heads, or in fact fogged them up.

Aaron's head was smudged with soot. "It'll all work out," he said. I turned and looked down at the small marina where six, seven boats were moored; our blue-pink spear was by far the largest. "We could always just sail the hell out of here," I said, and we retreated, smiling, to the coolness of the house they had bricked in under a pair of especially flammable pine trees. While Aaron started frying some goat meat in a heavy cast-iron pan he'd pulled out of a kitchen cabinet, I rinsed the scent of charred bark out of my hair in the shower and imagined, for the first time, what it would be like to stay with him forever, start a family together—could I imagine something like that? How would it be to do it *without* from now on; I fantasized about walking into the kitchen with my hair wrapped in a towel and saying to Aaron: "Honey, I love you, how about we forget those stupid condoms?"

My office door opened, and from the impatient squeak of the hinges I could guess who was on the other side. "Joy—five minutes?" Rusty's smile tickled me between my shoulder blades. I clicked away Aaron's website but did not take my eyes off the monitor. It was the end of the day, and I wanted to be getting home. When he started counting backward from five I turned around. Holding on to the doorknob, Rusty leaned into Room 203 (we'd never bothered to unscrew the red-painted metal hotel room numbers), and said: "Been crying?"

"Not since I was born. Why?"

"Two things." He walked over to the small conference table, pulled one of the heavy chairs into the middle of the room and sat down. Just like me, he crossed his left leg over the right one, but reconsidered, and planted his cowboy boots firmly on the carpeting a few feet apart. "First: why don't you do that interview."

"Oh?" I gathered my hair, twisted it into a knot, and pulled a rubber band around it. "If I feel like it, you mean."

"If you feel like it, I mean. Anyway, you've earned it. I'd do it myself, but I think you deserve it. And of course you feel like it."

The very opposite of feeling like it coursed through my nerves, a pre-programmed aversion to showing my hand, to being asked things by someone whose job it is to infringe on my privacy.

"Do you think I can mention the Barracks?"

"Difficult not to. Besides, it's for the magazine. Before they've printed the thing even Belfast will know about it."

"What if they pick the newsworthy bit out?"

"The *New York Times*? They won't. Too local. They'd sooner ditch an entire issue than publish a West Coast news item. What they're interested in is the phenomenon, the lifestyle, the success."

"Are they coming here? I mean, to Coldwater?"

"That girl's gonna be sitting in this very chair tomorrow morning at ten."

"What's her name?"

Rusty looked at me, concentrated, stuck two fingers in the air. "Double name. Wait a sec . . . Mary Jo something."

"And the other thing?"

He got up and walked over to a side window. He slid open the window sash, smeared thick with blue paint, and stuck his head outside, giving me a view of the worn-out seat of his jeans. Rusty must have read somewhere that a "founder," a genuine dot-com guy, should dress as casually as possible. ("Do I have a *suit*?" he said when I first broached the subject. "Yeah, my birthday suit." He did have one suit, a weird cobalt-blue thing with cactuses embroidered on it, a suit made especially for him by somebody named Nudie. "Who's Nudie?" "Don't you know? *Nudie.* Nudie Cohn. Hank Williams's Tailor. Nudie made Elvis's gold suit. Gram Parsons's Marijuana suit. She doesn't know who Nudie is.") And I have to admit: it worked. If Rusty and I went to an advertiser together, me in Gucci or the like and he as a freewheeler in one of his artistic shirts, we complemented each other and exuded just the right combination of anarchy and business sense. Now he belched. He brought his head back inside and went over to his chair. "I want to start filming in the Barracks in two weeks," he said. "Should be possible."

That was typical Rusty: he'd dig in his heels for months on end, procrastinate, run up against hurdles, then the about-face and, finally, overshoot his target.

"Are you kidding? No way. There's not even electricity."

"Then we'll improvise. Emergency generators. You just watch. And that journalist's name is Harland. That's her name. Mary Jo Harland."

I typed in the name on Google, 162,000 hits in twenty-four hundredths of a second, and the first was her own website. "She writes for the *New Yorker*," I said. "And for *Granta*."

"Great," Rusty said, "I'm going right out to *not* buy them and then I'm going to *not* read them."

"Is she pro or con, do you think?"

"Joy—we're gonna get shit either way. With your Barracks. Who do you think PR had on the line this morning? Louis Theroux."

A strange vibration high in my windpipe told me I should not do that interview: don't do it, why should you. Just as I was about to say that to Rusty, my telephone rang. An inside line. "Theroux's an asshole," I said, and switched the phone to speaker. "Hi, Steve."

Rusty made a gagging gesture. He had something against Steve, said he was "dry shite." I had snatched him away from Google, where he had obviously done good work for human resources.

"Joy," his voice echoed metallically through the room. "I'm just calling to say that Kristin called me to say you're scheduled for Wednesday, June 11th."

Rusty smiled and nodded at me.

"Why doesn't Kristin call me herself?" I asked. Yesterday at the Gold Digger, Kristin Rose took me aside and said that Isis had psychological problems, nervous tension, identity crisis, God knows what, and would be out of the running for at least a month, and would I consider filling in now and then. "You're my last resort, sweetie. And you're so *good.*" What irritated me was that I still hadn't answered and now Steve was on the line. Kristin was a director about my age and was there when Rusty had scouted me, and she'd started right in with that sweetie stuff. Her strategic friendliness worked wonders on Rusty.

"Because I need to know if I can book you for the usual fee," Steve answered.

"Have I said yes yet? Who's it with?"

"With, um . . . just a sec." Steve coughed, which the speaker translated into an ear-splitting grate. I wondered if he could tell he was being amplified.

"It's for girlslapgirl. Bobbi . . ."

"Bobbi Red," I offered.

"I think so, yeah," Steve said.

Rusty nodded wildly and gave a double thumbs-up. "Steven!" he shouted.

For a moment, only a hum. And then: "Rusty?"

"Steve—she'll do it, man. You should see her face. Joy's crazy about Bobbi." He sent me a warm smile. He was right, I was crazy about Bobbi.

"Steven," he continued, "as long as we're talking: have you drawn up that contract for Vince?"

"Almost," Steve said. "I mean: it's nearly done. In fact, I was just waiting for your answer. About my salary suggestion."

"Just make it seven," Rusty said. "Sweeten it up with secondary conditions."

"In Cleveland he got a percentage," Steve said.

"Sales?"

"Uh . . . profit. Half a per cent."

Rusty looked at me, I shook my head. "It's a deal, Steve," he said. "Print it out, send it off. Yeah? Do it. Bye, Steve."

He got up without putting back the chair, and leaned in the doorframe with his hand on the doorknob again. "OK, what are you up to?" I said after I hung up.

"Sorry," he said, "but that Vince—I've got to have him. You do too, take my word for it. By the way, did you know that Bobbi's gonna be on Tyra Banks next week?"

I was so taken aback that I forgot I was angry. "Really? What for?"

"Exorcism. Satan sent his daughter and her name is Bobbi Red." He glanced at his Rolex. "Feck! Joy, I've gotta go. Now. In two weeks you and the world-famous Bobbi will be shooting in the Barracks. That's a promise."

Bobbi Red—I let her stay at my place for a while in 2007, my hospitality tweaked by what you could call an atypical job application. It started with an open solicitation she sent to Rusty, not the usual slipshod e-mail we normally got, but a neatly folded, printed letter in a sealed envelope that out of fascination I've kept in my desk drawer. We got ones like this at McKinsey: a top-heavy letterhead, a Re: line and the textbook young-entrepreneur format that made you wonder if Bobbi, who still called herself Meryl Dryzak, was pulling our leg or really meant it, whether she was incredibly naïve or incredibly funny. "You gotta read this," Rusty said.

"Dear Mr. Wells," her letter began, "It has been my great pleasure to view your productions on the Internet over the past few years. I would very much like to join your company as an actress." The paragraph continued with the fact that she was attending a junior college in Denver, Colorado, where she studied voice and acting, film history, and modern literature, and while she found it all "extremely interesting," ever since her eighteenth birthday, the same age as the Federal Obscenity Statute, she thought the time was ripe to follow her heart. And her heart, she believed, lay in making pornographic films, preferably the kind of porn films we produced: "robust, realistic, and creative." The second paragraph began as the classic personal sketch. "I am generally considered reliable and a person with excellent communication skills. I have studied state-of-the-art X-rated films since I was twelve. I have extensive experience in anal sex, deep-throating, squirting, etc. During coitus I take pleasure in submission, but am equally comfortable playing the dominant role. Moreover I have many creative ideas to enhance your range and repertoire. In five years I would like to see myself directing; perhaps your company offers advancement opportunities? In closing, let me assure you of my capabilities as a team player and one who values a positive working atmosphere. I would very much like to visit your premises for a personal interview. Sincerely, Meryl Dryzak."

Rusty just about lost it. And that was even before he had seen Meryl's résumé. That she was poking fun at a genre, poking fun at Rusty himself, was obvious once you read her CV, which was constructed with the same pseudo-earnestness as her cover letter. Between her personal data and hobbies (sports and film, she admired Werner Herzog, Kurt Russell, Rocco Siffredi, and Michelangelo Antonioni) she inserted a section entitled "education and lessons," but where you would expect to find elementary school and high school, she listed her romantic relationships, including the exact dates, each entry in boldface, followed by concise accounts of what exactly she picked up in bed with "Rich" or "Josh" or "LaToya." She offered, if we so desired, three references, and to check whether the telephone numbers really existed Rusty, grinning from ear to ear, called someone she gave as "Joey F(ucking) Bastard." When he got an answering machine ("Joe Lightcloud Landscape Architects, for all your backyard decks and ponds"), he broke into a slow chuckle that carried on until well after the beep.

A week later Meryl Dryzak sat across from us in Rusty's office—not the girl *in* the letter, but a girl *like* her letter: decent but dirty. She wore a long, dark-green Led Zeppelin T-shirt, a wide belt with iron studs wound around her narrow hips. Her skirt was made of frayed camouflage fabric, her feet were packed into Nike high-tops. With her dark-brown braids and placid face, a pleasant mixture of the Mona Lisa, Kate Moss, and a heroine from a manga comic strip, she not only stood out from the typical debauched cheerleader type that overpopulated the Valley (no Botoxed lips, not covered in tattoos, not prone to uncontrolled giggling), but she also acted differently too. Intelligent and serious. She had a sensible, proper-sounding voice, a bit bored, but *what* she said in that languid tone was self-confident and, just like her letter, uncommonly sincere.

As usual, Rusty did the talking; he didn't like other people conducting auditions. "Meryl," he said after a few jokes about the kilo of sugar he dumped in his coffee, "your letter, your manner of speaking, your presentation, tells us you're an intelligent, talented girl. A girl who undoubtedly has what it takes to have any future she wants. I see you study film and literature, but I can imagine you could just as soon have chosen law or medicine or aeronautics. And yet you want to work for us. Can you tell me a little about your creditors?"

Rusty assumed she wouldn't catch on right away, but she understood just fine. "I'm not interested in money," she said without smiling. "Money doesn't turn me on."

And as though Rusty were Herbert von Karajan and she a violinist auditioning for the Berlin Philharmonic, she explained that, first of all, the business attracted her because of the intense pleasure she got from sex, a pleasure she wanted to explore to its fullest: "Pleasure is something very much worth pursuing," as she so elegantly put it; in close second place was her desire to share the fruits of her personal enlightenment with as many people as possible, she was something of an altruist, she regarded porn—"*good* porn," she clarified with her index finger raised—as an undervalued source of pleasure for plenty of people. She told us she came from Steamboat Springs, Colorado, a small town in the Rocky Mountains, where she spent eighteen years making a detailed study of everything that was boring and everyday and tedious. It was time for something new.

"Do you use meth?" Rusty asked. I could tell from his face this was getting too philosophical for him.

"I'm a fuck-junkie," she replied.

"Ho-kay." Rusty pretended to take notes.

We were used to anything here, from morning till night there was dirty talk at Coldwater, especially on and around the sets—but this? Without the vulgar spontaneity of her ilk (and who knows, without their typical snarkiness, their phony kookiness, their fickle unreliability too, which, I had to admit, seemed essential to a person's survival in this city), without the provocative prattle, the crass chomping of an entire pack of gum at once, it all sounded different, more surreal. *Harder.*

For the entire duration of the interview she held a Houellebecq paperback in her hand, her middle finger stuck in between the pages like a bookmark. When Rusty recommended she take on a *nom d'artiste*—coming from him, an idiotic term that made me laugh and betrayed that he was slightly intoxicated by her artistic-intellectual airs—she asked if he had a suggestion. Rusty took his time pondering it; he had a reputation to uphold when it came to artists' names. "Gigi Green," he said.

"How about Bobbi Red," she replied. That "Green" would typecast her, she saw it coming, she was already worried about it because of her wispy, girlish figure. "I'm, like, not planning to spend the next seven years showing up in white panties and plaid knee socks. *Daddy Fucked the Babysitter* number such-and-such, you understand what I'm saying?"

Rusty stifled a laugh. Normally he wasn't crazy about pips like her, normally he'd toss a chick with this kind of flimflam a pair of Harry Potter socks. "Good for you, Bobbi," he said. She was so pretty too. She was seriously beautiful.

After she'd got undressed and done the obligatory pirouette ("OK, kneel down on that chair, yeah, ass facing us, like that, yeah, drop your back, look at us—that's great") she told us she had flown to L.A. with $4,000 she'd earned waitressing in a steak restaurant in Steamboat Springs. She was renting a condo way up in the Valley, no air-conditioning, no stove, nothing. I imagined that poky room and the kind of life she was facing, and then pictured her on the sets where she'd be spending the coming months with those scrawny teenage tits of hers. I was overcome by a feeling I'd never had before in this kind of meeting: the desire to take her under my wing.

Rusty was possessed by another urge altogether: he flipped open his crocodile-leather diary to book her first shoots. Like always when a newcomer caught his fancy—and when did a newcomer *not* catch his fancy?—he scheduled himself as her first co-star. He was consistent in that respect. This is what he did it all for. Then the snuffbox appeared on the table: coke, Viagra. Wells was hopeless without his magic potions. Seeing as Bobbi considered three or four shoots in the space of a month a little scrimpy, he phoned up Kwimper Girls with her still sitting there. He praised her to Toby Kwimper, throwing little winks in her direction. Kwimper was a captain of industry from day one, and for thirty years had run his agency from a smoke-soaked Buick in which he crisscrossed the San Fernando Valley every afternoon until deep in the night. "Bobbi is a special lady, Kwimp, and you know what that means if I say so. Bobbi's got big things ahead of her."

These were prophetic words. Rusty thought so himself, and he was right. Bobbi Red, the former Meryl Dryzak, became a celebrity, a cult figure, a porn star of new and unheard-of proportions—still mostly underground, to be sure, but known far and wide, and completely crossover. "Bobbi will be the new Jenna Jameson," Rusty parroted *Rolling Stone*, but Rusty and *Rolling Stone* were both wrong. Jameson was "old school," an old-fashioned porn queen. Not Bobbi. Bobbi was not to be pigeonholed—Bobbi *demolished* pigeonholes. Although her films were no less hardcore (she won one AVN award after the other), this mysterious, profoundly shallow girl struck a chord outside the Valley. Internet trend-watchers were euphoric about Bobbi, top photographers wanted her to model for them, indie bands invited her to appear in their videos. She was on the cover of the Smashing Pumpkins' new CD. She let an editor from the *Los Angeles Times* follow her for six months. She posted video blogs on YouTube in artsy-fartsy black and white where she philosophized freely in that loose, serious way of hers about the rough life she led. And now she was going to be on Tyra Banks.

At the end of the interview Bobbi offered us a bony hand and got up to leave. As I accompanied her down the wooden stairs to the lobby I grappled with my urge. In the doorway, as she took out her cell phone to call a taxi, I offered to let her stay with me, free, no strings attached, so she could get her bearings. She looked at me, surprised, and politely turned down my offer—that, too, was atypical for her kind. But I kept insisting until she gave in.

Why? Every year hundreds of Bobbis washed up in the San Fernando Valley, damaged, grubby, dumb, shrewd, adventurous, broken, victimized sluts who infested the innumerable 1,000-bucks-a-month one-bedroom apartments between Ronald Reagan Freeway and Ventura Boulevard like baby-pink cockroaches. Depressing white stuccoed condos where they lay on their Wal-Mart mattresses, in the heat or the cold, waiting for the phone to ring, their agent sending them the next day, or even that very afternoon, to some anonymous villa with hideous sofas to appear in *Share My Cock 12* or *Cum Dog Millionaire*. Maybe I wanted to have a closer look at this kind of life. Maybe this girl triggered my big-sister gene, material that slumped jadedly on some dead-end side street of my DNA.

Bobbi stayed for two months. I gave her a large room with a balcony looking out onto Sunset and a view of the Pacific. Although I occasionally cooked for her—more nutritious meals than the tzatziki pizzas she otherwise had delivered, we spent at least ten evenings together at the dinner table—we never became close friends. She was either too aloof, or maybe she didn't think I was interesting enough. All I could pry out of her was that she was raised under the wing of a mother and an elder brother. Her father was killed in 1991 during the first Gulf War, friendly fire, she said drily.

She was constantly asking questions, but they were always practical ones, even when it had to do with my own past. "What did you study?" "Could you also be a director without having studied?" "Do you think about going back to Germany?" "Do you ever use an enema?" "Does that guy Rusty have a family or anything?"

"How did you tell your parents about this?" "How much was this house?" "How'd you get into the industry?"

When I answered that last question by showing her a handful of pictures I'd saved from the Enschede time, she laughed tenderly, maybe even teasingly. "Why, *that's* not porn," she said.

Bobbi could spend two hours in the bathroom, in the Jacuzzi with one of her literary heroes, the door open but in absolute silence. On the bathroom stool was a Louis Vuitton bag she took with her to the sets. One evening I snuck a look: washcloths, shower foam, perfume, mouthwash, lube, toothbrush and toothpaste, condoms, a telephone charger, dildos in a variety of colors and sizes, a hairbrush, the enema bag I suggested if there was an anal scene on the program. I caught myself subconsciously keeping track of how often Bobbi went out with that bag. When, after about seven weeks, she came to me with an apologetic pout on her face to tell me she'd found her own loft in Sun Valley, the counter was already on thirty-eight. Thirty-eight films, five of them at Coldwater; based on what she earned with us, she must have hauled in some $40,000 by now.

"Fifty," she said. "But it's not about the money, Joy. It's about the *oeuvre*," and with that word she let out a rare giggle. "About everlasting fame. It's neat, isn't it, that people can always see how I followed my heart." Oh yes, life in the Valley was everything she'd expected it to be, even *better*, and that was in part, she said sweetly, thanks to my hospitality.

On one of the last evenings she would make use of that hospitality, I returned from Coldwater and overheard, my hand on the front doorknob, muted voices coming from the living room. Unfamiliar voices conversing with Bobbi. I heard the word "Dad" and "absolution." I entered the room and saw a woman sitting next to my house guest and, seated on the sofa across from them, a dark-skinned fellow covered in tattoos. I remembered that Bobbi's mother and brother were planning to come visit her in her new city, an event that kept getting put off; Bobbi harbored a vague dread of this meeting, because she was planning to inform her family of her newly launched career. It was clear she had just done so.

"Hi, Joy," she said, smiling, straightening her back, "let me introduce you to my mother and my brother." The hulking young man, who stayed seated when I walked over and offered him my hand, was the exact opposite of his sister in every respect: everything about Bobbi that was petite, elegant, and feminine had found its masculine complement in this half of the Dryzak offspring. The guy was disproportionately muscular and had a gruesomely exaggerated nose and eyebrows; I looked down on a fully tattooed pair of shoulders that bulged out of a sleeveless T-shirt, the blinding white of the shirt inflaming the pitch-black eyes—eyes that, despite being housed in a pockmarked face, were obviously descended from the same jar of kalamata olives as Bobbi's. He didn't look at me, but stared angrily at the female wrist he held clamped in his vise-grip.

"I already called the manufacturer," Bobbi said, "but they don't have anything in stock. It might take a few weeks, I'm afraid."

Her mother was a sturdy woman with thick, lank hair and high cheekbones, and who, despite her jeans and leather jacket, resembled a squaw. To reach her I would have had to wade through thick hunks of broken glass that lay on my flokati rug like hailstones. So I didn't; we just nodded at each other. In her broad lap and on the floor by her feet lay wads of tissues from the Kleenex box that balanced on the leather armrest of the sofa. In the midst of this former family stood the matt-black aluminum tubular construction that once supported the glass top of my coffee table. At the bottom of the tubular cube, amid mounds of glass, Bobbi's silver laptop glittered, open and unhinged on one side. Across the room, in front of the open bathroom door, the Louis Vuitton bag lay like a duck shot down in mid-flight; scattered around it the tubes, the jars, the condoms, the enema.

"Joy's the director of one of the studios where I work," Bobbi said, more buoyantly than usual. When no one responded, she continued: "Well, I guess we'll be going."

Her brother stood up as though he'd been given an electric shock; instead of getting taller, he got broader. He strode over to me in two firm steps and pushed his flattened ravioli-nose almost against mine.

"You're lucky you're not a guy," he said with breath that smelled of sweet potato and fried calamari rings, "or I'd slit you open and rip your guts out. Being a woman and not a man shows that God hasn't forsaken you altogether."

After these words he disappeared into the front hall. You could hear his breathing as he waited for Bobbi and her mother to join him.

11

The Saturday afternoon after his pathetic quest through Aaron's house, they drive to Hans and Ria's, friends of Tineke from her Utrecht days. They spend two hours in their air-conditioned Audi, he at the wheel, most of the journey in silence. On Radio 2 an MP is debating the issue of fireworks permits with an industry lobbyist and a government inspector, he picks something up about an aerosol theory. Tineke's quivering thigh presses against his.

"D'you hear that?" she asks.

"Hear what?"

"About the nitrocellulose. Gun cotton. They found it right after the disaster."

"What *don't* they find." He has no idea what she's talking about, he does not know what nitrocellulose is, he has other things on his mind. It might be a good idea to listen, though: on Monday he has to meet with the Oosting Commission investigating the fireworks disaster. But he's preoccupied with that boat. He keeps asking himself what in God's name he actually knows about his children. A father who hasn't seen his son in years and whose elder stepdaughter is studying at his own damn university. What does he know?

This morning, while Tineke was at cardio fitness, he dialed the number on the marina receipt (on his cell phone, naturally); the chap who answered did not speak a word of English, it was dreadful, he couldn't even muster up "I'll call you right back" in schoolboy French. He raced upstairs to his study and looked up all the key words in a French dictionary, but when he called back the guy of course didn't answer. After a quarter of an hour he got him on the line again, and first had to lie that he was A. Bever's father, only to learn, in pidgin campground-French (the man who aspires to be Education Minister has to express himself in pidgin French) that Aaron was the *owner* of that boat, "*propriété de monsieur A. Bever, né le 8 janvier 1972 à Venlo—oui, c'est ça.*"

It was as though he himself had been side-launched, right into the Arctic Ocean. Following the initial shock, a painful strain on his chest, all sorts of images shooting through his head (drugs, Mafia, female trafficking, Dutch underworld, sex, sex, sex), he scurried into denial—he *must* have misunderstood, those two couldn't possibly *own* a boat worth millions, a boat you rent in Florida for a hundred grand a week? It was insane—*he* was going insane.

But now he believes it again. Because what do we really know about each other? What do fathers know anyhow? A *yacht*? Is it possible to hide a *sixty-foot pleasure yacht* from each other? What does a father know?

For the answer, he only has to shift the question a generation: what did *his* father know about *him*? He's just the person to ponder that. Suddenly he is no longer sitting in his car, he is back in Delft, in his parents' house on the Trompetsteeg, and like most other Sundays he is stiff with muscle pain and bruised from head to toe, and on this particular Sunday he doesn't give a hoot about the pain, because the previous day he became national champion in the Energiehal in Rotterdam. And his father? He didn't even know. He sat downstairs, stubbornly not knowing.

1962? 1962. Glowing from his achievement, he stared out of the dormer window in his boyhood room over the alley of a youth he had only just left behind. He most likely played one of his EPs on his Garrard portable gramophone to counteract the Sunday somberness that reached up through the narrow stairway, pawing the attic like a giant's hand, wishing he were back in the Kromhout army barracks. He and Ankie and their father had just eaten dinner in the kitchen, and following the circus act with oranges and full-fat yogurt their father had been performing for donkey's years—completely peeling and dismembering the orange, segment by segment, a messy half-hour exercise—he had gone upstairs counting the minutes until he could pack his duffel bag and cycle back to Utrecht. It was around seven in the evening, dusk settling over the alley, when across the way a front door opened and one of the Karsdorp boys crossed the black cobblestone street in his house slippers and knocked on the window.

"Ank," his father bellowed from the living room; he heard his sister draw aside the black-velvet curtain and squirm past the bikes to the front door. The greeting, voices-turned-murmur, Ankie on the stairs and her dark-brown curls poking around the corner. "Come quick," she whispered, "you're on television."

On his guard, he wriggled his feet into his army boots. Downstairs, in the dim sitting room, a delineated silence. His father sat at the table in his woolen Sunday suit, reading; the copper hanging lamp cast a searchlight onto one of his night school textbooks, bound in marbled paper; he perused the pages through his half-glasses as though the Karsdorp boy, who stood next to the table studying the worn spots in the carpet, was made of thin air.

"So long, Mr. Sigerius," said the boy, and he and Ankie followed him over the slick cobblestones to his parents' house. While they seemed even poorer than his own family, they were still the only ones on the street with a television set. "Watch, don't eat," his father admonished. Their living room smelled of cauliflower and fatty gravy and was chock-full of children and grown-ups, extra chairs had been brought in, and in the corner near the window the eye of a varnished television cabinet glowed with images of that afternoon's football match.

"Sit down, kids," said Mrs. Karsdorp, a mother with pale flesh and unruly red hair. Here too you could hear a pin drop, and afterward he thought he'd heard them go quiet when he arrived, sudden bashfulness, all eyes glued to *Studio Sport*, it seemed like they were bashful because of *him*, either because he was national champion or because of his military travel gear.

After the football came an item on a swim meet, but after that they really did see shots of the judo tournament in Rotterdam, the voice of commentator Jan Cottaar as he announced the title defender, Joop Gouweleeuw, also from Delft, the camera zooming on Anton Geesink, the world champion "who passed up the national title bout," and there he was himself, "the nineteen-year-old Simon Sigerius," at the edge of the mat for his final match against Jan van Ierland. Mr. Karsdorp, with whom he and his sister were squashed into a two-seater, was the first to open his mouth: "Won't your pa come watch?" he asked, and Siem could see that Ankie was about to answer, probably something apologetic. He beat her to it: "I don't think so, Mr. Karsdorp." His voice sounded heavy and loud. "My father thinks judo's a sport for traitors. He doesn't even know I'm national champion."

And that was that. No time for a reply, the action had already begun, "a battle of champions," according to the commentator, and everyone looked, each with his own uneasy thoughts, at the tiny black-and-white figure on the screen who just now, in real life, had uttered those strange words, but who now tugged at one Jan van Ierland, "and only in the third minute did serviceman Sigerius throw his opponent to the tatami with a lightning-fast tenth hip throw, securing the crown as Netherlands heavyweight champion."

Whether his father, like an insect trapped in amber in the lamplight, looked up when he and Ankie returned half an hour later, he couldn't recall, but there was a bottle of jenever on the table. His sister switched on a few lamps in the otherwise darkened room, he loitered a bit in the doorway, both of them waiting for something, for an explosion, for some terrible scene.

His father (who would die of a heart attack two years later) turned, his thinning hair damp from the pomade, and brought out three jenever glasses from the buffet, placed them on the table and filled them deftly until the liquor bulged above the rim. "Come, Ank," he said, "let's toast our Siem."

And when he and his sister stood awkwardly at the table, he handed them each a glass.

"I don't drink, Pa," he said.

"Lots of things you claim not to do." His father raised his glass by its silver stem. When he and Ankie followed suit he said: "To our double-crosser."

It was true. He'd been double-crossing them for years. His Judo training was like an underground movement: eventually everyone knew about it, his brothers and sisters, his classmates, the neighbors, in the end every *Delft Catholic Daily* subscriber—everyone except his father. For years he judoed in secret, first once a week, until the suit hung frayed on his body, then three times a week, and finally *four.* The whole time he maintained a tightly woven system of lies, backstreet routes, and accomplices in order to do what he loved.

His pa could get stuffed. He decided as much after a disastrous furniture-moving chore one ice-cold Sunday afternoon. He and his father had dragged a massive oak desk from the Trompetsteeg to the home of his elder sister Loes and her husband on the

Kruisstraat. It was a hand-me-down from his father's office that landed in their living room like a stranded galleon. "I'll take that beast," Loes offered. It was hard going; they had to set it down on the vacant street every fifteen meters.

He was red-faced from the exertion, but maybe also from the route they were suddenly taking *together.* For some weeks he had followed his father along these same sidewalks every Tuesday evening, cautiously, like Dick Tracy trailing a gangster, via the Beestenmarkt to the Moslaan, a paper supermarket bag under his arm. Before he turned onto the Kruisstraat his father's duffel bag was a dark-gray oval in the distance as he headed for night business school on the Raamstraat. Siem would ring Loes and Gerrit's doorbell, and his sister, half in the tiled hallway and half on the stoop, thrust his washed judo suit into the bag. Then he would run, hardly trusting his father's head start, to the Oude Delft to arrive at Uke-Mi's dojo on time.

Six months earlier, after some ten trial lessons with Mr. Vloet, he raised the issue at home. With a vague foreboding that his father might not share his enthusiasm, he had prepared his argument thoroughly; it would be most sensible, he thought, to bring up the philosophy behind his new sport, that judo was much more than just a kind of wrestling. Mr. Vloet, who had sparred with Japanese masters in Paris, devoted an entire lesson to the teachings of Professor Kano, judo's creator. A portrait of Kano hung in their dojo. What an amazing evening that was. Mr. Vloet could really nail you if he wasn't satisfied with your shoulder throw, "GARBAGE!" would echo loudly through the room, but when he *talked* he could be friendly and calm; they sat listening to him for a good hour, and that evening at the dinner table Siem found himself retelling, flushed with excitement, what he could remember of Mr. Vloet's words.

His brothers and sister listened as they chewed, and his father too listened in silence, the leather elbow patches of his cardigan resting on the embroidered tablecloth. He eyed him over a steaming pan of Savoy cabbage. His small, furrowed face looked overworked. Maybe because he had a sedentary life, both here and at the office, his bony shoulders hung forward and his neck seemed long and bare.

"So Pa," he said, "judo doesn't have much to do with fighting—nothing, in fact—with judo it's all about self-control and respect for your opponent. Professor Kano, the founder, didn't call it *judo* for nothing, judo means 'gentle way.' That the world would be a better place for it, that's what he hoped."

"Better?" his father asked. "Better, how?"

"From judo, of course," he answered. "Professor Kano never intended judo as a sport, but as a kind of, well, teaching. Kids learn judo at school, Papa, in Japan everyone learns the ideals and principles, the symbols behind it, at a young age, you see?"

His father did something out of character: he laughed. His raddled face twisted and creased; it startled Siem as though he were looking at his father's bare legs. It was not a cheerful laugh. What this thirteen-year-old boy couldn't put into words hung permanently in his head like an oily vapor: their father was a broken man. He and their mother had run an office supply shop on the Choorstraat, a low-key business that ran entirely on his mother's enthusiasm and went bankrupt soon after her inexplicable death, almost as though a plug had been pulled out of a bathtub drain. They had to move. Since then his father had lived with five children and sundry creditors in this crappy little house. He did his best, but he'd lost his spirit. He said: "There's no symbol *behind* anything, Siem. You can't say that. But go on, let's hear about those Japanese ideals."

"OK," he said eagerly, trying to recall Mr. Vloet's exact words. "Now, for Professor Kano, cooperation was really important. On the mat as well as outside, judokas are supposed to help other people."

Ankie stifled a yawn. Fred pretended to paddle. "Canoe," he said.

"Cooperation enhances people's well-beingness—"

"Well-*being*," his father interrupted.

"People's well-*being*. By being sportsmanlike and respectful, you enhance the happiness of others, Pa, and therefore your own happiness too. Unlike boxing. Boxers just bash each other's heads in. Judokas have respect for each other."

"So why do they strangle each other?" asked Fred.

"That's part of the game, you dork," he snarled. "We let go as soon as the referee gives the signal."

"Who would win," rejoined Fred, "Floyd Patterson or what's-his-name . . . that Anton Geesink of yours?"

His father stroked his thin neck with his left hand. "Siem here," he said to the others, "talks as though he has done this . . . sport for years now."

"No, really," Siem answered, shocked. He loved his father, because he was his father, because his father had the gumption to go to night school twice a week, because he was a widower, and in a way was their mother too. But he was also apprehensive, maybe because his father had been through so much.

"Patterson," said Fred. "He'd knock Geesink's block off."

"No, really," Siem repeated, "that's why I'm telling you all this, I want to ask if I can join. I *really* want to do judo. There's a good club on the Oude Delft. I've already had a few trial lessons."

At the words "trial lessons" a shudder surged through his father's body, as though he were in a train changing tracks. "And what might this teacher's name be?"

He often thought back on what his father once said when Fred had bored all the way through Jet Kolf's foot with a hand drill, the steel bit went right through her leather boot. Blood spurted out.

Someone went to get him, he didn't know who, his father came running to the Beestenmarkt without his coat. "If I've said it once, I've said it a hundred times," he growled as he slapped Fred upside the head, "I should've put the lot of you into an orphanage."

"You mean our *sensei*, Pa. That's what the Japanese call him."

"I asked you what his name was."

"Mr. Vloet."

His father shook his head, as though Mr. Vloet wasn't really named Mr. Vloet. "Boy," he said, "you shouldn't believe everything you hear. Wishy-washy nonsense about respect and virtue. That guy has no idea what he's talking about."

"Mr. Vloet is a third dan, Pa. That's a pretty high rank." He felt someone kick his shin. Daan glared at him, his mouth pulled into a tight little stripe, he shook his head almost imperceptibly.

"I don't give a shit which damn Mr. Vloet is or isn't," his father said, suddenly raising his voice. "What irks me is that know-it-all rubbish about the Japanese. Don't tell *me* about the Jap, Simon. Don't try it on with me about the virtuous Japanese. Or about another man's happiness. *God* help me."

And with the word "God" his father slapped his hand against the edge of his plate. It broke in half. First came the loud jangle, then complete and utter silence. Fred and Daan stared wide-eyed at their sausages, Ankie gawked with a full mouth at her father. As though his plate hadn't been cleaved in two, their father jabbed a piece of potato from the tablecloth, stuck the fork in his mouth and chewed. After he'd swallowed, he said calmly: "Listen, Siem. You tell that Mr. Vloet your father was a POW in Burma. You tell him: 'My father did forced labor on the Burma railway.' You understand? Then he'll understand why you won't be coming anymore."

• • •

Well over halfway along the Moslaan, he and his pa stood blowing on their fingers. It was as though there was a body *in* the desk.

"Going well, boy."

Sweat poured down his back—a mixture of exertion and fear. He trusted his sister all right, she wouldn't rat on him, but he wasn't so sure about his brother-in-law. Gerrit with his dirty fingernails from the workshop. He was an odd fish, Gerrit, a downright sneak, buttered up his old man until the stuff dripped off him. Had a story about everybody, things no one else ever mentioned. The exact cause of their mother's death, for instance—Siem had heard it from Fred, and Fred had heard it from Gerrit. His mother—his softhearted, sweet, pretty mother—had died, according to Gerrit, as a result of a *furuncle*. A furuncle in her nose. "A f'your uncle?" he asked, shocked, fyorunkel, fyorunkel? It sounded like that monkey the Russians shot into outer space. "But you don't *die* from it," he stammered, horrified. "A sort of boil," Fred explained, "you do so, if the, you know, the pus squirts into your brain."

He didn't like Gerrit knowing about him doing judo on the sly. That he was hooked. The afternoon he went by Loes and Gerrit's to ask if she would launder his judo suits from now on, a conniving frown passed over his brother-in-law's face. Gerrit sat him down to explain in detail why his father did not approve of judo. He did know about the war, yes? About the Dutch East Indies? What the yellow bastards had done to his pa? No? "Kid," Gerrit said with a grimace, "they brutalized your ol' man something awful. First he trudged 200 kilometers to Burma, barefoot, seven days and nights. And then spent two years dragging railroad ties, fourteen hours a day, no coffee breaks. Covered in open sores and lice. And the Jap with his billy club. Ever seen your dad's back?"

"No."

"Keep it that way, kid. When you were still in diapers your sister and me, we lived with your folks. Every night at 3 a.m., kid, it started. Bawled like a baby, your pa did. Slept in the alcove so your ma could get a good night's rest. Under his bed he had a, watchamacallit, one a them wog-cutlasses, a 'klewang,' and if your mother or me . . ."

Loes came in with the coffee. "What all are you telling the boy?"

". . . or your sister here, if we went in to calm him down, he'd stand up on his bed waving the damn thing. 'Out of here, dirty Jap! Ssssss—I'll slice you to ribbons.' " He grinned. "Ain't that right, Loes?"

His sister held a tin of butter cookies under his nose.

"Your pa went AWOL too, once," Gerrit said. "Escaped from the prison camp. Two weeks in the jungle. Oh yeah. A hero. Your pa's a hero." Maybe because he was only fourteen, had never had lice, let alone been beaten with a stick, maybe because Gerrit's venomous verbosity made him sick to his stomach, Siem had difficulty paying attention. "The Kempeitai, you've heard of that, right?" Gerrit asked. "The Yellow Gestapo, you could say. Your father, he walks straight into their arms. Poor guy. Spent the rest of the war in a metal box, a meter square. Home sweet home. Not sitting, not standing, not lying down. They'd let him out couple times a week so they could beat the crap out of 'im . . . Yeah, yeah."

Siem's head cooled down on his way home, it had iced over with recalcitrance. If everything Gerrit said was true, then it was awful for his father, really and truly, but what did a judo club in Delft have to do with the war in Asia?

He and his pa picked the desk back up, this time both of them holding it by the tabletop, so that they could take the corner with small steps, his father facing backward. Although his arms were trembling from the exertion, he still had time to ponder the whole judo issue. He couldn't *not* think about it. They had another twenty meters or so to go when his brother-in-law's dark-green Volkswagen came rattling around the corner. Gerrit parked across from No. 23. When his father set down his end and turned around, something in Siem's cranium started careening and crashing about. He watched as Gerrit climbed like a flightless bird from the dark-green dome. Gerrit had recently given his father a lift to Rotterdam. It was enthusiastic indignation that banged around inside his skull. Loes and her husband had a Volkswagen. A *German* thing, a car thought up by fucking Adolf Hitler. And his father was quite happy to ride around in it! In Hitler's car!

"I'll take over for you," Gerrit called from across the street to Siem's father, who was leaning with his back against the edge of the desk.

"Pa," he said, but his father did not turn around. "Pa," he shouted, "could you please tell me why Loes and Gerrit can drive a Kraut car, but I can't go to judo?"

It all happened so fast. In two steps his father was around the side of the desk, he'd never seen him so agile and athletic before. And then: exquisite pain. The palm of his father's hand landed mercilessly against his left ear, the fragile organ not yet cauliflowered by sixteen years of competitive judo. Tears sprang from his ducts, but he gritted his teeth, squeezing back the fluid with his eyelids until he could once again focus on the knotty wood of the desk. His father raised his arm and pointed down the street they had just come from. "Out of my sight," he said. "*Move.*"

Hans and Ria used to live in a small third-floor walk-up on a side street of the Antonius Matthaeuslaan; now they own a renovated brownstone overlooking Wilhelmina Park that Hans financed with the wholesale import of South African wine. They eat in the shady backyard. After a few glasses of Kranskop red, Sigerius debates the mathematical merits of chess with his host, a club chess player with black-and-white opinions. The obnoxious fanaticism with which he insists on his pet opinion (which he in fact borrowed from G. H. Hardy)—that despite its charm, chess lacks something essential, it is inconsequential as opposed to mathematics: "mathematics is elegant *and* relevant, Hans, you can't say that about chess"—makes him realize how much that boat is eating at him. He *must* find a way to get up into that attic.

The next morning, as they are saying their farewells, they accept the invitation to celebrate Christmas with Hans and Ria in their chalet in the French Alps. Tineke takes the wheel and drives, as they always do when they're in Utrecht together, down the Antonius Matthaeuslaan—but he hardly bothers to look. Should he go back to Aaron's house? He compares himself to his father, wonders whether, until that championship jenever, he really was completely in the dark. Of *course* he knew. He used to see his father's obstinate ignorance of his judo as pure weakness, as oversimplification and, as the years went on, as the plain indifference of an old fart. For the first time, he seriously tries to step out of that mindset and into the resentment his deeply humiliated father must have felt. This exercise in empathy makes him realize that his father tacitly tolerated his judo, despite his wartime trauma. When his pa died in 1964, Sigerius was secretly relieved—he dreaded facing the man after his training year in Japan, his relief was purely selfish. But in the hectic days after their weekend in Utrecht, that old feeling takes on a new taste; for the first time, he's glad his father no longer had to put up with it, for the first time, he's relieved *for his father's sake.* Shouldn't he do the same, just turn a blind eye himself? Just like his father, pretend everything's hunky-dory. Know but don't know. Until the neighbor's kid comes over one evening to say your son is national champion. But what, he wonders, what will they come over to tell him?

Wednesday morning the fireworks disaster commission meets, and at the end of the afternoon he grabs his chance. At half-past four he crosses the administration parking lot with his sports jacket draped over his arm. Humming, he gets in his university car and drives down the Hengelosestraat. He parks in front of the McDonald's on Schuttersveld and walks over to the hardware center.

A timid, pimply boy in a red polo shirt with the store's logo leads him to a display of grinding tools and bolt cutters. He buys the next-to-smallest cutting shears, which are still enormous, and drives back to campus. To his satisfaction he finds the farmhouse empty. In their bedroom, he removes his suit and goes into the bathroom. He takes a lukewarm shower. If he inhales deeply, his chest resonates with a pleasant edginess. He dries himself off, walks naked into the dressing room, puts on beige khakis, loafers without socks, and a pale-orange polo shirt. Not too theatrical? He checks himself out in the full-length mirror and decides to put his suit back on after all.

After a certain amount of searching he finds, in the bedroom cupboard, a large tennis bag; he stows the bolt cutter in it diagonally. He leaves a note for Tineke in the living room: "Hi hon, how was it with your sister? Afraid I can't get out of eating with the guys from that debating team. After that we'll watch France-Holland together. See you later, S."

Just after six he drives down the Hengelosestraat for the second time. Evening rush hour is thinning out, he's got both front windows halfway open and he's playing a Cannonball Adderley CD. It's a warm, windless evening, a large, languid sun paints over the city like a damaged maquette. There are lots of people about, bicyclists weaving in and out, men with rolled-up pant legs playing soccer in parks. But it is a film. Cannonball's elastic alto sax goes with this film—not with him. The warm evening breeze blows through his car, but he is entirely detached from Enschede.

He approaches Roombeek via the Lasondersingel. The fencing looks older than the city itself. He parks the car in the small lot in front of the low-rise apartment block, the bunker that protected Aaron's street from the shock wave. The athletic bag weighs heavily on his shoulder and grazes the overhanging conifers along the front path. This time the lock opens without resisting.

He enters the hall like in a recurring dream: the faint animal smell, the rustle of junk mail on the mat. He closes the door and listens with bated breath. A million dust particles exchange places, the whirl of silence. In the living room, a familiar tableau: the wall-to-wall curtains at the back are still drawn, the badminton rackets on the coffee table have not rearranged themselves. His mouth is dry, he drinks with long gulps from the kitchen faucet. He stands for a moment at the kitchen window. Aaron's bike leans up against the wide hedge of conifers.

With soundless adrenaline-laced steps he takes the stairs up to the landing. The smell of dust and washing. He sets down the bag, fingers the cotton of his judo suit superstitiously, and looks up. The eternal patience of objects. Does he dare? His battle plan is simple: snip open the padlock; if he finds nothing then he's made a monumental error, in which case he will leave this row house in jubilation and what happened to that padlock will remain a mystery forever; if he does find what he's afraid of finding, then the padlock doesn't . . . then *nothing* matters anymore.

He wriggles the bolt cutters out of the bag. The jaw is made of glistening, virgin steel. The rubber-sheathed grips are so long that he does not need a chair. His heart pounding, he raises the shears and places the jaw on the shiny U. It takes some effort to squeeze the tool, his upper arms quiver, the bolt cutter is heavy. He gives it one good thrust, and the blades glide through the steel as if through a licorice shoelace. To remove the lock from the rings in the trapdoor and molding he has to get a chair from the study after all, his legs tremble as he climbs onto it. With a dull thud the broken padlock drops into the athletic bag. He takes a deep breath and, the hatch crackling hellishly, he pulls down the folding stairs.

The rectangular hole leading to the attic: a soap film stretches between the wooden edges, a stubborn molecular membrane of last-ditch hope. The fervent hope of paranoia, the hope that things will turn out all right, a softly glistening skin that he puts to the test with every creaking rung—until his eyes scan the attic and the film bursts.

What else did you expect?

He mustn't fall. As though he's being crucified, he stretches his arms out over the bloodred carpeting, two nails through his palms. In the ensuing seconds he consists only of head and arms: his legs, his torso, the stairs, the house, Enschede—the whole earth has been swept away underneath him.

What he recognizes from the photos unfolds at lightning speed into three dimensions, what in the pictures was odorless, and essentially innocuous, now has the deadly aroma of unfinished wood, of dust, and of something soft, something feminine, expensive talcum powder. What he experiences is perversely akin to a mathematical proof, to what his beloved Hardy meant by revelation coupled with inevitability; to efficiency, elegance: the dazzling lamp that suddenly becomes illuminated when you hit upon a proof. Now everything blacks out.

He becomes aware of a distant, heavy panting—the rhythm of his own breathing. The attic is more spacious than he had expected, the red wall-to-wall carpeting chafes his arms. Twilight falls softly through a closed Velux roof window. In the middle of the room, a wooden bed in romantic country-cottage style, pillows with lace edging, a white duvet puffed up like fresh snow in a Dickens film. On either side, two tripods with flood lamps. The professionalism of those two scarecrows is devastating—this is no attic, this is a *studio.* The sloping walls are decorated with posters, carefully chosen posters, he appreciates at once, posters that deliberately have nothing to do with Joni and Aaron: a panorama photo of the Grand Canyon, the picture with the two kittens, Celine Dion in Las Vegas. Against the outside wall, covered in pink-and-white-striped wallpaper, he spots the bookcase filled with the American books, he recognizes it from the photos in Shanghai—a wave of bitterness and revulsion jolts through him: the calculated forethought, the devious perfection of that bookcase.

Off to the right, under the Velux window, he sees a small desk with a PC; lower, at eye level, where the sloping ceiling disappears into a sharp, dark corner, clothes spill out of canvas drawer units on casters: dresses, it appears, lingerie, so there they are, the sales boosters. Across the room, a green dressing table with an oval mirror; on it are various spray cans and roll-on deodorants, in front of it a nostalgic mannequin with, instead of limbs, a four-legged frame on wheels. Atop the faceless wooden head rests the straight black wig of his forebodings. Feeling as if he's been struck, he realizes that the objects on the dressing table are not deodorants, but plastic penises. His eyes well up with tears. Dildos. He can *think* the word, that far he can go, but he will never be able to say it out loud.

For a few minutes he stares, panting, at the peak of the roof, poisoned by the scent of talcum. A supporting beam runs across the entire breadth of the attic. Just swing a rope over it. The moment he realizes that his eyes are searching for a chair, he bangs both fists on the carpeting, hard, he almost loses his balance, the ladder underneath him wobbles and creaks.

He is a man who knows how much effort it takes to achieve something people will be impressed by, often for a disappointingly short time, perhaps because they do not appreciate the immensity of the preparations involved. The first time he detected a trace of that talent in Joni—the ability to work long and hard toward a distant goal—was in Boston. She had to prepare a final project on a subject of her choice, and this eleven-year-old girl produced a twenty-page paper on Dwight D. Eisenhower. While her classmates chose subjects like Afghan hounds or volcanoes or the Boston Red Sox, she gave an in-depth account of West Point, the Normandy invasions, the United Nations, Ike in the White House—knowledge she had collected from various sources in the MIT library, where, using his pass, she spent several afternoons perusing and photocopying illustrations and text. He was touched by Joni's project, for which she got an A-minus (that "minus" being the discrepancy between her own middling English and the too-perfect English of the excerpts she'd overenthusiastically copied from thick Harvard biographies—she admitted as much). It instilled him with confidence in her future.

The knowledge that she applied that same thoroughness, the same intelligence and tenacity, to concocting this Internet brothel . . . Is this why he encouraged her schoolwork? Taught her to follow through? To put together a fake bookcase? *To play the whore up in some attic?*

Behind him he discovers a rack of pumps. He recognizes the

shoes, right down to the last pair, the patent leather pumps in every jellybean color, the white ones with the little bows, the Burberrys, the ankle straps, the open toes. Shoes he's never seen his daughter actually wear. With great effort he reaches for the rack and just manages to flick off a black satin number, lifting it over with his pinkie. The heel is slender and delicate, above the toe there's a small, soft fabric rosette. "Karen Millen" is printed on the insole. He caresses the heel with his index finger. Then he hurls it across the room, it hits the bookcase with a hollow clack and falls to the floor.

He orders his numbed legs back down the folding stairs. On the landing he thrusts the bolt cutters back into the carryall, he wants to push the ladder back up, but reconsiders. To be alone for longer. No one around. Panic at the idea of having to watch a football match in a full students' union. Clutching the tennis bag he goes downstairs and walks into the deathly quiet living room. He puts the bag on one of the leather armchairs and sinks onto the purple sofa, gets up again and squats in front of a low oak cupboard with etched-glass doors; glasses on a shelf, bottles of liquor in the wooden belly. He pulls out an open bottle of Jim Beam, fills an old-fashioned tumbler and stretches out on the sofa with the bottle and the glass. He drinks with his eyes closed. And now? Now what? His thoughts, he realizes, have not yet gone beyond this point, all these weeks he has unconsciously firmly planted himself on the axis of the lucky break. That dimension has been pulverized, curled up, retracted: he is a flatlander, his new reality is level and bleak. He can no longer dodge the fact that his daughter and her boyfriend were . . . he is reluctant, no, he is *unable* to use the word "porn," it is too ignominious, the word itself makes him feel too wretched. He wants to tear it apart, letter for letter, burn each letter separately, scatter the ash on five different continents. He refills the tumbler to keep from flinging it through the television screen.

Above the TV hangs a large painting, a landscape with thick brush strokes, art on loan. Something has to be broken. Whiskey against canvas, in his mind's eye he sees the tumbler shatter, the alcohol dissolving the paint. Once, just once, he'd set foot in a sex shop, one of those places with blackened windows, a place that cannot endure daylight. Rent one of those films, Tineke's suggestion, no, a friend of Tineke's. You two should try one of those films. "Why do you discuss our sex life?" "What sex life, Siem?" So all right, he goes. But what a sorry sight. Walking into that blacked-out, back-street joint. Everything in him resists walking into a place with a nude broad painted on the front. But he does it. Once inside, the thought that soon he's got to go back outside again. The smell of plastic videotapes, man sweat, carpeting. The smell of semen. The louse behind his cum-counter. The displays of tapes, the plastic dicks, the men creeping out of the cabins like cockroaches. The *looking*, which film, hurry up, *decide*, for God's sake. And while he's standing there, roach among the roaches, awkward, miserable, horny, in comes a guy in a raincoat. Sets a stack of videotapes on the counter; "late," he mumbles. Out of the corner of his eye he watches the louse retrieve them and stab at a calculator. "That'll be 1,043 guilders and 30 cents." Just once he sets foot into this kind of joint and this happens. The raincoat digs around in his pockets, counts out eleven 100-guilder bills and leaves. *That* is porn, Joni.

The whiskey plows furrows in his throat. He has to try to address a number of questions in the right order. How bad is this? Start there. How bad is a daughter who prostitutes herself? He has to assess the damage. How bad is what his daughter is doing? And is it really prostitution? Yes, he thinks it is—and is immediately indignant: she, with her brains, with her opportunities. Your daughter sells close-ups of her genitals on the Internet. It's a disaster. She is bankrupt. *He* is bankrupt.

More Jim Beam, the gulp goes down like a dagger, try to calm down. It is a bottle he'd brought back with him from Shanghai—he realizes that he hasn't for a second thought of Aaron. What's his part in all this? This is *Aaron's* house, it is his attic, his computer, his photography equipment. Coercion? He lunges forward, grabs one of the badminton rackets and smacks the edge of the table. Is he coercing her? No—he knows those two too well to believe that, it's impossible. Joni can't be coerced, she is too headstrong, too dominant. The epitome of free will. Aaron is a follower—he thinks this to his own surprise. Only now does he despise himself for his *concern*. When he still hoped for a happy ending, he was mainly concerned for Joni, he loved his daughter so much that it was *her* future that mattered most. Was she mentally sound? Was she under pressure? But now: forget it. He is incensed, now that the truth spits in his face he's *livid*. What does that little bitch *think*? How could she be so stupid? So sleazy, so perverse. How could she? Do you realize what you're doing, Joni? The risks you're taking? Public risks? What if this gets out? How ostracized do you want to become, Joni Sigerius?

Drink and think. He sags on the stiff sofa like a zombie. For a moment he feels like giving in to the heavy, deep fatigue, but then bolts upright. Blood rushes to his head. *What about himself?* When this gets out? A Minister of Education with a double watermark on his stationery: murder *and* prostitution. A son who bashed a man to death and a daughter turning tricks on the Internet. Porn times murder, behold the formula of his life. Oh yes, they'll drag Wilbert into it for sure, everything will be dredged up. He'll be drummed out of office, they'll hound and humiliate him until there's nothing left of him. What did I do to deserve this? Has my luck run out? The sweat beads on his back, his legs are sticky.

Try to remain analytical. Think in terms of solutions. It is a crisis, not a catastrophe—not yet, at least. He still has almost a week to take measures. He has to come up with a plan of action before they return, a strategy to defuse this crisis that's not yet a catastrophe. Should he confront them? Take a hard line, give them a piece of his mind, should he unmask them, castigate them? Yes. No. He doesn't know. Perhaps it's better to collude with them; an enemy, he thinks, won't be able to talk sense into them. What they're doing is legal, they are adults. It isn't manslaughter, after all. Antagonize them and you've lost them. It will only egg them on. You have to confront them and negotiate openly.

Sounds from outside reach him through a rising haze of alcohol; somewhere in a backyard, football fans are gearing up for the impending match. He has got over the initial shock. His anger subsides, the whiskey relaxes him somewhat. His thoughts flow into another channel, again he arrives at his father. Could he be off the mark? Just like his old man was off the mark? Are there, like back then, two realities? Two truths colliding? Is he keeping up with the times? Is that attic room no more than a frivolous youthful indiscretion? Again he grabs the racket and slams a dent into the edge of the table. Don't be so soft, man! We're not talking about *judo*. This is damn well about . . .

And yet. Something's gnawing at him, a faint hypocritical nibbling, and the more he drinks, the more difficult it is to ignore. The ironic fact that he . . . that he happened upon this whole sordid business as a consumer, as one of Joni's *clients*, that he wasn't tipped off by a concerned third party, the fact is he *paid*, he transferred *money* to those two for exactly what he's now so vehemently condemning—the mind-boggling, tangled duplicity starts to dawn on him. The hard white light of his moral indignation strikes a prism and is refracted into a spectrum of nuanced and emotional doom.

The years of Joni's blossoming womanhood. His absurdly stilted efforts to avoid any semblance of erotic interest. Woody Allen's relationship with his stepdaughter, he and Tineke watch the evening news, and he furiously switches off the television, can't stand to hear it. Unbearable. How he prudishly stopped going in the bathroom while Joni showered, put an end to the tickling and roughhousing on the sofa or in the garden—memories he juxtaposes against the outrageous fate now confronting him, the awful awareness that this is the very same girl—woman—he has unwittingly been leering at and lusting after.

Anxiety about the Internet, which he has believed in since day one, which he even, as a scientist and administrator, helped foster, and that now has infiltrated his campus as a bordello. Grim thoughts of Aaron, of the young man who pretends to be his friend, whom he has admitted to his inner circle. Who is this Aaron Bever, actually? He glances around, takes a better look at Aaron's things, the expensive Luxman amplifier and CD player, the electrostatic speakers, the thousands of books, the furniture he suddenly notices as remarkably exclusive, pricey.

Disquiet about his role as a parent. What did he do wrong? Did he miss the signals? Focus too much on achievement? Did he *talk* to her enough? In his mind he tries a case of nature versus nurture; proposed settlement: it is nature *and* nurture. Did not raise his son, did not conceive his daughters—the outcome would make him weep if the alcohol hadn't tempered his nerves. Brooding over the year he had both of them under his wing, Wilbert *and* Joni, about his far-reaching suspicions regarding his own son, his concern for Wilbert's hormonal response to the sudden flowering of his younger stepsister. One question mixes like poison into the stream: what can you expect from a stranger's genes? *Is* she really his daughter? Who *is* Joni?

• • •

Meanwhile the whiskey also . . . softens him, eliciting a laissez-faire mood that's entirely unlike him. The corset of his respectability, the straitjacket of his status, the restraints of his . . . generation? start to slacken. He is relaxed. He loves them, doesn't he? He loves Joni, with all his heart, he even loves Aaron. Put yourself in their shoes. The seclusion and solitude of Aaron's house invites him to do just that. The sincere question of *why* they do it—why do they do it? Does it give them pleasure? The answer is obvious, of course it gives them pleasure. It turns them on. They're young, rich, reckless. They just do it. They do it out of lust and greed. And him? He likes Jim Beam.

It's a quarter to eight. He stands up, giddy, totters over to the liquor cabinet, places the whiskey with a crystalline smack against the bottle next to it. He dabs his lips with his sleeve. Another mood has now taken over, a dark mood, a mood that perhaps doesn't even matter. Shivers run through his body as he leaves the room. The stairs up to the next floor sound hollow. It doesn't have to take long. His heart racing, he closes all the doors on the landing, laundry room, bathroom, study, bedroom. He takes a deep breath, grasps the folding attic stairs, lets go again, wipes his sweaty hands on his trousers. Consumed by vicious self-pity, *I deserve this*, he begins climbing the squeaking steps. The sweet scent of talcum powder whets his resolve. He is *not* Woody Allen, he is *not* the Minister of Education.

The attic is an attic in Kentucky. Holding his breath, he closes the trapdoor and surveys the room. How to go about this? There are so many possibilities. The silence is profound, but he still hears it, a little tune reaches him from the far corner, it's coming from the shoe rack, the colorful pipe organ of high heels. Maybe the rack waited, let him blow off some steam first. Maybe it's been beckoning him all along.

He sniffs, undoes his laces, and kicks off his shoes; the carpet presses itself softly and gently into the soles of his feet. He can't swallow. His trousers and boxers rustle as they fall to his bare ankles; panting, he tugs his shirt over his head. He walks around the bed, gruesomely naked all of a sudden, there is a new nakedness that has concealed itself under his ordinary nakedness, and he picks up the satin pump from the floor. While holding his foreskin between thumb and index finger, as though his phallus were an inflated balloon, he examines the shoe from all angles. He presses the slender heel against his balls, traces a line along the underside of his erection. Something soft, panties, a slip. With the shoe in his hand he goes to the other side of the attic and squats down in front of the canvas drawers, pulling open the middle one: nylons, fishnet stockings, garters, body stockings, tops, skirts, bras, countless panties. He roots around, feels, looks, pulls out a sheer black stocking, thrusts his nose into it: that same dark, exquisite talc smell. Touching the infinitely fine-woven fabric catapults him back to the 1950s, he glides above Delft, descending into his sister's bedroom, and makes a belly-landing on her twin bed. Home alone, he controlled himself for as long as possible, but eventually reached under the iron box-spring and pulled out the hatbox where she kept her stockings. He examined them, felt them, inhaled the soft, feminine scent, in order to better imagine the feel and smell of the untouchable women's legs he saw on the street, in the tram, during Miss Rethans's English lessons. He was ashamed of it, thought he was sick, thought himself a deviant, especially once he found out there was a special word for his peculiar interests, a word he, still after all those years, detests.

With the stocking in his right hand, he gropes with his free hand in the drawer until he finds a pale pink elastic thong. Gulping back the tears, he steps into it, pulling it along his rounded judo calves and over his hairy thighs. The small triangle glides over his testicles, forcing his member up against his belly.

"There." His voice sounds heavy and close by.

He inserts his left arm, his arm of choice, into the stocking until it reaches past his elbow. The fascination. Perhaps it is the delicacy. The gossamer fabric that is more womanly than the woman herself. He crosses the bloodred floor to the shoe rack and drops to his knees. Eighteen pairs, he counts, each one more tasteful than the other. No cheap junk, no sleazy overkill. Stylish, feminine. He doesn't even bother with a photo series without them. In fact, stark naked doesn't interest him. He doesn't really even care for bodies. In that sense he is still a boy of twelve. He removes the shoes, one pair at a time, from the rack, arranges them around him as though they were Märklin model railway cars—

He desperately needs to pee. For a moment he tries to ignore the pressure on his bladder, but no, it's the implacable Jim Beam. He's on his feet, hurries down the groaning ladder, goes back down the stairs, his bare feet slapping against the steps. He ducks into the lavatory just off the passage. Evolutionary oversight: it's either urinate or ejaculate. To make himself go limp he studies the calendar that hangs next to the roll of toilet paper, *The Super-Scrub Household Calendar* it's called, nothing you'd expect Aaron to have, he looks up his own birthday, "SIGERIUS" is written in what must be Aaron's handwriting. As soon as he has softened slightly, his urine begins to flow, the thong still snugly around his testicles.

Before he's even finished his penis bounces back up like a spring, thwack, against his belly. He hears a nearby sound that makes his blood run cold. The jangle of keys, a lock opening—*the door.* For a moment he feels only ice, his blood has frozen in his veins. Shoes scuffing against a threshold. He has to brace himself against both walls to keep from fainting. The neighbor. Tineke. Aaron's parents.

"Gosh, lots of post." *Joni.*

In a reflex he switches off the light. His mouth wide open, as though in the pitch-blackness he hears with his mouth: footsteps. Someone brushes against the lavatory door. Cramp in his chest, he's having a heart attack. *He's dying.* He seizes his penis, mortified, he grasps it tight, if he lets go he'll disintegrate.

A door creaks open, the living room door? She goes into the room. Then: stronger footsteps, wiping feet. A hacking cough. *Aaron.* Every sound pierces through him. He's caught in a tiled trap: intestines are primitive brains, Aaron's and Joni's know they are home and will be wanting to relieve themselves. *Aaron is approaching.* But Aaron, too, disappears into the living room. He wants to exhale, but instead he breathes in even deeper and kneads his erection with his free hand, slick with sweat. *Think,* damn it. Nothing comes.

Run for it. You have to run.

Someone turns on the television, TV-station sounds, the voice of a commentator. "Let's unload the car now." Aaron. He ejaculates. A stabbing wave surges through his back. Footsteps in the passage. Warm semen falls onto his left foot, his own scent. Silence, then footsteps again, they're going outside. *They're out at the car.*

Run for it. Now is the moment. Go, *now.* The only way is through the kitchen. He opens the lavatory door and with three giant steps bounds into the living room.

"I'll give you a hand, honey." Joni, standing at the dining table, her back to him, examining something, a stack of envelopes and newspapers. Her neck is tanned, her pinned-up hair blonder than usual. The curtain has been pulled open. The room is bathed in devastatingly clear evening light.

"There's a postcard from your brother."

His teeth chatter. His daughter turns, the muscles in her suntanned face tighten, then slacken—and then shoot every which way. Her beautiful face dissolves. Joni herself collapses, she literally collapses. He sees himself in her grimace: naked, disheveled, one arm stuck in a nylon stocking. A raw scream comes splintering out of her contorted mouth.

"No," he shouts. "Not—"

"Not what, Dad?"

They are in each other's nightmare.

The backyard, he has to get away, he can't just stand here like this. Joni is sitting on the floor, her hands clamped like blinders against her face. She is shaking, her whole body shudders.

"It's not what you think," he says. And: "Well, that's it then."

He strides toward the light. He walks in a straight line, his body accelerates steadily. He is flying. His knee, and immediately thereafter his overheated forehead, are the first to strike the wall of light and air. A hand of glass pushes him back. The air is a glass wall—but even a wall cannot stop him. The sliding door gives a little, recoils and shatters like a tinkling waterfall; glass showers over his bare shoulders. Needles. Knives. He walks on, keeps on walking. Without slowing down he tramples through the high, lush grass. Curves off to one side, soft, loose earth under the soles of his feet. He hits something hard, something crashes to the ground. He writhes his bleeding body through the mist of conifers.

12

Spring even came to Linkebeek. The pivot window above his desk was opened all the way, a daddy longlegs stumbled inside. Aaron swiveled his desk chair in synch with the insect; it bumped into the ceiling, banged a couple of times against the molding where the room divider used to be, darted under the obstacle into the back room, and fluttered along the shelves packed with books he'd bought here and those he had managed to rescue from the Vluchtestraat incinerator.

He spun back and checked his e-mail. Still nothing. According to the travel alarm clock next to the monitor it was already past 10 a.m. in Los Angeles. Ducks quacked outside, he looked up, the church tower was now only barely visible through the light-green crown of the maple tree in his front yard. The mild weather tallied with his mood. He awoke mid-morning to an uncommon optimism charging through his nervous system. He frequently caught himself pondering Joni's life in California. The handful of messages he had received from her elicited in him a mixture of wistfulness and desire, a feeling he hadn't foreseen when he sent that first feverish e-mail. What was it exactly? A sentimental nostalgia for their long-gone Enschede time, but also some undefined, expectant yearning—both sentiments, he realized, as pitiful as they were absurd. But he couldn't help himself, he kept wondering how Joni was doing in that immense city, what her job was exactly in that Frisbee factory of hers, what kind of friends she had, where she lived, in short: what kind of life did she lead now? For all these years, self-preservation had held him in check, but he could no longer resist: he looked her up on the Internet. He typed her name into three different search engines, wrung the whole Web inside out, but came up practically empty-handed. The only hits included a couple of familiar *Tubantia* issues, the archive pages of her student club, and some PDFs of McKinsey reports she had written for firms like eBay and IBM. But these were all from 2001 and 2002. She wasn't on Facebook, did not have a LinkedIn account. There was a Joni Sigerius who traded on eBay, mostly shoes and dresses, some of which he thought he recognized and whose photos he copied to his computer desktop. The only other relatively recent "Joni Sigerius" hit was on a mile-long membership list of an inline skate club in Santa Monica. And that was it.

Strange. You had to pretty much encase yourself in lead these days to avoid showing up on the Internet—even a recluse like Aaron had his own website. For someone like Joni, this was totally out of character. She had been an Internet fanatic, even considered herself a pioneer—and wasn't she?

Her conspicuous absence fed his fantasies. Did this say something about her present state of affairs? That job at the Frisbee factory was obviously no great shakes, it appeared that, for whatever reason, her brilliant career had fizzled. He envisioned her in a part-time desk job in the accounts department. Maybe that was a pity, maybe not.

And thus an image of Joni gradually took shape in his head, a Joni who, like him (but in her own buoyant way), had meandered off course; he imagined, not without a certain pleasure, that she and Stol had got caught up in a dramatic divorce case, and she was stuck, penniless and thwarted in her career, in a drafty corner of Los Angeles, probably with a couple of fatherless children in her charge. On the other hand, wouldn't she also have cash left over from their website, or else from the *Barbara Ann*? Who knows, maybe she blew it all. Unlike him, not everyone buried themselves years before they were actually dead. She'd probably lived the high life in San Francisco, invested in the wrong Internet companies, gambled away millions on Wall Street—

Or was she with somebody after all? Maybe she'd married and taken her husband's last name. He reread her e-mails for the umpteenth time, but besides Stol there was no mention of men whatsoever.

He'd been so stupid. Last night he woke with a start from a nightmare that took place in a contorted Enschede. At the beginning of the oppressive little saga, Wilbert was his brother and they shared an apartment somewhere, don't ask why, but soon enough he had turned into Wilbert himself, and he rode a motorcycle down a long, lonely wooded path until he came upon a funeral in Venlo, something like that, he'd forgotten it already. Regrettably, he'd jumped out of bed and, still in a woozy haze, switched on the computer. In reckless abandon he foolishly related the dream in an e-mail to Joni. "Any word from Wilbert?" he inquired, and closed his letter with a semi-accusation: "Did you go see him, back then? Probably did."

This morning was devoted to damage control. Before breakfast—it was still only two-thirty in the morning in L.A.—he sent Joni an e-mail that at the time seemed relaxed and nonchalant. "Hi ex, it's springtime here in Linkebeek, it's not a village but a forest of weeping willows. You've got palm trees there, right? Send me a coconut and I'll plant it here." And maybe it *was* relaxed, but then, two hours later, he sent another, weightier message. "I've been thinking a lot about us the past few weeks," he typed. "It's weird, Joni, if you think of what happened to everyone. Your father, of course, to start with. You there, me here . . . Your mother remarried. I'm curious how you look back on it all. I'd like to catch up, either here or there on your turf! And vis-à-vis Wilbert: I'm just curious. Love, Aaron."

And meanwhile he'd been waiting for hours, first when morning had reached L.A., and still now. From 7 a.m. her time onward—maybe she checked her mail before going to the office—he refreshed his in-box incessantly, like a snake charmer. He swung between embarrassment and euphoria over his rash suggestion of going to visit her, he alternately blushed and rejoiced, while the knuckles in his index finger, his whole hand, the tendons to his right shoulder, had gone into a cramp as a result of his relentless mouse-clicking. It was nearly afternoon there already.

What was he hoping for? An unexpected twist. That Joni would take the bait, invite him there, or better yet: say that she'd be traveling to the Netherlands shortly, who knows why, maybe she'd reconnected with her mother, he had brought them closer together. And that she would offer, perhaps out of gratitude, to come to Linkebeek. There was much more behind that optimism, he felt it in his index finger, which by now was the same white plastic as his mouse; he secretly hoped that *she* also thought about *him*, that *she* enjoyed pondering *his* life and that she would also consider—

He got up and walked across the room, stood staring into space by the bookcase. He hoped that, for Joni, the idea of trying to get back together was not only special, but, as he also felt, meaningful. He breathed deeply. The mad but magnificent notion of he and Joni building a normal life together, the life a thirty-eight-year-old man is supposed to have, gave him a smoldering feeling in his stomach, he would like nothing more than to jump up and run outside, down the hill, and charge into the street with outstretched arms, sucking up all the oxygen he could. It seemed so . . . natural. He was euphoric, it gave him a, how could you put it, an "all's well that ends well" feeling. Who else but Joni was capable of *saving* him?

The daddy longlegs skittered past him; he grabbed it out of mid-air. He skated back to the window in his stocking feet and released the wriggler from his cupped fist onto the open window.

He had, in fact, already forsworn love. He was capable of living on his own, but "on his own" in effect translated into solitary, alone, lonely, abandoned. There had been girlfriends after Joni, certainly, he had tried, but while falling in love was asking for psychosis, cohabitation *guaranteed* it. A recipe for disaster. Lieke, a Flemish woman—a gem of a lady, civil servant at the European Commission—had lived with him for most of 2005. But she was stingy, pathologically tightfisted. So much so that she would shout "faucet off!" from their bed while he brushed his teeth, so penny-pinching that she checked the supermarket receipts to see if he had really bought the bottom-shelf brand, the B brands, no, the C brands. And as he stood at the stove warming up one of those Albanian delicacies she would crouch down next to him and glare suspiciously under the frying pan and invariably turn down the gas. She couldn't stand it that he didn't have a job. "I'm a fucking millionaire," he said when he walked into a restaurant without first studying the prices on the menu. "That's not the *point*," she whispered, "I'm simply not prepared to shell out thirty euros for a slab of meat." She'd rather piss all over the cellar stairs herself than spend money on a cat.

They quarreled about it. Fights about money which for him, as a matter of fact, *did* grow on trees. These shouting matches made him anxious, caused him sleepless nights, and the worse he slept the more anxious he became. After a few weeks it finally happened: he got up, left the house, and wandered through the undulating, tree-lined streets of Linkebeek, along the hedges and shrubbery, through the *Tiefschnee* of autumn leaves in all shades of red and yellow. He imagined they were euro banknotes. He dived into the leaf heaps in gutters and along sidewalks, laughing and crying at so much wealth—look, Lieke, look! He recognized the president of the European Central Bank behind the wheel of a Volvo station wagon and chased him for half a block. For two days and two nights he was AWOL, wandering aimlessly through the southern woods and estates in a hallucinatory frenzy: terrified of being robbed, terrified of being murdered, tortured, devoured. For a full twenty-four hours he hid in a ditch filled with rotting euros, his shoulders heaving in terror. On the third day he returned, gaunt, bruised, smeared from head to toe with blood and mud, hacking like a dog. He got the wheelbarrow from their shed and shoveled it full of cash. He wheeled it into the living room and dumped his riches out over the oak floor. "MONEY!" he screamed from the bottom of the stairs. "MONEY!"

E-mail beats Chinese water torture hands down as an instrument of agony. Not a damn word from her. In the old days you had that thin, blue, pre-gummed airmail stationery that you folded up on itself, licked closed, and, after a refreshing stroll around the corner, deposited in one of those red boxes on legs, and the rest of the week you could lead a normal human existence. He tried to restrain himself, but sent another e-mail anyway. "At least tell me if you went to see Wilbert. How was it?"

Smacking himself on his bald head, he put on a summer jacket and pulled the door shut behind him. He walked down the hill. It was still warm outside, the elder bushes in the gardens, the hawthorns and hornbeams, were starting to thicken. His neighbor across the way, a blond Dutch guy with an assortment of children, rounded the corner on his old-fashioned racing bike on his way home from work. They nodded at each other. He strode down the sun-flecked Grasmusdreef, followed the shallow curve of the Kasteeldreef, continued for a kilometer, and crossed the railroad tracks. He kicked a stone onto the shoulder. She could skate here too. You didn't *need* palm trees to skate.

A shortcut through a stretch of trees led him to a path that wound its way under a young but thick canopy of leaves. Mossy air that smelled of damp earth; he listened to his own breathing. After about 100 meters he could see, in a clearing off in the distance, the Roze Molen, a ruin of dirty white pumice that you could indeed call pink. He walked around the mill house and inspected the rusty waterwheel sticking out of the creek, just as it had done for centuries. Until a few years ago the place had been a youth hostel and had still generated its own electricity.

As he strolled across the rough, grassy meadow, he thought of Dr. Haitink: *she* had put him up to it, coming here to live. What else was he to do? Enschede was over and out, everything that bound him to the city had either emigrated, exploded, or—he was convinced—was after his scalp. "Just imagine being in a place where you're the most content, or once was": Haitink's advice for when he got antsy, a psychotherapeutic trick which he grumblingly accepted and which led him straight to this pile of stones.

Right about where he now stood, under the stringy branches of perhaps even this exact same willow, his parents, his brother, and he had stopped, entirely by coincidence, to camp one summer in the 1970s. Early one morning they ended up at this very spot in their raspberry-red Citroën van after fruitless attempts to find a hospital in Brussels. All night long, or so it felt to him, his father had dashed on and off the motorway, constantly getting lost in poorly lit suburbs, their mother groaning next to him in the passenger seat, while he and Sebastian sat silently in the back, staring at the impressive lump on her shoulder. They had left Venlo the previous evening, destination: campground in Brittany. He and Sebastian were expected to sleep in that clattering tin can, but instead they spent the entire trip teasing and taunting each other, bickering, hitting, spitting, until he ripped a fistful of pages from his brother's library book and their mother lost her temper and attempted to smack him with a backward fling of her arm. Dislocated shoulder. She wailed like a banshee. His fault.

So they drove around for hours, each pothole and bump sending his tearful mother into paroxysms of agony, he himself terrified that the ball of her upper arm would rip through the bloodless, tautly stretched skin. Finally their father just pulled over somewhere, jerked on the parking brake, and ran in barely concealed panic toward a dimly lit clump of stones, this mill house—to ask directions, they thought, but he came back with a huge man named Jean-Baptiste, who carried his mother into his big pink abode, his father close behind. There, out of the children's earshot, the two men rammed and jammed his mother's shoulder back into place.

That same afternoon his father and brother pitched their tents in the tufted grass where he now sat, while his mother went to Jean-Baptiste's doctor on the Linkebeek village square. His parents apparently clicked with the miller and his wife, because they stayed for a week. It was unforgettable. He and his brother befriended the daughter and son, twins about his own age, who took them to building sites, orchards, creeks, the ruins of a castle where they spent long evenings enacting knightly exploits. The girl was named Julie, she had fluffy brown hair and taught him, somewhere in these woods, how to "kino-kiss": two wide-open fish mouths that exchanged moist air, like in the movies. The next year, and the one after that, he already started dropping hints in April: Mom, Dad, can we go back to the mill this year? How about if we, etc., etc. They never went back. Years later, Sebastian told him that his mother had fallen in love with Jean-Baptiste. Their father found out they'd been corresponding via a post office box near her work.

Maybe Joni got found out, he thought suddenly. He had never considered the possibility. That aborted career at McKinsey—had somebody stumbled across those photos? There were bound to be pictures still circulating on free sites. Maybe someone recognized her, once it got out, she'd be finished, no way you'd keep your job after that in puritanical America. Could it be? It would explain her keeping her head down.

He closed his eyes. The rough bark of the willow chafed the back of his head. Compassion filled his tear ducts. He wasn't the only loser: 2000 had been a massacre. And *that* was why he longed for Joni, they could talk about it, he would comfort her. They shared a wild, disastrous past that together they could put behind them. Joni could come live with him; they could transform his absurd, empty, sad house into a home. She could easily find a job in Brussels, or in Linkebeek. Just last week he saw there was an opening at the library, not for a back-to-work mom but someone serious about maintaining the collection. And in Brussels there was plenty of office work.

He thought it was a great idea. She knew him inside out, knew him before he got sick. She could bring her children with her. He would raise them lovingly, just as *her* stepfather had done. And who knows. *Who knows*. How old was she now? Thirty-five? Thirty-six tops. He tried to imagine a thirty-six-year-old Joni. What did she look like? (All week he hadn't succeeded in recalling her natural, relaxed face.) He tried to envisage her . . . He tried to imagine how Joni, here in Linkebeek . . . how she would look *pregnant*.

Instead of that he saw something else, as so often when he

thought of her: that wide-eyed, stunned grimace—her expression during the last seconds that they had a future together.

She was sitting on the floor, half under the table. He came running into the room, alarmed, the neon-yellow Oilily bag with their dirty washing from Corsica slung over his shoulder, and there she sat, arms wrapped around her knees, the dining room table a canopy, as though she had taken cover from a shower of shards. On the table and on the floor around her lay envelopes and newspapers and slivers of glass, an orderly, serene still life compared to her face, which appeared to have been struck by something high up on the Richter scale. They gaped at each other for a few moments, her eyes bulged, her eyelids were bunched-up like sweater sleeves. In a thick voice she said that it was her father, that he knew everything, and that he just charged through the sliding glass door, "he just walked straight through the glass." She sat there stock-still.

Not Aaron. He dropped the Oilily bag, his heart kicking and pounding in his chest, he couldn't talk through his panting, did he hit you? he wanted to ask, she looked like she'd been knocked senseless, but he couldn't talk, he was dizzy—which is why he strode, with two big steps, through the splintery frame of the sliding door, out to the back terrace. "Blood," he stammered, there were thick splatters of blood amid the broken glass on the paving tiles. He walked farther onto the grass, "damn," he blustered breathily, "damn, damn, damn," but stopped abruptly, something moved, sunlight, he gestured defensively, *don't hit me*, bounded back in the living room, looked back into the yard, his breath rasping, and saw that it was only his bicycle, the sun reflecting off his bike. Joni was still sitting like a sculpture on the floor, her eyes bulging, staring blankly into space. She sniffled. He walked back, jerked the curtains closed, banged his shin against the coffee table, went into the hallway, and locked the front door without looking down the street. He stood with his back against the wavy glass. Then he launched into a lamentation, an uncontrolled stream of clichés, verbal diarrhea, this is what you get, they asked for this, fuck, Joni, *fuck*, they should have stopped, why did they even start, he stumbled into the living room grasping his sunburned head, "I was always afraid of this, why—"

"Shut your trap," Joni said. To his amazement, she stood up, plucked a sliver of glass from her shoulder. "You do understand," she said with unnerving calmness, "that we're stopping *now*. It's over, Aaron."

His arms slid off his head like rubber. He let out a sob, a deep sob—and nodded. Yes. Case closed. Not only did he understand what Joni said, he *knew* it. He knew it already outside on the deserted street, when he lifted the Oilily bag out of the trunk and heard the cacophony of breaking glass roll toward him from the front hall, he knew then that it was all over. A profound and irreversible knowing. He *knew* that it was Sigerius who had just smashed through his newly installed sliding glass door. A crystalline finale to everything, to Joni and him, their fresh start, his friendship with her father, life in the farmhouse, his adopted city. (Strangely enough, he told Haitink later, the *real* din was internal, his insides shattered. In his head too, something was smashed to pieces. He *himself* splintered into little bits. "You think so now," Haitink said. "I thought so *then*," he said. "*Now* you think you thought so *then*.")

The national anthem was being sung on the TV. They stared at the football players. "What did he say?"

"I'm going," she said flatly. "I need to be alone. Maybe I'll call you." She pulled some clothes out of the Oilily bag, took her rolling suitcase by the handle and walked outside. Was this really happening? Ten minutes ago they were like the little figures on top of a wedding cake, gushing over a future they had cut short their vacation for: California here we come! He believed it, and otherwise at least Joni did. The morning after the brush fire nearly drove them into the sea, she rose out of the surf of their little pebbled beach like his very own Ursula Andress. "You know what?" she had said as she walked over to him, wringing out her hair and tossing her flippers and snorkel at his feet, "I want to go home. We've got a million things to do. We'll watch the France-Holland match back in Enschede." And now she was just walking out of his life?

He spent the first few days and nights mostly frightened. Somebody who walked out like that could just as well walk right back in. Every hour of the day and the mostly sleepless nights he was aware that Sigerius could show up to settle the score. He lay on the clammy leather of his sofa in the darkened living room, cringing with every sound from outside. So as not to be caught off guard he took the telephone with him to the toilet, and while he showered the thing lay in his piss-stained washbasin. He went to the shed and dragged back the splintered panels the city had used to board up his windows the first time around, and nailed them over the new hole in his house. (The previous time had been no more than a foretaste, a harbinger.)

During that clumsy carpentry job in the full midday sun, he let the likely scene between Joni and her father expand into something monstrous, he continually replayed the moment where Sigerius smacked his daughter in the face, *take that, whore,* he felt it himself, a white-hot blow that in fact was intended for *him,* after which he pictured Sigerius, like a Viking in a suit, head-butt the glass door to smithereens. The violence of that deed surpassed his worst fears, belittled the visions of vengeance that he'd tried so hard to suppress during his moments of regret about the website.

When he stumbled upon a black tennis bag that turned out to contain a bolt cutter, it dawned on him that his father-in-law had been on a mission. Holding that leaden weight in his hands, he realized that Sigerius hadn't sent them abroad simply out of benevolence, it was a premeditated move. But how did he get into his house in the first place? The tool fell to the floor with a thud, it made him dizzy, he had to sit down: how long had his father-in-law been wise to their shenanigans? He avoided going up to the attic, spared himself seeing the ravaged room, upturned bins of clothing, dildos, wigs torn asunder.

Joni's departure left behind an abyss; occasionally he could touch the spongy, weedy bottom. The last remnants of his ability to sleep at normal times of the day dried up; his body only turned off when the empty batteries started to rust through. At night he lay on a sheet on the sofa, during the day blades of light pierced the splintered boards. Only when he'd entirely run out of provisions, down to the last crumb and last sheet of toilet paper, did he venture out. Everywhere he used to shop had either been blown to bits or burned to the ground, so he undertook longer expeditions by bike, returning from these other neighborhoods completely wrecked, more from nerves than from physical exertion. He saw them everywhere, sitting, walking, standing—Sigerius or Joni, or both. In his weakest moments he dialed Joni's number, but of course she didn't answer, and he did not know what to say into her voice mail. His grief turned into raging jealousy, and vice versa.

One day he found an envelope with the keys to their Alfa on the doormat. Their website had gone off-line, he noticed one night; he was surprised she was able to manage it on her own. He began to suspect that perhaps she had already left for America. At night—daytime there—he checked their joint bank account, he'd studied that astronomical seven-digit balance so often he could recite it like a telephone number—until, sure enough, the dollars started evaporating. From certain transactions he concluded that Joni had instructed their collection agency to refund money to clients. Withdrawals from Sunnyvale Plaza, purchases at Borders Books and Trader Joe's—amounts that approximated his own withdrawal of crisp 100s he used to pay the Italian or Chinese food deliveries—confirmed that she was indeed in America. He was crazy with mistrust. Did she have someone else there? One afternoon he called up McKinsey Amsterdam and invented an excuse to be connected to Boudewijn Stol. When he actually answered, Aaron waited a moment and then gently put down the receiver.

He hung in time like a jellyfish in the ocean, pulsating silently as though not only Roombeek, but also the entire world had exploded, and his living room was the sole entity revolving around the sun. He gave his insomnia free rein, day and night lost all relevance, his waking state gradually took on an inscrutable rhythm, drifting in and out of sleep. His dreams were intense. He now ordered all his food by phone, and the doorbell invariably shook him violently out of a turbulent underworld. Every now and then he got so sick of himself that he attempted to read something, or stared at the television, played a jazz record at full volume, only to wake up to the tick-tick-tick of the needle catching in the lock groove.

The few times the phone rang, he first had to get over the shock before he dared listen to his voice mail. Whenever anyone rang his doorbell—the postman, charity collections, even once his friend Thijmen—he would sink to his knees next to the radiator and peek under the curtains to see who was there to threaten him. The constant fear that it was Sigerius.

One day his voice mail overflowed with messages from Blaauwbroek. The jovial banter about putting out his barbecue, about rinsing the suntan lotion out of his ears, whether he was back in long pants—it was as though his boss was speaking a foreign language. He did not respond. Only after the third message, "Bever, stick some TNT in your ass and get over to the newsroom," did he force himself into action. Maybe, he thought, the world just kept on turning. He shaved, put on the only clean clothes he could find, and got on his bike.

His eyes no longer accustomed to so much daylight, he blinked his way around the fenced-off disaster area and cycled toward the Drienerlo woods. The brilliant sun burned into his retina, passing cars screamed in his face. His mouth was bone-dry. The campus still exerted a magnetic force on him, but now the poles were reversed. He cycled uphill, or so it seemed, he had to toss his cigarette away because he was gasping like a drowning man. When he reached the green corridor between the city and university he gradually slowed down, he couldn't catch his breath, even though he was almost standing still it was like he was being sandblasted. He was up against the sound barrier. Deafening noise, birds, leaves, insects, the stomping of ants. Up in the trees, libelous whispers. Everything on his body itched and tightened, his eyes watered.

A few hundred meters on, Sigerius rounded the leafy curve with a collie on a leash. Nauseous with dread, he swerved off the path, coasted behind an oak tree and into some low shrubs, coming to a standstill against a wall of pale-yellow sand. Still straddling the bike, he threw up. And there he stood panting in his shelter, spitting pukey saliva out of his mouth. The man and his dog walked past.

Cycling through the campus was out of the question. There was no way he would climb the cement stairs to the newsroom, that he would enter Blaauwbroek's office and take a seat across from him. Every Monday morning at exactly the same time, Blaauwbroek walked across the quad to the administrative wing and sat down with the rector for a "press moment." As long as this tradition continued, and continue it would, he could not face his boss; facing Blaauwbroek meant facing Sigerius, and the same went for every last soul on this goddamn campus, it was one huge pyramid, everyone supported, in one way or another, the capstone—except him. He had toppled off.

He wiped his mouth, pulled himself together, and pushed his bike up the sloping bank to the path. Go back. Just as he was about to set off, he noticed two figures cycling his way from the Enschede side. Murk van der Doelen and Björn Knaak. As soon as he saw them he looked the other way. Paralysis spread through his limbs. Not now. Knaak and Van der Doelen, he used to chat with them at keg parties and at gatherings of the debating society, student organizations and the like—mostly in a fairly drunken state, them, but him too. Contact within these groups was superficial, raucous, razzing, noncommittally chummy. The guys were in the same clique as Joni, he had witnessed them addressing fellow students from atop tables, bars, and other raised surfaces—brash, eloquent oratories, delivered with a panache he abhorred and envied at the same time.

They were the last people in the world he felt like bumping into. These guys had practically turned white from sheer cockiness, as scaly as an out-of-date chocolate bar. Knaak and Van der Doelen lived with about ten other Siemsayers in a swanky town house on the Oldenzaalstraat where they had 24/7 training in frat-boy superiority. He'd been in the villa about five times, mostly to photograph their top-drawerness in the run-up to the annual house ball, a self-satisfied fête "to put some pizzazz into the city."

By now they recognized him. Murk rode in front: a blond stack of Gouda cheese wheels, slouching on his bike like an old geezer. An expression of mockery spread over his bean-shaped head, which sat on his full-fat chest without any intervention of a neck. He was still standing there, bike in hand, so there was no avoiding them. Murk screeched to a halt.

"Well, if it isn't Aaron Bever," said Björn Knaak, coasting toward him until his front tire banged into Aaron's. Björn was a thickset fellow with a shaved head, mean eyes, and a low-hanging crotch. He was on the rugby team. Aaron had no idea what he studied, but it would have had to be something concrete and easy to grasp. Like Joni, he considered university the instruction manual for the business world.

"Hi guys," he said softly, and halfheartedly stuck out his hand. Handshakes were part of their obligatory protocol. Oh well, he didn't really hate them.

Murk van der Doelen took him in from head to toe. "Bever," he said, "are you dead or what? You look like you died of a lethal fatality."

Murk studied classical piano, the last thing you'd expect from him. Once, Aaron had heard him give a recital before some student gala: the picture of refinement, Beethoven, Liszt, Prokofiev, his fat fingers danced over the keys, elegant as anything, and afterward a too-long ovation and frilly nibbles on microscopic melba toasts. But deep down, Murk was a lout. Once a year he had his stomach pumped at the Medical Spectrum following the annual beer-drinking tournament in their wood-paneled old boys' society, a competition involving twenty-four bottles of beer which he, thanks to both technique and character, guzzled faster than anyone else. During the autumn "rush" of aspirant members, Murk defended the long staircase to the bar like a pale-skinned Hulk, cursing and screaming, his blubbery bare torso dripping with deep-frying oil, his arms around the skinny hips and necks of frightened eighteen-year-old runts who had envisioned something completely different.

"I'm on my way home from work," Aaron said. "I'm kind of under the weather."

"About-face, Bever," Björn said. "There's a party. It'll perk you up. We're going to celebrate your bachelorhood."

"Who says I'm a bachelor?"

"I do," said Björn. He wiped his hand over his muscled ferret-snout.

"Everyone does," said Murk.

"Your lady told me herself," Björn said. "Your *ex*-lady."

Actually, I *do* hate you guys, he thought. Maybe this kind of jerk was the reason he'd fled Utrecht, not a thought he'd ever admitted to Joni, who surely wouldn't have understood. Since you always saw Björn and Murk together, Joni gave them the amusing nickname "Björk." "I was at De Kater yesterday, and guess who was there? Björk." The complete ease with which she had these braggadocios in her pocket.

In fact, Joni knew little about the Utrecht debacle that had been on his mind these last few weeks. He kept all references to it vague. After high school his mother had packed a student cookbook and teddy bear for him, and off he went to study Dutch in Utrecht. It was a catastrophe. He flunked two-thirds of his exams, and due to unfinished hazing business at a fraternity he missed the department introduction, so that he didn't know anyone who could pilot him through the winter semester. He pined away in the room he rented from his great-aunt in Overvecht, a suburb with asbestos flats and its own station with two sets of rails to lie down on. Utrecht's nightlife was out of reach; from the sixth floor he stared out over a dark-green ocean of grass, his great-aunt's granite balcony was the edge of the edge. His insomnia thrived, he often woke at four, four-thirty in the morning, unlocked the door and sat freezing to death on a plastic garden chair for hours on end, until it was time to go to class. He would then grapple his way into town on his great-aunt's undersized ladies' bike, performing depressing slaloms through drafty Utrecht-North, which now reminded him of his cycling expeditions through post-explosion Enschede. He noticed from the pillowcases (also borrowed from his great-aunt) that his hair was starting to fall out, just like the bristles of her silky toothbrush that he used on the sly because he kept forgetting to buy his own.

"I talked to her a while ago," Björn lisped.

"Who?" he asked.

"Who do you think? Your lady, of course. She was in the Hole, a send-off from her debating team." The Hole: a dank underground drinking cave that literally bored into the Oude Markt. News about Joni in the Hole was always bad news. "One thimble of Bacardi," drawled Björn, "and she's pushing her tits up against you. She'll tell you anything you want to know. And also what you don't want to know. And forever pressing those party-knockers against you. Pity she's buggered off to America."

His big eyes were slanted, the whites were yellow. One way or the other, this ferret never failed to mention Joni's breasts. Knaak couldn't *not* talk about them. Yes, he hated Björn, even more than he hated Murk.

" 'I'll bet you're a free agent now,' I say to her. 'How'd you know that?' she says. You know how ladies say that at 4 a.m. in the Hole." Björn put on a girlie voice. " 'How'd you know *that*?' 'Well, I can feel it on two things,' I say. 'Two pointy pieces of hard evidence.' "

Murk chortled softly. Björn, who only laughed either out of strategic considerations or schadenfreude, put on a serious face. Aaron felt, to his surprise, no jealousy, did not taste the battery acid he used to taste, nor the explosive, childish rage over a pair of nipples poking into the wrong male body—only loathing. What he'd have liked most of all was to tell these two he was a millionaire, and which tits had made him just that. To check himself, he held the wide point of Björn's necktie between his fingers. The blue and orange tie was knotted in a full Windsor, which according to Ian Fleming was the mark of a cad.

"Paws off the tie, geek," said Van der Doelen, and wound up as if to slug him. Aaron decided to play along and let go. These ties were a symbol for the outside world that Knaak and Van der Doelen were officers of the Student Union, the crowning glory of their Tubantia years. Murk especially had a knack for looking back on his student years like an honorary minister, a twenty-three-year-old assessing his past over a good cigar. Of course it was Sigerius, as always, who had put the crown on his head. Three years ago there was a sudden and urgent need for an organization that would "steer all student activism." A student union, after the Anglo-American model. He had seen how Sigerius had screwed another administrative layer onto Enschede's student life, just like you sealed the lid onto a jar of canned peas. His hidden agenda was to counteract the exodus from campus. Students who were initially drawn to the compact, friendly, over-organized campus, usually thanks to enthusiastic parents, were now taking rooms in downtown Enschede, in a real student house near the bars and fraternities on the Grote Markt. It was 2000: you couldn't lock up Dutch college students in the sticks anymore. But now that once-provincial area was packed with hundreds of millions worth of real estate: student flats, faculty housing, a cafeteria and restaurant, a supermarket, an infirmary, a dentist, barber shop, swimming pool, library, pubs, theatres, basement party rooms, athletic fields, works of art—Tubantia *was* the campus. The Student Union was to be the engine behind it.

Sigerius budgeted a heap of money for it, and recruited Björk to mind the shop.

"Let's go, pussypants," Murk said. "Your daddy-in-law will be there too."

Aaron shook his head.

Björn laughed at something, but the sound was drowned out by the rustling of so many leaves surrounding them. "What," he said. "Sigerius *is* your pal, isn't he? Or are you chicken?"

Aaron suddenly went red-hot, the air that closed in on him felt like a furnace, it could ignite at any moment. He was *ashamed,* he was overcome by an explosive shame. But what for? From Knaak's and Van der Doelen's mugs you could see he had a strange look about him. His embarrassment had nothing to do with Joni's breasts in the Hole, nor with the fact that he had wholeheartedly distributed them throughout the world, boobs that would bob like driftwood around the Web for years to come—no, he was ashamed because the guys were right: he was chicken.

"What's with that Student Union?" he asked off the cuff. "It sounds so namby-pamby. In Utrecht it wouldn't ever get off the ground, in a real varsity town the frats wouldn't let themselves be bossed around by some student union. I thought that student associations didn't give a damn about the university."

As usual, he was only parroting Etienne Vaessen. To his friend, who had been something of a big shot on the Utrecht frat scene, he defended the campus tooth and nail, but as soon as he stood at the bar with guys like this he became a mini-Etienne and did his Utrecht veteran act. Sometimes he couldn't resist lying outright that he was a fratter, and if they pressed him he would bluff his way forward, delving into repertoire borrowed from Etienne. "A real frat lampoons the university admin," he said.

"Your point being?" asked Björn. As opposed to Murk, who was at a total loss for words, and whose body hung like a cheap sausage over his handlebars, Björn sprang to attention, his legs spread like a commando, the crossbar of his sticker-covered bike in his low crotch. He wore neatly polished, snug-fitting brogues straight out of the student handbook. His weird, glowing snake-eyes glared belligerently.

"Real fratters don't give a shit about how their university's run," Aaron said nervously. "They just do whatever they goddamn please."

Before Björn responded, he slid his pronounced lips up and down over that big set of teeth of his. "You hear that, Van der Doelen? Bever here is in the know. Now that Sigerius has dropped him like a piece of dog shit he's going to tell us just how things should go." He shook his disgruntled ferret-head. "The school newspaper photographer feels that we should do whatever we goddamn please." He looked straight at Aaron, mockingly. "For years he's got his head up Sigerius's ass and now he thinks *we're* ass-lickers. You hear that?"

"I hear it," Murk said earnestly. "Big talker in the bar, Siem this, Siem that."

His nausea returned. He might be five years older than these guys, but the world started spinning as though he were on a carnival ride, the rustling treetops became a green morass that whispered to him like a theatre prompter. *Go on, tell them.*

"Sigerius is leaving," he said. It sounded raspy; he cleared his throat. "He's through with your campus. He's going to be the new Minister of Education. I've known for months."

"Bullshit, Bever," said Björn. "Where were you at Sigerius's barbecue, anyway? Your bosom buddy doesn't even invite you around anymore."

"He's going to be a Cabinet minister. Still a secret, FYI."

Björn sniffed and spat into the bushes. "Now that his lady's off fucking Jim in America—" he said to Murk.

"Jeff," said Murk.

"Now that his lady's off fucking Jim *and* Jeff in America," Björn conceded, "and Daddy can't bear the sight of butt-kisser anymore, butt-kisser's gonna spread some secrets."

Aaron wanted to respond, but his stomach beat him to it. It clenched like a fist, so that the remaining gall made its way up his esophagus. Yellow bile oozed out of his mouth and dribbled over his handlebars. Björn yanked his bike backward.

"You've been boozing, Bever," Murk said. "Should've said so earlier." He laughed uneasily. "Go curl up in your basket, punk."

Björn, meanwhile, was back on his bike, and before he rode off he gave Aaron's baggage carrier a firm kick.

13

Brilliant June sunlight carved the linoleum floor of the former classroom into slices. We both sat looking at the grainy, glossy wooden crucifix on the white stucco wall, so colossal and three-dimensional that it persistently caught your eye. Jesus as hand-hewn athlete in the romantic Tyrol shepherd-with-flock style I recalled from ski vacations in Val Gardena. Every drop of sap would ooze out like blood.

"You hang him up?" I asked to break the silence. Wilbert seemed better at silences than I was. We sat opposite each other, me on an uncomfortable wooden chair, him sprawled on a formless thrift-store armchair covered in light-brown patchwork leather.

"Nah, the Romans did," he answered.

I didn't even realize he'd made a joke, that's how nervous I was. I can barely remember what we talked about for the first half hour, or should I say: what *I* talked about, agitated, high-speed, haphazard, like a wound-up toy mouse. Wilbert, cracking his knuckles, asking the occasional question. The whole time I saw myself through his eyes. I regretted my coquettish miniskirt, I detested my droning account of my internship in California, I cursed the *Quote* I'd bought at the train station newsstand and that had slipped out of the bag.

I focused on that crucifix, perhaps out of embarrassment, but also not to have to look at that other scene of suffering: Wilbert's face. What had *happened*? It was as though it belonged to two different people; the right half of his face, the undamaged side, showed a grim, ill-shaved man who was beginning to resemble his father: the same broad fleshiness as Siem, the same small nose whose right nostril moved when he talked. The eye was still black as crude oil, but duller and smaller than it used to be, accentuated by the gray bags underneath. I had trouble telling whether the healthy half radiated bitterness, or maybe even cruelty, because the gruesome left side demanded all the attention. It was twisted, almost *melted*. His left cheek and corner of his mouth drooped and puckered as though there were no skull underneath, the pale skin hung like an empty rubber bag. His lower eyelid sagged under its own weight, showing the reddish-white insides. When he blinked only the good side closed, the left side stayed open while the eyeball rotated to all white. Every couple of minutes a globule of drool threatened to escape from the corner of his sagging mouth, and he would slurp it back up. It was the sound I'd heard over the telephone.

"Do you have to be religious to live here?"

"Preferably not."

"Preferably not. OK."

As always, he was sizing me up, in so far that was possible with that one watery eye. "Sometimes I wonder," he said, "what exactly they do want. Why they take in megamorons like us. Nobody getting rich off us, see. They keep pourin' money in." He seemed to be mulling it over; I was relieved for him to be the one talking for now. "I guess their thing is to save souls. For them, every convert counts. And as long as they're at it, may as well be hardcore sinners. You have to be rotten to the core, otherwise you ain't gettin' in."

Although his Dutch had clearly deteriorated, his theory had something to it. And he knew himself well enough to use the term megamoron, a pretty accurate description, albeit an indirect one.

"Do you want to stay?"

"Sure. As long as I can stand it. You can't do nothing here. No smoking, no drinking. No drugs."

"Of course, they're helping you reintegrate, that's good." *Genesis: your bridge to society*—I had looked it up on the Internet before getting in the train to Amsterdam—Catholic, locations in ten cities. Applications accepted from prison; ex-convicts were only admitted if they were "motivated" to give their life "new meaning." Sounded all right to me.

"That's not the point," Wilbert barked. "I can fill in my own fucking forms. I can live where I want. I don't *need* them, see, I'm just *using* them, their, what do they call it . . . their compassion."

He yawned, stretched his arms above his head, and pushed his compact chest forward; the overwashed cotton of his T-shirt was yellowed in the armpits. He wore camouflage army pants and generic sneakers. His body was bloatedly muscular, a hard, round belly—a gift from his father—swelled between his thick thighs. On the dusty rattan coffee table in between us lay a copy of *Nieuwe Revu*, some dried-up tangerine peels, and a weird object: two short sticks, handles actually, connected to each other by a two-inch chain. "What's that?" I asked, nodding at it.

I spent the whole trip from Enschede to Amsterdam wondering what I was going to say to Wilbert. What to talk about with someone you perjured in court? Ten years had passed, I'd had ten years to think it over, and I couldn't come up with anything better than this?

"Karate sticks. Point is, they're different here. These religious people are selfless. Take Jacob, he's completely selfless."

"Jacob?"

"My mentor. The guy gets up at six every morning." He looked at me. What was I supposed to do, whistle with admiration?

"Then he bikes out here from Watergraafsmeer and sits in the kitchen waiting for the deliveries from the bakery and the grocery store. Every morning, see? He puts out the bread, the milk, the apples, and the bananas, drinks coffee. Only then does he have his breakfast. Half a loaf of *peperkoek* with butter."

I nodded.

"Spends the rest of the day fixing shit. Other people's shit. This morning two Yugoslavs showed up, they'd come to have a chat with one of our guys. He must've smelled them or something, 'cause he climbed out his window and shimmied up the drainpipe to the roof. Lay there flat against the roof tiles."

Strangely enough, I pictured *him* lying there, Wilbert, clinging to the steep, tea-cozy-shaped roof of the pretentious urban villa where we were sitting, a building that until the 1930s had housed the Free School. High-ceilinged classrooms with ornate woodwork, anthroposophical slogans etched into the tiled walls, once intended for children from the intellectual class. Today the villa was home to a very different sort of resident.

"And so Jacob has to get rid of these chumps. And then get a ladder and haul that dude off the roof. And that's how it goes, see, six days a week, for twenty years. If you ask him why he does it, he says: because Jesus loves me, and he loves you too. A selfless man. Doesn't even get paid, y'know."

That last part was hard to believe, that Jacob didn't get paid, in fact it all sounded pretty soppy to me, but, I thought, maybe he really was touched. I looked at the crucifix. Did he still believe? Once we all went to Drenthe, he and the four of us, a short vacation early on in his year with us in the farmhouse, we'd rented a National Parks bungalow, I think to get used to one another. So there we were in this forest ranger's cabin, sitting around a table that wobbled so much my mother flipped it upside down and took a bread knife to one of the legs—to Wilbert's amazement, because of course the only thing he ever saw his mother take a bread knife to was a cardboard carton of supermarket wine. And since it did nothing but rain the whole time, we played Risk and Monopoly and Trivial Pursuit, which pissed Wilbert off because even Janis knew more than him. His religious outlook, or what passed for it, revealed itself during those gaming hours: there was a question about Hinduism or Buddhism and Wilbert earnestly declared that there had to be something between heaven and earth, he did believe in a God, his mother's soul had to have gone *somewhere.* At which point Siem made an attempt to gently instruct him—but in fact he jumped down his throat; our live-in atheist was determined to convince Wilbert of the impossibility of an afterlife, tossing around studies done by scientists he "knew personally." It was a red flag to Wilbert. "Know-it-all," he said, hard as nails, and nothing else. I seem to remember hiking through the woods the next afternoon, could have been later, to a dolmen. Alongside that enormous pile Wilbert stumbled upon a rock with a cavity that had filled up with rainwater, and in that little pool we saw tadpoles swimming around. He asked if I saw the "fathead," that was Siem, he said, and the pool he was swimming around in was the universe he supposedly knew everything about. And those two other tadpoles, those were me and him, to whom Siem sat there hollering that nothing existed except our little pool.

"So do you still believe?" I asked.

"You sound just like Jacob," he said. "You wanna know where I got the hangjaw, don't you? Facial paralysis, the doctors call it. A busted facial nerve. Permanent."

"A fight?" I asked, wondering why he suddenly brought it up.

Wilbert laughed—the kind of laugh that doesn't let you off the hook. "You guys in that dollhouse of yours seem to think I go door to door with a bludgeon. Nah, run-of-the-mill ear infection. What you get when you sit in the slammer playing doctor with a plastic coffee stirrer." He leaned forward, brought his finger close to my face—for a moment I thought he was going to touch me. "There's this little cable, see, just a thread, a kind of nerve that runs from your ear to your cheek, and that thread makes sure you get to keep that smooth Barbie face of yours. Mine festered itself kaput. See that gauze?"

He pointed to a single bunk bed behind me, an IKEA assembly of untreated pine that went only halfway up the unusually high wall; his room was immense, the original classroom must have had two doors so it could be separated with a plasterboard wall. My eyes were drawn to the childlike desk under the bed; above a layer of tax papers and torn-open envelopes lay a wad of gauze and a roll of adhesive tape.

"Every night I have to smear salve onto my eye, see, and then tape it shut. Otherwise it'll dry out. But it spontaneously starts watering while I'm eating. Jacob, he wants me to look for a job, 'you've got to get back into the groove,' this and that, see. This here's one of their drawbacks—they're dreamers. Who's gonna hire a face like this, d'you think? Totally fucking *nobody*, that's who. Even that Jesus of theirs would hire someone else. If that guy there"—he stuck his thumb out like a hitchhiker in the direction of the crucifix—"had *this* face, somebody else'd be hanging there now."

"An operation?" I suggested. "Plastic surgery, I mean?"

"You paying?"

"Just trying to be helpful."

"Don't."

More spittle dripped out of the corner of his mouth, but instead of slurping it back in he caught the strand of saliva with his wrist and flung the glob of spit against the linoleum. "There," he said. "There's God for you."

There you had it: the loutish aplomb with which he transformed Daddy's little girl into an unmanageable teenager who considered anything not lethally dangerous extremely funny, and at least worth trying. But now I experienced what my father had to put up with for years: irritation at Wilbert's behavior, at his way of thinking, at his way of *non*-thinking. On TV I'd seen a Dutch bishop tell about how he was hit by some mysterious muscular disorder. For a while the Holy Joe couldn't walk, and his miserable time on wheels seriously shook his devotion. That's their take, the papists. Their whole life long they pray away earthquakes and genocide, but as soon as *they* get sick, weak and nauseous they start to teeter.

Wilbert stood up and walked with stiff steps behind me. "You want anything?" he said. "A drink or something?"

"Thanks," I said. As I spoke, I heard a dull thud. When I looked over my shoulder I saw him wind up for a second slug at a punching bag that swung, squeaking, back and forth on a long rope attached to a ring in the ceiling. Wasn't that twisted dribblegob more *proof* of God than not? An offhand, incidental show of higher justice? God had determined that he should go through life as the cliché murderer. I felt my irritation well up into anger. Wilbert did a few boxing moves, his body seemed to have become smaller and meatier, stronger too. He brought the leather cadaver to a standstill, unzipped it, and stuck his arm in like a vet into a cow. I saw his fingers root around under the dark-blue skin, and the one working corner of his mouth curled upward when he pulled out a small packet wrapped in toilet paper. He said: "Bit of a craving," and went over to a low cabinet, crouched down and pulled out a shabby washbag. Plopped back in the armchair, he took a shaving mirror and a Gillette razor blade out of the bag; the wad of toilet paper produced a ziplock bag of white powder, and I watched as he shook a small mound of it onto the mirror, cut it with short, regular motions, and slid it into a single line. He pulled a flattened ten-guilder note from his back pocket, rolled it up, and bent over the table, the tube up against his nostril. As he inhaled the powder in two mighty sniffs, I looked at his thin black hair, pulled back into a greasy ponytail. He flopped back in the chair. "Cooking," he said, satiated. "They teach you that here too."

A wave of indignation involuntarily forced its way out. "Why do you use that junk?" I heard myself snarl. "Tell me, Wilbert, why do you always choose the path of least resistance? Why are you sitting here doing lines on the sly? God damn it, why do you do the things you do—*Wilbert*."

His face hardened, his right eyebrow crept upward in provocative amazement. He hoarded aggression, I could see it. He closed his right eye and turned his head stiffly. He took a couple of seconds to loosen up his jailbird-neck. Then he opened his eye and looked at me in silence.

"*You* tell *me* something," he said. "Why were you in that courtroom? *You fuckin' skank.*"

The starting gun. Yep. What my father had warned me about ad nauseam was beginning at last. What he'd dreaded for ten years—and I, strangely enough, only now. I blushed, my mouth went dry. Is this what I crossed the damn country in ankle-breaking heels for? I was such an idiot. Why didn't I cancel? Why did I even call him in the first place? Questions, questions. But *his*—that was a good one. What *was* I doing in that courtroom?

"Telling the truth"—so said my father. "Just tell the judge the truth." We were sitting opposite each other in the Bastille's otherwise empty bistro. That's all he asked of me. So what *was* the truth? According to my father, the truth was what Vivianne had told Maurice, and Maurice subsequently told him. And that's what he was going to tell me now, so that I could then relate it to a lawyer, months from now, who would then put it in, what did you call it, a brief? All of it without hearing *his* side. Just tell the truth, kid.

It was the Monday afternoon following the not-so-laconic telephone call from Vivianne's laconic boyfriend; my father and I on campus, seated at a table with red paper placemats on an old-fashioned thick white tablecloth, it felt more like a Chinese restaurant than a French bistro. He had phoned my school and achieved the desired Professor Sigerius effect: the vice-principal stood waiting for me, beaming, outside the chemistry lab. My father was already seated at the window, waiter at fifteen paces, when I showed up at the restaurant, sweaty from the bike ride and the jagged stone steps. He ran his hands through the full black beard he had back then, and only saw me just as I was about to sit down.

"Take a seat," he said, clumsily formal, as though I wasn't his daughter but one of his doctoral students. There was an empty coffee cup on the tablecloth, next to a saucer emblazoned with the Tubantia logo. He looked tired, and in the bright sunlight his suit looked rumpled.

"What'll you have, honey?"

"Dad, I've got sandwiches."

"Throw 'em out. I'm having the steak sandwich. It's delicious here. How'd economics go?"

"Went OK."

He closed the leather-bound menu, beckoned the waiter, and ordered two steak sandwiches. He said something about our vice-principal, uptight man. And then, more to himself than to me: "All right. Now then."

Without a segue he related what Maurice had told him last

Sunday. He tried to, at least: first he got all tangled up in a woolly introduction, and for a moment it looked like he was just going to drop it, but then he cleared his throat and got down to it. His head like a hornet's, he told me about the handkerchief, still euphemistic and clumsy, and when he got to the scarf, to the shower curtain, and what Wilbert had been up to behind it, the whole thing just ground to a halt: his message, it seemed, was a round peg and his mouth a square hole. Why is discussing sex with our parents so awkward? We sat there embarrassed, both of us, but me most of all for him, until he picked up a hammer and bashed his way through the misery that had cost him a good night's sleep.

I think I said something like "jeez," in a slightly surprised tone. A mild kiddie-curse resulting from at least two emotions that tugged at me during my father's tortured account. The worst one was my urge to burst out laughing at what sounded like Wilbert's constant efforts to exponentially augment his repertoire of tomfoolery, which I was starting, deep down, to consider more and more fascinating and arousing—certainly in this "blue" area, one that involved what girls and boys could get up to together. At the same time, this was exactly what *kept* me from laughing—I was watching my step. Yes, that second emotion was apprehension. My father was clearly allergic to Wilbert in general, but of all his irritations I think the most deep-rooted and now the least visible was Wilbert's—how to put it?—lack of inhibition. It was more than just confidence. His aggression, his sloth, his boldness (his *stupidity*, according to my father): these things you could quite reasonably fight about, I'd seen them do so with great enthusiasm. But the fondling and the filthy language, that non-stop hormonal surge—since his arrival the farmhouse had turned into a particle accelerator. Wilbert and the girls, it made Siem nervous, set him on edge. Before the prodigal son had returned to Daddy's hearth and home, four-letter words were like electric fencing; within a radius of 200 meters our little throats slammed shut, Janis and I were struck dumb with cuss-aphasia. But from the minute he sets foot in our house, Wilbert calls everything "cocksucker" or "fucked" or "jism" or "ho" or just "shit," there's no stopping him. After just three weeks he brings a girl back to the farmhouse one Saturday night; the next morning an unfamiliar red and blue granny-bike is leaning against the chestnut tree next to the terrace. The whole Sunday my parents sit there like some Bible-belt couple waiting to see what comes downstairs, but nothing at all comes down the stairs, until Wilbert and the girl saunter into the living room, half naked, at five in the afternoon: "We've come to score a couple of fried eggs."

But instead of just letting them fry up a couple of eggs, my father, covertly pissed off, hisses that the kitchen is closed—shower and beat it, both of you. So that was the last we saw of his one-night stands, from then on Wilbert did that elsewhere, but what we did see more of was skin mags flung about, and boxes of condoms. One day my father storms into Wilbert's room with a gigantic phone bill—itemized, of course. "06" numbers. That sort of to-do in a house which, pre-Wilbert, you could raze to the ground without finding even one single unillustrated and footnoted sex-education manual, let alone anything remotely titillating. Not even a *Panorama.* Weren't you two from the sixties? God, the prudishness! The complete absence of sex in our house. Yeah, they had a Jan Wolkers novel on the bookshelf. But the wrong one.

"Jeez," my father repeated with a mouthful of steak and Italian bread. "That idiot, the jerk, the *scum*bag, molested your French teacher. In our bathroom, in *my* house." Now he was angry, indignant, I could see it on his face, but that Vivianne and her

Maurice, they were livid, especially Maurice. He talked about lifelong traumas *and* about a lawsuit. And my father didn't blame them—on the contrary, he agreed with them entirely. "And if they don't do it, I will."

"Wait a second, Dad—you want to sue your own *son*?"

"Enough's enough, Joni. That creep is ruining us. All of us. Your mother, me, Janis, you. Your sister can't sleep. Janis is afraid of everything. And you . . ."

"*Me?* What *about* me?"

But first he finished chewing. Grinding up that hunk of beef, swallowing it, collecting enough saliva to be able to continue talking, appeared to require more effort than fattening and slaughtering the cow itself. Sweat beaded on his forehead. "You, I worry most about," he said.

"Dad, what. Why do you worry about *me*? What does that kid have to do with *me*?"

He did not answer, but looked at his right hand, the one holding his water glass. Was he just thinking? The sight of this tired, bearded, brooding man made me uneasy; I could tell he was struggling with something he found much more taxing than mathematics.

"Sweetheart," he said, "you know you never have to be ashamed of anything in front of me. Never." Something unlike him: he laid his hand on mine.

"How should I say this. Mom and I get the feeling that Wilbert is . . . uh . . . very fond of you. Do you get my drift? We get the feeling that he's . . . *more* than just fond of you. And that he probably . . . how can I put it decently . . . Mom and I get the feeling that he . . . that you two . . ."

"Dad! What do you *mean*? What are you trying to say?" I yanked my hand back out from under his and shoved my chair back. "Don't be ridiculous, Dad. You mean . . . No, of course not! How dare you!" Although I knew I was overdoing it, I got up and slapped my hands on the table.

"Joni!" he whispered. "Sit *down.* Wait. Sit. Calm. Listen to me. Often, when someone is the victim of this kind of thing, they're ashamed, maybe they're *so* ashamed that—"

"Dad! Shut. Up. Don't say another word."

"Just *listen* to me. And keep your voice down. I hate having to confront you like this, but your mother—"

He got choked up. To regain his composure he used the last bite of bread and meat to sop up some gravy, jabbed it, but it fell off his fork onto his lap. Without cursing, without a laid-back chuckle, he plucked up the wayward morsel and set it on the edge of his plate. "Your mother and I *know* you two are . . . together a lot. We know he takes you out with him, and that's, that *was* . . . fine. I can't tell you how much I . . . appreciate the attention you've given him. You're my daughter. You've done your best to make Wilbert feel . . . to feel at home."

To my shock I saw his eyes welling up. Moisture was collecting in a place that was supposed to stay dry. No! Do not start crying.

"Sweetheart, listen." He appeared to pull himself together. "Of *course* he likes you, I understand that completely, *all* the boys like you, so he . . . so Wilbert *cer*tainly does. That's to be expected. But it's unac*cept*able. It's dangerous; *he's* dangerous. That boy doesn't know the difference between liking and . . ."

"And?"

"Joni." His voice was suddenly sharp. "Answer me. Has Wilbert ever . . . *molested* you? That's what I want to know. It's not such an outrageous question. And that's what the judge is going to want to know. Be honest now."

No. No way. I was not going to tell him about the few times

we came back from town on a Saturday night and plopped down together on the sofa, tipsy, exchanging stories with muted voices, or just making stupid jokes, channel-surfing while the rest of the farmhouse slept. And that it was *me* who put the moves on *him*. At fourteen I was perfectly capable of making a boy of seventeen get all hot under the collar, nothing could be easier—seventeen-year-old boys seldom found themselves on a sofa in the middle of the night alone with a girl who felt *this* comfortable with herself in their sultry presence. Not even Wilbert Sigerius. And so I would quasi-nonchalantly pull up my knees, or just the opposite, spread my legs far too wide while I laughed at what some guy panted in my ear back in the joint where Wilbert had sat at the bar watching me on the dance floor. Or I'd shake my hair loose with a sigh, twang the rubber band into his crotch, and lay down on the sofa with my legs across his lap. When he'd finally put his hands on my bare legs—too hesitantly, if at all—I'd pull myself up on one of those fantastic arms of his and climb, play-insulted, onto his lap, my knees straddling his thighs, I dug my hands into his firm hips, tickled him—"bitch," he would hiss, and I'd poke my index finger under his discreetly stubbly chin, "look at me—what'd you just say, boy?" while we both felt my terry-cloth crotch push against the fly of his jeans—sorry Dad, *that* is all I could think of.

But that was about it. No more than that.

"Dad—you know what you can do?" I said, loud enough so that the waiter looked up. "You go ahead and lie to your lawyer. Tell them Wilbert molested *you*."

His full, thick lower lip trembled as he nodded and stood up. "Be right back," he said and shuffled, in a tragic parody of his hobbling gait, to the men's room at the back of the bistro.

• • •

My legs were covered in goose bumps. Above the enormous windows that looked out onto a schoolyard basketball court were elongated pivot windows. They were open. Soon, after I'd cleared out, Wilbert would close them with the long aluminum pole I saw lying under the radiator. So what was the fuckin' skank supposed to answer?

To my surprise he started talking himself. He had slouched back into his patchwork chair, his hands clasped behind his neck so I could see his leached-out armpits. With his good eye focused on me, he told me how he'd had ten months' juvenile detention, which I already knew, of course, and that they'd put him in De Hunnerberg on the outskirts of Nijmegen, this I knew too, and that he was surrounded by retards, and that he hated me. This last piece of information, I had only assumed.

"When they dragged us out of bed at 7 a.m. and kicked us into the shower, then I took either an ice-cold or a scalding-hot one. That was the only way to spend five minutes *not* thinking of revenge, see. As soon as I turned off the water, I thought: I hate her."

He stopped and sniffed loudly. I crossed my legs. I didn't know what to say.

"I imagined you all having breakfast in the farmhouse. Your mom in her bathrobe, your dad counting scoops of coffee, you and Janis—fuck, I hated you all. I was dangerous." He slurped saliva, and shook his head, grinning.

"But among all those retards I had one friend, see. Big ol' blond dude I sat next to in those classes they made us take. Manners, something with emotions, whatever. Ronnie. Ronnie Raamsdonk. Seventeen, armed robbery. Says he's a nephew of Pedro van Raamsdonk, this and that, but what happened to the 'van,' I ask. He looks at me like I've said something really comical. 'Where's the "van" then, pal? Your name's Raamsdonk, right?' Well, he didn't know, that's just how it was. Anyway, I told him how you fucked me around. You have to talk, you—"

"Wilbert," I interrupted, my head spinning from his declaration of hate, "I wish you knew how sorry I am, I—"

"Just listen," he said. "Don't talk." He waited awhile before continuing.

"So I told Ronnie I hated you. 'You want to even the score,' he said, 'you want to get out of here so you can even the score with your stepsister.' He was right about that, I got all sweaty and jittery at the thought of it. He told me there was 17,000 guilders buried in the woods near Zwolle. He thinks about that money every minute of the day, sometimes out of desperation he tries to count to 17,000, he says, that's how much those Gs are on his mind, this guy was *dumb*. He believed he had to get to those woods before he turned eighteen, otherwise the stash would be gone, see. 'We're gonna help each other out,' he said, 'and I already know how.' "

Their outdoor exercise space, Wilbert told me, was surrounded by a four-meter-high steel fence, untakable without a pole vault, but there was a sort of bus stop shelter up against it for when it rained. If Wilbert were to give Ronnie a boost, he'd pull Wilbert up onto the roof. "This hombre had the meanest arms, see. You hadda see what that guy pumped in the gym. We'd go to the woods near Zwolle together, and I'd get a thousand smackers from him."

"Why on earth would you want to escape?" I asked. "Ten months, weren't you already, like, halfway? I don't get it—really, I don't."

He laughed noiselessly. "You have no idea of time. You've never been mad for more than an hour. You have no idea of anger. What it's like to be eaten up by anger for a week, a month, three months.

You should just keep your trap shut. For weeks I lay awake till dawn"—he made a pistol with his hand—"it got light outside and I stuck this here in your mouth . . . *Bang*."

So one freezing-cold January evening he and his hulking friend smashed a bathroom window and within three minutes they were standing on the other side of that fence. They sprinted down the Berg en Dalseweg and got on the train, without a ticket, to Zwolle. He had cut his shoulder pretty badly but did not feel it. Revenge, see.

"But you—"

He shot me a sharp look.

But you weren't entirely innocent. You *are* a dangerous lunatic—goddammit man, *didn't* you molest Vivianne? *Didn't* you bash a guy to death? The sentences forced their way up to my molars, but I sent them back. As I stared at him they transformed themselves into something more dangerous, a deeper thought. How was I supposed to explain what came over me when our father, long ago, had retreated to the men's room in the Bastille in order to get a grip on himself? What was my reasoning? I only half understood it myself. In my five minutes alone at that stiffly set table I made a hasty decision. I decided to betray Wilbert. My father came back and sat down as an old man. Without batting an eye, I said: "You're right, Dad. It's true. Wilbert's been hassling me." Why did I say that? *Why?*

"But I what?"

"Nothing," I said. "Go on."

"So me and Ronnie, we hike out of Zwolle from the station. Only reached the woods in the middle of the night, see. And him searching, searching, searching. For hours! Behind every damn tree in those woods. It drove me crazy, it drove *him* crazy. It was *freez*ing. He starts punching trees with his bare hands. 'Easy, big fella, relax,' I say to him, 'we'll just wait until daylight.' "

Why? Had that fuss in the bathroom shocked me more than I cared to admit? Or was my concern tinged with jealousy? His attention to Vivianne? Could that be it?

"And guess what, next morning that jerk-off just walks up to it. As though he'd been raised by wolves. Ronnie digs a leather handbag out of the cold earth, unzips it, voilà, 17 Gs. And whaddya know, he gives me one. 'For you,' he says, 'cuz we're comrades. And now we're gonna go to Enschede. You're gonna take it out on your stepsister, I know it, man. I want it too.'"

He paused and looked at me.

"Why're you stopping?" I said, while trying not to listen. Maybe the answer was much simpler, that it had everything to do with the sight of my father walking off. The defeated exhaustion of a man who, before Wilbert showed up, used to amaze us with his vitality. It started back in America, on Bonita Avenue, when in the morning I'd leap out of the bed Siem had tucked me into the night before, tingling with a zest for life that echoed my new dad. Despite reaching his mathematical apex in Berkeley, you'd sooner think he spent his days somewhere on that campus hooked up to an enormous battery-charger. Siem was incredible. In the weeks before Christmas he waited until Janis and I were in bed, and knocked together and painted a dollhouse using my mother's tools. On Sundays he cooked spaghetti with red sauce. He could construct a kite out of a garbage bag and plywood strips in less than an hour. Once we were back in the Netherlands and newly installed in the farmhouse, he built a chicken run in the backyard for five Leghorns, and a rabbit hutch that he disinfected with Dettol and boiling water every Saturday, humming all the while. We watched breathlessly as he fetched a trailer full of old bricks from a demolished youth center behind Boekelo, marched them around the back of the house and—again, humming—built a huge planter using homemade mortar. By the end of 1989 there wasn't a drop of fuel left over in him. Burned up on Wilbert—I think *that* was what hit me when my father returned from the men's room, and sat back down across from me like an empty, dented oil drum. That kid had to go.

"Ronnie could go to hell," Wilbert continued. "No way did I want that monkey tagging along, see. So I say 'no way,' and he says 'yes way,' and I say 'fuck you,' and he grabs me by my throat, pins me to the ground and says 'money back, asshole,' so I say, 'OK, you can come too, but it'll cost you an extra grand.' So he lets me go and gives me another G. God, he was stupid."

And slow, says Wilbert. A sluggish hulk whom he had easily outrun in the Cooper tests at the detention center, and so he stepped it up, walking toward the highway they had come down the night before. When he got to the bike path he intentionally took a wrong turn, not back toward Zwolle Station, but away from town, and Ronnie stood there shouting: "Man! You're going the wrong way!" And then Wilbert broke into a run, a jog actually, at a good clip, farther and farther until ol' Schwarzenegger gave up and gradually became a dot on the bike path. At the first town he got to he broke one of the thousands at a supermarket and took a taxi to Almelo—not the train, he was afraid Randy Ronnie would get the same idea. Once in Almelo he killed time in the freezing cold until the shops opened. He bought some clothes at the V&D department store, and a heavy coat he kept on. At the hardware store he got some rope, a box cutter, a kind of machete, "half a sword, man," a roll of wide black plastic tape. At the sporting goods outlet he bought a gym bag into which he deposited his purchases.

"Is this all true?" I asked. He sat there dishing me up a sexual fantasy, he was inventing it on the spot, one of his jailhouse wet dreams. "I don't buy it. You're making this up."

He smirked at me, pulled his T-shirt out of his trousers and wiped the spit from his mouth. "Yeah," he said, "I'm a born liar. I make things sound better than they are, that's me. Trying to spare you some, see. She doesn't believe me. And the face? The ear infection? D'you believe *that*?" He pinched his rubbery cheek and tugged it back and forth. "That crap about my ear, *that* you believe, but not this." He shook his head pityingly. "This here"—he tapped his right temple—"this was a present from this black dude I sold smack to. Diluted heroin, complete junk. The fuckin' jungle bunny. Guy always paid too late, see. Constant shit with him, so I give him shit back. One day Sambo's waiting for me at my car. This and that, y'know. Wants his money back. Go fuck yourself, I say. Bam, he goes and smashes my windshield with a claw hammer. So I jump over the hood and grab him by the neck. But yeah, the fucker slams me on the head with the hammer."

And sure enough, there's a red half-moon on his right temple. He suddenly looked terrible.

"Broken temporal bone. When I came to I was lying in an ambulance."

I wanted to say something, but Wilbert said: "Shhh." He leaned back with a look of contentment. "OK, so months later I'm walking my dogs on the beach, Zandvoort, see, and who do I see but that same guy. Dude's walking along the empty beach eating fish nuggets. So what do I do, I sneak up behind him, let out a scream, and grab him by his moss head and drag him into the ocean. The dude totally doesn't know what hit him. I give him a few head-butts and hold his head under water. Kept doing it until he's half drowned, see." He looked at me, satisfied. "*That's* what I do with dudes who fuck with me."

See, y'know, see—I'd had about enough, see. I was *through* here.

I didn't want to spend another minute in a room with Wilbert and his *see.* I got up, could've just walked out the door. But instead I went over to the window. Behind me I heard him scuff his chair.

There were two small framed pictures on the windowsill, I picked up the first one, a black-and-white photo of a laughing young woman. She had tufted-up dark hair and was standing in a yard with a white fence. Must be Wilbert's mother. Without realizing it, I'd started crying, silently, calmly. In the other frame, I saw through my tears, was the same woman. Margriet, years older, sitting on a plaid sofa in an eighties living room, pixie haircut, her face unnaturally thin. Next to her: Wilbert. About eleven years old, square buck teeth, shaggy hair, cheerful and serious at the same time. Man of the house. So this is what he looked like while the people who dumped him were living in America. I had to sit this out. *Grant him this.*

Maybe he read my mind, because he said: "It was a Thursday. I knew you had that job at the stables on Monday and Thursday nights—you went, no matter what. That last stretch through the woods and fields, pitch-dark, no houses, for a kilometer or so. Your route that night. No doubt about it."

God, he was right—I never ever missed it. Never. If I stayed home sick from school, I'd make sure I was back in shape before it was time to go to the stables. I saddled up horses, broke in newcomers, hosed down the troughs. At fifteen, nothing could beat this.

"Out before nine, back after eleven. And that's when I was gonna drag you off your bike. I hung around in Almelo until after dark. In the library, in the V&D, in a restaurant right near that fucking courthouse. I blew a hundred bucks on food, see." He chuckled and said he'd taken a taxi "with his pants undone" to Enschede and had the driver drop him at the wooded bit between the campus and town. He chose a gentle curve with high bushes to hide in. Still had a few hours so he walked into the fields out back. Hard beds of gray sand, dead roots on the ground. In the distance, frozen water, and next to a dock there was a small shed. "All sorts of junk in there, including a rubber inflatable boat. So I blew it up, lay there a bit, see. Maybe an hour. I was totally . . . *horny.*"

He'd taken the tape and knives out of the gym bag and walked back to the curve. Bike lamps visible from afar, but whether it was me or not, he couldn't tell. Then he recognized me, blond hair sticking out of my winter cap. "How you lean over your handlebars when you bike, see."

I went back to my chair, sat down and sniffed. "You're crazy," I said. "You're completely crazy."

His breathing became agitated, his fingers clawed at the loose leather of his chair. "You were just a few meters away from me, bitch." The difference between the right and left side of his face was greater than ever. It was impossible to say how he looked at me. "And then I saw somebody cycling behind you. Some fat bitch without a lamp. I hesitated."

"You *hesitated*?" I said. "You're fantasizing. You're talking crap, Wilbert. Nothing like this ever happened. Who do you think you're kidding? You can't even come up with a decent ending."

Yeah, that's how it went. I'd forgotten how angry he got. He jumped out of his armchair with such force that it fell over backward with a huge crash, iron legs up in the air. "Bitch!" he shouted. "*Bitch!* Fucking *bitch!* I should've slashed you to ribbons—god damn it to hell, what a bitch you are. I should have *fuck*ing slashed you to ribbons when I had the chance. I *smelled* you, your Judas-smell. I got a whiff of that goody-two-shoes, your loyalty to Daddy, loyalty to your safe little nest, your—"

"Siem and I don't see each other anymore," I screamed above his tirade. I surprised myself. I'd jumped up too, we were standing face-to-face, four shins against a rattan coffee table. I hated myself. Hadn't I resolved not to let it get out of hand? "I'll never see him again, *ever*, d'you hear me?" I barked. But why? Why did I say that? To impress him? It was just like back then, him taunting me for being a daddy's girl, and my need to disprove it. I could see Wilbert prick up his ears, he pursed the good half of his mouth.

"Oh yeah?" His voice was calm, as though he hadn't just lost his temper. He extended his arm, put a hand on my shoulder and let it glide off with a vague stroking motion. "Let's hear it."

I slumped back into my chair. "I'm not as . . . goody-goody as you think."

"So what's that got to do with him?"

Catharsis. Just the simple fact of telling it out loud, relating the drama that had taken place on the Vluchtestraat, the still-fresh horrors I'd been feverishly keeping to myself for days, putting into words what we had been up to for four years like a pair of counterspies—that alone provided me with a strange, intense sense of relief. But the real pleasure came from the amazement on Wilbert's face, the mouth-watering awe, he even seemed shocked, he called it "bizarre and pretty gross." He'd put his chair back upright and sat listening to me with his hands in his lap. "You loaded, bitch?"

"Nah."

"Course you are."

"Really, I'm not."

"OK. So tell me what *he's* got to do with it. I tell you stuff too, see."

The acuity of his argument. Maybe I was just relieved he'd stopped asking about money, maybe I realized he did have a point. I told him the straight story: the vacation, us coming home early. The sliding glass door.

"*What?* So he knows everything?"

"Yup. What I'm telling you is two weeks old, you get it? We come home earlier than planned and there he is. And I realize right away: he knows everything."

"Why you telling me this?"

"And then he walked straight through the window," I said. "And now I'm going to America. He just marched straight through it, *bam*, straight through the glass."

"But bitch—why are you telling me this?"

14

He's bleeding like a pig. Vague throbbing under his left foot, tingling in his hip and lower arms, if he lays his chin on his right shoulder blade he can see the gash that runs diagonally over the ball of his shoulder—but he feels almost nothing. His physical pain is smothered by a much broader malaise. Why did he get undressed, why didn't he just leave? The regret that descends upon him feels like a chronic condition. He pushes his back flat against the blind brick wall behind which Joni and Aaron are, *must stay.* He prays they won't come after him. His brain is a bazaar after a bombing, thoughts are ripped-off limbs. His nakedness is infinite. From the blood prints on the gray paving stones he sees that he walked a little way into the alley, then back again. His entire existence is reduced to this alley, with the Vluchtestraat on one side, the Lasondersingel on the other. In his initial panic he almost ran out onto the boulevard, a powerful flight reflex. Not long ago he helped lead the town in a silent march through these streets, now he is standing stark naked in this alley. Naked in an alley with his ass in his daughter's panties. *Please let this be a nightmare.* He shuffles along in that procession and sees himself emerge from the alley without any clothes, through pairs of 100,000 eyes he looks at himself: a raving lunatic. His clothes are lying on the attic floor, but going back in there is out of the question. He keeps seeing himself standing in the living room, sees his nakedness through her eyes. Where did they come from? The recurring image of Joni collapsing to the floor in shock. Think for a moment. You must get out of here. But you can't. The brick wall is making his back itch. Just think of one thing at a time. Wait for it to get dark. And as though someone is reading his thoughts, the light dims, he looks that way: a silhouette at the Vluchtestraat end of the alley. He is briefly glued to the wall, a sculpture in a ludicrous place. The echoes of a bouncing soccer ball, it is a child, it runs for a few steps, picks up the ball, and looks. He jerks into motion, drags himself through the alley, the sole of his left foot suddenly on fire, after a few meters the brick walls become a green wall of conifers. He can only think of one thing: without hesitating he wriggles between two man-sized conifers at the edge of Aaron's neighbor's yard, for the second time this evening he squeezes himself among countless pricking fingers, the grainy sand sucks itself deeper into the hole in the sole of his foot. Stay standing in the narrowest spot. Make yourself small. The sand wants to suck him dry, the itching of the branches in his ears, between his buttocks, in his navel, the intense smell of sap. He turns his head toward the backyard, the branches scrape, he sees a terrace, the back door is open. Automatically he shifts slightly back into the alley, and listens. Footsteps, the echo of the bouncing ball, every sound wave ricochets ten times up and down between the walls, the child is approaching. He squeezes his eyes shut, listens, himself a conifer, all he hears is the rushing of his blood. The echo recedes, the steps become slow, almost inaudible. Wounds throbbing in unison. When he opens his eyes and looks through the dark-green tangle of branches, he sees the child, it's standing in front of him, it's orange, it's wearing a Holland jersey. It stares wide-eyed in front of him—at his chest?

"Go away," he whispers.

It cowers, it is a little boy, he sees, he drops his ball in fright, grabs it as it bounces away and sprints with hollow footsteps toward the Lasondersingel. He remains stock-still, waits before exhaling, a trembling sigh. Slowly his hearing sharpens again, he hears a bus drive by, he hears soccer coming from the houses, the voice of a commentator, fans. God bless football. *Keep my alley clear.* He allows his tension to ebb slightly—but then stiffens again. He's overestimating his invisibility. These people only have to walk into their backyard. And Aaron and Joni? He's still bleeding like crazy, a tepid stream trickles down his biceps. He needs to think more clearly. He can't stay here. But then what? A sudden roar rushes sweat to his skin. Shouting inside the house, cheering from all the backyards: the hordes are coming to get him. A goal. He realizes he's still clamping the nylon stocking in his fist, he shakes it loose as though it's a rattlesnake. The branches are armies of ants. What can he do? The streets are abandoned, emptier than this it will never get. He tries to control his breathing, shifts his feet and visualizes the Vluchtestraat. Maybe he can ring somebody's bell. Say he's been robbed. The thought of himself on a garden path in these panties. But he can't very well take them off. *Everything is ruined.* He is humiliated, *she* is humiliated. Is she really? *Must get out of here.*

He considers: half of them are on vacation. He visualizes the low-rise apartments at the end of the street with all his might; museum on the left, block of flats on the right, wooden garden fences behind. Can he get up to one of those balconies? And which one? Is there a logical approach? Closed balcony doors mean the occupants are away. Open: football, closed: away. Can he sprint there? Peek out of the alley, choose your moment, make a dash for it. He tries to estimate the distance. Forty meters. Fifty. Six seconds. And getting up onto one of those balconies? For a second he thinks of home, of the tangle of grass behind their farmhouse, of the tranquillity, the shelteredness. It has to be pitch-dark before he can . . . walk home? Christ on a crutch. Must he *walk* home? *You're in a dream, you're in the mother of all nightmares.* A short-cut, maybe? All the jogging paths he's seen in the past twenty years unfold simultaneously before him, a knot of wooded paths and loose sand. But there's the city in between. A taxi? *You don't even have a phone.* No keys, no money, nothing. His thoughts turn to Tineke. He can't face her. He mustn't even *get* home before midnight. Is there a spare key in the garden?

Got to get onto one of those balconies.

He turns his head 180 degrees, bristles rub against his eyelids and cheeks, his neck is strangely stiff. His chin tucked against his own blood, he looks over his shoulder, down the alleyway, and listens. On this side the world is quiet. Again he is struck by the indifference of objects: gray paving tiles absorbing his blood, the indifferent exterior walls. He inhales as though he's about to take a dive and glides out from the trees. *Run.* Adrenaline dissolves in his blood, is discharged from his wounds. The air on his bare skin. Every few steps he looks back, tries to suppress his panting. Behind that brick wall: *them.*

The street clutches the setting sun. He is overcome by the sudden spaciousness. The purple sky is infinitely high, his nakedness is intensified. He peers around the corner of the brick house at the apartments, the wide balconies, it's farther away than he had hoped. The balconies are fronted by orangey-pastel panels; that's where he wants to be, behind one of those panels. Across from the entrance door with the letter slots is a large concrete and steel bin, a mini-bunker for garbage bags. Already now, from his trench, he feels the warm asphalt under his feet, pebbles in his open sole. A car turns into the street, with a groan he darts back into the alley. Holds his breath until the unhurried machine has passed. So close to their front door. The street is empty.

Now.

First the cement sidewalk, then with five long strides diagonally across the asphalt, don't look back or around, the apartment is getting bigger, casts a shadow. He jumps up onto the massive concrete container like a baboon, bags of smoldering garbage bulge out from under the metal lids. Don't think, *act.* Why does he keep seeing himself? A naked man clambers over the squeaking lids, curls his toes over the edge of the concrete. He estimates the height: a meter and a half separates him from the railing of the nearest balcony. If he loses his grip he'll land in somebody's front yard. He flies, he's a flying monkey! He'll make noise. They're watching football. His knees bang against the pastel-colored panel, his fingers grasp, one hand flies loose, the other grabs the edge of the rail. His body dangles, stretches. His weight pulls on the fingers of his right hand, it feels as though his shoulder is being torn open even farther, as though the skeleton will glide out of his skin, he throws his second hand over the railing. For a moment he hangs totally motionless, his belly pressed against the warm panel. Cutting straight through the pain is the vision of himself dangling there; the disgust energizes him. He's hung on a high bar plenty of times, did the parallel bars, the pommel horse: he was the best gymnast of them all, better than Snijders, better than Geesink—but that was forty years ago. He pulls himself up with all his might, works himself up until his elbows are locked. The balcony door is closed, the apartment is dark. He swings his left leg over the railing, clambers over, lands on the cool concrete floor. He crouches behind the panel.

He sits like this for a while, panting like after a fight, his good shoulder against the panel, staring at his toes on the concrete. Wait a bit. If someone is home, then they'll have heard him, the door will fly open any second. He waits. His breathing relaxes, from the neighboring balconies comes the reassuring sound of the football match. Has anyone seen him? On the street? Good chance that the police are on their way. His right shoulder is bleeding again, dripping blood onto the concrete. He inspects the bottom of his foot. In the ball of the foot, just back from his big toe, is a star-shaped hole. It is his short leg: feeling never really returned to his foot after the scooter accident. Now he doesn't regret it. He pulls out a splinter of glass. New blood wells up.

He gradually persuades himself that no one is home. He looks around, this time in more detail: the balcony is a meter or so deep and runs the breadth of the apartment. To his right is a dark-red door. From a crouch he can just peek into the living room: a green-and-white plaid sofa opposite an old bulky television; farther in, an ironing board and behind it, a kitchenette. A student flat? What would be worse, he wonders: a Tubantia student who recognizes him or a regular Enschede resident face-to-face with a dangerous lunatic?

On the balcony itself there are two plastic chairs, alongside them three empty Grolsch swing-top bottles and in the far corner boxes of waste paper. Opposite the boxes, a yellow drying rack hangs on the railing: *laundry*. He crawls past a chair toward it. Two dishcloths, a towel, a pair of pink and black ladies' socks, a pair of red knee-length men's swim trunks. He wriggles out of the panties and, still sitting, puts on the bathing suit. A wave of euphoria and relief streams through him. He stuffs the panties in one of the back pockets. He lays the drier of the two dishcloths over the wound on his shoulder and ties it with endless fumbling under his armpit. Having no other choice, he tugs the stiffly dried socks onto his feet.

Then he lies down on his back. The concrete supports his

weary body. He lies like this for maybe half an hour. The panel doesn't extend all the way to the floor, if he rests his chin against his bandaged shoulder he can peer through the gap. By turning slightly farther onto his side and pressing his chin farther into his flesh, he can even see Aaron's house. In the distance he sees the shrubbery at the foot of the path and the top of the front door. Heavy with regret, he looks at it for a while. He gradually becomes calmer, his reasoning takes form. How big was *this* coincidence? he wonders. The chance of being caught like that? Caught at the most wretched moment of his life. The modulations of fate: coincidences are usually smaller than you'd think, the football match he'd just thanked his lucky stars for probably played a role in his downfall. Undoubtedly. Without the soccer alibi he wouldn't have even come here tonight, not at this exact time—and knowing those two, the same is true for them. They drove here with the match in mind. Switched on the TV the minute they got home.

Above and alongside him, a new outbreak of cheering. Although he feels relatively safe on this balcony—it gives him a rudimentary sense of security—he's itching for it to get dark. It's his younger sister's birthday. The longest day of the year. Any thoughts about the consequences—what does all this mean for Joni and him, for his family?—he tries to postpone. I've got the longest birthday, Ankie always said. Get these old bones of his into his own bed.

But time on this stranger's balcony clots, the events repeat themselves like TV clips, immutably sharp, he keeps seeing himself crash through that glass door. And with each rerun of that image he realizes what Joni saw, and he wonders how *grim* her conclusions are. Disastrous, for sure.

• • •

It gets dark, finally. A breeze brings him the first goose bumps of the evening. He prepares to lower his bruised body off the balcony. By way of disguise he wraps the second dishcloth around his head. He knows which getaway route he'll take, but his patience is being tested once again: the match is over, their team has obviously won. People begin to stream outdoors. From all sides he hears men talking excitedly, a car door slams. Wait until things die down again. But: the chance that the resident of this apartment thanks his hosts for the fun evening and climbs onto his bike—he's already up. Without feeling his body, without feeling the concrete under his feet, without touching the railing, without touching the grass on which he lands, he's standing in front of the apartment, and immediately breaks into a run. He scuttles off like a rat, scoots along the fencing toward the Deurningerstraat, ducks into the peaceful residential neighborhood.

His foot strains and stings, but the pain has a cleansing effect, he stays as much as possible in the ever-deepening shadows. In a pinch, he decides, he'll feign drunkenness. He keeps walking, each step is a step closer to home. Cyclists pass him without so much as a second look, nobody pays him any notice. The sole of his foot is killing him, but pain has meanwhile risen up into his calf. He chooses quiet streets, walks past elegant houses with the curtains drawn. When he reaches the Horstlindelaan he feels a guarded sense of relief. He sits down on a bench but springs back up again.

It's a strange sensation, as the landscape passes him slowly by, his bare chest exposed to the mild summer evening, this walk puts nearly everything in a different perspective, the immediate contact of his feet with the earth, the gravelly asphalt, the spongy moss on the edge of the road. The starry night sky is perfectly clear, his eyes seem more sensitive than usual, he reads the surroundings like a night animal. He hears a marten burrowing under a bush, in the yellow light of the moon the trees and meadows seem more intensely colored than before.

It's the second time, damn it. The second time in his life he's been caught with his pants down. And just as it did back then, the foundation of his life has shifted. As he walks along the wooded path to the campus like a criminal he thinks back on the other time he was caught red-handed. Maybe he's recalling Tineke's long-ago birthday party in Utrecht in order to distract his short-term memory. Tineke Beers-Profijt she was called back then—the very idea that his wife was once married to the downstairs neighbor. He and Margriet had been invited; together with about fifteen other neighbors and friends they sat in the ground-floor flat inhabited by Tineke and that vague husband of hers, a weekday cocktail party for the neighbors and colleagues from her furniture workshop; wine, beer, and Campari and funnily enough Tineke's sister from Amersfoort kept putting on yet another LP by Mojo Mama, Theun's band, he never saw him anymore, a curious choice of music, Theun was conspicuously absent, as though he hadn't been invited to his own wife's birthday party, or, more likely, just didn't bother showing up. This was Tineke's midseventies rock 'n' roll marriage.

His own marriage was, if possible, even worse. He remembers the whopper of a fight that broke out between him and Margriet just before the party, they were at each other's throats in their kitchen, their floor was the ceiling under which Tineke was welcoming her first guests with beer and liverwurst (how old were they? twenty-five?), and he can still recall the exact anger in their bodies as they walked down the stairs from 59B and rang the doorbell of number 59A. Memories of the actual gathering, no, not really—the Antonius Matthaeuslaan was a regular party street in those days, and since everyone had a workday ahead of them, most had already left by midnight, with the exception of a few hangers-on, including Margriet and him. And when the hangers-on had pushed off, Margriet started tugging at his sleeve (the booze was finished), but, contrary to his usual way of doing things, he suggested, no, he *announced*, that he was going to finish his own drink and, entirely contrary to *her* way of doing things, Margriet went home alone, upstairs. "I'm going to turn in, honey," she said to Tineke.

After which things took a turn for the worse—or the better, of course. As soon as everyone had gone and he and Tineke were left alone and he stayed sitting next to his fresh-faced, good-humored, intelligent, interested neighbor, next to each other on Theun's orange three-seater, among the empty glasses and the full ashtrays, his leg against hers, a broad, warm thigh against that still-slender thigh of hers—precisely at that moment, the incident that had been two years in coming, came. Before they knew it Siem was on top and Tineke underneath, kissing, intensely, without so much as a chuckle or introductory mumbling, a transgression that had been brewing ever since he lay plastered together in his bed, from the first time Tineke had paid him a daytime visit, offering him companionship while he recovered from that scooter accident. Why did she come, actually? Just because, just to drink a cup of coffee with someone *different*, with a *man*, not to have to talk about the kids of friends of friends? Even back then they were preparing to take this leap.

And when they'd found themselves without passports in those sublime, overwhelming foreign lands, they decided, with no discussion, to stay there longer. They stood up, he and his stable, friendly downstairs neighbor, kissing with ever more abandon, *we can't*, he whispered—*can't what?*—*do this*, but it was only a half-hearted protest, more passionate than guilty, and they staggered toward the bedroom, through the narrow passage, and one door farther (and yet another door farther, who was sleeping there? Little Joni), turned the handle, stumbled into the bedroom, flopped onto the double bed that had stood there waiting for years, a bed under a humongous Kralingen poster, he recalled, Mojo Mama in between Dr. John the Night Tripper and Tyrannosaurus Rex, there you are, Teuntje Beers's triumph that the upstairs neighbor did not register, a triumph that paled the moment he laid Tineke down on the crocheted bedspread.

Although the shortest route is tempting, to be on the safe side he stumbles with his gnarly feet in ladies' socks around the campus rather than through it, takes the now-darkened path through the woods north of the Langenkampweg—the harbor in view, but which harbor? He knows Tineke well enough to be sure she'll be asleep when he gets home. But what about tomorrow? He's got to tell her *something*, even if it's just to be a step ahead of Joni and Aaron. Entirely unpredictable what those two will do. Will they assume he talks to Tineke? No idea. He carefully touches his shoulder. Can he even keep it under wraps? *Can* he lie yet again to the woman to whom he once, long ago, had to give his radical, blind, immediate trust?

For they had made a mistake. They neglected, in their overactive, dizzy state, one small detail. How *human* of them. The front door is not shut. They were too busy to notice that it was ajar—left that way by Margriet from upstairs, simple Maggie Sigerius, maybe a tad less fresh-faced, interested, and intelligent than the woman he is feverishly undressing, but not born yesterday. A drinker, and emotionally labile—but not blind.

And Margriet goes all the way upstairs (at least that's how he reconstructed her movements, in retrospect, in detail), climbs the steep stairs to their cramped apartment, and then goes straightaway to the upper floor, into the front bedroom (who is sleeping there?

Wilbert, sucking his thumb), and, holding her breath, she looks at her little boy, for maybe a full minute, as though she's listening to his dream. A good mother. *Am I?* But actually she's not thinking about Wilbert, in fact her hearing is directed two floors below, to the downstairs neighbor's open front door, and walks slowly back down—but stop, first into the kitchen, she *forces* herself to go into the kitchen, where she pours herself a glass of wine and commands herself to drink it *slowly,* calmly, give them time, five, no, *seven* minutes' more self-control. And while she drinks, one glass, two glasses, her ears are lying like rubber dinghies on the kitchen floor. After seven torturous minutes she takes off her boots and walks silently down the steep stairs to the front door. *Hi, I'm back.*

He reaches the Langenkampweg, walks past the first four detached houses that look out onto the street, averting his gaze, he hardly talks to these people anyway, the hell with 'em. As soon as the leafy canopy reveals the front of his house he stands still. There's a light on downstairs, a faint glow, she's left a light on for him.

Margriet Sigerius, twenty-three years old, walked in the direction of the sleazy, sordid sound that she could just hear above her heartbeat—her heart, too, was bigger than usual, her heart is a pounding machine, but cutting through that pounding she *hears* it: the far wilder banging from the room adjacent to the still-warm birthday room with the showy wicker-and-beanbag interior. She stands at the bedroom door, clammy hand trembling above the handle, but she chokes. Can't go in. She listens, petrified. Then she takes a deep breath, and screams. Melted together with his downstairs neighbor for the first time, Sigerius hears his own wife screech at the top of her lungs, "SIE-IEM"—she screams his name three times, and then: "*What are you doing, what are you doing, I hate you.*" Like stiffened corpses they lie on top of each other, he and Tineke, the rapture never existed. Out in the passage it goes quiet. Dead still. *Maybe we're dead ourselves?*

Then the door flies open, smacks against the wall, the frosted glass shatters into tiny fragments. He looks into Tineke's wide-open eyes. *She's watching them.* "You're never setting foot back in that house, asshole. Never, do you understand? Don't you dare try coming back home, goddammit."

He remains silent, his impudent tongue lies in state in his mouth. They do not hear her leave, the front door slams all the more deafeningly, a grenade. The door to 59B, her own front door, hers and her little boy's, formerly also of Siem Sigerius: she bolts it shut.

The farmhouse, finally. He takes the gravel path around the back, shuffles onto the grass of the backyard, too dark to see his hand in front of his face. Thanks to Janis's habit of leaving her house keys in Deventer there is a spare key hidden in the bird house at the far end of the terrace. He finds it without much trouble and walks over to the garbage can next to the workshop. He bangs mercilessly into the tree stump for chopping hardwood, clenches his teeth against the pain, and removes the worn-out socks from his feet. The left one is drenched in blood. He wraps them in the dishcloth from his head and squashes the wad as deep as possible under the cardboard boxes and scrap wood in the plastic bin.

Strangely enough he yearns not so much for the security of his house as for Tineke, he yearns to curl up against her sleeping body. But he's not there yet, not by a long shot. In the kitchen he removes the dishcloth-tourniquet, impatient blood immediately fills the salmon-pink gash in his shoulder. He binds it with gauze and adhesive tape. His body is covered with clotted blood, his feet are as brown as goat's hooves. He switches off the table lamp in the living room window and walks toward the bedroom, his feet now in his running shoes. He creeps into the room, whispers "hello, sweetheart" to make sure she's asleep and in two steps is standing in the bathroom. He showers, avoiding his shoulder as much as possible; it takes him twenty minutes, his foot stings and throbs.

Tomorrow he'll have to lie about *her* daughter, it won't be easy, an intense anticipatory regret elicits a deep affection for his wife. He turns off the tap. It's *her* daughter we're talking about.

The summer dies down. The months following his descent into hell are uneventful. So uneventful that it makes him nervous, this uneventfulness is a relentless burden. Tineke was not aware of his degradation, he's relieved for that, but her ignorance only augments his isolation. He never mentioned the wound on his foot, he bluffed about the gash in his shoulder, told her it was the result of an unlucky spill at a glass-strewn frat house, he really should have dropped by a first-aid station. Not a word from Joni. Aaron no longer comes to training sessions, good, correct, he canceled their dan exam by letter to the judo association.

Joni plays it neatly by flying off to California while they're vacationing on Crete. Tineke is flabbergasted, but he defends her sudden departure, McKinsey does not wait for Mommy and Daddy to come back from holiday, he says, meanwhile biting his nails: every day of their vacation he plans to spill the beans, tell his wife how he really got those strange wounds, to be *totally* honest, but he holds his tongue. In fact he never really comes close. They're eating souvlaki when Joni phones Tineke's cell, he forces a cramped smile as his food goes cold; even when it's clear that mother and daughter are carrying on a neutral, normal conversation he can't manage to swallow a single bite.

Back in Enschede he is greeted by relatively good news,

confirmation that he did the intelligent thing: just keep your mouth shut, wait and see what happens. And what happens: that website of theirs has frozen, no new photos for several weeks, and then it vanishes from the Web entirely. Apparently they were making the best of a bad situation. He relaxes somewhat. Or is it because Joni is in America?

Meanwhile things are very quiet indeed. Not a peep from California. It is Tineke, of course, who is most surprised. She thinks she understands why Aaron is making himself scarce, although he hasn't yet dared tell her the judo sessions have stopped. "Siem, honey, Joni's keeping awfully quiet, don't you think?" This opportunity to open up, he lets pass by too. What's more, he does just the opposite. To his own amazement he is prepared to do anything to keep Joni from blowing the whistle on him. He undertakes something extremely gutless and futile. Not to mention risky. He creates a fake e-mail address for his daughter on Yahoo and from that cursed phony out-box he sends brief messages, sometimes longer ones, to his own e-mail address. "Dear Dad and Mom and Janis, it's terrific here, been over the Golden Gate Bridge, no phone yet but fortunately there's e-mail. McKinsey is great but intensive, love, Joni"—that sort of drivel, and because Tineke doesn't use e-mail herself, he prints out these stinking lies of his for her. It fills him with disgust and self-loathing, but he does it all the same.

As though he's being punished: no word from The Hague. He peruses the newspapers and journals until his fingers are black, reads memoirs of illustrious statesmen at bedtime. Rumor has it he's in The Hague's waiting room, there's been a leak somewhere. On a Radio East talk show someone—a college student, no less—says he's going to become Minister of Education, and the next day he has to shake off four journalists.

Annoyingly, this vacuum fills up with self-doubt, it just happens. Isn't he being overly self-righteous? Sometimes he thinks it downright stupid to equate that Internet site with prostitution, it's just not the same thing; these are the moments he considers himself a narrow-minded old fart, but a minute later the taboo takes his breath away again, he almost wants to scream with misery, and he treats himself and his wife to another phony e-mail. Then, again: am I being too uptight? Am I not the one who's a moral and ethical stick-in-the mud? A frightened, sexless man?

While he runs the university on auto-pilot he thinks about his children. He can get his head around Wilbert's downfall, with a mother like that, with a *father* like that, a father who ditches his family. He's asked for a son like Wilbert. But Joni is another story, he tells and retells Joni's story, which is his own story: a girl destined by him for happiness and success, a daughter to whom he offered security, gave all the attention a self-fulfilled man like himself has to offer—partly to ease his guilty conscience about Wilbert, he readily admits, but in the end she *did* receive all his love, not to mention *reaped* it, far more than he got in his own youth.

Wednesday, October 11th. As he and Tineke sit watching the evening news, dinner plates on their laps, De Graaf rings. In a two-hour conversation, Sigerius learns that D66 will officially withdraw support for Hildo Kruidenier after the weekend, maybe earlier; the inside story is that this public hazard is dragging the party down in the polls, it's untenable, he has to go. Kruidenier will resign, there is no other option, and therefore De Graaf wants to present Sigerius the next day as the new minister. Is he ready? More than that, he answers, and yes, he'll be able to get to the Prime Minister's office tomorrow morning, Kok wants to see him. Does he mind if the Interior Ministry does a security check—of course he doesn't mind, bye Thom, for sure, thank you, I'm very pleased too.

The next day, on his way back to Enschede following a relaxed interview with the PM, De Graaf phones again. He hears, in euphemistic terms, that the National Security people came across Wilbert, and they want to conduct a limited security investigation to rule out the possibility of blackmail.

Blackmail—the word triggers him. During a sleepless night he ponders which of them, Wilbert or Joni, is more of a liability; he asks himself the perverse question: which is worse, murder or porn? For the first time since his undoing he gets out of bed and looks at the young women on the websites. He thinks about them. About the mystery of their choices, about Joni's choice, about the choice of all these girls; he looks them in the eye intending to read desperation, self-destruction, insanity perhaps, regret, deep-seated sluttishness, rotten teeth, traces of abuse and neglect, or else simple, honest-to-goodness stupidity—but the only thing he sees is beauty. They are all, pretty much without exception, beautiful. Not concert pianists or doctoral students, maybe, but above-average attractive women; you could also say: as looks go, successful young women, thoroughbreds in possession of eyes, hair, feet, legs, hands with which they could make it out in the civilized world, could snag themselves potent, healthy marriage partners, land themselves decent jobs. He is no sociologist, nor a biologist, but couldn't these girls have in fact been born into decent families? To good-looking parents with balanced, sturdy genes, with genetic material that produces daughters that every man wants to have, or touch—or barring that, at least *look at*? Behind every nude photo worth paying for are parents who conceived a desirable child. Behind every sex site is a man like him.

A man like Theun Beers—who'd have known? The next day he does something off the wall, something he never thought of before all this mess began. He goes into a record shop, tries to remember the name of Joni's begetter's band, and when he does dredge up the name he goes through the bins of LPs in search of Mojo Mama, against his better judgment, but what do you know, he finds one. *Stupid City Blues*, it's called, a battered copy from 1973; on the cover, a photo of the Utrecht Cathedral tower, with—undoubtedly a scissors-and-paste job—an equally tall electric guitar leaning up against it.

With a fascination you'd sooner expect from Joni, but which she always denied—so with borrowed fascination—he studies the photo of the man whose appearance he'd nearly forgotten, but whom he immediately recognizes as her father, because good God, she does resemble Theun. The same healthy blondness, the same proud, self-confident expression, the broad face, the erect posture. The spitting image of that virile, dark blond fellow who on the back cover of *Stupid City Blues* is shown walking along a river, probably the Vecht, the guitar from the front cover slung over his shoulder like a Viking sword, a rock 'n' roll guy who named his daughters after Joni Mitchell and Janis Joplin. *This* is family. The DNA drips off it.

Before listening to the LP on the turntables and headphones up front, before determining that Theun Beers has a flat, uninteresting voice, he stares mesmerized at that picture. According to the caption, the figures a few steps behind him are a drummer, bassist, and pianist: like Beers, twenty-somethings with sideburns and floppy hats or Sandokan turbans over their long hair, but guys who pale in comparison to their frontman in charisma and photogenics.

Theun Beers wears leather pants, and between the lapels of his open suede jacket glows a brazen torso as leathery as his trousers.

On Sunday he and Tineke stroll pseudo-relaxed through Het Rutbeek, they discuss the immediate future and how he will inevitably be sleeping in a pied-à-terre in The Hague on weekdays. Suddenly it's all moving so fast: on Monday morning he hears from Kok himself that the Cabinet very much wants him, "we've got a green light"; the next day the eight o'clock news opens with Kruidenier's dramatic exit. Current affairs programs spend the rest of the evening speculating on a successor, his name keeps coming up. He has already informed his university deans and the key members of his staff by telephone. He and his spokesman go through what he will have to do tomorrow afternoon, after the news from The Hague. A special meeting of the Board of Directors and the trustees has been convened to address the changeover, there is champagne, he makes a farewell circuit through the administrative wing, starts removing things from his office walls.

At two o'clock that afternoon the hurricane starts swirling; the campus is swarming with news media, he gives the same brief reaction a few times and leaves the administrative wing via a side door. The next morning his new chauffeur picks him up, and to his surprise his department secretary is sitting on the backseat. Conversing calmly, they drive to Huis ten Bosch, where after his swearing-in he drinks two cups of tea with the queen; the world is spinning again, but now at double time.

He recognizes the pattern. The first weeks are killingly hectic, he puts in fourteen-, fifteen-hour days, hurtles between Zoetermeer and The Hague, sees more civil servants, advisory panels, and union officials than is good for a person. He endures his first parliamentary debate, wades through stacks of dossiers—but his head is calming down. This is how he's always done it: smother private problems in demanding work. He enjoys his new arena, the responsibility, the national interest that, like a horde of hooligans, storms the Cabinet where he is suddenly a member.

Back in his apartment on the Hooikade, as he showers off the new reality, Aaron's house on the Vluchtestraat seems farther away than ever, and he can hardly imagine he actually smashed through that sliding glass door. From his cozy Hague apartment, that balcony where he lay bleeding seems like a fantasy, a dream, a nightmare. For the past few days he's been toying with the idea of calling McKinsey, asking for Joni's e-mail address, the *real* one. Maybe he'll muster up the courage to send her something, something sensible, something . . . fatherly?

But then he himself is the recipient. The text message comes in on his private cell phone during parliamentary question time. The Christian Democrats' education expert has summoned him to the sitting with a query about the competitive position of Dutch research institutes. He is early, it is only his second time in this situation, before it's his turn the Defense Minister takes questions about the Joint Strike Fighter. The practically empty chamber seems immense, bigger than on television, questioners walk in and out, the minister's response elicits another question. Kok comes in, walks behind the television cameras. The PM grunts something that sounds like "how's it going," sits down next to him and thumbs through a stack of paper. To kill time during the ensuing airplane discussion between his colleague and a defense specialist, he takes his phone out of his pocket. "Unknown sender," just an 06 number. He opens the message.

Wanker listen. I know you're fucking your stepdaughter on the Internet. Want me to keep your jerk-off secret quiet?

He glances at the PM. The electrical field surrounding the boss of the Netherlands: its force dissipates. Which throws Sigerius off balance. He has to grasp the veneer tabletop so as not to tumble over backward. But he forgets to first set down that instrument of calamity, he just lets go of it, the phone bangs against the edge of the table and clatters to the floor. He grimaces sheepishly at Kok, who glowers at him, he slides his chair back a bit and disappears under the table. His temples throbbing, he gasps for breath.

Christ. Now the shit's gonna hit the fan.

He sees the gleaming phone, half of it anyway, the anthracite back panel has come loose, it's lying on the floor between Kok's feet. The Speaker of the House calls his name, it's his turn, he looks up at the PM like a puppy dog, mumbles "sorry" and points under Kok's desk, "I'll just get that." He grabs the bit of plastic from between the heavy black leather shoes, robust labor union footwear that would cost a Berlusconi in the polls, and struggles to his feet. He sets the dismantled cell phone on the desk top and hurries to the Speaker's lectern. A capable body double answers the questions that are fired at him.

As soon as he is liberated, he leaves the parliament building without so much as a glance in any direction, and has his Volvo deliver him to his department in Zoetermeer. Only once he has closed his office door behind him, high up and deep in his department, does he reassemble the phone. It comes to life, searches for a network, and immediately starts vibrating: two new messages. The first is from, of all people, Isabelle Orthel. *Hey, just saw you on TV, long time no see. How's things?* The second is from the same unknown 06 number. *Went all pale, didn't you. Shit-scared, you fucking wanker. Make me an offer.*

He slams the cell phone onto his desk, stares at it for a bit, and picks it up again. He's got a meeting with his department secretary and under-minister in five minutes; instead of preparing for it he fumbles a reply.

Who are you?

For the rest of the week he agonizes over that question. He dials the number about four times, each time gets put through to a female voice who reads out the numbers, followed by a beep. Once, he leaves a message, firm and clear: Identify yourself, friend, or drop the goddamn charade. Once, somebody answers but doesn't say anything, he keeps asking who he's dealing with, until, following a derisive chuckle—a gruff man-laugh—they hang up.

His options are few. Aside from himself, only Joni knows of his "involvement," maybe Aaron too—and *he'd* sooner bite off his tongue. He rules out either of them being behind these perverse texts. So one of them must have blabbed. Or is he underestimating Aaron? Could he have pissed Aaron off? *What were you doing in my house? What kind of vacation did you treat us to?* Something like that? No, it can't be. The kid isn't crazy. No, one of them talked. The person who is hounding him is well informed, knows that Joni is Linda *and* knows about him—in other words, knows *everything*, and that infuriates him, he's mad at the asshole himself, but at Joni and Aaron too: why did they talk?

Wait a sec . . . He scrutinizes the text messages again. Could they be from someone who recognized Joni, just like he recognized her—why not?—and is now taking a shot in the dark? A wild guess? Who would do something like this? Somebody at Tubantia? A student?

In any case, it hits the mark. His old fear returns, a paralyzing combination of panicky self-preservation, that first and foremost, and an overwhelming fatherly concern. Not only is his ass on the line (a mutated ass, Siem Sigerius's ass has expanded into a network of interests, contacts, expectations, responsibilities; a reputation like a crystal chandelier that under no circumstances may be allowed to come crashing down), but Joni's too. The illusion that Joni would come out of this unscathed, that everything would eventually return to how it was, a cautious flicker of hope that has provided him with some relief these past months, has been destroyed.

During his next obligatory question hour, exactly what he is afraid of happening, happens. Perhaps that is why the text message hits him right in the gut. *I can see you, wanker. You're looking pale. Been jerking off too much or just sleeping badly?*

When, later that afternoon, his chauffeur drives him through an autumn storm to Utrecht, where he has to address a meeting of the national Student Union, he asks him to stop at a roadside restaurant. Although he has resolved to ignore the stalker, he retreats to the men's room and, trembling with rage and hardly in the mood for a friendly chat, calls his old secretary. Who has asked for his telephone number recently? Only journalists. No one else? No, not that she can recall, and anyway she never gives out telephone numbers, he knows that.

He's completely at a loss. That evening, as he sits in his furnished apartment, the walls start to close in on him. Rain falls in sheets on the sidewalks in the depths of the Hooikade and he stands with his legs against the warmth of the radiator. He is imprisoned in a glass cell, he has never been so visible before, so vulnerable. All eyes are fixed on him, he is fighting for the confidence of parliament, of the media, of the party, of the voter. His stalker has chosen his moment well, he's got to hand it to him. He tosses and turns, the wind whistles around his foreign, anonymous bedroom, he thinks of home, of Tineke, of their life before—and suddenly it hits him.

Wilbert. *Who else?*

God, *that* took him long enough. How could he be so blind? His son gets out of jail, his son calls for Joni. The only man on earth who has a score to settle with him. He switches on the lamp next to the bed and looks into the small bedroom. He can't say the thought puts his mind at ease. "Dumb bitch," he hisses. Could Joni have told him? *How incredibly, terribly, unbelievably stupid.* The room is chilly and yet the sweat is pouring off his shoulders.

Or did Wilbert first threaten *her*? If it's him at all. So there he is, in the dead of night. He stares into spacc for several minutes. Then he takes his cell phone, locates that 06 number, and dials.

"Wilbert," he says after the beep, "I know it's you, kid. Apparently you're angry. After ten years you're still angry. I respect that. I'm angry too sometimes. But realize you're playing with fire. On top of it, you're talking crap. You insinuate all sorts of things, but can you prove anything? Of course not. There's nothing to prove. Get a grip on yourself, kid. Get a life."

15

The dreams were relentless. They picked at him with their sharp beaks, and when he woke up the ravens landed on the lampshades, waiting for him to doze off again. He found himself everywhere: in bed, on the sofa, at the table with his stubbly cheek in a cold slice of pizza, on the stairs with a cramp in one of his feet.

It felt as though he didn't sleep for more than fifteen or twenty minutes at a stretch, but sometimes it was suddenly pitch-dark, or conversely, an unexpectedly bright ray of light sliced through the gap in the curtains. He made space-time journeys through all the houses that had featured in his life. Often he was at home in Venlo with his parents, in creepy variations on the row house he grew up in, and there was always someone—usually his father—who was pissed off about something; then he lived with a malignantly or terminally ill Sigerius family member in his little room at his great-aunt's in Overvecht, or he lay on his own deathbed; he often had the same dream, in a room in the otherwise abandoned farmhouse. Sometimes awoke to guinea pigs pissing on him, having placed them on his chest in another epoch. He listened to distorted sirens in the city.

Twice he had visitors. Somewhere in time he woke with a start to an electric drumroll that repeated itself three times as he lay on the sofa, swallowing and blinking, a container of lukewarm pasta carbonara on his chest. He slid to the floor and crept toward the radiator. In the shadows he could make out a pair of figures, a man and a woman. The man wore a blue suit and tie, the woman an ash-gray ensemble, they both had scarves around their necks but no overcoats. They each gripped a leather portfolio under their arm. Jehovahs. He would keep an eye on them until they pushed a *Watchtower* through the letter slot and then tried their luck with the neighbors. But they didn't. The man's gaze glided up and down the front of the house, the woman rang again, louder, it seemed. Aaron ducked farther down, kept so quiet he could hear them whisper. When they rang for the third time he got up and went to the front door.

His visitors introduced themselves with names he forgot straightaway. They claimed to be from the Ministry of Justice, they wanted to ask him some questions about "Mr. Sigerius." For a brief moment he was certain they had come to tell him his ex-father-in-law was dead.

"Do we look that gloomy?" the man asked kindly. He looked sympathetic too: well-meaning wrinkles folding across his rock-hard head, but his handshake betrayed him: a hydraulic vise-grip. He smelled like a mixture of subtle aftershave and the brown oil he used to grease his firearms.

"Your friend has been nominated for an important position," the woman added. She did not smile, but slid the toe of her shoe over the threshold. Something told him he had to make a solid, upright impression on these people. "Come in," he said.

In the passage he distinctly heard the woman inhale sharply through her triangular nose. "Horses?" she asked as he led them into his house; strangely, it was as though all three of them were entering his house for the first time. He was dreaming, it seemed, he dreamed the smell of fresh manure, a scent he'd hardly noticed until now. It felt like he was watching himself from the sofa, he saw himself walk into the freezing-cold living room, and immediately noticed that he looked very strange indeed, in Sigerius's judo jacket, which he wore like a bathrobe that used to be white but was now smeared and stained with bits of old food. He also realized, from his racing heartbeat, that his living room did not exactly radiate stability and solidity; he was busy emptying out his bookshelves, everywhere there were stacks of books he was planning to use to stoke his multiburner the coming winter, it was getting cold and his central heating got tepid at best. On top of it, he needed to buy garbage bags. "Don't mind the mess," he said, in fact to himself.

The man kicked some guinea pig droppings out of the way, producing a high-pitched rolling sound. The woman raised her painted eyebrows and looked around. He hurriedly removed a stack of pizza boxes from the armchair next to the curtain. "Take a seat," he said, gesturing toward the purple sofa, the only unoccupied place in the room because he himself was not lying on it. He set the boxes on the coffee table, on top of a brickwork of books, and sat down on the freed-up armchair. The container of pasta he'd been eating from was lying on its side next to the woman's right foot, a congealed tongue of beige-colored sauce oozing out.

"You're the boyfriend of Mr. Sigerius's stepdaughter, is that right?" asked the man. He sat on the sofa like it was a gas station toilet. "According to our information, you and Mr. Sigerius are well acquainted." He pointed to the badminton racket that stuck out from under a pile of boxes. "You work out together and are close friends."

"That's right." He saw no reason whatsoever to go into the

situation in detail. How would he explain it? That everything was ruined was none of their business.

"We're interested in Sigerius's son," the fellow said. "His only biological child."

Aaron nodded. The division of duties was clear: the woman sat with a notebook on her lap, poised to write down everything he said. He noticed her looking interestedly at the fence post. It was leaning like Gulliver's toothpick against the emptied bookcase.

"Not so much in the son himself," said the man, "but in his relationship with Mr. Sigerius. What can you tell us about that?"

The man's tone switched between formality and familiarity like a traffic light. He simmered with aggression. In his own office, deep in the sub-basement of some concrete complex with endless corridors and security portals, a bright, monochromatic lamp dangled above the table.

"No contact," Aaron said. "Zero. As you're perhaps aware, he's a bit of a, um . . . how can I put it nicely? A strange guy."

The man nodded earnestly, but the woman, reacting to his last words, emitted a brief chuckle, which she tried to disguise with her hand. Seeing that he was on to her, she asked: "What is that pole doing there?"

"I need it during my expeditions," he said, too eagerly and too earnestly—he regretted it immediately, and as he did not elucidate further, they all sat staring at the muddy fence post he had unearthed in a park on one of his trips to the supermarket. At the top, where a steel cable had once been threaded through the nails, he had tied a length of rope.

"Expeditions?" the man asked. He enunciated the word as if it did not have a scientific connotation, but a menacing one, a threat to national security, which he moreover seemed to take personally.

Aaron nodded. "If we just wait for government agencies," he answered as truthfully as possible, "we'll never get to the bottom of the fireworks disaster. That's why I'm devoting my free time to investigating the underlying explanation of things."

The guy locked his gaze onto him, red-hot steel that Aaron had to let loose. "In the eschatological sense," he explained, looking at the woman. She smiled at him as though he were lying in a crib. "And what does that pole have to do with it?"

Everything. Was he supposed to tell them that sometimes, when his neighbor's lights were out, he would drag his fence post to a stretch of painted fencing across from the Rijksmuseum, prop it against the partition, climb up onto it and pull himself onto the top rail? Then he'd hoist the pole up by the rope and jump down into pitch-black ruins. A few times, he wandered around, sneezing from the ashes his feet kicked up, shining his flashlight on chunks of rubble. Agonizing about the meaning of it all, the myriad consequences, all of them causal, he poked around the colossal vehicles that clean-up crews drove around during the day, studied the foundations of demolished houses like a dentist. When he became exhausted, or frightened by the din in his head, he went to the crater where the SE Fireworks bunkers once stood, now a sandpit cordoned off with plastic barrier tape. And then lay down on his back, stared up from his observatory at the stars, allowed himself to be trampled by the stampede in his brain. It was a scary place. Was it wise to tell these cops about it? The fear in the focal point of his sooty enclave. In the distance, a halo from the unwitting city.

"Nothing," he said.

"Do you recall any conflicts between Sigerius and his son?" the man asked. Eschatology didn't seem to interest him one iota.

"Oh yes," he replied. "They fought about everything. Even about a glass of Coke."

"You just said they had no contact."

"Did I? They don't; haven't for a long time. It's not something I'd say lightly."

The guy fired a barrage of insinuating questions at him, fishing for signs of problems between Wilbert and his father; he was after something. As though what he'd most like to have heard was that Sigerius and Wilbert had had fisticuffs right here in this room and smashed, the two of them, through the sliding door. Meanwhile some details came to mind. I could blab, he thought, I could tell them what I know about the court case against the kid, and the deceitful role Sigerius played. For now he let the man talk, heard himself give evasive answers, and was surprised to notice himself flagging, almost nodding off. Or were those in fact his waking moments? He wondered other things too, like who Sjöwall and Wahlöo reported to, and would Sigerius find the transcript of this interview on his desk in the morning? The he-man had guaranteed him anonymity at first, it was a routine screening, he claimed, but the secret service often kept things from you.

"Who's calling themselves the secret service?" he asked.

"How about if we ask the questions," said the woman. The secret agent got up with a sigh, squashing pizza boxes with his Italian shoes. Shivering from the cold, he walked alongside the bookshelves. "This is nothing," Aaron said. "It's supposed to freeze tonight."

"You moving or something?" the guy asked, his chin pointing like a urinal toward the stacks of books piled here and there. No, he wasn't moving, but he just couldn't stand it anymore, the thousands of spines staring at him from the shelves.

"Maybe," he answered. He used to like to stare back, but these days it only depressed him, even now that his broad-shouldered friend stood at them, rubbing his hands, his back squarely in his jacket, on the verge of instigating one of his forays: crouched down, on the balls of his feet, asking questions, a steady stream of questions. Had he read them all? What did he think of that Vestdijk? Had he read *this*? What're they worth, all these books? Why didn't he lend them out? How did he keep them alphabetized? What was the point of a first edition? And Naipaul, was he worth reading? And bam, there was Sigerius again, holding up one of the thousands of novels he had dragged off to his nest in the years after his Utrecht debacle, a mountain of never-to-be-read books that had exerted such an attraction on Sigerius. Why did he think this or that author was so good? And this one, isn't he overestimated? So I should read him? What do I *have* to read before I die?—limitless interest, Aaron at first wondering whether it was genuine, or if Sigerius was just returning the favor for his own boundless curiosity about jazz.

The fact that Sigerius kept coming back proved he really meant it. He apparently missed their exchanges. And yes, he did have some catching up to do. Literature was his blind spot, he was ignorant about the oddest things. The man who'd stared at his books and now turned to look at him thought Dostoyevsky was a composer. Grew up among sailors and construction workers. Faulkner? No idea. In his speeches at the opening of an academic year, Sigerius never skimped on quotes, Ibsen, Isherwood, Irving, Ishiguro—everything with the I for Important, but decorative and discretionary. Suddenly he felt like commenting on it, a strange virulence washed over him. "You've read so little," he said. "Practically nothing."

For his part, all he did in the weeks, months, years following his Utrecht disgrace was read; out of pent-up anger, out of sheer frustration, he read hundreds of novels, in many cases asking himself, even before he'd met Sigerius: why? Are you done trying to prove yourself yet? When will you admit defeat? It was Sigerius who had given his reading frenzy, in retrospect, a clear significance. "Aaron," he had said, "I'm not an intellectual. Help me catch up." The intense realization made his eyes brim with tears. He got out of his chair and took a step toward Sigerius, prepared to embrace him—

". . . asked you something," said the man.

Aaron's eyes went wide. He hadn't heard a thing. Had he fallen asleep? Or was *this* a dream? He looked at the man. "Sigerius and I have a very close relationship," he muttered desperately, his voice trembling more than was acceptable, "sometimes it seems like *I'm* his son."

Unfortunately the woman did not write this down. She fastened the top button of her blouse. These two weren't here to screen Sigerius; he had *sent* them. They were his agents, he understood perfectly well that Sigerius was already a minister, probably Prime Minister by now.

"Well, what do you know," said the guy. He was perched on the edge of the sofa like a dandy. "And what does that say about Sigerius and his *real* son?"

The woman glanced at an unusually large white-gold wristwatch. *But was it really a watch?* An inky cloud of fear shot through his veins, several organs simultaneously kicked into wartime production: panic overruled his sentiments of a moment ago, how suddenly they could change! He clenched the leather armrests of the chair with his clammy fists. That watch, it was probably a device, a webcam tested by NASA, and Sigerius and his wife looked at each other right now, judgmentally, our friend here thinks he's got us figured out, not knowing he also had *that* figured out. The great shadowing had begun.

"Wilbert plays no role in our lives whatsoever," he said as softly as possible. "Sigerius abandoned him very early on." Now that he had them figured out he noticed that Sjöwall wore a huge signet ring, his clenched boxer's fist looked like the head of a cyclops, he stared into the eye, a diaphragm opened. No one played a role in anyone's life any longer, he realized all over again. He heard clattering, a gust of wind brought the boarded-up back window to life. All three of them looked. Sigerius had abandoned him too, and how. Strangely enough, he couldn't put his finger on the exact reason, there must have been a motive of some sort, anyway his friend had well and truly left him out in the cold. A wave of irritation washed over him. What possessed Sigerius to make a habit of abandoning his family? He was being spied on here, but you could also turn the tables, why didn't he take control of the situation? This was his chance, the line was open, this was the moment to get it off his chest. As a real son it was his duty to tell Sigerius, preferably over Thomson and Thompson's heads, a thing or two. It wasn't going to be pretty, but in time his friend would thank him for it. He wanted to say that he loved Sigerius like a father, but that he felt terribly abandoned, and he said so, but what came out of his mouth was so muted and muffled that the guy leaned his granite-head forward.

"What did you say, son?"

He started. Suddenly he smelled Sigerius's unnerving power, a tingling, fresh chewing gum smell. His tears were already mobilized, now they flowed freely, he cried miserably. The man asked him again what he was trying to say, pushed his small, flat ear almost against his mouth. Aaron whispered the words about fatherly affection and being unappreciated.

The man sank back, looked at him. "I'll bet it's not that bad," he said. The woman slapped her notebook shut. She looked around the room, her nose scrunched upward. "We'll be off then."

• • •

Time passed according to the laws of nature. The weather became grimmer, wheezing storms blew rainwater and curled-up autumn leaves into the house. His guinea pigs quietly scratched about, he listened attentively to the gnawing and shuffling. The nights got longer.

On the evening of the second visit—or was it the early hours?—the sound of the electric doorbell plowed through the syrupy silence that enveloped him. Was he awake? Yes, he stood with the bathroom doorknob in his hand. Had he ordered food? He couldn't remember, and besides he had to go to the toilet. Instead of doing the sensible thing—locking himself in the bathroom—he hurried to the living room, crouched down next to the cold radiator and peered outside from under the curtain. His view of the front path was blocked, so he pushed the left-hand curtain aside a tad and pressed his temple against the ice-cold windowpane: was somebody standing under the wooden overhang? The answer came from a series of loud bangs on the door; he fell backwards onto his butt from fright. He crawled back to the gap underneath the curtain. The shadowy figure—a man, judging from its posture—was definitely impatient, took three steps back and looked up, went back to the door and rattled the letter flap with a deafening clatter. He had something on his back, a small knapsack. His mouth puffed out agitated little clouds.

Aaron's intestines gurgled. Why hadn't he just gone and sat on the toilet? Something dark flashed across the front of the house, he held his breath, the man stood squarely in front of the living room window. What was going on? The next moment a merciless banging on the window. His heart shot under the sofa like a dog. Two flat fists, like a child's feet, against the window, between them a circle of condensation. Losing his balance entirely, he fell forward, only just avoided bashing open his chin on the granite windowsill, but his knees slammed against the radiator with a dark, metallic thud. When he looked up, he was staring into two deep-set, restless eyes. They were Sigerius's burning oil fields. He immediately turned away, dug his chin into his chest. Had the moment of truth arrived? There he sat on his haunches, paralyzed, fighting against the wind like Hans Brinker, in a desperate struggle with the afterimage. What had happened to Sigerius's face? Was that from the glass door? Anguish, devastation, humiliation? It was contorted, caved-in, as though a demonic mask had been made of his old face.

Was he dreaming? He felt tears glide down his cheeks. Shatter this window too, he thought. Go on, smash it. And then smash my head. He was numb with fear: his knees, his legs, his whole body, they no longer existed, all his nerves had amassed in the very top of his skull, awaiting the blow. Hit me!

Breaking glass. He fell backward, groaning. He heard the tinkling of the shards, unnervingly far away and at the same time frighteningly close by. But: no pain. No cracking of crushed bone, no gushing of warm blood. He felt nothing! Instead, he heard the front door bolt slide open. Relief made way for new fear: *he's coming to get me.*

But again, something else happened. Sigerius did not enter the room, but stormed up the stairs. His ass glued to the floor, he listened to the sounds coming from upstairs. After a brief silence he heard the creaking of the folding attic stairs, and then: footsteps. Sigerius was up in the attic! He hadn't dared go up there since that terrible evening in June. Once or twice he'd stood in the hallway, clutching the bolt cutter in one clammy hand and a staircase tread with the other, staring tentatively up through the hatch, planning, surely, to smash the whole caboodle to smithereens. But he couldn't.

What was Sigerius doing there? Had they come home before he'd had time to rummage about properly? Had he left something there?

"Siem," he said softly.

His teeth chattered as though he were in a cold tub, he bit his lower lip as hard as he could. What was he going to say?

After an eternity that seemed to last no more than a second, he heard the steps again, the creaking, a loud thud. Did he jump the last few treads? Heavy shoes came crashing down the stairs. He was furious!

Aaron cleared his throat. "Siem," he whispered, he could not get any volume into his voice. He raised his hands in defense. He wanted to scream—but instead he shat himself. His boxer shorts streamed full with warm shit. "Siem . . . ," he whimpered. "I'm sorry. I'm so sorry." The shit oozed from the bottom of his shorts, poured between his thighs.

The front door slammed with a massive thud, footsteps retreated down the paving stones of his front path. He exhaled. A car door thumped shut, an engine started, and it drove off.

When he jolted awake it was still pitch-dark. It stank in his dream too, but what he now smelled was unbearable; he gagged. His excrement had cooled off and stuck like caked lava between his bottom and the seat of his jogging pants. He stood up, bile in his mouth, holding the lukewarm pile in place with both hands. Choking with disgust, he crossed the room and went into the passage. He stumbled up the stairs, turned on the shower tap (the water only grudgingly started running; it was days since he had stood under it), and undressed in the shower. He dropped his soiled clothes and stamped on them as though he were treading grapes. The hot water splashed heavily, he kept on treading, squirted endless amounts of shampoo and bath gel between his feet, half an hour, an hour, as long as it took until all the foaming sewer water had disappeared down the drain and all he smelled was Palmolive.

Only then did he soap himself up, scrubbing his groin, his shoulders, his arms, his belly, his legs, until his skin flushed. He washed the congealed sweat from his armpits, and squirted Zwitsal baby shampoo on the thin strip of hair around the back of his head.

He dried himself off slowly, mechanically. Then he wrapped a towel around his waist and went out on the landing. Taking a deep breath, he took hold of the folding steps and climbed up to the attic. It was a disaster area. The rack with Joni's shoes appeared to have been kicked over, the pumps lay scattered around the floor. The white baskets had been wheeled into the middle of the room, panties, tops, and stockings lay strewn about. The drawers of his computer desk were open. He went over to the tussled bed and bit into the waterlogged heel of his hand. What had Sigerius been doing here? Hadn't he been up here once before? Or had it been like this for months?

His attention shifted to a pile of clothes next to the opening in the floor. Men's clothes. A light-gray pinstripe suit: jacket, trousers, an entire outfit. Under the trousers a pair of white boxers. The white button-down shirt had soft pink stripes, the cuff links were still in the buttonholes. Those shoes . . . they were Sigerius's expensive Greves, unmistakable, one of them had a heel lift. What were his clothes doing here, for God's sake? Had he brought them over with him? *Why?* He felt the pockets of the trousers and jacket. Keys, a loose house key, a wallet, a dead cell phone.

He walked back to the bed and flopped down on it. And lay there, God knows how long. Maybe he slept. Anyway he was chilled to the bone when he got up and walked over to the heap of clothes. He dropped the towel and, shivering, started to put them on.

16

The first weekend of December he only gets back to Enschede on Saturday evening. Tineke is disappointed that they're "not doing Sinterklaas" this year, so he bought a silver bracelet with freshwater pearls for her at a jeweler in The Hague. She takes him to a recently opened vegetarian restaurant on the Hengelosestraat, and after they've ordered she tears open the marbled wrapping paper. Her reaction strikes him as more surprised than pleased; her eyebrows raised, she wriggles the bracelet around her fat wrist. "This isn't like you," she says, and that's true—spontaneous gifts are not like him, there's always something behind it. These are penance pearls, a single pearl is equal to one year less of purgatory. He sits grinning like a freshwater swab.

He fills her in on Cabinet doings. They eat something with pak choi and chickpeas. He nearly chokes when she says: "I spoke to Joni."

"Oh? Did she phone you?" The restaurant is dark, he hopes she doesn't notice he has to pull himself together.

"I pho—"

"But we don't have her number." Don't get too agitated, he thinks, nothing to be done about it now.

"I was tired of waiting." She wiped her mouth with a paper napkin. "I know time flies with her, but really, I think five months is—"

"Four. You phoned from Crete."

She's taken aback, looks at him. "What's the difference. All right, four. Anyway, I think four months is long enough. So I called McKinsey. Just on the outside chance. And sure enough."

He rubs the rough of his chin, hoping to rasp away his nerves. He wishes he could hear exactly what they said to each other, word for word, not from Tineke's mouth, but rather from a cassette tape he can play at his leisure and rewind when necessary. He needs time to plot his course. It was all going so well. For a few weeks now, he has tried to convince himself that his nighttime offensive paid off. Since bluffing on Wilbert's voice mail—at least, what he assumes was Wilbert's voice mail—things have been quiet. But he is not reassured. He has not, for instance, been back to parliamentary question hour.

"And?" he smiles, "what did she have to say?"

"Oh, you know. We kept it short, of course. I caught her off guard. She sounded tired. But it seems like her internship's going well. She thinks they're going to offer her a job."

"She coming to France?"

"Probably not. She'll be tied up all month with a big client."

"Then she'll be doing overtime during the Christmas break," he says. He tries to hide the relief he feels breezing through his insides. "Where's she working?"

"Where? At the office."

"Which company, I mean. At Christmas."

The nonchalant way his wife considers his question puts him at ease. "IBM?" she says. "Yeah, IBM."

"Oh well," he says. "I wonder if Hans and Ria are really her cup of tea anyway."

"She always likes skiing. I discreetly asked about Aaron."

"Aha. And?"

"She said it's better this way."

• • •

They drive through the drizzle back to the farmhouse. Sometimes, come evening in The Hague, he longs for Enschede, but now the thought of Tineke rambling around this empty, embalmed beast, day in and day out, makes him itch to return to the intoxicating flurry of his department. He parks on the gravel driveway, they use the back door, the utility room smells of warm washing. Tineke opens the drum of the machine and pulls out the wet strand, he walks into the darkened living room, switches on lamps.

"Was there much mail?" he calls, but Tineke does not hear him. He goes to the front hall, smells the familiar scent of slate and soaked wood stain. He turns on the light above the chest of drawers, the stack of envelopes and magazines reaches to the edge of the Marseilles photo, next to it, the newspapers he's asked her to save for him. Among the envelopes is a packet containing a book he'd ordered a while ago, there's an envelope from Japan, the new issue of *Pythagoras*, a smattering of belated congratulations on his appointment, two *Football Internationals*, bills, a letter from the Royal Academy of Sciences and a lumpy, middle-sized padded envelope whose address has been crossed out with red pen, under which Tineke has written "addressee unknown." There's something hard inside. He gasps, his vocal cords vibrate, as he reads whom it is addressed to. "Mr. F. Wanker," written in a childlike scrawl, Langkampweg 16, 7522 CZ Enschede—"Langkamp" instead of "Langenkamp."

First his hand goes hot, then cold and clammy, his sweat soaks into the paper of the envelope. So his wife does not think Mr. F.(ucking) Wanker lives here. The urge to run to the utility room and embrace her, confess everything, say he's sorry, and at the same time the fear that she could just walk in on him—he's paralyzed. He stares at himself in the photo in Marseilles: a hunk cradling a tree trunk. *You won't get me, pal.*

He presses the envelope against his chest, goes into the bathroom, sinks down onto the toilet. While he lets his bladder go he tears it open at the bottom, because the top is sealed with wide brown tape. His trembling hand pulls out terrible things: black fishnet stockings, red panties, a clump of cotton fabric, a wadded-up handkerchief—*his* handkerchief, he sees through white lightning bolts of shock. The cotton feels crusty in the middle, maybe from snot, but probably from something else, something that infuriates and saddens him at the same time. A hard object slides out of the envelope, falls to the rubber toilet mat with a loud *tock.* It is a lifelike black fake penis.

He exhales deeply, flabbergasted, furious. And afraid. The brazenness shocks him. He gets up, sits back down. "Asshole," he mumbles. This is taking things pretty far, he thinks, it's taking things to their limit. Was that jerk up in the attic? He can hardly imagine it. When he says: you have no evidence, then the kid gives *this* as an answer? Was he really at the Vluchtestraat? Or did this packet come from . . . from *Aaron*? No. No? He just doesn't fucking know. Did Aaron let Wilbert in? Or did the lunatic break in?

He picks up the veined dildo from the tiled floor and tries in vain to break it in half. Then he wraps it up in toilet paper, in the naïve assumption that he can flush it down the john, and the rest too, all of it, get rid of it—but he reconsiders. Tineke will wonder what happened to the envelope. He's going to have to watch his step.

Only now does he look *in* the envelope, something is still wedged in the far corner, a letter, he fishes it out, lined notebook paper, he unfolds it. Crude handwriting that corresponds with the jagged letters on the envelope. "Withdraw 100,000 guilders, wanker," he reads. "Show some ministerial accountability." He is instructed to go to the beach at Scheveningen—"I'll make it easy for you, wanker, right near your jerk-off den"—on Thursday,

December 14th, at 8 p.m. and bury a bag containing a hundred 1,000-guilder notes at the edge of the dunes directly across from coastal marker 101. "If the money's not there then some pictures are going to get sent around."

Again he breaks out in a sweat, out of anger, but also out of nervousness bordering on panic. Damn it, this isn't just harassment anymore, it's blackmail—high-stakes blackmail. He is being shaken down by his own son. Shouldn't he make a beeline for the police? Yes. And yet . . . *no.* His calves harden, he clenches his teeth until they almost crack. So *this* is what blackmail feels like.

He has to deal with this shrewdly and methodically. Calm down a bit. He can't go into the living room like this, carrying this envelope. Upstairs, to his study. He hurriedly shoves the contents back into the bubble wrap. He'll take all the mail up with him, stash the envelope there. He listens for a sign of Tineke; only once he's sure the coast is clear does he flush and sneak out of the bathroom. He grabs the stack of letters and magazines and bounds up the stairs.

His study is chilly, he sits down, pushes the regular mail to the corner of the desk. Before he locks the poisoned package in one of the green steel drawers he removes the blackmail note, steers his eyes once more through the brief message. At the words "ministerial accountability," doubt sneaks up on him again: is this terminology that his son would use? And: does he have such disdain for his son that he doubts whether the kid knows the term that is, after all, his job description? Yes, he does.

He folds the note and shoves it deep into his wallet. With a nominal sigh of relief he turns the key and for a few moments stares out into space. The small windowpane above his desk is pitch-black against its chrome-green frame. He swivels his chair to face into the room, but what should be familiar and trusted, the only square meters in the world that are his exclusive domain, his cave, his thinking space—this very space reminds him of his tormentor. That snake slept here. The serpent he flung out of the window with a stick. Now, ten years later, here he sits, sweaty, stressed, strung out. Now that bastard is letting *him* feel what power is.

Enough. Basta. He takes a deep breath, slaps his thigh with a flattened hand. He has to tell Tineke *something* at least. Tell her some or other half-truth, this is the moment. This time it's an envelope full of underwear, next time it'll be the lunatic in the flesh—and what then? His twisting and scheming has already put Aaron in danger, which in itself ticks him off, his reflex is to protect Aaron: in the insane soap opera his life has become, he has to protect his near-son-in-law from his *son*? It's time for a confession.

She's not downstairs. That usually means she's in her workshop at the back of the yard. In the kitchen he drinks a glass of water. He gazes indecisively into the darkness beyond the utility room, switches on the outside light and walks through the overgrown winter grass where, he sees, thistles are growing. Halfway there he can already hear the buzz of the circular table saw and the vacuum. He opens the heavy door and remains standing in the bricked opening. About twenty meters away, under fluorescent lights suspended on thin cables, his wife is piloting a plank of wood along the blade. She does not notice him, she's wearing hearing protectors.

How to begin? He inhales the pleasant, constructive scent of freshly planed wood. He is grateful she doesn't notice him. As always, he admires her creativity, his wife thinks up something, sketches it, lets it materialize from her fingers, sells it. As he watches her—she is concentrated, focused, swift; her overweight body seems to work to her advantage among the machines, as though it were a precondition of her mastery—the urgency ebbs from him like a receding tide.

Should he approach her? Tap her on the shoulder, honey, come sit down, there's something I have to tell you. What touches him at this exact moment, this impossible moment, is her cheerful pragmatism in standing by *him* all those years whenever it came to his son. As catastrophes small and large piled up around the boy, she was always the one who put things in perspective, she was the one who offered solutions, saw points of view without which he'd have sunk into something that might have turned into a depression. Where on earth would he have been without her? She's the first one to dismiss that thought, sweep it off the table, just like she does with the curly wood shavings now; he sincerely believes that without this woman he'd still be lying on the Antonius Matthaeuslaan, plastered leg in traction for eternity, with a beard reaching all the way to the Willem van Noortplein, wallowing in his thwarted Olympic ambitions.

For months there was no getting through to him. One look at his judo suit and the tears welled up in his eyes. Sometimes he and Margriet heard her bursts of laughter, loud, light, irresistibly cheerful, right through the kitchen floor, straight through their own sullen, disgruntled silence. A combustion engine had moved in under them, a female force that made their windowpanes rattle in their sashes. After he had that accident with the scooter and Margriet, by necessity, went out to work, and the woman from downstairs had started making ever-so-friendly house calls, from that moment on he forgot his wife and little son. He has to admit it. They ceased to exist. He lay on his cot, and next to him sat Tineke.

Now too, he is well aware of why he fell in love with her: that vitality. Her lust for life, her exuberance. The way she stood there at that machine, the one they bought together at a factory in Münster, where she apparently knew everything there was to know about brands and model numbers, interrogated the salesman in fluent German about rpms and blade positions. She was his new beginning, she repaired his willpower. That is why he cannot walk over to her now and disassemble himself in front of her.

Not only did Tineke's morning visits draw him out of his syrupy self-pity, but also without her he would never have discovered mathematics. She rang the bell at least once, sometimes twice a week, mostly when Margriet was sitting at the mail-sorting machine across town, and then he would yank the rope that disappeared via a pulley into the stairwell, down to the front door bolt, and she clumped up the stairs, with or without Joni on her arm—blond, large, attractive, cheery, interested, intelligent. She emptied his thermos into the kitchen sink and made fresh coffee, helped him onto the balcony if it was sunny, sometimes brought a loose chair or table leg that needed sanding, sat next to his bed and chatted to him about her day, her life, about how the construction of Hoog Catharijne was coming along downtown. On one of those mornings she came to cheer him up she brought him a box full of reading material: *Libelle*, *Ariande*, *Privé*, *Panorama*, a home and garden magazine, and some of it such junk he wondered why she read it, why that blues singer of hers read it.

"From my mother," she said, and told him that her parents lived in Tuindorp, the neighborhood where she'd grown up, and only later in the week did he rummage through the box, and maybe already then, or later, three small moss-green books with Olympic rings slid out, it was a symbol he couldn't look at without going all bilious, and those rings nearly prevented him from thumbing through the rest of the books.

Mathematics. Arithmetic. Long ago, in Delft, algebra and geometry came easily to him, which was the only reason he did MULO-B in high school: as few languages as possible, but all the so-called difficult subjects, *they* were a breeze. No time for anything but judo. Everything—his penchant for motorcycles and cars, his chess set, the high school, where his father had hoped he would study—took the backseat to judo. In retrospect, it was remarkable that no one, including himself, found it the least bit strange that he passed math and physics exams without doing any homework, without studying, yes, *without prior knowledge*. Let's see, what do they want from me—that's how he took an exam. Got an eight out of ten by inventing the wheel on the spot; right there in the lecture hall he figured out how to factor a quadratic equation.

It may have been his boundless boredom, with the mother of all wet blankets having been tossed over his life, that made him take a look at the problems in those booklets. He saw mathematics for the first time in twelve years, for the first time since the Oranje-Nassau MULO. He skimmed the word problems, the geometric figures and illustrations. There were five problems in all. He took a ballpoint pen and, on the cardboard cover he'd torn off one of the magazine folders, he tackled the first problem, fussed around with the data he'd distilled from the question, made a rough sketch. Just like a joke occurs to you, or the idea for a limerick, a solution welled up in him. OK, it's got to go like this. And if not that, then like this. After forty-five minutes he had cracked the first problem, his solution was spot-on, he knew it for sure. He went straight to the second problem, and then yet another, until soon enough he himself throbbed with spot-on-ness. If he hadn't been confined to a plaster cast he'd have bounded down the stairs to ring Tineke's doorbell and show her what he'd accomplished.

Usually he just sat out the tedious hours; in that kitchen it seemed like evening would never come, and when evening did come it seemed bedtime would never come, but now, suddenly, Margriet was standing there in front of him with Wilbert, who wasn't at school yet and spent days at his grandmother's in Wijk C. It was already getting dark, but everyday reality passed him by, he'd misplaced it somewhere, he was lost in an opaque, radiant world where closely related phenomena were either true or false, with such clarity it filled him with a thrilling energy. Rather than staring peevishly out into space, or picking petty arguments with Margriet—this wasn't her choice either, to be cooped up with such a bitter old fart—he spent the rest of the evening engrossed in the moss-green booklets, and part of the night too; it was cold, he still remembers, it froze in the kitchen, but he let his arms and fingers go numb, and when he'd answered all the questions he went through them again, solved a few in an even better way, out of camaraderie with the problem itself—what kind of feeling was that?—and honed his scribbled calculations or improvised embellishments.

One of the problems stuck with him ever since, not so much because of the Olympic connotation, or its inventiveness, but because he came up with a variant of his own: "ada/kok = .fastfastfast . . ." was the given, and the question was which digits could replace the letters so that the equation would be correct. He licked that one pretty fast, but had to work much harder to give Ada a friend: "pele × play = kick × goal," the fruits of incredible mental acrobatics that kept him awake until he heard Margriet showering upstairs.

Pelé and his goal was the first thing that Tineke's father wanted to talk about. Unannounced and totally to his surprise, a week later the man stood next to his makeshift bed; he was more gentleman than anything, he wore a distinguished lemon-yellow spencer and had soft white hair that looked as though it had been washed and touched up on the way over. "So this is the culprit," said Mr. Profijt, his future father-in-law, mathematics teacher at the Christelijk

Gymnasium on the Diaconessenstraat. The elegant hand that sported a slim wedding ring held up the fully scribbled magazine cover that, he gathered, Tineke had brought him. "Young man," he said earnestly, "I've spent my whole weekend on that Pelé kicking a goal. I can't crack it. Save me." Whereby Tineke's father squatted down next to his bed and Sigerius explained, step by step, in a ring notebook the man pulled out of a leather attaché case with a flap, how he constructed the brainteaser.

"Beautiful," said the man who was Joni's grandfather. "Robust. And elegant at the same time. Playful too. My daughter claims you're not a mathematician. She is mistaken. Where did you study, if I may ask?"

"In Delft," he replied. "Oranje-Nassau MULO."

A moment of silence. Then: "That's impossible," Profijt said. Tineke's father had a friendly voice in which he wrapped schoolmasterish sentences. "It is *not* possible that you've only done MULO."

"I'm afraid so, Mr. Profijt."

"Then you must have had help. Is this your handwriting? Do you know what these are?" He tapped one of the moss-green booklets.

"Math problems?"

"These exercise books contain the second-round problems from the National Mathematics Olympiad, 1969 edition. These five open questions, young man, were devised by the brightest mathematical minds in the country. The most talented A+ high school students train for a year, only to bang into this wall of mathematical ingenuity."

"Aha."

"The majority of that elite corps, the flower of the nation, one could well call it, scores two out of five. At best. Twenty points out of a possible fifty. Those students can go home well pleased. The top ten score between thirty and forty. Sometimes, but only sometimes, once every five years or so, there will be an exceptionally gifted boy among them, sadly they are always boys, a lad who gets almost everything right. Only once in the history of the Olympiad, I believe in 1963, did someone get a perfect score. Like you did. Zero mistakes. Fifty points. Flawless."

"Nice." From the middle of that little kitchen, which he now saw as unbearably filthy, musty, and shabby, Tineke stood beaming at him as though he'd just been knighted. She resembled her father, their faces had the same disarming roundness.

"It is not *nice*," said Profijt. "Because it is *impossible*. I've studied your work with extreme interest. At times it's brusque, mostly surprisingly graceful. And always efficacious. It appears that certain operations and standard formulas have been derived—no, *designed*—on the spot. On this piece of cardboard are two, I repeat, *two* different proofs for Pythagoras." He stopped briefly, weightily. "One of them, I've never even seen before. The other is three centuries old. If what you say is true, then I must congratulate you."

"Dad," Tineke said, "of course what Siem says is true. Come on, give them to him."

Her father extended his hand. "Congratulations." This was the first mathematician whose hand he shook, hundreds more would follow, perhaps thousands, but Tineke's father was the very first. The hand was not calloused like a judo hand; it was also unlike his in-laws' hands, which were clammy and jittered if they weren't holding a bottle.

"You'll be laid up another couple of months?" Profijt brought his attaché case to his lap and carefully removed a small stack of books. "I shall take responsibility for providing you with nourishment." In addition to four Olympiad booklets he called "snack food," Tineke's father gave him something he had saved since his own student days: books sheathed in brown paper on integral calculus, on linear algebra, on integer theory, but also *A Course of Pure Mathematics* by G. H. Hardy, a final-year gymnasium textbook, Struik's *History of Mathematics,* and even a satirical mathematics novella called *Flatland.*

"Work through them and let me know how you make out. Promise me that. And when you've finished I'll bring some more. In return I would ask that as soon as you can walk again we pay a visit to the Uithof."

"The Uithof?"

"The Utrecht mathematics faculty. And get well quickly, if you please. You've no time to waste."

She sees him. She switches off the saw, takes off the ear protectors. "Coffee? Yes, please!" she calls out, laughing; slaps her work gloves onto a workbench outfitted with a variety of vises; glides, smiling, past a futuristic cabinet. She approaches him—carefree, unaware. His thoughts bounce over their countless discussions about Wilbert, with the late '80s as desperate nadir, arguments that challenged everything they thought they knew about parenting. After the court case their marriage nearly fell apart, worn out as they were by that nut case. Yes, once Wilbert was out of the way they started arguing with *each other,* about everything. As a result she bloated up like a balloon, abandoned all discipline. After a hostile year she went off to a summer course in England, a top-notch academy for furniture makers, "the chance of a lifetime," but in fact it was pure escapism. She spent three months in Dorset and he missed her terribly. So badly that before she got back he invested a small fortune transforming the abandoned stall into a studio:

troughs and timber out, table saws in, storage racks, compressors for the vacuum, staple guns, a whale of a veneer press.

"What's up?" she asks cheerfully, looking at him under halogen lighting so bright that he's afraid she can read his thoughts.

Here? Now? What a mistake to think that he can spill out his pathetic, putrid news here, under the rafters of this hopeful hut. For ten years now, this workshop has symbolized the success of their marriage, every piece of furniture that has emerged from it reminds them that they have a grip on their lives, that they do have the power to influence events. And he's going to tell her here, of all places, about Wilbert and Joni? Maybe because he doesn't answer, his mouth just a slit from which he can see his breath, Tineke picks up the conversation. "You know what I was just thinking?" she says, taking his hand between her surprisingly warm fingers. "Wouldn't it be a great idea to fly to California in February, around carnival time? Surprise Joni? I think that would be such fun."

She has rented two films, it's his choice. *Secrets and Lies* doesn't seem like a good idea (he does not say why), so they curl up next to each other on the sofa for *Magnolia,* which is not unsavory enough to keep him from dozing off. What he dreams, he doesn't know, he's in a stifling quagmire, he's in The Hague, but also in the Delft of his youth, he doesn't know.

"*Y'KNOW,*" her voice suddenly blares in his ear. He bolts up with a start, she sounds so close by, the crown of her head tickles his chin. "You know what I forgot to mention?" She pauses the DVD.

"I was sleeping . . ."

"The mail," she screams, or does it only seem like she's

screaming? "This strange envelope came last week. Have you had a look at the mail yet?"

He tries to talk and inhale at the same time. "No," he says in a weak stammer, "well, yes, glanced through it."

"That brown padded envelope," she continues, "the fat one. Did you see it? Sent to the wrong address. There wasn't a stamp, no return address either, I only realized later. Somebody must've delivered it by hand."

"Why's the movie stopped?"

"Because this suddenly occurred to me. Monday, I think it was. I didn't know what to do with it, so I opened it up. A *really* strange little package, Siem. *So* strange." Her voice sounds alarmed, as though a suppressed fear is rearing its head. "I tried to phone you about it."

There is sand in his mouth, he can't get a word out, and still he hears something: "What was inside?"

"I'll just go get it," she says, and makes a move to get up. "I taped it back shut. It's not really—"

"Wait," he says, wide awake now. "It's upstairs, I think. I took the mail up to my study." Before she can respond, he's up off the sofa, walks toward the hall without looking back. "Want some wine?" she calls after him.

Numb, he stumbles up the stairs, his head is a reactor vessel. Throw the envelope out? Confess everything? Play dumb? Has she read the note? Like a zombie he opens the drawer.

"Ah," she says as he returns to the living room, "so you've already opened it." She sets two glasses of red wine on cork coasters. "And? What do you think?"

"Haven't looked yet," he says. Before he's even sat down she grabs the envelope out of his hands and shakes the contents onto the sofa between them. The stockings, the panties, the handkerchief, they fall noiselessly to the seat cushion, the jet-black object bounces and lands on the back of his left hand; as though it is a huge insect, a giant caterpillar, a black widow, he yanks back his hand, the thing leaps up, clatters via the coffee table to the tiled floor.

Silence.

He is deft, socially speaking. He knows just how to look when he's taken a swallow of scalding tea while standing face-to-face with the queen, he can debate in parliament, he can debate in parliament even while being called a fucking wanker. But now, he's stuck. He slumps back with a groan, his burning back against the cold leather.

Hours later, walking across what is no longer his campus, he tells himself that the story he dished up was consistent and in a certain sense more logical than the truth. Although it was a pretty rough evening, the end of which is not yet in sight—tonight might never end, he thinks, Tineke is going to start brooding, she won't leave it at this, he knows her, she's going to fret as well, maybe she's fretting already, she's gone to bed, lies there staring up at the ceiling—at the same time he experiences both the relief of confession and the satisfaction of a well-told lie.

A late-autumn breeze drives waves over the athletic fields, the campus is a turbulent sea of curled leaves, the scent of damp dirt and rot forces its way into his stuffed-up nose. Removed from the world, he crosses the wet gravel of the dimly lit 400-meter track, sheltered by a wide ring of dancing alder and hazel trees. He put all the blame on Wilbert—of course he did, without any scruples. The son of a bitch deserves it, finally he's of some use. Now that he can think it over in relative peace and quiet, Wilbert's intrusion seems, all things considered, not so bad after all—as long as *he* keeps a tight rein, of course, he mustn't forget that.

The ensuing quarrel was out of his control. Tineke's conviction that the package was not intended for them turned out to be a form of vague self-deception. "Siem?" she said at once. "Are you mixed up with this? Don't tell me you know something about this."

The solution presented itself like a mathematical proof, logical, irrefutable, organic . . . "Yes, dear, well, I do know something about it," he admitted, but instead of starting at A he started somewhere around Z, quite naturally, he thought, and yet careering forward, whispering to himself to keep as close as possible to the truth. In a somber tone of voice he told her that the text messages had started that summer, scarcely a week after that reception where Menno Wijn had shown up. At first he had no idea who was sending them, nor what they referred to, but he was hardly pleased to get them. Joni was a whore, that's what it boiled down to, and did he know, and it was just what he deserved—yeah, it was awful. Some time later—"and here it comes, Tien, brace yourself, this isn't pretty"—one of those texts contained a website address, advising him to have a look. So he did.

"And? Well? Where are you going with this? Siem—quit being so sinister! What did you find?"

"I'll explain, honey," and he took her hand in his. She reacted quite calmly to his account of the website, perhaps because he presented it so calmly, euphemistically, avoiding the word "porn," while distracting her with his alleged concurrent suspicion that Wilbert was behind those texts—go on, shoot the messenger. "Well, I got the shock of my life," he said. "Tien, it *was* one of those sites, I couldn't believe my eyes, although at first I couldn't believe I was looking at Joni."

The strange part was that her indignation was not directed at

Wilbert (that's how accustomed she was to his monkey business, no doubt), nor at Aaron and Joni (she only seemed to partly realize it), but at *him*. Why wait till *now* to bring it up? It was a lot to handle all at once, of course: the nasty erotic junk lying there between them, all that "wanker" stuff. ("Why does he call you that?" "You know what a filthy mouth he has." "Are you keeping something from me? Siem? What're you up to?" "Me? Nothing, darling, just calm down.") Yes, the *why* of his long silence, she made a point of it, the cavernous gap between May 2000 and now. "*Six months*, Siem."

He reaches the embankment that separates the campus swimming pool from the athletics track. Up the path he climbs, through low shrubs and nettles, to the highest point, where one of his predecessors had, with great ceremony, installed a thinking-bench. In the old days he'd come here to sit and contemplate when there was an important decision to be made.

Tineke asked: "Did you confront her?"

"Yes," he said, because didn't he, in a way? His wife sat an arm's length from him, staring ahead in what appeared to be utter astonishment. Then: "But where do you get off not telling me? Do you think that's *normal*?"

"I wanted to spare you, sweetheart, I wanted—"

"You wanted to spare me *what*? The truth? Facts? What the hell!"

He offered a spineless apology; she should keep his own worries in mind, and what a tricky subject it was to broach. Besides, after he'd given Joni a talking to, the website was history.

"So what's *he* after then?" She picked up the stockings and threw them back down.

"Those photos still exist. They're out there for good."

Instead of responding to this disquieting remark she wanted to know exactly what he had said to Joni.

"Oh, you know . . . ," he sputtered, "the kind of things you say in a situation like this, we kept it short, actually." An answer that did not satisfy her. Rather, it elicited a tirade that rampaged over the real problem, a centrifugal rage that was not about Joni, but about the two of them. She made him out to be the prudish old fart that he essentially is, a fool so devoid of sexuality that she seriously wondered about the scope of his edifying little chat. "You didn't just give her some sermon, I hope," she said. "Well, *now* I see why she's not coming to France this Christmas." And: "Are *you* surprised those two split up?"

He felt the need to stand up for himself, not so much because she doubted his tact—go on, say it: his parental aptitude—but because she just didn't seem to get it. "Do you realize what we're talking about?" he asked. "I'm telling you our daughter has put herself on the Internet as some or other . . . what's the word . . . some kind of *slut*. Do you have any idea what that means?"

"And do you hear your*self*? Who are you to call my daughter a slut?"

"Tineke . . . ," he said, taken aback by her raised voice, by that "my daughter."

"Let's see that website. Am I entitled to my own opinion?"

"Pictures. There's no websi—"

"Pictures, then. Let me see them. Probably nothing at all. For example. I don't think you have the foggiest idea of what's a slut and what's not. Let's see them, damn it."

"Sweetheart, *please*. We're not going to sit here examining that garbage. It *is* bad, believe me. Just because I, because we don't . . . you know . . . that doesn't mean I don't know what . . ."

"Well?"

"What porn is."

"Porn? Now suddenly it's porn?"

This time he was the one to explode. "Why do you think that bastard's sending me all this crap?" He swiped the lingerie off the sofa, the panties landed on the coffee table, slid across the tabletop. "Because of vacation snapshots?"

"Let's see them. Now."

"Tien—I'll send you a few on Monday. I can't do it. Not here."

When he wakes up the next morning, she's already up, there's a note on the breakfast table, she's gone for a walk, she has to think. He's glad of it. After breakfast he builds a fire in the living room fireplace and installs himself in the sunroom with a pile of dossiers. But all he does is think up scenarios: say she calls Joni again, say she asks her for an explanation, what's the chance that their daughter squeals on him? And what if he were to call Joni himself? Keep one step ahead? He tries to imagine that conversation: him trying, one way or another, to make clear to her, to convince her, that he . . . that he doesn't . . . *lust after her.*

He tries to figure out how to get his hands on that 100 grand without anyone noticing. There's still a U.S. bank account with twenty or thirty thousand dollars, MeesPierson manages the rest of his Spinoza grant, plus a few hundred thousand in savings. He turns on the TV, tunes into a current affairs talk show, but can't keep his mind on it.

How about making a deal with Wilbert? The very idea—negotiating with his son—infuriates him. Is he going senile? Luckily he is reasonably certain Tineke did not see the blackmail note. Suddenly he yearns for The Hague. Immerse himself in his department. He calls his chauffeur and asks if he can come and pick him up that evening.

It's already afternoon when Tineke gets home, packed tightly in a cap and his scarf, but still she's freezing, with eyes that have clearly been crying. He warms up pea soup for her, she seems less upset than yesterday evening, she asks why he doesn't go to the police, the threats seems serious enough, they've come from a recidivist, give me just one good reason why not?

"Joni."

"Joni?"

"Yes, Joni. Just think of *her,* will you. She's done her best to keep that website a secret, and now you want to go to the police with it? We'll have to tell them everything. There might be a court case. We'll have to talk to *her* about it. Exactly what she doesn't want. Even Wilbert understands that. Not to mention the danger of it leaking out."

She stands with her broad back to the fireplace, palms of her hands turned toward the fire. "Those people are bound to secrecy."

"Tineke," he says theatrically, "don't be so incredibly naïve. She's the daughter of the Minister of Education. You want it juicier? OK. Then ring up Bill Clinton."

"Cut it out, Siem."

"Honey," he says, "we're talking about Joni's future. *That's* what concerns me."

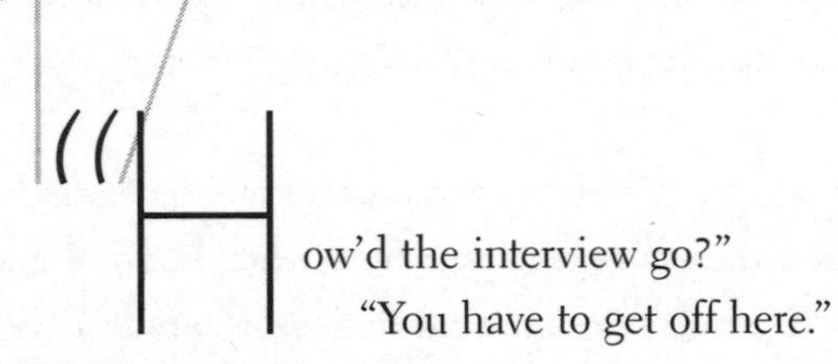

ow'd the interview go?"

"You have to get off here."

"Was she bitchy?"

"*Off here*. Not especially. She was clever. Interested."

"But she's a woman. Women have ulterior motives."

"Course not."

"A woman talks nice to you and only sticks it to you later. Once she's back home sitting at her laptop with a cup of tea, she'll skin you alive."

"Speed limit's fifty here."

"Skin *us* alive."

"Rusty, I'm a woman too, remember? You're talking crap. FYI, I know exactly what I said."

Too much, that's what. That Mary Jo Harland was a pro; first she plied me with intense empathy, then she tipped me over like a tub of dishwater. Within half an hour she'd got on tape that my father had committed suicide and I hadn't gone to the funeral. It took a certain amount of wangling over the phone to see that this didn't get into the article. That compassion of hers was probably still lying in the rental car.

"Did you give her a tour?"

"Of course I gave her a tour. *You* invited her out to Coldwater. What: 'Sorry, off limits, we're making WMDs here'?"

"I assumed you'd take her to whatsit across the street. Or to Starbucks. That's what *I'd* have done."

A couple of minutes of silence. Then I said: "Take Alameda here, get onto Harbor Freeway only after Little Tokyo. Why aren't we picking Vince up? He lands at LAX, right? Might have been nice."

Rusty's protégé ran his own site somewhere in Cleveland, Ohio. The first interview was a bit strange; Vince seemed like a capable guy, he expressed himself clearly and concisely—*if* he expressed himself, that is, because he was as taciturn as an oracle, and so bone-dry and listless that I was afraid he'd slip into a coma. On the open notebook page in front of me during the interview was a single, boldly inked word: "DULL."

"You think I'm nice, Joy? Let 'im take a taxi. So what'd she say?"

"Who?"

"Harland! What did she say? Y'know, when you showed her around."

"Not much, really, Rusty. This article was all *her* idea. She was crazy about it, believe me. She knew our sites, so there wasn't a whole lot she hadn't seen already. I hope Bobbi realizes she's going to Compton, though."

"Oh? Do I hear worry? Ha! Joy's worried about our swanky new location. Now that's interesting."

I kept my mouth shut. Of course nobody was dying to move to Compton. A week before the closing somebody left a *Gang Territory Map of South Los Angeles* on my desk, the area divided into red and blue blocks. According to the key, the blue areas were Crips territory, the red ones Bloods. Some anonymous chickenshit had naïvely printed out the map on one of our color printers:

within three minutes I'd spoken to a systems manager who told me it came from Deke, a black cameraman who lived in respectable Burbank with his family, but looked like he'd been born in an NWA T-shirt. "You watch too much MTV," I e-mailed him, "South L.A. is a product, Deke honey, it's today's Disney. Twenty years ago you could buy those Fuck Tha Police pics of yours all over Europe, even out in the sticks. Ever noticed how much Snoop Dogg looks like Goofy? So don't be such a wuss."

"I'm not *worried.* I'm just wondering how she'll get in."

"We should be getting there first."

The words were barely out of his mouth when traffic started slowing down, until we had almost stopped. Rusty lowered the window of his Maybach and wriggled out up to his waist. Gas fumes wafted into the red-leather interior. The police were cordoning off the two left lanes. Now Bobbi would probably have to kill a half hour on the streets of Compton—not a pleasant thought, I had to admit. Of course I was bluffing with Deke. What did I know? L.A. was a metropolis of ten million people, nine million of whom pretended that Compton and Hawthorne and Inglewood didn't exist. I never set foot there. Three times a year I sped through that rotting cavity on the way to a girlfriend in Long Beach, and that was that. Deke and his gangland guide had me worried enough to spend a whole evening watching Bloods and Crips posts on YouTube, and I had to admit that Goofy wasn't his good old self anymore. The Compton Goofys strutted bare-chested and bandana'd through their down-and-out neighborhood, toting sawed-off shotguns and yelling whom—in random order—they were planning to murder or fuck. (The police, our bitches, us.)

Rusty flopped back into his hand-stitched bucket seat with a springy slap. "A semi jackknifed. They're pulling a rice rocket out of the guard rail." That's what he called Japanese cars, in fact all cars smaller than his—this grotesque German tank of which there were fewer than 100 in the whole of America, most of them belonging to elderly millionaires for shuffling to and from their gated communities. Rusty's Maybach was finished in black gloss with gold-leaf trim, a hearse for transporting wedding cakes.

"Did you see Bobbi last Friday?" he asked once we started moving again.

"On Tyra? Sure did. She was good."

"So do you believe it?"

"Believe what?"

"What she said about that movie."

"Could be. Bobbi's no bullshitter."

"She's shooting her mouth off, I suspect."

"I'll bet they've called her. This exit."

Rusty looked over his shoulder and swerved, cursing, around an SUV with blacked-out windows that had "Music is my life" printed on it in swirly letters. "We might still be on time."

Even for the tenth time the sight of it was impressive. From the sharp curve of the crumbling concrete off-ramp we had a bird's-eye view of the Barracks on the white-hot horizon. Alongside us, a dented mocha-colored Dodge sped up and then slammed on its brakes. In the passenger seat sat a black kid wearing a cap made out of a stocking, staring at the Maybach like it was a grilled chicken. Half a mile later, after passing Rosecrans Avenue's derelict low-rise buildings, vacant sandy lots, boarded-up fast-food joints, and a gas station pretty much rusted down to nothing, the side view of a dark fortress stretching a good 100 yards long by 150 wide rose up on the corner of Avalon Boulevard.

"*That's* where *I* work, Mama," said Rusty.

As we approached, the hundreds of narrow windows in the bastion wall came into view; every one of them, without exception, was smashed. I had worked myself into a tight corner: during a tough talk with the city council I'd promised to have the glass replaced and the frames painted within a year. I guaranteed that the bare sidewalks—where the drug-dealing and streetwalking started right after *Sesame Street*, and which were strewn with cardboard packaging, broken glass, dog shit, *human* shit—would be planted with young trees. The exterior walls would be fitted with stainless-steel lighting fixtures so that the residents of this urban jungle—the crazies, the homeless, the junkies lying around in doorways—would no longer have to rely on self-made fires and could have a nice read before settling down for the night.

"There he is," Rusty said. Instead of Bobbi from Steamboat Springs standing at the main entrance, it was Vince from Cleveland, yawning, dwarfed by the high brick doorframe. Rusty raced past him and braked in front of the large, half-cylindrical roof that arched over the drill square.

"You gonna park inside?"

"No time."

The heat poured like liquid into the Maybach; I instinctively held my breath against the stench of urine. A sinewy dog on a leash sniffed at my foot as I felt for the curb. "Afternoon," Rusty said to the hefty black woman who jerked the dog back as though she were yanking life into an outboard motor. As we approached the building, Rusty's gaze strayed up the side of the immense brick wall. "Did you know that Joe Louis and Rocky Marciano once boxed in there?"

"Yeah," I said, "I'm the one who told you."

I thought I caught Vince's diffident puppy-dog gaze and waved, but he didn't react. When we reached him, Rusty extended his hand to the new man. "Maestro," he said jovially, "how's the form? Good flight?"

Vince nodded.

"Great, nice. You're looking tip-top."

Vince looked decidedly un-tip-top. He looked like he'd just been mugged, not by Crips or Bloods, but by the Little Rascals. Instead of the ill-fitting suit from last time, he wore faded, baggy-kneed trousers made of jogging-suit material. Thick chest hairs on his pear-shaped figure curled out from under a Hawaiian shirt with enamel snaps. Despite the blazing heat he wore heavy black steel-toe boots. His equally pear-shaped face, a genetic echo of his idle body, was unshaven; jet-black stubble climbed up his hamster cheeks. Apparently for Vince a "follow-up interview" meant "come as you are."

Rusty hummed as he unlocked the cast-iron doors and swung one heavily open. You could drive a tank through it. "Come on in," he said in a homey chirp. The three of us entered the cool reception hall. "We've got lights," Rusty said as he reached for the old-fashioned wall switches; after a slight delay three pendant lamps struggled their way on. "Here, at least." The gleaming floor segments that spread out before us were made of flamed gneiss outlined in black granite. Withered balloons and clusters of paper streamers were scattered here and there, remnants of last week's opening party. The beer tap still needed to be returned. Six stairways gaped like the pockets of a billiard table, between each pair were two wide polished oak doors.

Vince sniffed the stony, sweet-rotten smell with an inquiring frown. "I smell ground water," he said.

He bugged me. Rusty had "scouted" him, as he put it, in some or other hot-sex issue of *Cosmopolitan* where Vince had tied up some models in a way that admittedly betrayed skill and imagination.

"Sensitive nose you've got there," I said. "There's an underground branch of the Los Angeles River running under the foundation. Parts of the basement are under water."

Vince briefly touched his nose. He studied the walnut wall paneling in silence. After his first interview I had taken him to a bagel joint on Ventura Boulevard, and by mostly keeping quiet and asking brief follow-up questions I managed to find out more about this forty-three-year-old. For instance, that he still lived at home; for the past fifty years his parents had applied themselves with unassuming and, I gathered from his words, maddening devotion to the Cleveland Indians. Vince's mother manned a souvenir kiosk at the stadium and his father was the revered equipment manager of generations of baseball players who had all achieved something that Vince Jr. certainly did *not.* Maybe that's why the son had racked up an impressive series of apathetic failures: after an exhausting outplacement from a security firm (chronic sleep rhythm disorders that led to depression) and subsequent years of unemployment (a handful of attempts at new careers, including mechanic and welder, notwithstanding), Vince had managed to get himself diagnosed as disabled due to rheumatism and psoriasis.

Rusty crossed the room and stood with one foot on the stairs opposite us. "A short tour," his voice echoed. "I see our guest has worn his hiking shoes." I let Vince go first.

It bothered and amused me at the same time, the pseudo-expertise with which Rusty showed his new friend around, his eagerness to share the structural details of the Barracks—*my* Barracks too, you could say, but you wouldn't know it from watching Rusty. He spelt out his plan to beautify the place with his art collection, a "eureka moment" he had while in the Getty. I could just see him up on that Olympic mount, his pet-Rembrandt glowing at his back, Los Angeles spread out at his feet, daydreaming of his very own museum, a hedonistic *anti*-museum in the ugliest place on earth, in the most inward-looking, dank, poorly lit pile of bricks imaginable.

Vince trudged behind him with an expression somewhere between complete relaxation and a dopey smile. Every so often he would nod approvingly, or offering up some irritating monosyllable: "high," "low," "wood," "rust." Back in Cleveland, he had told me, he spent a few afternoons a week in a harbor warehouse his parents thought was a welfare-to-work center where he cabled machines, but in fact, together with two partners, one business and the other artistic-perverted, he cabled young ladies, the only skill he had truly mastered in all those lonesome years.

Vince's story might have moved me if I hadn't found him so repulsive. He was unsavory in the physical sense, but a bit musty under his scaly skull as well. Contact with women did not suit him ("scabs and flakes," he mumbled, "all over," gesturing with his hands over his torso and shoulders like a magnotherapist); he had only ever had one girlfriend, a brief romance that came to an abrupt and panicked end when the girl's parents asked him at the front door to take off his shoes. But his deep-rooted desire to tie up women dated from much earlier; even as an eleven-year-old kid, he confessed tearily, he got an erection when "a broad" with a wad stuffed in her mouth lay waiting for Roger Moore. The Internet had liberated him. He survived puberty, he mumbled, and in fact early adulthood as well, thanks to Japanese bondage mags he picked up in Cleveland's Asiatown. Up in the same attic room he still occupied he rehearsed and refined the art *on himself.*

"On yourself? You mean you tied yourself up?"

He rubbed his scaly eyes and nodded. "Who else?"

Did I have any grounds to object? Not really: from today onward, this Barracks was wacko central, everyone was nuts in their own way. And Rusty was brazen-faced: he didn't give a damn whom he worked with every day, as long as they shared his licentiousness, and he was right. Just like us, Vince had migrated to a city that applauded anything and everything as long as it was impermanent, reckless, and outrageous. We lived on uncertain, decadent ground, on shifting tectonic plates, in a city that could collapse any minute with one great shudder and vanish into a gash, indifferent to one little Vincent more or less.

My feet started to hurt. Just as I was about to excuse myself—"gentlemen, I've got a job to do"—my phone rang. Squinting at the display, I left the vault where we were standing. I was surprised to see it was Boudewijn. I answered, but before the thing reached my ear the line went dead. He'd apparently already tried a number of times. Boudewijn never phoned unless there was a crisis with Mike. The last time was more than six months ago, and the next day I was at my son's bedside in a San Francisco hospital: meningitis. I tried calling back but there was no signal. Taking off my shoes, I headed with softly flopping footsteps down a long, unlit corridor. On both sides were Brazilian rosewood doors leading to abandoned horse stalls and dripping boiler rooms whose immense, rusty machinery had been sparked back into service. In the distance, daylight from the stairwell. As I climbed the cool granite steps I tried in vain to reach my voice mail. Concern came first, then the internalized guilt. My uselessness as a mother was unarguable; I had come to terms with it. But of course it had its price. For the time being I paid with nightmares where the most terrible things happened to Mike: accidents, drowning, always the worst possible scenarios, but one day these nightmares would come true—death had made this much perfectly clear by now.

The stairs led to a granite corridor, a sort of circuit, I figured. I took a left, turned another corner thirty yards later, and immediately recognized the narrow windows of the exterior wall: handy for those looking to hurl themselves a few stories down. The floor glittered with broken glass, so I put my shoes back on, and as I turned the corner I heard, above the echoing click of my heels, a mechanical hum that intensified when I turned another corner and continued under a broad arched construction. I retried Boudewijn's number, but again no luck. Boudewijn was the primary parent; for years he had been giving the boy his undivided attention and devotion. And Mike was crazy about Boudewijn, he never went willingly to his mother. Perhaps it was better like that. The decision, the entirely *natural* decision, to leave Mike in Boudewijn's care, was for all parties the best choice.

The space widened unexpectedly, and with it I caught a whiff of iron and sand: I had entered the immense drill square and become as small as a chipmunk. At the left of the concrete floor, under an arched roof supported by Eiffel Tower–like trusses, three toy cars were parked. Diametrically opposite I saw one of our trucks and an unfamiliar pickup, and next to them a couple of generators on wooden pallets vibrating at high frequency. My cell phone gasped desperately for a signal. I whipped off a text message ("smt w/mike?") that took three tries to send. I already knew that Boudewijn wouldn't understand why I'd texted rather than call; compared to his ceaseless care, whatever interest I showed came over as secondhand and spineless. I was happy to admit without reservation that he made a fantastic father, from day one, and even before that: during my pregnancy he outdid me with nearly academic knowledge of what was going on in my womb. He drove to San Francisco for homeopathic morning sickness pills, organic cosmetics, and dandelion tea for water retention, which he then made for me with concentration and precision. "Sharon, one of the secretaries, says the prenatal yoga classes on Valencia Street are terrific." He was probably so on top of things because he rightly suspected me of prenatal depression, and was afraid I'd throw myself belly-first down a flight of stairs.

I took my shoes back off and walked around the mobile power station. No one was manning it, the machinery functioned on its own. With half an eye on my cell phone I followed the thick black electricity cables.

"There she is," Kristin said. I had cut through a dusty gym with rings and climbing frames and arrived, after yet another long brick corridor, at a scene of noisy activity. She and Q stood in the doorway to the ballroom I recalled from the tour with Sotomayor's assistant: an expansive space with narrow strips of parquet flooring like an old-fashioned dance school. Inside, the guys from lighting were setting up a powerful stage lamp.

"Hi doll," Kristin said. "This place is amazing."

"Thanks," I replied.

"You know how cool I think it is that you're going on film again? Are you psyched?"

"Can't wait." I smiled at Q, who lowered his eyes and ran a big white hand down his cheek. The truth be told, I was dreading it like the plague. After Boudewijn's call, I was feelng anything but sexy. Maybe Bobbi had some cocaine.

"Where's Rusty and the new guy?" Kristin came right up in front of me and took my face in her hands. I could see her contact lenses.

"Checking out the building. Wells is turning it into a guided tour."

"Go ahead and change," said Kristin. "Nice blouse." Through the satin she pinched my left nipple with her thumb and index finger, gently twisting it in circles like I was a radio that needed fine-tuning.

"Macy's," I said. "Sale bin."

She smiled. "That door. Bobbi's here already. It's all kind of makeshift, Joy. Can you make sure she puts on something cheerful?" She took obvious pleasure in giving orders to the woman who had cut her off at the pass. When I first met Rusty at the reception of the independent film festival, he had introduced Kristin as his right-hand woman. A half-hour later he catapulted me, to her unconcealed chagrin, pretty much to co-director. Since then, she'd become *my* right-hand woman.

The washroom block had none of the warm coziness of Coldwater's dressing rooms, no deep-purple velvet wallpaper, no lacquered make-up tables, no theatre mirrors surrounded by soft-white bulbs. The white plastered walls reflected the harsh fluorescent lighting, the floor consisted of a honeycomb of hexagonal tiles that thousands of officers and cadets had once traversed on their way to the battery of urinals in a break from the military regime, a moment alone with the yellow fluid and the smell of grainy soap from a bucket. Someone, Q probably, had laid a couple of wide planks across a row of twelve washbasins as a sort of improvised make-up table. Two rickety chairs—on one of them hung a pair of jeans and a T-shirt—stood in front of a long mirror, which was half misted up, an undercoat of rust showing through. To the right were two galvanized racks with kinky stuff I recognized from the Coldwater dressing rooms. Lavender soap and steam tickled my nose. To the left, an open door with cracked frosted glass led to an abattoir-ish shower room with eight drippy showerheads dangling from the ceiling. In the middle of the room, a girl stood on the wet tiles, drying herself off with a large white hotel towel. Bobbi glanced skittishly over her shoulder.

"Hello . . . ," she said with faux bashfulness. She had obviously read Kristin's script.

"Don't move."

I walked across the wet floor and studied her back and remarkably narrow hips. Since living with me she had got two stars tattooed on either side just above her buttocks. The one was red with a thin black outline, the other black with a red outline, probably something Jekyll and Hyde-ish. You didn't find many under-twenty-fives in this town without a tattoo.

She made a move to turn around, but I gave her a hard slap on her left buttock; she drew a deep breath, a shower cap fell to the floor.

"Did you hear me?" I grabbed her buttocks—both of them now nineteen years old, the left one emblazoned with my handprint in red—and squeezed them. "Legs wider." She shifted her feet farther apart. I squatted down, stuck my thumbs deep into her butt crack and pulled her cheeks apart; her cleanly scrubbed anus opened up like a monkey's mouth. I spat on it and eased my thumbs inside; the sphincter closed around them in a sucking reflex.

"Hello, Bobbi, nice to see you again."

Since the coffee table incident, which seemed to have encouraged rather than embarrassed her, we phoned each other every few months. If I was at Coldwater whenever she did a shoot for one of our websites, I'd drop by the dressing room, if she hadn't stopped by my office on the way to say hello.

"Yes . . . ma'am," she said. "I'm so pleased to be working with you at last."

"I wouldn't be so eager if I were you," I said. "How'd it go with Tyra, Bobbi?"

"Tyra Banks is a . . . bitch," she replied. "D'you see it?"

I pulled my left thumb out of her. "*Ma'am,*" I said, and gave her four vicious slaps on her left buttock. "Did you see it, *ma'am*?"

As she let out her breath she said: "Did you see the show, ma'am?"

"You were great."

"But Joy," she said, suddenly matter of fact, "that whole fucking show was, like, fucking fake."

I let go of her and stood up. She turned toward me. She was putting the game on hold.

"Oh yeah?"

"They film it in New York, you know?" she said. "On the phone beforehand one of the production assistants says: wear whatever *you* think is nice." She shivered for a second, walked over to the chairs by the mirror, and sat down. I took the towel from her and dried her shoulders. "So I fly to New York a whole day early for those people," she continued, "and spend the afternoon shopping on Madison Avenue. Skinny jeans, a top, earrings. I kinda want to look good on that sofa of hers on national TV, you know? I buy two pairs of Christian Louboutins because I can't make up my mind, all of it with my own money. Next morning I show up at the studio, and what do you think?"

You're phenomenal, that's what. As I got undressed we eyed each other in the mirror. God, what an old tart I am alongside you. Bobbi's deep-brown eyes were, as always, half shut, and a geisha-like smile floated around her small mouth—controlled mockery, the maximum indignation her stoic face would allow. She was stunning. Hardly surprising that this cult bombshell had caught Steven Soderbergh's fancy—that is, if what she said on Tyra was true.

"So, what's with Soderbergh?" I asked. "Did he really offer you a part?"

"Hang on," she said. "So I get there, and those jerks from production go: this isn't how an eighteen-year-old girl looks. That's right, I say, it's how a *nine*teen-year-old girl looks. Maybe, they say, but today Tyra's talking about teenagers in the porn industry, and that's why you're here. So they bring me over to a rack of children's clothes. Oilily. They made me dress up like . . . like . . ."

"Gretl von Trapp. Pass me your soap?" I walked toward the showers.

"Did you see that pink sweater?" she called after me. "And those flats? Even the earrings had to go. That production bitch gave me little pink studs."

I picked up the shower cap and twisted the calcified faucets. The showerheads vibrated and sputtered, the slushy stream of hot water splashed onto my shoulders. She stood in the doorway and watched as I soaped myself up.

"Hair pulled back in a ponytail, hardly any eyeshadow, too much blush, you get the picture. I thought: Just you wait, you fuckers."

She did look like the Virgin Mary on Holy Saturday, but in fact that only enhanced her performance. What charm, what icy composure. Without getting worked up, she explained her decisions, just as she always did, you couldn't even call it defending herself. Tyra, with all her prescripted questions, couldn't poke even the slightest hole in her argument. As always, Bobbi spoke in a dry monotone, her words as salty as beef jerky, the vowels flat. Her speech was filled with street-smart wisdom, she exuded a faint disdain that even put that Tyra on edge. ("Bobbi, you don't have to answer this, but I'm going to ask you anyway: were you sexually abused when you were young?" "Me? Oh no. I had a terrific childhood. Why? Were you, Tyra?")

But the knockout was that Soderbergh movie. Right after a censored compilation of Bobbi in action, Tyra asked how long she was planning to stay in the business, and when she answered that she'd keep going until she stopped having fun, Tyra asked how she saw her life *after* the porn industry. She replied that she was considering a mainstream acting career, and when Tyra only just managed to stifle a patronizing titter and asked Bobbi if she really thought Hollywood was sitting around waiting for her, she said that of course she didn't know for sure, but that she'd be having lunch on Broadway tomorrow afternoon with Steven Soderbergh.

"Steven Soderbergh?" Tyra said. "You mean the *director* Steven Soderbergh?"

"*Ocean's Eleven, Twelve, Thirteen,*" Bobbi answered, "you know, with Clooney and Pitt?" And when Tyra gawped at her for a few seconds like a bumper car with a dead battery, she continued: "*Sex, Lies, and Videotape*?"

"I know who Soderbergh is," Tyra snapped. "You have an audition, I take it?"

"A role. I've got the lead in Steve's new movie."

Just the wrong starlet to bring out to New York. What a delight to watch the desperation glide over Tyra's smug face. In the audience, a shell-shocked delegation from the Anti-Porn Movement: a Bible-basher and a feminist, both of them with a Ph.D. on the psychological and sociological damage that people like Bobbi and me and Rusty inflict on society. Are we supposed to believe this teenage floozy? This depraved cocksucker whom the underworld plebs of L.A. elected SuperSlut 2008? Who has won awards for the year's filthiest blow-job scene, the year's filthiest threesome, the year's filthiest whatever—are we supposed to believe this doe-eyed skank? You saw Banks thinking: why don't I know this? Why didn't my editors know this? And the desperation spread over the rest of the audience, and then onto us, the viewers at home. Is she lying? But in the studio there was no time for that, the show must go on, so the question just hovered there like a buzzard over Tyra's head: is this *possible*? Or has she been fucked so senseless that she's delusional? And *if* she's telling the truth, what's the point of this whole show? What exactly am I trying to tell America?

I turned off the faucet. It was Q—I hadn't heard him come in—who handed me a towel. I was struck, not for the first time, how much his craggy face reminded me of Larry King, but without the glasses.

"So is it true?"

"Is what true?"

"The movie, Bobbi."

She chuckled. "I thought it couldn't hurt to do a little PR. Of course it's true."

I walked over to Q, who was fussing with a plastic crate he'd placed on the improvised make-up table. "So how'd this all come about?"

While Bobbi told me how she'd received a message on her MySpace a few months ago from someone claiming to be Steven Soderbergh—not just one message, but four—and who turned out to really *be* Steven Soderbergh, Q hoisted a sort of leather harness onto my hips. A week later she had "Steve" on the phone, he knew her work, that's how he put it, he'd read about her in *Los Angeles* magazine. Steve was looking for someone for his new project, a movie about a high-class call girl in Manhattan. It wasn't a bit part, as she initially thought, but top billing. She was the first person he'd thought of. She did not believe him. The next day they met for coffee in the L.A. Zoo, and while the man did look just like the director Steven Soderbergh she still didn't believe him. The plan was for the movie to open the Berlin Film Festival in February.

His knees creaking, Q sank to his haunches and buckled the belts around my waist and thighs. With a face like a gravedigger he fished a green hard-plastic penis out of his crate and screwed it into a notch in the corset right above my mound of Venus.

"It was in *Newsweek* the day before yesterday, by the way."

"Did you know this before you went on Tyra?"

She smirked sarcastically. "Well yeah, how else could I have told her about it?"

"I know that. I mean, at the time of the phone call. Did you keep your mouth shut on purpose?"

"I kept my mouth shut on purpose."

There was a knock on the heavy industrial door, and right away it swung open. A slim-built black guy in a shiny blue shirt came in.

"Ladies; sir."

"Hi, Ralph."

"Because you knew you'd get your chance."

"Those jerks were just itching to tell me I'd blown my whole future. *Itching* to. From the very first minute I was sitting there with my finger on the trigger." She extended her arm, her dainty hand formed into a pistol. "*Bang*. Tyra got it right between the eyes."

Ralph went over to the washbasins and laid a brown leather case on the plank. He grabbed my penis, pulled me toward him, his lips pursed and eyes closed. I gave him a kiss. Only then did he unsnap the case and bring out brushes, eyeliner pencils, and little oval make-up boxes.

"But is it a serious role?"

"*Soder*bergh?" she said with an uncharacteristic edge. "Of *course* it's a serious role. I've read the screenplay, it's subtle." She picked up Kristin's script between thumb and index finger and dangled it in the air. "Not as subtle as this, naturally," she said with a snicker.

The set teemed like an anthill, everyone was moving—everyone except Bobbi. From the hall I could see her kneeling crosswise on a bed that looked as if Oliver Twist had to sleep on the floor tonight. Vince was tying Bobbi up with a length of thickly twined rope. Her wrists were bound tightly behind her back, the rope wound around her upper body, cutting into her breasts, which hung out of her puffy red blouse. She was wearing cute embroidered canvas peep-toes with huge cork wedges, linen ribbons crisscrossing up her calves. Her fragile wrists were pulled upward by a cord that ran to a ring in the ceiling.

Two cameramen and a photographer circled around the Oliver Twist bed. Kristin studied a bird's-eye view of the set on a laptop. Clint, a guy whose card read "floor assistant," crouched on the far side of the bed, where Bobbi's head hung awkwardly over the edge of the mattress. He joked with her some, and occasionally poured a swig of his Red Bull into her mouth.

Vince was completely engrossed in his first job. Despite the chill in the ballroom he was sweating profusely, flooding the beaches on his Hawaiian shirt. With the speed of a catamaran sailor, he brought the rope around Bobbi's left knee, which rested, like the right one, at the long edge of the bed; he tossed it around the outer left bedpost, threaded it back and pulled it tight, tying it deftly in a sea scout knot. Bobbi's buttocks glowed like the head of a sphinx in the glaring floodlights. With his back to me: Rusty, monitoring the goings-on in his new office.

No one noticed me. I stood half in the brick doorframe, about twenty yards from Bobbi and Vince, a distance that seemed to fold in on itself, leaving me a total outsider with regard to the bed tableau. Something—perhaps I was hoping for a message from Boudewijn, or maybe it was Bobbi's last comment, which struck me as arrogant, a tad too much disdain for my taste—kept me utterly detached and unexcited. As much as I tried to get caught up in the moment—I impatiently slapped my legs with the whip Q had given me, trying desperately to work myself into the state of mind needed to perform my duties on that iron-framed bed in a few moments—as much as I tried to concentrate on Bobbi, my brain marched on, a paradox whirling in my head, two contradictory thoughts twisting my consciousness from my body like a wing nut. On the one hand this fort was like a Faraday cage: I was totally blocked from external signals, off the radar, non-existent to my ex and even my son, whose phone calls and messages bounced off the shield. And on the other hand, Bobbi Red lay there waiting for me; like it or not, my thoughts X-rayed her impending fame, which did not yet exist but soon would, a fame whose exact form and scope were still uncertain. The idea that the ingenue who stood at my bathroom sink on Sunset washing her anonymous little ass would become Soderbergh's new muse, that in six months she'd be traipsing down the red carpet in Berlin with that man, and who knows, might wind up in the Kodak Theater with a gilded statue in her hands—from now on, *any*thing was possible—made my head spin. The movie would probably disappear into the DVD circuit, I comforted myself, and Bobbi into obscurity; no, it would almost certainly bomb, she would be panned, written off, laughed out of town. But something told me it was going to be a very different story. This was going to be her big break. She'd emerge as a star the likes of which Hollywood hadn't seen in a long time. Bobbi would become a radioactive twenty-first-century Mae West, a Nicole Kidman that exploded in your face.

Kristin spotted me and signaled. "Joy—three minutes."

Just say it *did* happen, I thought as I walked into the ballroom to the hollow click of my heels, what did that mean for the scene we were about to shoot? *Her* role was clear: this would become a piece of Bobbi footage that contributed to her cinematographic double whammy, a film clip that everyone would want to see, maybe just to satisfy a basic lust, but maybe more to make a study of Bobbi

Red, that strange, beautiful geisha whom no one knew how to take. Bobbi turned the brick Barracks into a glasshouse, Bobbi threw open the curtains, Bobbi lifted the manhole cover off the gutter, and then the outside world would see . . . *Mike's mother*?

Rusty had just pulled the Maybach away from the Barracks when Bo's texts and voice mail messages appeared on my phone, one by one. *Cut it out*, a voice in my head snarled, *leaving Boudewijn was absolutely the right move.* The three of us sat on the backseat: me behind Rusty, who despite his manic edge still drove like an old lady, Bobbi in the middle, and Vince on her right, Kristin up front in the passenger seat talking loudly. No post-shoot downer here; the mood, as usual, was congenial and relaxed. We were on our way to Coldwater to catch the end of two other sessions. *Leaving was the best thing you ever did.* Bobbi slid her slender fingers between mine and pressed up against me, maybe just to be as far as possible from Vince.

I would have died of boredom. Before Mike was born, Boudewijn and I were at least *both* unhappy in San Francisco. Those months of wandering aimlessly around our new city, wounded and homesick, seeking each other out for comfort and companionship. Misery loves company. But after Mike came, Boudewijn was suddenly contented, he read out loud to Mike (about the only times I heard him speak), enjoyed his hobbies (the only outings we had were long, statewide car trips, sometimes even as far as Nevada, which invariably ended in the barn of some farmer in slippers who pulled a blanket off a half-dilapidated jukebox), and picked fights. Conflicts here, conflicts there, after two years with Boudewijn Stol I couldn't hear the word "conflict" without breaking into a rash. When I'd get home from Silicon Valley in the evening, he'd already be sitting in his satin pajamas, typing scathing complaint e-mails. To his co-directors at the Golden Gate Park Golf Club, to the personnel at Mike's nursery school, to his partners at McKinsey, to the divorce lawyer on whom he'd sicced another lawyer. The only person he didn't fire electronic grenades at from his trench was me.

"F-ing call ASAP" was the first text message I opened. A new jolt of panic shot through me. Mike go-carted a lot recently. Or maybe it had to do with money. Had I missed a payment? No way was I going to call San Francisco from the backseat of this car: I was too chicken, too hung-up, too inhibited, scared to death that Rusty might yank the phone out of my hand and jabber something into it, the kind of thing he'd been jabbering for half an hour already, things he meant as compliments (and, in a sense, were) but would get me barred from parental custody once and for all.

"*Feck*, Joy, you are one hard woman," Rusty exclaimed right after the shoot. He called my performance "fascinating," almost alarming. He was briefly worried about the bloodred welts on Bobbi's thighs, hopefully they'd heal before she had to strip for Soderbergh. I was wise enough not to let on how I'd mustered up the requisite sadism; that Bobbi-doll with her cheek resting on my shoulder might not have even understood. What it boiled down to was that I had succeeded in hating Meryl Dryzak for who she was. Out of *envy* for who she was. I had mobilized all the jealousy in me to hate her for her ambition, her flair and pluck, and the unapologetic way she went out and became, at age eighteen, exactly what she wanted to be, without pretense, without cowardly, costive *shame*: this is me, take it or leave it. And look where it got her. And, moreover, look where being just the opposite had got *me*. My half-assed spinelessness had cost me dearly, but I was still leading a double life, I still had everything to hide. I let the *New York Times* interview me, but without a photo. Try explaining that to Bobbi.

(I hadn't explained a thing to Boudewijn either. I just buggered off and tendered the fake excuses later by phone. After two and a half comfy years up in our Russian Hill eagle's nest, the little one tucked under his down covers, I simply up and left.)

His second text hit me like a bullet. "Aaron Bever called us. WTF?!" I jerked my hand out of Bobbi's and clapped it to my mouth. Startled, she looked up.

"You OK, honey?"

"Yeah, sure," I stammered. "Sorry . . . something just occurred to me."

"What, hon?" She kissed my shoulder and felt for my hand.

"I think I've . . . uh, left my back door open." Was Aaron in America? Was he on his way to Boudewijn and Mike?

"Prob'ly not," Bobbi said. "And anyway, if they loot your place, you can always come stay with me." She let her head sink back onto my shoulder. I looked out of the window: on the horizon you could see Watts Towers, two black pointy hats made of junk and old iron. I dialed my voice mail and pressed the phone as hard as possible against my far ear. Why on earth did I trade in my family for this bunch? You and your intuition, so much for all those McKinsey decision-making models.

Boudewijn spoke to me—in Dutch, the only person who still did—via my provider's voice mail chip. I had to do my best to understand what he said, what with Vince in the background discussing his moving plans with Rusty and Kristin. "Joni," Boudewijn's voice said, "this is not good. Bever got Mike on the line."

Bobbi was still holding my hand; as I squeezed it I felt her eyes bore into me. "Have they cleaned you out?" she asked.

"Do you know anything about this?" Boudewijn continued. "He managed to wangle your address in L.A. out of Mike. What's Bever up to? Call me, damn it."

18

Before he lies down in the extra-firm twin bed, Sigerius reaches into his laptop bag for the CD-ROM with the website photos. He finds the disc he managed to fool himself with last spring in Shanghai; fighting back melancholy and self-censorship, and with a sour taste in his mouth, he selects five images and e-mails them to Tineke, as per their agreement to the Hotmail address he once opened for them but which they never use.

The next morning there is consternation at his department about an editorial on last weekend's political talk show. He had missed it; the columnist held forth on a controversial education plan for which he was called—they've wasted no time, have they—a *turncoat*: he is about to implement a policy which as rector he vigorously opposed. This is true. He and his spokesman formulate a strategy; afterward, alone in his office, he phones MeesPierson, his private bank, where his call is taken with the customary discretion. Saying the amount out loud ("Michael, listen, I need 100,000 tomorrow, cash") sounds definitely shady, as though he's ordered a shipment of explosives from Kandahar to blow up the Prime Minister's residence. He chooses a branch in The Hague where he can pick up the bills early tomorrow morning. "I'm afraid I have to ask a few intrusive questions," the fellow says.

"Because?"

"The law, Mr. Sigerius. I have to regard your withdrawal as an 'exotic' transaction." Apparently there is a form that has to be sent to a national data bank. He asks if he can call back tomorrow, he has to go now.

After he returns from an obligatory dinner with the Culture Council, Sigerius gets a phone call from Janis. He's uneasy: it's not about those pictures, is it? First they discuss the TV editorial (a number of newspapers have followed up on it), and then she tells him that she and Tineke will be going to Val-d'Isère a week early; they are at the farmhouse and plan to leave first thing in the morning. Not with the Audi, but in her own car, the skis are already up on the roof rack, does he mind driving down alone? "I'll have to grin and bear it," he says.

After they've hung up he's almost sorry it wasn't about the pictures. He likes Janis's straightforwardness. He's curious what she would have to say about it, just as he wonders what she would think of the blackmail he's about to succumb to. In bed he recalls the serious talks they've had: you could count them on the fingers of just one hand, but they were always, how would you put it, *clarifying*. Janis is a girl who can lie sprawled on the sofa watching the Tour de France for hours on end, and just before the finale switch off the TV and ask: "Hey Dad, why'd you marry that Margriet, anyway?" It was a rainy Sunday afternoon, they were home alone; she barraged him with questions, and by the time he was through with his reconstruction of that disastrous marriage it was too late to go to their favorite Chinese take-out.

With Janis's voice still resonating in his head he tosses and turns for hours under a too-thin blanket, barraging *himself* with questions, *her* questions: but why have a *child*, Dad, why have a child with that woman? Sleep? Forget it, his restlessness disguises itself as a dream, and in his agitation the images are relentless; they are linked together like a chain that begins with 100 grand hush money and ends at that marriage he'd been conned into. How did he manage to get himself into such a mess? He tries to block out the memories, but there's no holding them back: there she is, Margriet Wijn, her raven-black hair put up like one of The Supremes, her eyes always slightly hazy. *What did you see in her, Dad?* Of course he retaliates, don't give me such a hard time, young lady, I was twenty-four, damn it, what the hell did *I* know. They'd married him off, that's what it boiled down to, his sister-in-law married him off. *Right, Dad, blame somebody else.* She was right—why did she always have to be right? *Your sister-in-law married you off? Go on, I'm listening.* All he wants is to sleep, but his memory gives his younger daughter what she wants, no, it wakes the dead; instead of sinking into blackness himself, he dredges up old ghosts. He'd just left to spend six months in Japan when his father died suddenly—while hanging a lamp, Janis, your grandfather (well, my father) came crashing off an end table, heart attack, a bolt of amperes straight through his heart. Months later he arrived back in Delft (having missed the funeral, of course) to find that the Trompetsteeg 14 had been confiscated by his brother Fred and his wife, a pair of late-twenty-somethings who'd installed themselves in the barely cooled-off living room acting like they were his parents. He and that Mieke get under each other's skin, she'd send him to the bathroom with a bucket and rag, "You shower too often and too long, Siem, once a week is plenty, and from now on take your judo suit to the Laundromat—right, Fred?"

On Saturday evenings she more or less shoves him out of the door—"go on, Delft is full of cafés, do you want a girlfriend or don't you?," followed by that incessant "right, Fred?"—so to get them off his back he admits he knows a nice girl, Menno Wijn's sister, from Utrecht, where he still goes for judo four times a week. One Friday afternoon he gets home from the athletic training school where he teaches and gets the shock of his life: *there she is,* Maggie Wijn, sitting straight up in his late father's easy chair, shooting the breeze with Mieke like it's the most natural thing in the world. She looks different, he explains to Janis, less blue-collar; she's ladylike, she's used hairspray, there's eyeshadow on her limp lids, she's holding a white leather purse on her lap. Mieke's been meddling again, but for once he's grateful; until now it's never got any further than awkward stammering at the back door when he stopped by to fetch Menno. Now they sit here chatting for a couple of hours, it's even fun, they talk about beat groups she likes, about the liquor store on the Oude Gracht where she works as a cashier; she has a low, melancholy voice, but when he cracks a joke she laughs out loud, more than at Fred's sarcastic remarks. At nine-thirty Mieke gives a little clap. "Siem, walk Margriet to the station, won't you?" She'd have preferred to have Fred hand over the wedding rings there and then.

He does not remember much of what must have been an engagement period. Meeting Margriet's parents, a nerve-racking gathering in a smoke-filled living room, where, he hears later, he gobbled up all four slices of buttered cake; Sunday strolls in Amelisweerd Park where they did their best to chat casually until their well-earned necking behind the dike.

They were married three months later. It took him somewhat longer to understand who it was he was now bound to, a bit like when Margriet only discovered his tattoo on their wedding night: the two blue-green Japanese characters he had had emblazoned on his chest following a tournament in Marseilles, and which Menno said meant "judo." ("Egg foo young, you mean," she says, one of her flimsy jokes that he has to laugh at.) What do they know about each other, really? He ejaculates before he knows it.

She turns out to be insufferably lazy. On the days he teaches self-defense in Amsterdam in the morning, arriving back at Utrecht Central at one-ish and cycling home to grab a sandwich before his afternoon training session, he notices as he approaches the house that the bedroom curtains are still drawn. Like practically every other weekday morning, Margriet is still lolling in the bed they inherited from his father, on the bedside table a soup bowl with dried remains of the spiked eggnog from her former employer. When he criticizes her slothfulness—he's spent time at a Japanese drill camp where they slept briefly and deeply on mats as thin as carbon paper, got up with the rest of the jungle animals, and ran six kilometers before breakfast—her reaction is one of impassive penitence.

He subjected her to what is nowadays called a vocational aptitude test, and subsequently enrolled her at a local sewing atelier: make your own dresses, pin up jackets, stitch a suit out of a bolt of fabric she could, he found out, pick up for a song at the Saturday textiles market. He bought her a Singer with his sport-school salary and installed it on the kitchen table next to the electrical outlet. It's a hit, she loves it, she says, the teacher's great, he's treated to news items concerning the other women, mostly intrigues, intricate tales of love and betrayal, Margriet has apparently become the confidante of the atelier. Every now and then she comes back with a self-made skirt, or a jacket, sometimes something for him—she's got talent, it's as good as store-bought, and it is difficult to describe what goes through his mind when, a year later, he finds out they *were* all store-bought, purchased with her household allowance, from her *lesson* money, because Margriet admits without blinking that she'd only been to that atelier twice.

The truth is staring him in the face: he has got himself a very strange wife indeed. A sardine who does nothing but sleep and drink. And prevaricates, by which he means a creative form of lying; Margriet Wijn does not spin half-yarns, or concoct ordinary lies—she cultivates new realities.

"And you get a woman like that pregnant." Janis.

"Yeah."

He lists all the ways he had back in 1970 of not making a child—nip out for some cigarettes, jump on the first merchant ship leaving town—and adds them up, the most important tally of his life, he realizes, and to his amazement the sum total says: *get her pregnant*.

His phone rings at six-thirty. Tineke. He takes a few deep breaths before answering.

"Why're you calling so early?" His voice is hoarse. He has hardly slept a wink, and doesn't know what to expect.

"Janis is in the shower. We're about to leave."

"What about the pictures?"

She laughs, a commiserating chortle that sounds forced to him. Then she says: "You're kidding yourself. She's a pretty girl, I'll give you that, and a cheap little hussy on top of it, and yes, she does look a bit like Joni. But it's not her."

He listens, dumbfounded.

"Aside from that it's just not her," she says, "this girl has bright blue eyes and totally different hair. It's someone else." She laughs again. For a moment he considers playing along, just as one laughs along with a lunatic; pretend he only now understands, finally sees the light. Instead, he sighs.

"Is that all you can say? This girl is American, Siem. Your sex babe. Where *did* you find these pictures?"

"Don't be so stupid," he snarls. "I've talked to her. Whether or not it's her is not up for discussion. Have you lost your mind?"

"Have you lost *yours*? You misunderstood her, that's all. I think you panicked. Misinterpreted everything. It's Wilbert, he's thrown you off-kilter. It's a tasteless joke. *That's* what *I* think."

Although he expects this veneer of self-deception to crumble to pieces at any moment, she holds her ground. She *means* it. It is not even self-preservation, she is actually *convinced*. "You said yourself it was a short conversation," he hears her say, "and of course you were shocked, maybe even furious, whatever. Wound up into a frenzy by that damn son of yours. You're mistaken, honey. Really. Shall I phone her?"

"Don't you *dare*!" he barks. She does not reply—stunned, he assumes.

"Sorry," he says. "I'll call her myself, dear. Let me take care of it. You just go and enjoy France."

Soon he has to leave for Leiden to open a conference of the National Network of Women Professors. He switches on the bedside lamp, sleep is now out of the question. He steps onto the cold floor and takes the speech someone has written for him out of his briefcase. Back in bed, he leaves the bundle of papers lying in front of him on the covers.

Is he really planning to bury 100,000 guilders on Scheveningen beach?

An hour later he directs his chauffeur not directly to Leiden, but first through the city's rush hour to the MeesPierson branch.

He has reluctantly invented a pretext for the money, something about paintings and auction houses in Nice and Marseilles, dealers who insist on cash transactions, which turns out to be sufficiently plausible. While the Volvo idles he goes into the office with a small leather Puma sports bag he bought downtown. The receptionist makes a phone call, a smiling young woman appears, she brings him to a room that smells of new carpeting. There she counts out—her nails are painted with little palm trees—a hundred 1,000-guilder notes, a stack not even an inch thick; he is embarrassed by his stupidly amateurish gym bag.

About an hour and a half later he gives a speech to 300 professorial women with 100 grand stuffed in his breast pocket. He fields questions about the dismal Dutch participation statistics on the world stage, about the transparency of the appointment process, social exclusivity in academia's upper echelons—and strangely enough, there, up on that stage, during the open questions, he experiences a kind of deliverance. Is it that simple? he asks himself. Now of all times, with a microphone in front of his nose, standing in front of 300 skeptical women, he has a revelation. Joni's own mother does not recognize her! He says: look here, I'm sorry but this is your daughter, and she replies: get your head examined.

"What we in the Netherlands have to move away from," he says from behind his lectern, "is professors being appointed by deans and department chairs. In countries like America and Norway you start as an assistant professor, and whether you move on to a full professorship depends on how much you've published, not on your boss."

She does not recognize her own daughter. Are you still someone if no one recognizes you? Maybe not. If Tineke, after a confession like his, after that dildo in the mail, still believes that the girl in those photos is not Joni, then it's *not* Joni. He's the only one who single-handedly recognized her, and then only once he actually stood there in that attic room. It's her and it's not her, a case of being *and* not being, wave *and* particle. "In Norway and the USA," he says, his heart nearly exploding with elation, "one person does not hold another person back, and that must be our goal here in the Netherlands as well."

Of course it's not her! The applause that washes up over the podium encourages him, legitimizes his grin, drenches him in relief. Drop dead, Wilbert! *It's not her!* Don't you see that? Call your stepmother, you bum. You got shit in your eyes, or what? You can *see* it's not her, can't you? Wilbert Sigerius, now *him* they'll believe. Well, if Wilbert Sigerius says so. Glowing with triumph, he accepts the bottle of wine and thinks: if I could only talk to Joni. If he had her number he would call her right now: listen, sweetheart, let's just forget what happened. I don't know if you've heard yet, but it's *not you.* Mom and I are sure of it. Please come to France, bring Aaron with you. Tell him it's *not you.*

Exactly a week later he takes two last phone calls on the electrically warmed backseat of the Volvo. Outside, the city streets, with their sunken tram rails and stately town houses, gradually glide into suburbs and glossy black office parks. The quiet December evening, already deepening into night; the silent strength of his chauffeur at the wheel, who calmly drives him toward the A12—very soon he will be, for a week, a non-minister. He yearns for what the Kingdom of the Netherlands so promisingly calls the Christmas recess; the government car that drives him from The Hague to Enschede is a lever on a mixing console; with each kilometer he is transformed into a family man, the worse for wear perhaps, but still hankering for the French ski village where he'll celebrate the holidays.

Although he can't wait to glide down an alp behind Janis, he first looks forward to an evening alone in his own house, listening to his own music, sleeping in his own bed. For the next seven nights he'll be free from his satyrs, but even freedom can be tiring. Several ecstatic days followed the female professors' applause, days of excited confusion, his thoughts were already taking a ski vacation of their own: that same evening he quenched his exultant fury with the bottle of Cabernet Sauvignon they had given him at the conference, and then sat down to pen a *mea culpa* to Aaron and Joni, in duplicate, on a ministry notepad, a letter he had genuinely planned to mail; but upon rereading it on the freezing-cold toilet the next morning, he tore it up and flushed it without hesitation.

It was the day of the beach. He would *not* be standing at beach marker 101 at eight o'clock sharp, he had decided, and would *not* bury any bag of money. This was the result of that blissful inspiration Tineke had triggered. He no longer considered himself a blackmail target per se, and in order to bolster this idea he worked stealthily in his office on a serious letter to Joni in which he related Wilbert's extortion attempt, asking if he could count on her to back him up, form a united front, should Wilbert ever try to put his threats into action. But whether it was just the bustle and constant interruptions, or whether he simply blocked it out, the sliding door incident never made it to the keyboard.

Perhaps because of this, he felt his mood dampen in the course of the day, the triumphant buzz faded, he became softer, squishy, maybe even sentimental. The direct threat dispensed with, he crept out of his bunker and noticed, for the first time in years, a need to put himself in his son's shoes; we were talking about a guy of twenty-nine after all, a boy really, about the same age as he was when he dropped Margriet like a hot brick. His tongue ran over the words "ministerial accountability" like a molar that's lost its filling. Everything was fine back in his office in Zoetermeer, his brain saturated with the day-to-day urgencies, but on his way home he played reruns of the past, with his son in various roles: Wilbert perched in his child's seat on the front of the bike, him looking down on the boy's soft hair, testily pedaling through an abandoned Utrecht because he couldn't bear the sight of their national team's humiliation in the World Cup final; then the panther-like kid with his fanatic horseplay, who some fifteen years later came to liven up his girl-heavy family, and who playfully grabbed him by the wrists behind the farmhouse: the impressive strength of that adolescent body, he felt *himself*; the sullen, sagging head in the courtroom less than a year later. What was my part in all this?, he thought. How does the kid live? And for what? For whom? Unwittingly and unwanted, blades of pity started sprouting in him.

The flurries have begun, the Volvo makes its way through swirls of snow. His department secretary phones. As they speak, snowflake-speckled signs—towns, distances, exits—emerge from the darkness, at Deventer he signals his chauffeur to pull into a McDrive. They eat their quarter-pounders and fries in the parking lot, calmly chatting about the impending frost, about skiing regions and the best time of year to go.

Jesus—your own flesh and blood. He even attempts to understand Wilbert's unbridled rage, an enervating exercise in empathy, it is partly meant to anticipate future troubles, naturally—of course there's an element of tactical thinking; they *both* got a life sentence, he realizes now—but also to take stock of himself: what mistakes did *he* make? He tries to imagine how it must have been for a seventeen-year-old kid like Wilbert to be plopped into their family, from that fucked-up food-stamp life in Wijn's attic to their majestic farmhouse nestled in a poplar grove, inhabited by stable, well-fed, energetic achievers.

He spent that last week at the department with these kinds of thoughts on his mind, and when his chauffeur dropped him off at his flat on the Hooikade he knew what he had to do. He changed out of his suit into jeans and a fleece sweatshirt, and took the rickety ladies' bike from the downstairs landing out to the street. Off to the beach after all. With nervous resignation he cycled out to Scheveningen, without the money, but with the steadfast resolve to wait at beach marker 101 for his son. Surely Wilbert would come dig up the loot that same evening. Eye to eye it should be possible to engage him, maybe talk some sense into him. He was prepared to chance it. He would try to assess the danger, see how aggressive the kid looked; before he left he had stood in his expat-kitchenette holding a tomato knife, but thought better of it. Naturally he wanted to convince Wilbert he didn't have a leg to stand on, that this was not a blackmailing family—but without force, and intending to assure him that he belonged, that he was part of the family, no matter what, in spite of everything, in spite of the past. He conducted that odd tête-à-tête in his mind, a father-and-son conversation that would begin awkwardly and would probably end awkwardly too. And yet he wanted to extend his hand one more time.

So there he stood, on December 14, 2000, at eight in the evening, on the pitch-black Scheveningen beach, shivering from the cold, but in fact mostly from nerves. The wind at his back, he paced around marker 101, giving the briny wooden stake the occasional kick just to release tension, rehearsing what he was going to say, scanning the shadowy dunes until he had differentiated the various shades of black, and finally concluding from the total lack of movement in that teeming darkness that Wilbert was not going to show up. He waited until ten, eleven o'clock, the sea approached him—the *sea* did, yes—and then he declared himself crazy. A sentimental, naïve dickhead.

That weekend he stayed in The Hague. Not much point in hanging around in Enschede on his own. He worked a bit on the table in a living room that wasn't his, his sandy shoes on a newspaper, and to his surprise all was quiet: no text messages about not-buried bags of money, no sign of life, nada, and when the last days before the recess steamrolled over him, long workdays laced together with end-of-year cocktail parties and last-minute Cabinet decisions, a vague, almost existential doubt crept over him: maybe he was being paranoid, who's to say he was dealing with Wilbert after all? Couldn't he have fallen prey to some anonymous nutcase who one way or another had stumbled across Joni's online mischief and decided to give him a run for his money? Welcome to the reality of The Hague. He felt strangely provincial on Tuesday when he went to return his untouched 100 grand to that same MeesPierson girl. Maybe he had been living for weeks now in a phantasmagoria of guilt, maybe he had let himself obsess about his insane progeny to the point of narcissistic personality disorder.

He and his chauffeur have worked out a way to play music in the back of the car but not in the front. He listens to *Everybody Digs Bill Evans,* his favorite trio album, virtuosic up-tempo numbers alternated with skillfully contrasting, Satie-like, um, what are they, nocturnes? Aaron—wonder how he's doing. On the last stretch of freeway he renews his pledge to e-mail Joni, preferably before he leaves for France tomorrow. It has to be a combination of the serious, fatherly approach and that drunkard's rant he flushed down the toilet last week, a message in which he'll sort things out in an intelligent, tactical way; he must make it clear that he's kept her secret to himself, that he has got past being judgmental, that everybody commits youthful indiscretions.

His driver drops him off at the main entrance to the campus; he wants to walk the rest of the way. His laptop in one hand and his doctor's bag full of documents in the other, he passes the administration building and looks dispassionately at the picture window of his old office; his successor keeps the blinds shut, a faint light burns inside. The campus is a frosted Christmas cake, the fields resign themselves to the blanket of snow, only the widest stretches of asphalt still resist. In front of one of the dorms, a group of boys are engaged in a rather premature snowball fight; you can see their breath, their raw yells are echoless. He passes the sports complex, through the patch of woods, and reaches his street, the Langenkampweg. Snow swishes around the high streetlamps, all he hears is the crunch of his soles and a muted silence that thanks to thousands of slamming snowflakes can hardly be called silence.

There it is, the farmhouse, *his* farmhouse, swathed in white, patient, immune to the vicissitudes of life. Pain shoots through his bad leg: the exhaustion of the past few days, the exhaustion of the past six *months*, it's excruciating, he is broken, yearns for a glass of wine, for a scalding shower.

When they bought the house back in '85 there was a glossy wooden plank on the front with the words *MON REFUGE* burned into it, and after closing the sale he promptly unscrewed that smug piece of kitsch from the wall and—how appropriate—stoked the fireplace with it the whole evening. At first the impressive spaces, the luxurious finishes, took some getting used to—who'd have guessed he could grow old here, in aristocratic style? He, whose father had dropped dead in that hovel on the Trompetsteeg.

Tineke would have asked him to go around to the back with

those snowy shoes, but he doesn't have the energy. Sighing, he pushes open the heavy front door, one of the cats darts outside. He stomps the snow from his shoes but decides to take them off anyway. He feels the underfloor heating through his socks. His skis are propped up against the dresser under the stairs, Janis has brought them down from the attic for him. He scoops up a handful of Christmas cards from the doormat, walks into the living room, sets down his bag full of work papers between the magazine rack and a large floor lamp that gives off a warm, soft light: after Tineke's workshop was broken into three years ago (the booty: an electric drill, some 200 hand-tools, and pretty much anything liftable and with an electrical cord) she insisted on installing a light-timer in the house, an apparatus he prefers not to fiddle with. In a sudden urge for domesticity, he switches on the Christmas tree lights.

He takes an opened bottle of red from the wine rack next to the liquor cabinet, pours himself a full glass, and flops down in the corner of the sofa, his feet on the coffee table. He is hardly ever alone here. Dog-tired, he looks around the wide, sparsely furnished room and feels bad about leaving Tineke to her own devices here during the week. A copy of *Nouveau* lies open at his feet. On the other hand, maybe she loves it.

He takes his laptop from the bag and turns it on. The letter. Do it now, have to get an early start tomorrow. This afternoon at the office he plotted his route, Metz-Nancy-Lyon-Grenoble, more or less the route to Sainte-Maxime. He is planning to allude to that boat of theirs, but doesn't yet know how; perhaps in slightly shocked terms? In Val-d'Isère, anyway, he wants to be the bringer of good news; provided he can hit on the right tone, he's planning to close his e-mail with Tineke's idea of visiting Joni in Silicon Valley in the new year.

He nods off before he's even opened Word, how long his catnap lasted, he can't say; snippets of dreams, they are like memories of memories, shoot through his head, he dreams of a boy with deep-set eyes dressed in a body warmer. When he wakes with a start he is thoroughly zonked, his face is sticky—heavy stubble, he really must shave—and his bad leg is asleep. He's hungry again, there's a vague cooking odor in the house, a greasy smell he didn't notice before. It's half-past nine, he shoves the laptop aside and decides to shower first. On his way from the living room he ponders how to formulate the rapprochement part, attempt to explain his naked presence, or however you'd put it, in Aaron's house. Maybe he should be as honest as possible, just write it down the way it happened.

In the hallway he is reminded of a comment of Tineke's two weeks ago that had taken him aback: "I'm so glad everything we need is on the ground floor," she had said, "because my knees just about explode every time I climb those stairs." Maybe they should have a talk about taking drastic measures, a stomach bypass or something, but he's not sure how to package a suggestion like that.

Well, it is handy, he thinks as he undresses in their bedroom; it was one of the pleasant surprises of the house: the master bedroom, bathroom, and dressing room all connected. Yes, handy. He shivers from the cold. The curtains are still closed, their bed has been slept in on his side—the idea that his wife sleeps there when he's gone is not so much moving as poignant, only a step away from pity. With a sigh of relief he undoes his trousers, that junk from McDonald's has bloated his stomach, he looks at his body in the mirror next to the bathroom door and absently rubs his hand over the tattoo on his chest.

What if he made a detailed account of it? A few sheets, like a narrative? From the evening in his hotel room in Shanghai, when he first thought he recognized her, to his ransacking Aaron's house . . . or maybe further back . . . He fills one of the washbasins with lukewarm water and uncaps the shaving cream. A confession like this has something ludicrous about it. Since yesterday he's been troubled by a painful reddish spot on his left nostril, the skin is taut and irritated. Back in high school, when his brother had taken to harassing him with the story of their mother's deadly boil, he didn't dare even touch the pimples on his face, let alone eliminate them. But he's over that now. He places the tips of his middle fingers on his nostril, leans toward the mirror, and squeezes. What is the essence of the situation? The skin around his nostril tightens, changes from red to white, the pain is a pinpointable, promising pain. The point is to make Joni realize it's not about *herself*—

In the upper-right corner of the mirror he sees something move. Focusing close-up blurs his vision at first, he sees only a pink splotch. *Someone is standing behind him.* The arc of muscles that connects his cold toes, via his buttocks, to his hunched shoulders, freezes. He drags his gaze like a granite block to the upper corner of the mirror. Breathless, he stares into a contorted face.

"*Fucking dog.* Time to pay up."

As these words explode in his ear canals, the air is filled with a swishing sound. His right side and rib cage are struck by something so hard that it feels white-hot. The object Wilbert wields causes him a stinging pain in his lower body, a pain that easily eclipses the twinge in his nostril. His hands slap downward, he grasps the edge of the washbasin, its seam crackles, the soap dish clatters to the tile floor. He has to hold on with all his might to keep from falling over.

"You've already got undressed."

He answers, but has no idea what.

"Who'd you expect, wanker? Your stepwhore?"

The second time, the nunchuk hits him numbingly hard in his neck: pain shoots its way to his jaw. (Nunchuk: the overestimated, vulgar weapon he is being assaulted with, two sturdy steel handles connected by a short chain, a double flail that owes its dwindling popularity to Bruce Lee films. Once favored by skinheads with testosterone overload who went to public festivals or football matches looking for a brawl.) As he gasps in pain he sees in the mirror that Wilbert wants to say something. The bastard thinks there's time for that. He couldn't be more mistaken. *If you only knew who you're dealing with, asshole, then you wouldn't stand so close.*

Funny how it works, but he makes all the necessary approximations in the first second. Right after the first slug: a chain of assessments. The distance between him and the doorpost. The relative strengths: his opponent is a fighter and is armed, he himself is relatively well trained, but old and tired—a brief jolt of uncertainty: can he put up a good fight against a violent ex-con in the prime of his life? His vulnerable nakedness might seem like a drawback but, humiliating as it is, it's also an advantage: he is nearly impossible to grab. The moment: this scumbag *wants* to fight, he has chosen his exact timing, and that's *now.* At the same time he suspects that he's just woken Wilbert up, when he walked through the hall, that this pig had mussed up the covers of the master bed—a thought that *recharges* him.

"Been patient long enough, wanker, it's payback ti—"

He pushes himself with a groan from the washbasin, his left leg takes a giant step toward the doorpost, he drags the other one with it, and with his left shoulder lunges like a battering ram against the thickset chest, a firm mass that only grudgingly gives in, but the push is unrelenting. They commence their fall and, programmed as he is, he claws at his adversary's pant legs, his hands clutch at the loose-fitting cotton around the calves and the knee hollows, grab it *low,* and straightaway he yanks the bastard's legs out from under him, lifts him up, it has to be explosive, this is a tried-and-true, brutal technique. As one body they tumble into the dressing room, Wilbert has no time to grab hold of the doorframe, an indivisible moment later the back of his head smacks against the low shoe rack opposite the door, a loud, dry wallop, and again his shoulder drills into the fleshy chest, something cracks, squeaking vocal cords, the smell of alcohol fills his nose.

They lie there, dazed, both on their backs, he on top of his assailant.

Then something hard and cold slams against his chin: the chain of the nunchuk, the links chafe his skin. He reflexively tucks his chin to his chest, the metal glides over his stubble, the pain is direct and sharp. The chain slips to his neck, the fingers of his left hand immediately grab the iron chain, his fingertips lodged between the links and his Adam's apple. Wilbert pants loudly in his left ear, spit dribbles with it; growling, he tugs on the handles, Sigerius's Adam's apple is being crushed. He swings his arms backward, hits Wilbert's shoulder with his elbow, delivers a series of hard pops to the shoulder and upper arm, by now his air is getting cut off, he hawks, blood collects in his buzzing head. He was afraid of this, has been for a long time, from the moment he realized that the kid was out of control, knows no limits—that he is no match for him.

In a surge of exertion he contracts his stomach muscles, he has the stomach muscles of a gorilla. His knees shoot upward, he throws them back with all his might, the right one lands with a soggy thump in Wilbert's face, *take that, you bastard*—the bang is intense, the kid groans, his left hand lets the nunchuk fly, it slaps against Sigerius's chest with a leaden thud. Sputtering, spitting mucus, he grabs Wilbert's left arm, clamps both hands on his wrist, and as if in a dream—*it's like he's dreaming about judo, just as he so often dreams about judo*—executes the technique he excelled in long ago, a classic armlock, a *juji gatame*, words that well up in him like the first and last names of an old friend. In a flash he turns his own body perpendicular to Wilbert's, throws his left leg over the meaty chest, the right one over his throat and shoulders, contact, *control*, it is a fluid motion, at right angles to the body, his crotch under the left shoulder blade, *a crowbar of muscle.* Euphoria: the nominal resistance reminds him that there's only *one* judoka here. Wilbert thrashes with the nunchuk, the steel handle whips his thigh, but he hardly notices. The sweaty wrist is locked in the vise-grip of his hands, he forces Wilbert's arm—a strong, well-trained arm, he feels that all right—across his own stomach and chest, it goes so quickly, a perfectly outstretched, no, *overstretched* arm; if he wanted to he could bite off the thumb. Not necessary: all he has to do is tighten his back, hollow it just a tad, so that his hard stomach rounds itself under the elbow, and anyone will sing. Wilbert raises his bloodied face, tries to bite his lower leg, kicks wildly against the shoe rack. He removes one hand from the wrist and jerks the head back by the flaxen hair. He tightens his back. Right away Wilbert screams, a fierce cry from the bleeding mouth—yeah, it hurts, he knows it, nobody can stand it, not Geesink, not Ruska, not *you.* The screaming becomes shrieking, but he feels no sympathy, only deep satisfaction; he hears the joint crack. Or is it pleasure? It is pure gratification. Infinite, sadistic pleasure. "*Sto-o-o-o-o-o-p, sto-o-o-o-o-o-p, dirty fucker*"—he keeps going, until he passes the point where in the past he stopped hundreds of times, the shrieking becomes inhuman, go on, scream, no one hears you, as if in a dream he crosses the boundary, presses his belly mercilessly far forward, his heels dug deep in the carpet. What he hears is a dull, gruesome crack, wreathed in hoarse screams, bone breaking like a table leg, the elbow breaks completely through, makes an unnatural angle of nearly ninety degrees, the arm loses all its strength, a floppy rag, the sweater sleeve becomes drenched in blood, he feels the warm moisture on his belly, and something sharp, a bone has probably been thrust through the skin.

"That's what you get, *God damn it,"* he screams. First he gives the underarm a furious twist, as though it's got to come all the way off, then he kicks the screaming marionette away from him. But it springs into action, like a spasming chicken. Wilbert struggles to his haunches, his hideous face is frozen in shock, his mouth is a squashed tomato. He is wailing so loudly the pain must be excruciating, it sounds like tearless crying, putting up any more of a fight seems out of the question. He stares, awestruck, at his ruined elbow, squeezes the splintered joint with his good hand, blood trickles over his fingers.

"I'm gonna kill you," he blubbers, but instead of doing so he starts crawling out of the dressing room like a crab. He trips over the leg of a galvanized steel rack holding Tineke's dresses; accompanied by a loud clatter he rolls around in the glistening fabric, clambers upright, sputtering and panting, and disappears into the bedroom.

Should he go after him? Sigerius stays lying on his back. A second later, the moaning and groaning echoes through the hall, a thumping, hollow gait. A door slams shut with an angry bang, the living room door—the enemy is *there,* he is *here,* flat out on the dressing room carpet.

For a good few minutes he lies there for dead. The rising and falling of his chest. His teeth chatter, from the exertion, from the stress, from the cold: there's a sharp nip in the air. The chill bites into his wet body. Then, with a shock, he comes to his senses: the bastard might come back. With a knife. Or a gun. How could he be so stupid as to let him go? He should have held on to him, here, in a headlock. Jesus, he let a psychopath escape from a headlock. "*Damn,*" he whispers.

He gets up—everything hurts, his tendons seem shortened by half, he's covered with welts and blood, his chin is bleeding, the skin's been chafed off—and walks through the bathroom into the bedroom. What was he supposed to do? Hold on to the bastard until after the holidays? Listening keenly, keeping an eye on the open door leading to the front hall, he dresses as quickly as possible, pulls on his underwear and his pants, grabs a boating sweater from a chair in the corner of the room, his eyes glued on the doorway. He pulls on his socks, wriggles his feet into his shoes. He hears noise in the distance, banging in the living room, like heavy falling objects—what's that lunatic up to? What should he do? Call the police?

Regardless of whether he *wants* to, or whether it's wise, all the phones are in the living room. His keys too. He could leave via the front door, get himself to safety. He could walk to the campus. Or to the neighbors. But then what? Tell all? He ties his laces without losing sight of the doorway. No. He decides to do nothing for the time being. He crawls onto the bed and gropes around the floor on Tineke's side. Good, that hockey stick is there after all. Joni's old stick that Tineke has kept there since he moved to The Hague. But he changes his mind and goes back into the dressing room. The nunchuk is lying on the floor among the shoes scattered around the rack.

With the weapon in his hand he goes to the bedroom doorway and peers around the black curl of the stairs into the dark abyss of the front hall. There is light at the other end, a yellow glow through the frosted glass. He waits for several minutes. At times he imagines he hears something above his own panting, a soft shuffling, footsteps. He's taken a pretty fair beating, he's a purplish blue where the iron handles hit him, his ribs are bruised, maybe broken. He is so cold that he crouches down, as close as possible to the warm floor tiles. He keeps replaying the scuffle, that unreal sensation of the moment he let rip. The convulsing, suffering body of his son underneath him, his smell, the defenselessness of that arm, the snap.

He can't stay crouched here forever. Gripping the nunchuk loosely in his hand he tiptoes toward the living room. There is an irregular trail of blood specks on the slate floor. He passes the front door, realizes he's locked it from the outside: he can't even get out of the house—well yes, like a thief through a window. He stops at the living room door. With eagle eyes he peers through the thick glass, but sees nothing. Wait a bit longer. Give him time to bugger off, maybe he's gone already, given in, beaten, cured of his vengeance once and for all—maybe everything will just resolve itself. Maybe he should quit thinking that.

There is blood on the door handle, he pushes it downward, the sweat that wells up out of his fingers cools off on the cold brass. He gives the door a shove and takes a step back. From the hall he gazes into their living room, once a haven of comfort and security. It is quiet, it exudes warmth. No one is seated in any of the chairs, the sofas are empty. Here and there, flecks glisten: blood. The only place danger could lurk is directly to the right, next to the doorpost. He takes a step forward and lashes out with the nunchuk, the handle smacks against the brickwork, mortar rustles to the floor. Three strides and he's standing in the middle of the room, he looks around.

The sheetmetal drawers of the buffet against the far wall have been pulled out and shaken empty—good work for someone with just one arm. The floor is littered with paper, binders of household statements, pens, a hole punch that has spewed out its confetti. He smells the sharp odor of alcohol. The liquor cabinet, on the opposite wall, is open, two splintered bottles lie on the stone floor in their bodily fluids.

Wilbert could be in the sunroom, or the kitchen. Or in the wine cellar. His cell phones are lying on the coffee table, just where he left them. The house telephone isn't in its cradle, he doesn't see it anywhere. If the kid has a weapon, then this is the wrong place to stand: nowhere to take cover, a perfectly illuminated target. But if he does have a gun, why didn't he use it in the first place?

"Wilbert?" he calls. His voice sounds murky, unsteady, he clears his throat and waits. The snow beats gently against the windowpanes.

"Wilbert? I know you can hear me." Without any forethought he has just started talking. How deep is his conviction that words are preferable to physical force? How naïve is that conviction? "If you're still here," his voice echoes, "then I know you're listening. You don't have to say anything. Just listen to me. I don't have that money. It's back in the bank. But listen. If it's about money"—he is out of breath, the tension is getting the better of him. He swallows, pauses.

"If it's really about money," he says, "then we should talk. Man to man. We've already fought. I'm done fighting, believe me."

The silence is consummate. His brain produces primal screams and gunshots, but the silence persists.

"We shouldn't fight, Wilbert. We should talk. About you, about the future. Wilbert?"

To show he really means it, he crouches down and slides the nunchuk away from him across the floor, a meter, it's a halfhearted gesture, entirely improvised. He raises his empty hands to chest level, palms facing the dark hole of the sunroom.

"Wilbert. I've been thinking about you. Maybe you don't believe me, but it's true. Not just now, no, but for the past few years. What am I saying—I've thought about you from the very beginning. Do you hear me?"

He stops talking. This is pathetic. It's too late.

And still he continues: "I know you hold a grudge against me, I know that. But it goes both ways. I also blame you. But listen, we're still young, both of us. But you, you're *really* young. I've realized that. When I was your age, Wilbert, you hadn't even been born yet."

This is not entirely true, and he wonders if what he wants to say *is* in fact true. It feels like he's onstage, he's observing himself from a box seat, and what he sees is a mediocre actor, a man standing there trying to save his own skin with untruthful, poorly rehearsed lines. And yet he means every word of it.

"It's not a lost cause, in fact nothing's been lost. You're a free man, and I am your father. Wilbert. All I want is for you to go out there and lead a normal life. And I want to help. Do you hear me? Let's just consider this . . . altercation as us having hit bottom. We've hit rock bottom. Let's—"

At that moment the telephone rings. The electronic chirp of the landline gives him such a jolt that his heart nearly stops. The ring begins in the empty cradle and reverberates as an echo from the kitchen—the cordless handset. Is *he* in there too? The electronic melody goes on forever. Is he standing there holding the thing? The answering machine clicks into action, the speaker is turned on as always, they've never been able to figure out why. He hears his own low, strange, self-satisfied voice recite their names and ask the caller to leave a message. The beep, and then his wife:

"Hi honey, how are you? I thought I'd just phone to wish you a good trip tomorrow . . . but I guess you're already in bed. You're bushed, I'll bet. I hope you get a good night's sleep and feel rested

tomorrow in the car. Now, um . . . everything's fine here, there's a good layer of snow. Hans and Ria got here yesterday, we're having a ball. We miss you! Well . . . See you tomorrow. Make yourself a hot-water bottle. It's colder up there than here, Hans says. Bye, sweetheart. Drive safely." When she hangs up it sounds like a slap to his ear; a nervous busy signal echoes through the living room.

Unease creeps over him, his wife's voice has sobered him up, the intimacy of her message, but most of all her voice: the familiarity, the soothing tone, and at the same time her ignorance of his woes: everything underscores the insanity of the evening, his inane drivel in the darkness, the crack of Wilbert's elbow. Tineke's voice versus that crack.

He takes two steps to the liquor cabinet, glass crackling under the soles of his shoes, a bottle of Baileys, he squats down next to it with his back against the ice-cold stuccoed wall, listening, waiting. He runs his index finger through the brownish liquid and licks it off.

How long does he sit there? An hour? He's not sure, his legs are asleep, the balls of his feet have gone numb. He stays sitting there until he's stopped believing. The kid is gone. In the emergency room by now, even patched up already. He is alone in this house.

He gets up and walks to the sunroom, gropes for the switch to the table lamp, an explosion of light: nothing. He sits down at the table, panting from the strain. On the glass roof is something darker than night: snow, of course. He sees his reflection in the picture window. Immediately he gets back up and dims this display case he's standing in. Snowflakes stick to the glass. How dangerous is a man with one arm, with one hand? Harmless, even with saws or hammers. He walks stiffly, but with the same aplomb, into the kitchen: no one. The under-cabinet lighting is on, a box of paracetamol is lying on the counter, next to it a blister strip from which four tablets have been punched out. He feels his chafed chin, dabs the bleeding wound with a piece of paper towel. He takes three tablets.

The phone is lying in the sink—*in* it, strangely enough—and next to it a liquor bottle. Rum. It was part of last spring's anniversary gift basket, a liter of "Lust Rum," bottled especially for Tubantia, it's cheap rotgut. He picks up the bottle and sees that it is three-quarters empty. It was unopened before tonight, he's certain of it. There is, he notices in a flash, a knife missing from the wooden block next to the microwave. He swerves around, looks around. Relax. That knife is safely stowed in the dishwasher. He's gone. Still, he pulls a stubby steak knife out of the block. He walks over to the cellar stairs, turns around, goes back to the counter. Everything hurts. He takes a swig of rum, it's poison, and walks back to the hole in the floor. The stairs creak, he's hardly been down here these past few months; from the dust on the cement floor he sees that no one else has either. Still he checks behind all the racks.

Finally he stumbles into the utility room, it's cold as anything in there, little puffs of condensation glide out of his mouth. The door to the terrace is ajar, one of the windowpanes has been smashed. So that's how he got in. He pulls the door shut, turns the key, and removes it. He fastens the deadbolts.

And now? He is exhausted but sleep is out of the question. He could power his car all the way to France on adrenaline alone. The thought of drawing the curtains, turning down the heat, and crawling into bed is ludicrous. He has read enough insipid thrillers, seen enough Hollywood movies, to know that this house is the last place on earth he can afford to be unconscious. Pajamas on, teeth brushed, and lie there waiting for the plot to unfold. A fire, ignited with gasoline from Tineke's workshop. An ice-cold gun barrel in his neck as he starts his car tomorrow morning. An axe—he'll wake with a start in the middle of the night, a finger tapping his forehead, tick, tick, wake up pal, upon which his skull is cleaved with the same axe Tineke uses to chop wood every autumn.

He must clean the place up. Figuring it out takes some time, but finally the drawers of the buffet roll willingly into place. He stacks the envelopes, sweeps the confetti into a dustpan, scoops the pens and pencils up off the floor. With each movement his ribs swap places. He plucks shards of glass out of the puddle of Baileys, mops the floor with a wet dishtowel. He doesn't dare vacuum, he has to be able to *hear*. In the utility room he tears off a piece of corrugated cardboard from a wine box and, shivering from the cold, tapes it over the broken windowpane.

He has decided to set off tonight; that is, as soon as possible. As he expunges all traces of that grotesque scuffle—he scrubs away the blood stains in the front hall and living room with all-purpose cleaner, hangs Tineke's dresses meticulously back in place, arranges the shoes on the rack, wipes the blood from the edges with a wet rag—he becomes calmer, and muses on the plotlessness of this evening. An unfinished tragedy took place, a tragedy without a glimmer of a catharsis, nothing was resolved, the bleakness has only deepened. And now? Now he is expected to join his family at Hans and Ria's, they will greet one another, and then? Christmas will come, he will either confide in Tineke or not, and then? In the new year he will return to The Hague, and when his staff ask how his holiday was, he will answer: invigorating.

19

Aaron had taken the early-morning train to Brussels and stepped into a travel agency on the way to his appointment with the psychiatrist. Seated at the round multiplex table, the travel agent stuffed him like a Toulouse goose full of brochures about California: scenic drives down Highway 1, must-see national parks, Death Valley, and much more. Only after the girl had finished her spiel did he mention his specific interest in Los Angeles.

Nothing had been booked yet, he was still just exploring possibilities. His plan was to spend part of the summer in Santa Monica, perhaps take an apartment on the beach or, if need be, a hotel; he'd enroll in a photography workshop—that was how he tried to sell it to Herreweghe later that morning. But he didn't buy it. Herreweghe—the psychiatrist he'd been seeing for about eight years, on a referral from Elisabeth Haitink—was not the observant type, but rather the correctional: a doctor-as-curator. The humorless, businesslike Herreweghe *managed* your psyche.

The padded treatment room struck him as typically Belgian, furnished as though Jung or Reich were standing in an adjacent room mixing opiates; heavy, immovable furniture, authoritarian elmwood bookcases, the leather-bound medical journals behind the glass reminding you that you knew nothing about your own piddling ego. "You haven't set foot outside Belgium for years," Herreweghe said.

"Venlo," Aaron replied.

"Venlo. And now Los Angeles."

He wasn't quite being straight, which said something about the nature of his plans. He told Herreweghe about a friend who had emigrated to America, how inspired he was by what she wrote about her new home, her enthusiasm rekindled a lifelong desire to visit America, and more such drivel, and it almost looked like he'd get away with it, they were already talking about a medical passport and emergency numbers. It was none of this guy's business that he wanted to go to Santa Monica to see Joni. He knew that Professor Herreweghe worked for a government stalker-rehab clinic—obsessivos delivered to him by the Ministry of Justice—so he was wary of the s-word, ungrounded of course, but probably hard to avoid.

"What's her name, your American friend?"

He tried to come up with a fake name. Unfortunately, with this man a single twitch could trigger his snare.

"Is it Joni?"

"I have no plans to look her up." He felt himself blush. And yet in a sense he was telling the truth: an arranged meeting with Joni was out of the question, she was keeping a polite distance, not even that, she was actively avoiding the issue, and maybe an official visit *was* too much of a good thing, he thought, too emotionally charged. So he would go to Los Angeles on his own, stay there awhile, have a vacation, what was wrong with that? And from that relaxed situation he might try to make contact with her.

"But you do have her address."

The imperative question, that was Herreweghe's forte. Pretend there's a question mark coming, but at the last moment spit out a period. Aaron couldn't recall ever getting an open question from this guy.

"No. How come?"

14023 Sunset Boulevard, Santa Monica, on the outskirts of Beverly Hills. He'd pulled that one off pretty neatly. The tone of their e-mails was not conducive to asking for her address outright, and anyway it would have spoiled all the spontaneity, the possibility of a surprise visit, for instance, or a chance meeting in front of her house—the idea appealed to him. Since she wasn't listed in any phone books he had to think of something else, and came up with the clever idea of looking up Stol in San Francisco. Say what you like, but Stol at least had the decency to be listed, phone number and all, on the Internet. He would honestly be able to say he was just ringing about a practical question, but he also relished the subtle undertone of revenge this phone call would have.

Instead of Stol himself he got a boy of about seven on the line, who said his father was out golfing, giving him scant time to get used to the notion that those two had spawned. Is your mother at home then? he asked, theatrically naïve. "She lives in L.A.," the boy answered. "Is your mother Joni Sigerius, by any chance?" He tried to sound as unfazed as possible, but after the kid's affirmative reply he started right in about her address, too eagerly, for suspicion crept into the child's voice, "Who are you?" the boy asked with touching directness. Slightly flustered, he repeated his name.

Herreweghe's bluntness was like having a spade thrust squarely into your soul. Joni—he wanted to hear how she was, her name set off alarm bells all these years later. The man glanced at his watch. "I take it you'd like to look her up," he said. "Tell me about the last time you two saw each other."

He made the mistake of taking the question seriously, of succumbing to Herreweghe's X-ray vision, of calling up the month of December 2000. This is a man who specializes in restraining orders. It was an episode he never dared to look back on, it was a dateless fog, an abstract mishmash of frightened impressions and manic low-flying passes over what he once thought of as a life—just give it a try, Herreweghe prodded (swimming instructor on the high-dive might have also suited him), when did you talk to her last, and how was it?

How was it . . . Did Herreweghe really want to know? Being nearly dead was enervating in a way. But it was Joni who came for him this time, Death took a rain check. How was it . . . the nosedive of December 2000. Is this really necessary? Now? I'm sitting here with a bag full of travel brochures. She had rescued him, that much was beyond a doubt. First she phoned him, from the States. Yes, that phone call too is lodged somewhere in his memory, it was a miracle she didn't give up trying to reach him. What would have become of him without Joni? She had dumped him and then she came back.

In the meantime, sheets of ice had buckled over Roombeek. Freezing temperatures and early dusk were the result of fallout, the atmosphere was full of particles that wouldn't settle, the fallout held in an indefinite suspension by the Coriolis effect. It looked threatening. The sun twinkled like a dying star above the bomb crater, but only sporadically, and ever more fleetingly. Abandoned steam shovels and bulldozers stared lifelessly at the epicenter, rusting away in peace. The cold entrenched itself. Not a soul dared to go outside, but everywhere there was a restless rustling: irritably waving conifers, loosened roof tiles that, moments later, spattered like grenades; the wind drove plastic bags and newspapers along the gutters. For weeks the lukewarm radiators in his house had rattled like mad, until the *hammerklavier* suddenly went silent, dead, cold, and his teeth took over the chattering. He heard doors slam in half-crumbling houses.

The flame in his multiburner was constantly on the verge

of going out, he knelt down in front of the cast-iron mouth, the jointed black doors hung open like black crab claws, condensation escaped from the two copper ornamental knobs on the cover. Every so often he fed the flames with strips of cardboard he tore from the scattered boxes. Meantime he hastily thumbed through the book he had condemned to death, diagonally scanning the pages for anything he deemed worthy of a reprieve. The books printed on flimsy paper, laid open, burned like peat, at least as long as chair legs and cupboard shelves. The vital pages he tore out with a series of short jerks, folded them in half and stuffed them, coughing and gasping for breath, in old bank envelopes.

The gunpowder dust was almost unbearable. His eyes itched, black soot inflamed his windpipe. He had first smelled it months ago, a vague odor that reminded him of his earliest childhood, the smell of spent firecrackers, of cap guns, a smell that little by little became a stench; since winter had set in the fumes often hung visibly in his room, the sulfur molecules wafted in from outside, a chafing, heavy vapor that took over the entire house.

It frightened him. He would suddenly panic that he was choking. Sometimes he woke up with a parched throat, his mouth wide open like a coffee filter brimming with gunpowder. Occasionally it penetrated his lungs, his clothes, his *consciousness* so deeply that he forgot the stench altogether; he smelled only the separate elements—charcoal, sulfur, saltpeter, and finally nothing at all . . . was it gone? At those moments, when his mortal fear subsided, when he smelled nothing, he was calm. Everything was worse in the crater, he dared not go there anymore, it was bad for you, and cold as hell besides, even if he wore three layers of clothes—underwear, pajamas, a sweater, Sigerius's suit, the judo jacket, a padded Gaastra coat, ski socks, hiking boots, mittens on top of gloves—even then, he froze.

So he stayed at the hearth despite the risks of an open fire; he knew that if the saltpeter concentration got too high, the whole neighborhood would be blown sky-high. Sometimes he wished it would happen: one single, devastating bang putting an end to everything, and yet he maintained his source of warmth as much as possible, small, compact, and kept his eye on the alarm the authorities had installed. When it did go off—a shrill electronic screech that frightened the bejesus out of him—he leapt up, stumbling and slithering into the kitchen, filled a frying pan with water, and dumped it over the flames.

It was a telephone. A plain old telephone. *His* telephone? Alarmed, he struggled up from the sofa where he had buried himself and waded toward the sound of the siren in the back room. Holding his breath, he peered at the closed curtain. What the—? The piece of plastic behind it was a potential intruder, he only had to lift it up and it would metamorphose. Something from outside would force its way in. That Limburg woman who had tried to interrogate him earlier? He groped behind the curtain and picked it up. Deep in the plastic, electrons teemed.

"Hello?" a voice said. He waited, listening acutely. "Aaron? It's Joni. I'm calling from America."

It was a stethoscope, Joni had tricked him into placing the instrument against his skull, for a brief moment he knew exactly how it worked—they had laid a transatlantic cable, miles and miles long, across the ocean floor, across pine forests and into his house, a military operation in order to diagnose him—but the image faded as quickly as it had materialized, maybe because the voice upset his frame of mind, a mental state that had settled like sediment at the bottom of an old wine bottle, one of her father's bottles? The voice shook him hard, memories drifted to the surface, blurred his focus on his month-long battle against the elements.

"Are you there?" the voice said.

He hawked soot out of his throat. "Yes," he said. But where was she? Was she really in America?

"Hey. Phew. Long time no see. How are you? I have to keep it short."

He nodded. He had not spoken to another human being for so long that he was unable to respond, she had to understand that, he was so used to listening, to the blabbing in the supermarket where he actually never went anymore, to the squeaking and scuffling of the animals under his sofa and chairs, to the recriminations emanating from his bookshelves, maybe it was the quiet in the house, his own silence that provoked the hissing and groaning, he only had to glance at any random spine on the bookshelf and it would explode in a tirade—toxic manipulation it was—and he allowed himself to be slandered, he bore it submissively; at times it went no further than minor accusations ("buy some normal food, you shit, something you have to peel and cook yourself!") or just ordinary cursing ("deadbeat! you stink of puke!"), but often they were vicious personal attacks ("traitor, Nazi, you should die, *die!*")—rhetorical choruses he fled from, huddled in bed or cowering in the shower, but the cold always drove him back downstairs, the same cold that gave him the wicked idea to kill his tormentors, a funeral pyre—

"Aaron? The balance on my calling card is low."

Balance? *Bank balance.* They drove him up the wall, those balances. What was she trying to say, he tried to grasp the gist of her words. The balances fluctuated like crazy, every envelope he used to fill with reprieved book pages once contained bank statements, the place was overflowing with bank statements, envelopes poured out of upstairs drawers and cupboards, or he shook them out of lead-gray binders up in the attic: opaque, oblong windowed envelopes from banks in the Netherlands but mostly from Luxembourg; the one announced an overdraft of 284.30 guilders, the next a balance of $2,438,749.63, after that he had to make do with five guilders and fourteen cents, it baffled him, he could lie there for hours fretting about it, where'd that damn money go, where'd it come from? "I'm doing my best," he said. "But it's still difficult."

He heard nothing, only white noise. "I understand," a voice said. "It was hard on me too, believe me. Anyway, I have good news. I've found a buyer. For the boat."

By your boat . . . in his mind a smooth, black ocean stretched out before him, a sunken ship, trillions of ice-cold water molecules beneath the faint moonlight, hardly any waves, he held on tight to a piece of slimy driftwood, around him he could see the tops of heads, bodies floating against the sea's ceiling.

"I wondered if you might want to drive to Sainte-Maxime with me. Take the Alfa down to the *Barbara Ann*. I've got lots to tell you."

His confusion capsized into fear. A moment ago his heart had felt too big for his body, but now it caved in altogether, his heart became as small as a cherry, creating a vacuum in his chest cavity, an implosion which, obeying age-old laws of physics, drew in the entire room: the walls were sucked inward, the smashed back window was a mouth that inhaled gallons of rust-brown vapors. They sat in the Alfa, he stepped on the accelerator, but they drove *away* from the yacht. They raced northward, to the Netherlands, to here. To glass that had to be broken.

"OK," he stammered.

"That's great," she said. "I've got a ticket for December 21st. I can be in Enschede in the afternoon."

He coughed, cleared his throat, and spat out a thick wad of dusty phlegm.

"OK."

Before or after, he wasn't sure which way they were traveling, time still flew, or had she crashed?—anyway at a particularly cold moment he picked up the chestnut-brown object by its narrow protruding edges and lugged it, groaning from the effort, over to a wall. Halfway there the side of the chestnut-brown object flew open like a small door and its guts came crashing out. They broke like glass, he screamed from the shock, penetrating odors rose from them. Like a coiled spring, he bolted into the next room.

He awoke with a start, and couldn't see a thing. In the darkness he groped for the rectangular opening and stared through it long enough to make out the chestnut-brown object. It did not move. He stumbled cautiously around it, felt through his mitten-covered gloves for the smooth edges. It had become so lightweight he fell over backward. As though gravity did not pull at it. He put the corpse against a wall.

When he opened his eyes again, everything was visible. Me, here? With a Magic Marker between his teeth he climbed up onto the liquor cabinet (had he put it there?), suddenly high up off the ground, the empty bookshelves intimately close, the edges pressing not unpleasantly against his chest and thighs. Trembling, he took the marker from his mouth and spat the cap into the room.

In large, open block letters he drew an "A" on the wallpaper and filled it in red. Then he drew "ROOM," it was slow and tough going with his double-gloved hand. Before he finished filling in the second "O" he had to get down because his arm quivered and his shoulder ached. After that it was dark for a long time.

Outside, a layer of white ash covered the remains of houses and flora. Something terrible must have happened, a nuclear disaster of which he was the sole survivor. The ash, white as snow, had come fluttering down from the sky for hours on end. He had probably survived the atomic blast because his house was at a particular coordinate, a thermodynamic singularity impervious to the heat. The entire cosmos was burned to a crisp, everything except the houses on his street. Something, or someone, still appreciated his worth.

"WITH A"—he was still coloring in the second lonely "A," a letter that evoked his intense sympathy, more than the first one, he had to fight back his tears, when he smelled that smell. He immediately saw why: the uppermost shelf was covered with an alarmingly thick layer of gunpowder. All of his muscles contracted in a simultaneous spasm, with a yell he shoved himself away from the wall, his body flew through the air, he floated, perhaps he could fly outside between the planks covering the windows, but before he could change course his left arm slammed against a hard object. He landed with a muted thud on the ground, his head was flung back. He calmly rotated with the charred earth, taking note of the throbbing pain in his buttocks and lower back.

• • •

Later, someone spoke. When he opened his eyes, he looked up at a figure in the semidarkness. He pressed the palms of his hands into a boggy substance. The creature stood in the middle of the roofed space. It took a step, extended a gloved tentacle that held a weird, glimmering ball. “Easy does it,” it said. With kicking movements he pushed himself back, shouting, sliding on his back across the floor until his head banged into a wall.

It was puffed up, it wore a kind of space suit, the garments of an alien bomb-disposal squad, he did not recognize the face, it kept morphing. In the shadows it looked like a gas mask made of human skin, a face with big round eyes and a rubber snout. The fiery sphere was a neutron bomb, it emitted golden flames, the creature was offering him Armageddon. It took another step in his direction, he pushed off again, hard, scooted up farther against the wall.

“No,” he whispered.

“Aaron,” said a voice of soft velvet. “Calm down. It’s me.”

20

When he heard my name his eyes shot back and forth like hockey pucks, he wrenched himself farther away, babbling gruffly, kicking at the debris like the back legs of a scurrying dog. It looked like he wanted to press himself through the wall.

"Don't be afraid," I said in a small voice, unsure if it I meant it for him or myself. I held out a gift I'd bought him at the airport, a giant chocolate Christmas ball filled with hand-made Belgian bonbons and wrapped in cellophane and gold ribbons. Half a kilo of utterly misplaced goodwill, I realized at once. It stank too much in the darkened room to even want to *think* about chocolate.

He sat jerking his head from side to side until he suddenly looked straight at me. I was so shocked by his face—eyes like spark-spattering transformer stations—that I let the chocolate ball roll out of my hand. It landed with a hollow thud on what sounded like cardboard. Aaron's reaction was as unexpected as it was terrifying: he let out a shriek, threw his arms over his face, and cowered as though there were a tarantula at his feet, or the devil himself. "Take it away," he screamed, his voice breaking, "TAKE THAT THING AWAY!"

The only thing here that urgently needed taking away was him. To a doctor, and fast.

"Stay there," I said, "don't get up," and staggered backward in panic toward the front hall, dragging my roller suitcase behind me over ankle-high junk out into the sunlight. Panting, I stepped into the snow and pulled the front door shut, the same door I had to open with my own key a few minutes earlier. I had rung the bell but there was no answer; if I hadn't heard a vague murmur from behind the broken door pane, I'd have assumed he forgot our date and was spending Christmas in Venlo. In retrospect it was clear why our phone call two weeks ago had sounded so strange. What I took for bitterness—he came across as piqued and out of sorts—must in fact have been pure psychosis.

I went into the alleyway alongside the house, took out my cell phone and called Boudewijn Stol, my tower of strength these last months—to my surprise, he had even met me at the airport, just because, out of curiosity for the person he'd been e-mailing every day—and asked him to look up the number of a mental health hotline. "You want me to come out there?" he asked, "drive to France with you? What did Arend have to say about it?"

"About what?"

"You know—*it*."

"Nothing," I replied. "All he did was scream."

At the crisis hotline I got a woman with a surly Twente accent who made it clear they were not going to come and pick Aaron up, but that I could bring him to the outpatient clinic at the Twentse Tulip, a psychiatric hospital on the south side of Enschede. During our exchange unnerving howls emerged from the living room. I walked farther into the ice-cold alley and peered between two conifers at the back of the house. There wasn't much to see aside from the moldering planks where the sliding door used to be, and the greasy glass of the kitchen door. I hurried back inside, the snow was powdery but treacherously slick, I nearly slipped just before reaching the front walk. Again I waded through the unopened mail and waste paper on my way to the living room. I felt along the wall for the light switch. What hadn't entirely sunk in before, in the semidarkness, was now perfectly obvious. The mess was unimaginable. You could hardly see the carpeting; the place was strewn wall to wall with litter. Cookie packages, potato chip bags, sweaters, French fry containers, towels, empty milk cartons, wads of paper towels, junk mail, torn-open envelopes, half-eaten sandwiches, rotting fruit, plastic bags in every shape and size, countless pizza boxes, the gnawed-off crusts sticking out from under the same grinning green-and-red pizza man. But the furniture was littered with rubbish too, as though it had *rained* garbage. All sorts of gibberish had been scrawled on the walls with Magic Marker, I saved myself the trouble of trying to decipher it. A partially charred wooden fence post lay on the love seat. The bookshelves, once his pride and joy, looked as though they had been emptied at random; there were books everywhere, *hundreds*, some of them ripped to shreds or lying open, squashed facedown. They hadn't been read, they had been murdered, butchered. The old Aaron used to practically wear white gloves to read a book. Now I saw, in the cast-iron multiburner, a stack of scorched, half-charred blocks: *books*.

This was television-style dereliction: those awful voyeuristic programs about people with no connection to the species. But what they didn't show on TV was the guinea pig shit. That beat everything. Guinea pig droppings everywhere, thousands of tiny, slightly curled turds, all exactly the same size, like giant chocolate sprinkles in the corners, along the baseboards, and around the table legs, crushed into a dark-brown mud in the doorway. The guinea pigs were nowhere to be seen—just like Aaron. He had disappeared.

I walked back into the front hall and stood at the foot of the stairs. Just as I was about to go up I heard the shower—a welcome, promising sound. Maybe he wanted to clean himself up. Had he remembered who I was and what I had come to do? In the meantime I'd have a look for the keys to the Alfa. In the midst of that dung heap there was only one place they could be: the cocoa canister on the mantelpiece, he always used to keep them there. I pulled open the front curtains for more light. The windowpane was covered in red smears I had vaguely taken note of outside, but now I recoiled with a gasp. On the windowsill lay a hairy, bloody cadaver. The black guinea pig. Decapitated, in fact scalped, and cut open lengthwise. I took a deep breath—through my mouth: the stench in this cesspit, that little animal—and tried with all my might not to gag.

In shock I went back to the mantel and stared at the empty take-out containers and the rest of the garbage. At the same time I was overcome by intense pity and equally powerful guilt: I spent my six months in California feeling so sorry for myself, and gave precious little thought to what had become of *him*. He'll be OK, I thought. He's loaded, right?

When I had pulled myself back together I found the cocoa canister and dug out a sealed envelope—the same envelope I had shoved through his letter slot six months earlier—with the keys still inside. The idea that Aaron hadn't driven in *six months*. I tucked the envelope into the inside pocket of my winter coat and walked back to the foot of the stairs. He was still in the shower. I had to coax him into coming with me.

I braced myself, went upstairs, and stopped at the landing. Across the jumble of clothes and towels I called out "Aaron, I'm back," and knocked gently on the bathroom door. There was no reaction, and after a little while I realized the jet was loud and steady—too loud and too steady. I pushed open the door, steam came billowing over the landing. On the tiled floor, amid hairy, nondescript filth, was the cellophane and the gold ribbon from the Christmas ball. The shower curtain was dirty but still transparent;

you could see there was no one behind it. As I pulled it aside I burst into tears at what I saw—an odd reaction, in fact, the melting chocolate ball was peanuts compared to the wretchedness downstairs—but anyway, what was left of it lay on the floor of the shower in a bath of gurgling chocolate water, the carving knife that had been stuck into it (rammed, I imagined) lying disappointedly on the drain. The hot water had melted a conical hole in the ball; all that remained of the pralines inside it was their filling. This is not where I wanted to be. *Not with this belly.* I felt a brief urge to curse Boudewijn out, blame him for everything. Thanks to *you* I'm standing here, without *you* I wouldn't have this damn belly. Sniffling and swearing, I turned off the shower.

Only now did I hear Aaron shouting. "FUCK OFF!" he yelled hoarsely. "FUCK! OFF!" I followed the sound of his shrieks, fighting the temptation to do just that, to fuck off for good. I opened the bedroom door. He was cowering on the mattress, knees tucked up to his chest, hardly even recognizable with the grubby fringe of hair tracing a line around the back of his head. Between shouts he babbled at top speed, his shoulders and head shaking in violent spasms. As soon as I entered the room he began to shriek, he held the bare, yellowed comforter up to his chin with white-knuckled fists. "Please," he whimpered, "just leave. Leave me alone. You have a snout." As if I were braving a hurricane, I climbed onto the double bed and softly took hold of his leg through the comforter. Howling and sobbing, he bit into the cotton blanket, his eyes rolled back in his head and he palpitated as though I'd prodded him with a red-hot fire poker. Now gasping with fright myself, I let go.

"Please. Go."

In order to restrain myself a second time, *not* to go, to flee from this hellhole, I tried to picture him on his black Batavus. Remember who this is. I saw him sitting on that big bike with its double crossbar, his sheepskin coat open, a silk shirt underneath that could just as well have been a ladies' blouse, this nonchalant grasshopper on a bike, oversized boots half sliding off the pedals, leisurely cycling off to buy this very bed with me. With that Aaron in mind, I laid my hand as gently as possible on his sweat-drenched thigh, and called him "sweetheart." It was with *that* Aaron in mind that I'd come to Enschede, with *that* Aaron in mind I'd decided to keep it.

For weeks, Boudewijn was the only one who knew I was pregnant. I was avoiding all contact with Enschede (and Enschede with me), and at McKinsey I kept mum about it as long as I wasn't showing. From Day One of my internship in Silicon Valley, Boudewijn and I e-mailed each other daily, a routine with which he rounded off his afternoons in Amsterdam and I began my mornings in California. At first they were mostly jokey, corny e-mails, sometimes unexpectedly candid, with an unambiguous undertone on his part that I rather enjoyed. "You're the only person I trust," I wrote one day in October. "Of course, of course," was his almost gilded answer, so I told him I was pregnant and confessed right up front that I was considering an abortion. "Considering" was my euphemism for the appointment I had already made at the Stanford University Family Planning Service. That sure cured him of his corniness; he turned into a sponge that wanted to soak up everything with exacting precision, so I told him everything with exacting precision—but how precise was it all *without* the sliding glass door and the website?

His reaction caught me off guard: he explicitly *forbade* me to go to that Stanford clinic. "Put off your decision for as long as possible," he wrote, "ask for a cooling-off period." "I've got one already." "Then ask for another one," and he reminded me I had *responsibilities,* not only with regard to the "life" but to the father as well.

Excuse me? Really, he was dead serious, he considered having an abortion behind Aaron's back, "how can I put it mildly," he said, a *crime*. "But I don't want anything to do with the guy," I protested. "That's beside the point," he wrote, "who says you have to have anything to do with him? Who says he wants a child?"

What Aaron wanted was a tranquilizer dart. His fear itself was terrifying, and still I persevered: little by little I made progress, unhurriedly caressing his thickly clothed arms, his shoulders, until his dread seemed to gradually subside. Both bedside tables, the open drawers, the floor—everywhere, actually—were littered with pill strips and liquor bottles, all of them empty. After rummaging frantically through one of the bedside tables I came up with two sleeping tablets. "Here," I said, "take these." But he spat them out, and again I wriggled the soggy capsules into his mouth. I found a bottle of jenever with a swig or two left, put it to his lips and he swallowed. He let me nestle up against him and I continued stroking his arms, his face, his chest, until his breathing relaxed. And only then, when I had calmed down some myself, did the reality of the situation hit me: *he didn't notice.* Even if I were to take off my heavy winter coat, even if I took off *all* my clothes and climbed onto his lap with my six-month belly, even *then* Aaron wouldn't notice I was pregnant, let alone *comprehend* it.

It was a job and a half getting him down those stairs. He thrashed about and wedged himself between the wall and the railing. His body odor made me gag. In front of the house he fell to his knees in the snow, and while I hastily swept the snow off the Alfa he lay there curled up in a fetal position, wailing and ranting; I smiled at passersby while coaxing him, patiently but firmly, into the car.

We arrived at the Twentse Tulip before dusk; I had never been there before, it was surrounded by woods and had a huge Christmas tree in the granite foyer. After a good deal of pleading and explaining on my part they agreed to keep Aaron overnight for observation. I watched as he, meek as a lamb, gulped down two bright purple antipsychotics with a large glass of water; it was as though I was quenching a week-long thirst myself. Only when they asked me for his particulars—parents? employer?—did I realize how extraordinary it was that he'd managed to get to this stage. I'll bet no one had been at his house in months. His parents lived down in Limburg, and they phoned, as far as I knew, infrequently. And what about his work? Was this the fate of a freelancer? I found Cees and Irma Bever's number in my cell phone and gave it to the staff nurse.

I wanted to get out of there. Move on. While Aaron was being examined by one of the psychiatrists, I slipped out of the building. I looked up at the snow-covered oak trees and sycamores, the endless depth of the stone-cold sky above, and thought: this is as good a place as any for insanity to evaporate.

Driving south through salty slush, coat buttoned up, window open, dazed, I thought: did I really just go through all that? I only braked in Liège, soon after midnight, and checked into the most expensive room I could find. Should I have seen this coming? My suite had those little pillows a pregnant woman can prop under her belly while lying on her side, but sleep evaded me nonetheless.

I think it was already September by the time I realized it. I lived in a sort of student pueblo with undergrads, foreign post-docs, and beginning consultants, situated in the woods between the Stanford campus and the office park where McKinsey had its local division. I shared a top-floor apartment with two somewhat disagreeable

French girls who had allotted me a square bedroom looking out on three sides at the tall, pointy pines. For the first few weeks I was lonely and depressed, I missed Enschede, I missed Aaron, I missed my father. Now that I was alone, guilt got a foot in the door. Hadn't everything gone haywire essentially because of me? Wasn't it my greedy exhibitionism that had driven us, a three-way bond with the strength of a water molecule, apart? I saw Siem crash through that glass door more often than I wanted to, I realized all too well what exactly had been smashed to smithereens—but at the same time I was liberated; the newness of being on the other side of the world banished the darkest thoughts of Enschede, distracted me from the irrevocability and hopelessness of the situation. On weekdays I worked long hours; at the weekends colleagues took me with them to San Francisco, where we spent days on the beach and nights in the clubs. This is good, it is good you are in California—and as soon as I started thinking this, sometimes even saying it out loud, I discovered I was pregnant.

"Prosaic" is too nice a word for how it all went. The youngest intern there, I was sitting in on a conference call with a McKinsey team for a page-by-page review of a final report for an Asian client; I was nauseous and the itch on my breasts was driving me insane. Don't scratch, don't scratch; if somebody had asked me anything I'd have answered, "don't scratch," but no one asked anything, giving me plenty of time to put two and two together: the itch, my late period, and all that the Enschede palaver had truly made me forget—that back on Corsica Aaron and I had had unprotected sex.

I got up, white as a sheet; the associate principal who chaired that witches' coven asked if I was "OK" and whether they should call a doctor. Yeah, an abortion doctor, I thought, but left the conference room with my hand over my mouth, took the glass elevator downstairs, nodded weakly at the receptionist, and walked straight to the drugstore on Palo Alto Square where I bought two different pregnancy test kits and peed on them both, one after the other, back in the pueblo. Fat pink stripes. I sat there on the toilet until my legs fell asleep. Damn it to hell, I was pregnant by Aaron Bever.

I lay in bed for the rest of the week. Too sick to work. At night I puffed my sniveling self up into a zeppelin of self-reproach, and when I jolted awake in the morning from muddy dreams, that ink-black airship hung above the pine trees, casting a shadow and on the verge of combustion. I only got up toward afternoon, ate a little something, and marched through the woods, furious, overwrought, stamping pine cones to splinters. My atheism teetered: it was difficult not to see the punitive hand of some god or other behind this new ordeal, that damn God of Wilbert's. I cursed the hunk of wood on Wilbert's wall and at the same time prayed for a miscarriage: Dear Lord, please let me be rid of this, I don't want it. Internet pregnancy forums list all kinds of things mothers-to-be should expressly *not* do, and so I worked overtime, slept too little, drank as much alcohol as possible, at home, up in that little room, wine, whiskey, vodka. Weekends I ate with those two pocket-sized French girls, who chatted with each other in incomprehensible Parisian, perhaps about my cooking (they invariably sliced open the meat I had cooked for them, scrunched up their tiny noses and brought it back to the kitchen to finish the job), perhaps about my constant nausea. I called the Stanford University Family Planning Service. I e-mailed Boudewijn.

He phoned while I was sitting in the empty breakfast room in Liège eating Nutella on French bread.

"Where are you?"

"Liège."

"And. How did he react? They gave Arend a downer—and then? What'd he say? Tell."

"And then nothing, Bo. There's nothing much *to* tell. My ex-boyfriend's got a psychosis, a whopper of a psychosis. He thinks the sun is made of yellow jam he can smear on his toast. It's really awful."

"So he's not going to miss the little one for the time being."

Only months later, when I was less self-absorbed, when I wasn't afraid Boudewijn would find out I'd been trying to unload a $1.5 million boat, when I no longer dreaded seeing my parents, when we were already safely ensconced on our hill in San Francisco—only then did I figure out what he had been up to. In retrospect I understood his loyalty, his empathy, the earnestness of his e-mails, how he managed to get me to cancel the appointment at that Stanford Family thing and think "for at least five minutes per day" about "the joys of motherhood," a phrase that leapt with surprising ease to the lips of this fifty-year-old childless man. In retrospect I understood his satisfaction when I passed the twelve-week mark and announced my pregnancy at McKinsey. The story behind his smile at Schiphol Airport, where he whisked me into a business-class lounge I called "louche" and why he, in the middle of that joint and with a mouth full of crab salad, had laughed so hard. "I've got really sad news," he said, "Brigitte and I are splitting up. I've filed for divorce. We're driving each other bonkers." Then he put me on the train to Enschede and as a farewell laid his ringed hand briefly on my belly. (And *still* I hadn't caught on, no idea that he'd already started finagling his transfer to San Francisco, no idea that he was already planning to cradle my head during delivery. A few years ago I dug up some old e-mails from that time, and sure enough, there it was in black-and-white: in October 2000 Boudewijn wrote that Brigitte was making a big deal—rightfully so, he felt—of his infertility.)

Now he said: "And soon, your parents. Be sure to greet your father for me."

"I'll do that."

That boat. The fucking *Barbara Ann.* We really had to get rid of it, preferably in one shot, one viewing, because I was not about to travel back here from the States a second time. She was moored in the marina where we'd left her the previous summer. I was to meet the potential buyer the day after tomorrow in Sainte-Maxime, a wealthy American ICT guy I had met through McKinsey who spent his winters in Monaco and had recently been on the lookout for a Palmer Johnson like ours.

I crossed into France well before noon and decided to push on until Lyons, so as to arrive in Sainte-Maxime early the next day and take my time readying the boat. The *route de soleil* was, on my own in the Alfa, a different experience altogether: a bleak, monotonous streak through restlessly leafy hills, the sleepy *aire* restaurants and parking lots, no sunflowers, no traffic jams, no expectations. I had to do my best not to constantly think back on the Vluchtestraat and what I'd seen there. Why did things always go differently than you expected? Hours of dark toll roads later I found myself in Christmassy downtown Lyons, booked into a hotel with a sagging bed where I didn't get a wink of sleep.

At the end of November my mother called me at McKinsey. She caught me so by surprise I didn't even have time to die of shock. Suddenly I was sitting in a full office courtyard with my mother on the line—I had no idea what to expect, and in fact I've never figured out whether she was just pretending everything was hunky-dory, or if everything really *was* hunky-dory. She was as sweet as pie, gave no indication that she knew anything about the glass door incident. She asked if I would come to Val-d'Isère for Christmas. The half-second delay allowed me to invent an excuse: sorry, Mom, tons of work to do over Christmas. A few days later I really *was* sorry, because since deciding to keep the baby, something else was growing in me as well, an idea, a plan, a notion that I had started to cherish as though I were carrying twins. I took folic acid to strengthen them both at once.

The next morning, completely wiped out, I drove through Provence. Despite the mild weather I was still cold; a profound melancholy began to seep into my bones. At Chambéry, the exit I would use tomorrow to head back up to Val-d'Isère, I saw a bright speck of light. A minuscule hole in my perception, as though an extra-intense white heat pricked through the day's movie screen. I glanced at the dashboard, at my hands on the sporty three-spoke steering wheel, and then back to the road.

"Fuck."

Here we go again. I'd been asking for this for weeks, I was well aware of that. The last one was before the fireworks disaster, so I'd had, believe it or not, six migraine-free months behind me, I had warded them off with abracadabras and incantations. But the day of reckoning had arrived. Within minutes the illuminated speck spread into a fist-sized, swirling diamond of light—more eager than usual, it seemed, as though someone wanted to fast-forward the misery. The aura phase, the doctors call it. I had been familiar with the routine since high school: fifteen minutes from now all I'd see would be fireworks, everything would become a dancing, burning, full-screen light show. After a while the diamond would disappear, followed by a half-hour respite. Then the migraine would hammer a nail into my temple.

Too nauseous and blinded to drive, I maneuvered the Alfa into the first possible lay-by, turned off the engine, and rested my head on the steering wheel. All I had in my purse was paracetamol, no Imigran, which is what I needed now. The box was already empty before I left for California. There might be some ibuprofen 600 on the boat. I put on my sunglasses, but the frenzied flickering was on the inside: thoughtburn. I swallowed three paracetamols and concentrated as best I could on Christmas in Val-d'Isère.

The baby would fix everything. I didn't tell Boudewijn, simply because he didn't have a damn thing to do with it—but this idea did, in the end, keep me from having the abortion. Night after night I lay on the communal sofa of the pueblo, tossing pine cones into the fireplace (the strange hardness of the scales, their crackle and hiss as soon as the flames flared up and made short work of them), brooding, reasoning, *feeling*; and the more my waist vanished and my belly swelled, the more I realized what a *trump card* I had in my hand. For the first time since the sliding glass door I allowed thoughts of Corsica in, tried to recall the emotions of the vacation. We knew full well what we were doing when we made love. On the boat, on the way back in Nancy. *We wanted this child.* It wasn't conceived by mistake. I knew Aaron would acknowledge paternity at once, he would put everything aside to raise the child. And damn it, it was on its way—irrevocable. And wouldn't this irrevocability cancel out that other irrevocability? A child, Aaron's and mine . . . Did I realize what I was doing? I lay there on a sofa in Silicon Valley making Siem a *grandfather.* And after fully realizing that, I knew without a doubt: this thing in my belly would be stronger than what drove us apart. We'd become father and mother and grandpa. I would birth us back together.

The fires of purgatory subsided. I drove 160 kph all the way to Hyères, where the freeway ended and the headache began. The coastal road that looked so enticingly short on the map turned out to be a small intestine: endless hairpin turns and rocky cliffs, I had to constantly alternate between gas and brake. Rather than its azure sparkle, the Mediterranean showed its true colors: an indifferent black drink. I lowered a window, the ice-cold sea air screwed itself into my throbbing temples. Saint-Tropez exit, now that's more like it. As soon as I reached Sainte-Maxime I'd coast straight to the marina, park the Alfa as close as possible to the *Barbara Ann.* In my thoughts I dived into the water and swam like a dolphin toward the medicine chest.

I wove around a cliff and suddenly, way down to the right, saw the slender little white boats alongside what looked like endless tables set for dinner. I drove too fast across a bridge and descended to where the tortuous *route nationale* turned into the beachfront boulevard. By now I was howling from the pain, a monotonous yammer.

Winter was very much in charge here; chairs were stacked and parasols tightly wound shut on the café terraces opposite the moorings. I had my choice of parking spots. I killed the engine—silence at last—and rolled my head and shoulders. For a few seconds I knew for sure I was going to throw up. Breathe calmly. Hair loose, *now.* Catch your breath, swallow, just swallow it back. I took a swig of mineral water and got out.

The sea wind blew straight through my coat and what little I had on underneath. Where was that sloop? The glazed kitsch that the marina exuded at the height of summer had gone into hibernation. The rows of winterized yachts displayed themselves at their hardest, the pleated white plastic, the polished wood, the tinted windows that were meant to express speed and exclusivity—floating insults, that's what they were, we'd given the middle finger to soberness and self-restraint.

Aaron threw a wrench into everything. What kind of father would he make? Who would let that kind of guy become a father?

It had all seemed so logical, the two of us showing up in Val-d'Isère unannounced, you couldn't really call it a surprise anymore, it would . . . I walked along the stone paving to the marina office, a low white building with a roof deck. The door was locked: in off-season it was open only between three and five. So much the better, no stammering in French to an unintelligible harbor master. I had pictured us making our surprise entrance at Hans and Ria's, waltzing into that gingerbread house of theirs, serious but excited. I glanced at myself in the reflection of the office window: spikes of tousled hair framed a face like sweaty old cheese that begged for sympathy. The same girl that cycled from home to the campus in a free fall to Mommy. I'd inherited the migraines from her, but she gave me no sympathy. "I get headaches too sometimes, Joni. You really *can* talk *normally*."

If he saw me like this, his elder daughter with a pregnant body, everything between us would simply evaporate, I was sure of it. We needn't say a word about last summer, or maybe in fact we *should*, those million-year-old mountains might be just the place to get it out in the open. We could do whatever we wanted. We would do what was best. And after New Year's, Aaron and I would get into the car and drive to the farmhouse. And just like after the fireworks disaster, we'd stay. And I would give birth in my parents' farmhouse.

My temples throbbing, I fished the keys to the cabin out of my purse and walked up the third pier; if I remembered correctly we were moored at the very end. And yes, around a forty-five-degree bend in the walkway, among the rest of the big boys, I spotted the undulating of a familiar tush. *Barbara Ann*'s high-class ass. I picked up speed as I walked along the black water, gritting my teeth against the screech of a million seagulls. The painkillers were up on the deck, in one of the compartments in the wheelhouse, or else in the bathroom of the big cabin in the nose of the boat. "Hi Babs," Aaron would always say as he climbed onto the stern, and I caught myself parroting him. The steps up to the sun deck were covered in gull shit; brownish water had collected in the gutters and corners. If only I could pull the tarp off the purple sunbeds and lie down. Instead, I opened the doors of the pilothouse. Not without regret: I recalled how the Palmer Johnson instructor had taught Aaron and me how to maneuver these twenty meters of luxury safely in and out of harbors in just a week.

I sat down on one of the leather captain's chairs and opened a cupboard next to the rudder. The first-aid kit. Band-aids, gauze, scissors, Aaron's temazepam—*ibuprofen*. I ripped open the sachet and washed it down with a few gulps of mineral water. And now, flat out. The guy would be showing up in just over four hours. So what if it's messy. I pictured myself on the large round bed, felt the luxuriant lift of the mattress, shades drawn, telephone off.

I went down the stairs, too fast maybe, because as I passed the U-shaped sofa in the salon I had to grab the edge of the table. Vomit filled my mouth. I staggered into the kitchen and puked into the sink. The fancy faucet ran as though it was last used yesterday; I rinsed my mouth, hoping I hadn't puked up the magic powder. In fact it really was a hell of a mess down here, you could see we took off back home in a hurry: two crumpled-up swimsuits of Aaron's; dishes, washed but not put away; tools I had no idea we'd ever used. On the dining table, an open bottle of uncorked rosé.

How sick was Aaron? How unwelcome was this surprise now? What was I supposed to tell them about the father of my child?

Beyond the salon was a guest cabin you had to pass through to get to the master suite, a roomy sluice with two sofa beds, never used, ditto the smallish shower cubicle. I squeezed through it and opened the door at the other end. Only now did I smell my own puke-breath: a heavy, sweet-rotten smell. A few steps later I reached the bed; on it was a pair of high heels and, unfortunately, just a thin sheet. I dropped the water bottle, sank onto my left side and buried my head into one of the pillows. I lay there for only thirty seconds, until I nearly suffocated.

So would it be "all's well that ends well" after all? Would a grandpa and a mother alone be enough to make this work?

Don't think, just relax. I took my head out from under the pillow. God, what a smell. The sound of the seagulls, the rustle of the waves in the bay farther up, the traffic on the quay had all but vanished, and I sank away as though gravity doubled over on itself; I was driving in a car along dark, narrow roads, familiar surroundings, it looked like the campus, I plowed the Alfa through arid farmland, it was rough going, the wheels got stuck, strangely enough I became incredibly tired. In the distance I saw someone whom I recognized as Aaron, his bald head gleaming in the moonlight, shining over the sand beds like a second moon. He looked happy, his sheepskin coat was wide open. "Where have you been?" he called out.

It felt like I'd slept for hours, but was probably more like a few comatose minutes. The headache spread to my shoulders and neck, I turned my head the other way.

Maybe it was that unreal smell that drew my eyes along the glossy wood of the wardrobes toward the floor, the hesitant start of an exploratory glance. A piece of clothing caught my eye, it lay like a red river of fabric on the cream-colored carpeting. Intriguing, that hundredth of a second, the fraction during which unsuspecting becomes suspecting. Your brain sends SOS messages at neuron-speed to all parts of your body, to your muscles, your sweat glands, your heart, your lungs—I had to catch my breath. My eyes followed that river upstream: the coat—it was a heavy red coat—was lodged in the matt-glass bathroom door, forcing it ajar. It did not belong there. I kept staring at it, paralyzed. I lay there for six months, maybe even a year, my eyes glued to that coat—and then I slowly got up.

My headache was gone, that's how fast the blood drained from my brain. There was someone in the bathroom. A junkie with Christmas plans. A serial killer with Christmas plans. With two soft steps I stood at the door and pulled it farther open. The same terrible stench hit me like a ton of bricks. The bathroom was disproportionately huge, design overkill that played on the nouveau-riche thirst for luxury: suspended toilet, his-and-her washbasins, bathtub, water-tight shower whose sliding glass door, I noticed at once, was open.

The next moment there were flies—a swarm of metallic flies, a pestilential cloud that lifted off and, as if on command, alighted again. Pinching my nose, I approached the shower. The flies clung to a body that hung from a noose of orange nylon, the rope we used to fasten the boat. It was clothed; the torso was like soaked fruit in a lambswool sweater—it looked set to explode. The shins—swollen, festering, moist—bulged above the thick-laced hiking boots. The inside of the cubicle was smeared with dark wetness; in the corner, a toppled bucket. The head—*his* head. The rope, tied with a sturdy knot onto the hinge of the open vent, pulled it skew, the neck had an unnatural kink. The face—

I choked back my vomit. Aside from being bluish-green, the face was swollen, the tongue stuck out of the twisted, grimacing mouth. On the chin, a whopper of a scab. The left eye was closed, but not the right one, it bulged out. It was more out than in. It stared as though it had collected all the torment and agony that a person could suffer.

I puked before I reached the toilet. The contents of my stomach sloshed onto the plastic floor tiles between the cubicle and the bowl. I squatted, gagged twice more and stood back up. My head. My heart was up in my skull. I went over to the washbasins and turned on the faucet.

"Don't cry, God damn it. Don't."

Cold water. I rinsed my mouth and my face. I stared into the drain. Paper: a piece of paper stuck out of his breast pocket. Had I seen it right? An envelope, a napkin?

I mustered all my courage and turned around. I took a step toward the shower. Without looking at the face, I reached for the breast pocket, first came up against the dead chest, felt the sluggish weight, and jerked back my hand. Panting, I grabbed hold of the doorpost. "Dad. What–" Then I took the body by the hips and held it tight.

It was an envelope. I brought it with me through the bedroom and upstairs to the deck. I sat down on the bench in the pilothouse and caught my breath. I tried to breathe normally, focusing on a red buoy off in the distance, where the bay met the ocean. Only when I started freezing—half an hour later, an hour?—did I look at my hand that still clasped the envelope. It was a standard size, it looked like it contained a postcard. My belly felt heavy. I tried to tear it open, but my fingers were trembling. And my head was about to explode. I laid the envelope on the table and got up. *Suicide?* What had happened to the fighter? I tipped a second packet of ibuprofen into my mouth and forced the powder down with spit.

Suddenly there was the barrage of questions, stupid ones and idiotic ones all jumbled up together. How did he get in? Did he have a key? Why did this have to happen? Did he already have the key when we got back from vacation? Did I have a knife? Or scissors. Couldn't leave him hanging there like that. Why did he do it? Has anyone missed him yet? Mom? His department? Those flies had to go. Is it my fault? I had to lay him on the bed. That rope around his neck. Call the police? *Why didn't you call me?* I had to go into Sainte-Maxime to find a police station. I had to call Val-d'Isère.

But I didn't get up, I stayed put. "If you really had such a problem with it, Dad," I said, "why didn't you *fuck*ing come take it out on me?"

With barely functioning fingers, I opened the envelope. There was indeed a card inside, a repro of an old Sainte-Maxime poster, I'd bought it that summer and left it lying there, Jugendstil with a palm tree and a beach. Something was written in pen on the back; through my tears I could make out his surprisingly childlike handwriting. Instead of reading it, I tore the card into little pieces and threw the scraps overboard.

21

At Venlo he crosses the Meuse. Large ice floes hug the edge of the graphite water, a long barge carrying mountains of beige sand keeps a middle course. On both meandering banks he sees the provincial clusters where thousands of families will soon be waking up to the gray December light; for yet another consecutive night the snow covering has thickened. Aaron's parents: didn't they live in Venlo? He met them once, in their son's house. Mild people with mild opinions. He should call Val-d'Isère, he had promised to call before leaving home. A message from a mild husband with mild opinions. As long as it keeps freezing. He rolls down the back window a bit farther.

Fumes penetrate the Audi, morning rush hour is under way, the roads become increasingly congested with truck traffic, heavy tires lisping their way through the salty brown slush. Since Duisburg he's been stuck at a snail's pace behind an Italian eighteen-wheeler, but he is still early. He hadn't the energy last night to install the roof pod, so his skis are lying on the flattened passenger seat and the suitcases are in the back, stuffed with unironed pants and shirts; only now does it occur to him that what he's wearing—a moth-eaten lambswool sweater, a dubious pair of jeans, and hiking boots—is out of character; he is, to put it mildly, quite a sight.

Day breaks off to the east, the ashen morning sky is like a ponderous announcement of the mining region he's about to drive through. *Don't think about it.* The image, it seems, is stored in countless caches in his memory, it comes hurtling at his retina from unexpected corners of his subconscious. Book a hotel in France. He forces himself to imagine a bed in Metz or Nancy where he can actually *sleep* for a couple of hours. Prepare himself for the normality of Val-d'Isère. A showered guest, duly attentive to his host and hostess. A few curative hours in a hotel room. Near the Belgian border he stops for gas, wipes snow from the windshield. Inside, in line for the cashier, he spreads his limbs in order to absorb as much warmth as possible. He strikes a strange pose there in line, halfway turned toward the car, never once taking his eyes off the Audi. He buys chewing gum, puts three pieces into his mouth.

His breathing is shallow. He crosses the border, nodding to a pair of chatting customs officers as he passes. Shouldn't have drunk that rum. The moment he's out of sight he floors it. For the past hour or so he has felt an unprecedented anxiety, his nerves are off-kilter, like somebody is jerking a brush through the tangled dendrites. He grits his teeth, but as soon as he releases the pressure his teeth start chattering. Avoid Liège, his rule of thumb: they always used to get hopelessly lost in this chaotic city. Drive around it. He wants to go to an anonymous place, an illogical place, somewhere that takes some trouble to reach. Belgium is reliably illogical; he has already taken a detour in order to be here.

The snow chains, why didn't he bring the snow chains? They're lying on top of the cupboard in Joni's old room; earlier that night it seemed too risky to go upstairs, and after that it had slipped his mind. And now he's driving in the Alps without snow chains. *Or is it already thawing?*

He is on a kind of ring road around Liège. Instead of heading south, to Metz, he decides to go west, he takes the A15 to Namur. It is impossible *not* to think about it. To block out the image he evokes substitute thoughts—pleasant thoughts, under normal circumstances—visions of off-piste skiing, of the copious meals Hans will prepare for them, of complex mathematical formulas—but they flutter away, they are too flimsy to accomplish much. He racks his brains for something stronger, something potent enough to convince himself that he is doing what he *has* to do, but he comes up empty-handed. He jams his index finger into his skinned chin.

After Namur he exits the freeway. Taking the country roads, which soon become stony paths, he passes craggy, leafy woods, hardened snow around the gray tree trunks. This is another world, here the earth is bleak, just as it is bleak almost everywhere except in his own country; in the Netherlands nature dives underground like a metro and only resurfaces in Scandinavia. His life is bleak. Sometimes that life races down a village street with houses as gray as stringy rags, and then covers long stretches without seeing a single building, only woods and farmland, every so often a spotted tile roof deep down in a valley.

On the way down a hill he turns onto a snow-covered dirt road that leads to a green-black pine forest. A few minutes later, completely surrounded by the tall fir trees, he parks as far off the path as possible. He sits there for a quarter of an hour, too tired to move. Tineke, he really must phone Tineke. He enters the number and listens to the ragged foreign ringtone. After the seventh ring he hangs up. Blood is pounding in his ears. He tries to rehearse the conversation: what, in fact, does he plan to say? Before he's come up with some platitude, she calls back. "Hello dear," he says hoarsely. Just let her do the talking. They are having breakfast, his wife tells him, they're looking out over the slopes, the trails are still being prepared—but he hardly takes it in. She wants to know when to expect him, he says it will be late, he's just leaving Enschede, count on midnight. She's taking ski lessons, she says: news meant to counter his own silence, so he mumbles something enthusiastic, but his thoughts slip away—he almost gags. *The black pinky, think of that burned-off gangrene finger.* "What did you eat yesterday?" she asks. "Did you remember to turn down the heat?" While he inhales and exhales deeply she rattles on, maybe because Hans and Ria are within earshot, maybe because she's suppressing thoughts about the photos he's nearly forgotten already. She says he sounds tired, "did you have a cold night?" No. Yes. He mustn't warm himself on her normality, on the stubborn unchangedness on her end of the line—not yet. Soon. Later.

"Did you get everything in the roof pod?"

"I'll try now," he answers, and as soon as they've hung up he calculates how long ago it was that he left the utility room with his skis under his arm. Six hours? Could just as well be six years. He lets his cell phone sink into his pocket.

He had already walked around the side of the house to the Audi a few times, his footsteps crunching, first with his travel bag, then his laptop and attaché case, cautiously forging a path in the light that shone out from the sunroom onto the softly ionizing layer of snow. He tried to recall his mood at that moment, the weary restlessness that accompanied him on his last inspection of the farmhouse, looking for blood stains or anything out of place, before he carried his skis into the utility room. Cautiously optimistic relief? He had turned on the outside light—only then?—and in the yellow glow saw the entire terrace light up. The snow was falling harder now; he opened the kitchen door and stepped outside. White powder fluttered from the thatched roof and the crown of the chestnut. As the icy wind cut through his clothes he looked at the trail of his footprints running parallel to the sunroom; only now, though, did he notice a second, much narrower, trail branching off into the backyard. His eyes followed the snow-dusted footprints. They led to a hump at the edge of the terrace, about six meters from where he stood. *Something was lying there.* An oblong, snow-covered object, right about where the patio stones met the grass. His skis slipped out of his fingers, the slap muted by the snow. Fucking hell, *he was lying there.* He took a step back and watched closely. Wilbert. On his back, the broken arm bulging up under the bomber jacket. Snow was starting to cling to his clothes, the legs were spread slightly, feet pointing outward, the toes of the shoes were white. His head was facing the farmhouse, bent backward at an odd angle. He could see the battered face, the left eye was open a crack. The nose, he observed with a shock, puffed out little clouds of vapor.

The thought of that face. Pressing the slimy wound on his chin, he looks around. Think of something else, damn it, think of . . . *Joni?* He sits panting in a parked car on a forest lane in the Belgian Ardennes, on the verge of fainting. Think of something . . . *good.* The game Joni used to play on Bonita Avenue, a game she called "America's Good-time Girl." She'd poke her little blond face around their bedroom door, the new day shining on her face like fresh dew, and chirp: "Dad and Mom, OK, Round One. America's Good-time Girl. Stay in bed." He lets his head fall back against the headrest, allows his eyelids to droop for a moment, and immediately they suck themselves against the white of his eyes. From their bed they'd hear her downstairs in the wood-paneled kitchen, squeezing oranges, making coffee and toast; there was an evening variant too, when she'd whirl through the cramped living room like in a fast-motion film, a busy little bee lighting candles, closing curtains, the adorable fumbling with a corkscrew and a bottle that wouldn't—

It backfires. His happiest memories plunge him into a deep

gloom. He opens his eyes, rolls down the driver's window and stares out into the woods for several minutes; the black trunks are close together, he can't see any farther than thirty meters or so. In the depths: darkness.

He couldn't move, he could only stare. How long had that bastard been lying there? It looked like he had slipped, he must have lost his footing, maybe he fell on his head, or on his arm. Did he try to get back up? The surrounding snow looked raked about. *He's sleeping it off.* Was that it? The rum—he was completely blotto, he fell, thrashed about with his one good arm and when nothing helped he thought: nighty-night. The idiot was sleeping off the rum at 13 below zero.

He debated with himself. How often had he debated with his better self lately? This time they quickly reached an agreement. He stood for a moment longer, his gaze fixed on the sleeping figure in the freezing cold, and then he turned away. He picked his skis up out of the snow, put them on the brushy doormat in the utility room and meticulously locked up. Back in the kitchen, he took the carving knife from the block again. He went into the sunroom, out of habit switched on the light, then turned it off again. His eyes glued to the body, he walked around the long table without banging into anything, turned a chair with exaggerated care toward the glass wall and sat down, knife in his hand, his hand on his lap. His son had an ugly, balding head.

At first he did not know exactly why he was sitting there. Was he guarding his fort? Or did he have other intentions? As the minutes ticked by he was interested in only one thing: condensation—in the furthest reaches of the outdoor light he saw the damp discharge of Wilbert's breath. Shivering, he zipped his ski jacket up over his Adam's apple. He watched the breathing obsessively. He noticed his own reflection in the glass, faintly, like a watermark, a contour ten times weaker than the illuminated face out there in the snow, a strange, skewed face that belonged to a blind-drunk, hypothermic body, a body in need of assistance.

Become a monk. How can you stare at the same thing, attentively but devoid of all thought, for an unlimited amount of time? He pressed his left knee up against the icy windowpane. There was nothing but condensation, soft little puffs filled his consciousness. Switch off your thoughts, you've thought enough by now. And yes, it worked, his head cleared immeasurably, no more unfinished thoughts, no reflection, only snippets, *what fifteen blows of a sledgehammer could do*—they slipped out of his brain but he quashed them in the cloudlets outside. Not once did he take his eyes off the volcano that kept smoldering, emitted those puffs of sulfur—they kept on coming, low, tirelessly. Still, it was freezing out there: cold in, warmth out, cold in, warmth out . . .

. . . he lifted him up and cuddled him, a dry, ribbed chin against his sweaty forehead, then the man whom he didn't know carried him to the edge of the spongy mat. He lay on his back, deep in the mat, other boys were standing around him, they were silent, only nodded at him, except for one thin, bawling blond boy. He noticed that his own face no longer had its old shape, he felt it, he was swollen all over, small warm tomatoes, everywhere, it felt hot and gigantic. "Don't fetch my wife," he wailed. "Oh yes," said Mr. Vloet, who, he saw now, was an aged version of a neighbor, their elderly neighbor from the Antonius Matthaeuslaan, who walked across the dojo that changed into his office in Zoetermeer, only larger, emptier—

He woke to a metallic clatter. Where am I? Until he saw his own reflection he swirled aimlessly through a pitch-black universe. He rubbed his hands over his face. The carving knife had fallen to the slate floor. His muscles felt tense from the cold when he retrieved it and grasped it in his fist; skittishly he scanned the terrace. His short leg was asleep. The night was still black, but paler. The face was still there, it seemed to have turned slightly, for a moment he thought the eyes were open, he rubbed his own eyes to clear them.

The breathing had stopped.

He stayed put. For at least a quarter of an hour, he guessed, he sat in that chair as if frozen himself, staring at the immobile body in the snow. Non-thinking was not out of the question, every incipient thought burst into a garland of triumph *and* guilt, he allowed the confusion to blossom, as though it were not his own . . . *So you're a murderer. You're both murderers, but you're alive and on the run, the one who got off scot-free* . . . He stood up and opened the sliding glass door, it was sticking, like the lubricant was frozen. *No, don't prettify it, don't call him a murderer* . . . His feet sinking into the snow, he walked over to the body, stood close to it and looked. *Mustn't kill him, mustn't slander him either, he wasn't convicted of murder* . . . Blood had leaked through the jacket, the snow under his left side had become a slushy brown. *Manslaughter, fifteen hysterical blows, fifteen death blows within a minute, but it wasn't murder, you must be precise about it. You're the murderer in this family, you murdered him* . . . Was he really dead? He inhaled, held the cold air in his lungs, nudged the right shoulder with the rounded toe of his hiking shoes, cautiously at first, then harder. No reaction. He gave the thigh a kick. His knees cracked when he sank to his haunches. He took a deep breath and rammed the point of the knife into the palm of the outstretched hand.

He gets out of the car. The slam of the door thunders through the frozen silence of the surrounding woods. He opens the rear hatch, wavers for a moment between the backpack and the tent bag, in the end lugs the tent bag out of the trunk. He clamps the load under his right arm while he locks the car. The canvas is frozen, and yet he knows it's thawing outside, and in his head as well: something is changing up there; what he was able to do all morning, in fact all night—cold-blooded reasoning, followed by cold-blooded action—is becoming increasingly difficult. He looks around again and walks into the woods, the bag clamped to his chest. It's rough going, there is no path, here and there he has to wriggle between drooping branches. The snow on the ground is thin and hard, he continually stumbles over roots, his ungainly coat keeps getting caught on the bristly thicket. There are no birds to be heard. Crackling branches and needles under his hiking shoes, the occasional rustle of unseen forest animals, but most of all: his own heavy breathing. The thirty, maybe forty kilos in his arms want to sag, he's got a poor grip on the bag—this is bad. And again he thinks of the face, his hands begin to perspire, he has to stop. *Replace it with another gruesome thought.* The elbow, think of the elbow cracking. The resistance in the wrist; bending, struggling cells; the moment of capitulation, *the snap*. And keep walking.

He had damn near just driven off. After he knew for sure that Wilbert was dead he had simply turned around, picked his skis up out of the snow, and loaded them in the car. Just leave him there: he died like he died. From the one moment to the next he was high on testosterone, he felt a victory flush that almost made him afraid of himself. I'll just say I was sleeping. Like any normal person I went to bed at night, and while I slept the bastard froze to death—that's how it goes. Drunkards freeze to death when no one sees them. And the next morning I got up and left for my skiing vacation. I didn't see a thing, it's as simple as that. He was already turning off lights, the radiators and underfloor heating were already set to anti-freeze mode, when it occurred to him that it *wasn't* as simple as that. There is nothing simple about a dead body in your backyard. How could he not have seen Wilbert lying there? The footprints on the terrace—the snow was crisscrossed with footprints leading to that body, *his* footprints. And even on the outside chance that they'd melt in time, that bastard wouldn't melt. Never.

Dog-tired and desperate, he lay facedown on the sofa. He no longer needed to close his eyes in order to picture himself on the ski slopes when the detective called: Mr. Sigerius, we've found a corpse in your backyard; he could see the red-and-white-striped barrier tape around their farmhouse at the end of a killing homeward drive. He began to shiver like someone with a bad fever, an unstoppable tremor of something, fatigue, grief, *fear.*

Yes, he was afraid. From hightailing it out of there he catapulted to the other extreme: report it. Contain the damage and go to the police at once. Enschede police headquarters, have them write up an acceptable version of the events. I caught my criminal son as he tried to break into my own house, we got into a fight, a life-or-death struggle, and then he buggered off. And just now, as I'm about to leave for my skiing vacation, there he is, lying on my terrace, under the snow: dead, frozen. For a moment he considered this a lucid, plausible story. He stood in the living room with the phone in his hand, had already dialed the number, when he thought: but why didn't you phone right away? You wanted to go *skiing*? After an incident like that? Why didn't you call the cops right away? *Sir, that was hours ago—why only call now?* It is the first question they will ask him, a question that begs answering. And what is he supposed to answer?

As he lies half asleep on the sofa, he is startled by a soft motorized sound. A scooter? The paperboy's scooter—it approaches, stops, pulls out again and fades away. Was it that time already? The world will be getting up in a few hours, *in a few hours his neighbors will be getting up.* The Teeuwen girl, she's coming for the cats, she was going to take care of them. He could already picture her in the yard, dumbstruck, hand over her mouth.

Get rid of that body. Breathing rapidly, he stood up, went to the utility room, put on a duffel coat from a couple of winters ago, and slid his hands into a pair of woolen gloves. The starless cold bit into his face. He walked past the corpse without looking at it, farther into the crunching darkness of the downward-sloping backyard. He cursed the snow into which his hiking shoes sank; he was doomed to leave a trail behind. At the back of the yard he slipped, banging his knee hard against the massive table on the terrace next to the workshop. He groped his way to the padlock on the wooden door, undid the bolt, felt around for a light switch. He surveyed the suddenly brightly lit space: islets of sawdust on the concrete floor, the professional tools hanging on their pegboard racks, the machines oblivious to the cold. He could stash the body behind the veneer press.

He walked back by the light of the fluorescent tubes, teeth chattering, following his own footprints that showed up as dark shadows against the illuminated snow, and crouched down next to the body. His toes were already numb; these must be the coldest hours of the night. Illuminated by the outdoor lamp the face looked surreal, it was the color of newsprint, the blood under the nose was black.

Never drag a dead body. Crime shows are a turn-off, he avoids watching reconstructions of murders and rapes, and yet somewhere he's learned that drag marks are the worst. He planted his feet perpendicular to the body and squatted down. The smell of rum, and something musty—he put his revulsion aside, wriggled one arm under the shoulders, the other under the thighs. A wet chill had soaked through his woolen gloves. He tried to straighten up, a sharp pain shot through his bruised rib cage. The load came loose from the snow, but behaved in a way he did not expect: instead of giving in the knee joints and midriff—as a sleeping daughter does when you carry her from the backseat of the car to the house, up the stairs, and into bed—the body resisted gravity like a railroad tie. Its center of gravity was in a strange place, he had misjudged it: the legs, stiff as boards, sloped toward the ground; he had to squat down again to keep from losing his balance, the corpse's heels landing in the snow with a thud, he slid forward anyway, banged his knees against the leather jacket. It felt hard underneath, as though he'd fallen onto a rock in a river.

The second attempt went better, although the outstretched hulk was heavier than he had expected. Treading cautiously, he carried it to the workshop, had to turn it sideways to get it in. He went to the middle of the concrete floor, turned hesitantly around, and even before deciding to hide the body behind the veneer press after all, he knew he had made a mistake.

How could you be so stupid? How could you be so stupid as to lug a dead body around? The realization of what he was facing made him dizzy, he had to sit down. How logical it would be to pin it on him, to suspect him of murder. The obvious assumption that he had deliberately dumped Wilbert out in the cold. He staggered over to the band saw, a kind of overgrown sewing machine, and slumped down onto the leather seat attached to it. Through the eyes of the prosecutor he saw himself hoist the unconscious, wounded body into a fireman's lift and carry it into the backyard, the motives fluttering out of his sleeves like playing cards. A frozen stiff with a torn-off arm? And then drag it into the shed? Why? He didn't have a leg to stand on. On top of it, that is how it *was.* He *did* abandon Wilbert to his fate. He knowingly let him die. He laid his head in his hands and stared at the blood spatters on the cement floor.

The corpse had to go. *Dispose of the body.* As he fingered the wound on his chin the stupid ideas came, the easy, obvious solutions that were everything *but* solutions. Bury it behind the workshop, in the weedy bit where the kids used to have their vegetable patch. Yeah, and spend the rest of his life next to his son's grave? He squeezed his chin in anger, the pain was gratifying, the wound oozed fluid along his stubbly neck. Then it came to him: the Rutbeek, of course, the *Rutbeek*. It would be dark for another few hours, he could weigh down the body, drive out to the lake, and dump it. He pounded his knee from the stupidity of it all. *You can't just go driving around with a corpse.* He shouldn't have touched it in the first place. Dump a dead body in a recreational area? Damn it, people *skated* on the Rutbeek.

Keep on walking. The first time he looks back, the Audi seems far off, a barely visible silver speck beyond a tangle of branches and tree trunks. And him? Does he stand out in his bright red coat? Do the Walloons come here? Of course they do. One day they will. And where will he be that day? It feels like the tent bag is hanging by hooks on his ribs. Keep walking. Despite the pain he sees it before him; he *must not* think of that mug. *Feel the moist splinters on your lips, on your forehead.* Fifty heavy meters into the woods, the ground suddenly slopes downward. He is standing on the edge of a sort of pit, a hollow several meters deep. At the bottom, bird footprints dot the snow. At the ridge of the cavity he sees a large pine tree, leaning forward as though taken by surprise as the ground gives way at its feet: the wreath of roots hangs half over the edge. He descends, his back to the pit, with a few cautious, slipping steps, and glances under the roots. Yes, there's enough room. A hollow to stuff his conscience in.

First he went to fetch the bags. He had ordered himself back into the farmhouse and walked upstairs. The bathroom door was open, the small fluorescent light was on. Muddy feet on the green tiles; in the toilet a wad of tissue floating in an oval of urine. He gave the flush knob a smack and went into Joni's old room. The pink curtains were drawn. He smelled something sourish-sweet, but refused to consider the notion that the bastard had been in here too. At the bottom of her wardrobe he found his old backpack, the one he took to gymnastics camp and on InterRail vacations as a teenager. One door farther, in his study, he removed a hatch where they stored the camping gear; stretched out on his belly, he reached through the dust and pulled out a dark-red oblong bag holding a family-size tent, shook out the ground cloth, the moth-eaten canvas flysheet, and the poles. With both bags under his arm, he went back downstairs, took a roll of garbage bags out of a kitchen drawer, went back across the yard, and laid it all out on the long workbench in the shed.

In the hard light of the work lamps he went over to a blue steel rack holding about twenty planks of wood, all different sorts, waiting to be planed, whittled, or sawed. Flaky wood, a kind of chipboard, a fibrous, absorbent plank. He took a sheet of pressed sawdust the size of a double door off the rack and carried it, wincing from the pain, over to the table. How did Tineke do this again? He rested the sheet against the workbench and nudged the adjustable rip fence made of green hammered steel, picked up the sheet of wood and laid it onto the frame just as he'd seen her do. The purposefulness of his actions made him think of the way he could pack a suitcase following an argument: demonstratively, decidedly, but not believing for a minute that he would actually leave.

He walked around behind the veneer press and studied the contorted, rigid body lying on the floor. Was it still cooling off? Did it freeze all the way through? Could a person freeze solid in six hours? What would he do if—

There were no "ifs" anymore. He squatted down next to the body, his knuckles against the concrete, and lifted it up for the second time. Ignoring the shooting pain in his ribs, he released it with a bonk onto the chipboard. With some joggling and prodding—the load was on the heavy side, the squeak of the bearings told him—he managed to roll the horizontal surface so that the saw was at right angles to the left hip. He went over to the long workbench and found a roll of silver duct tape in a plastic bin. With long, gummy lengths of tape he fastened the corpse in various places to the wood.

For the first time he saw it close up and fully lit: the lopsided white sneakers, laces double-knotted; the blood-spattered jeans; the battered face—the pleb-face that Koperslager had warned him about all those years ago—and yet: *his* features. The congealed blood stuck like caviar to the cracked lips. The edge of his ears, the flat boxer's nose, the right cheek—black and wrinkled as prunes. The right eye was open. A smog of alcohol still wafted out of the twisted mouth. The fingertips of the visible hand were black too, the withered pinky resembled a burned match.

Again he experienced an alarming satisfaction with his deed—or was it a non-deed? Until now he had steadfastly performed the ultimate *non*-action, just as he had made a point of steering clear of that rotten life. With a jab on a red rubber button he set the saw in motion. The teeth whistled in the cold, dry air, gave off a slight gust. The motor produced a sonorous, frighteningly loud tone. He glanced back anxiously at the workshop door: how far does this noise travel? With a separate switch he turned on—and then back off—the exhaust arm. He was overcome with revulsion: instead of sawdust, bits of . . . *flesh* would fly around. Organic blobs, scraplets that under no circumstances must be allowed to get into the exhaust system, they would decompose, rot, stink to high heaven. Every scrap, every splinter, he would have to clean up meticulously, without forgetting a thing, like a reverse proof in mathematics.

Hang on tight to your nefarious sense of satisfaction. Think of the headaches he's caused you, the stress, the shame, year in and year out. Every time, yet another slap in the face, another disappointment, another misdemeanor, another, another, and *yet* another—he poured all this misery over himself like a ton of fish waste, and before he knew it he was shoving the panel into the saw with all his might. With a screech, the blade slid into the flaky board, sawdust sprayed, he smelled the false scent of construction, in less than ten seconds the steel shark fin had chewed its way to the hip. I'm not planning to bleed for you any longer. *I'm not going to fucking let it happen.* The circular saw sank its teeth into the worn-out denim, there was no sign of resistance; without balking, the spinning blade chewed through the frozen thigh bone, the shrill sound did get augmented by something darker, a damp, almost gurgling undertone, whitish and dark-red spatters flew off the saw blade. Screaming as if it were his own leg, he rammed the saw even deeper. The motor seemed to slacken a bit, the upward spattering increased, a hailstorm leaving a trail over the board and his coat. He felt soft flicks against his neck, against the corner of his mouth, his cheek, his right temple—and he recoiled.

Is this me? Is this us? As though he were on fire, he swatted at his face and neck, cursing and sputtering, in an attempt to rid himself of the gunk. In a wild panic he yanked off his sweater, buttons burst off his shirt, he could feel the scraps of sticky-wet flesh sticking to his hands. Spitting, spastic with disgust, he lunged at the saw and slammed the rubber button, silencing the machine, and then hurried out of the workshop. Blinded by tears—something inside him was starting to thaw—he staggered through the darkness, marking out figure-eights and zeros in the snow, until he slipped and landed with a smack, facedown, on the cold deck. Lying there in his mold, he pressed his sullied face into the snow and felt his tears freeze. He squeezed his eyes shut and scrabbled upright. The cold burned his face, he walked, moaning, to the utility room. In the living room he pulled his shirt over his head and undid his belt. Still sputtering, he went through the front hall to the bedroom and then into the bathroom. He furiously undressed. Naked, he rinsed his mouth at the washbasin and let the shower run hot.

The tent bag is lying like a blood blister on the edge of the pit. He clambers back up the incline a bit, grabs the drawstring and pulls at it until the bag rolls over the mossy edge. He catches it and lets it slide the rest of the way down to the bottom. He stands panting for a few seconds. Just as he is pushing and wriggling it into the rooty crevice under the pine tree, his phone rings.

The ringtone is so incongruous in that morning silence that he surprises himself with a grin, his facial muscles are taut and rusty. With a sigh he sinks to the ground, stretching his legs out in front of him in the snow. He just sits there, absently, until the ringing stops. For a moment the woods are noiseless. Then his phone starts ringing again, and this time he takes it out of his breast pocket. It is his advisor, Hendrik, the old hand who had been banished to Education in the wake of the Bijlmer inquiry. Through his infinite exhaustion his mouth once again curls into a sort of a smile. This dedicated soul, who from a parallel universe has reached him in the depths of his misery.

"Morning, Hendrik."

"Hello Siem, sorry to call you on a Saturday. Am I disturbing you?" The voice fills his consciousness like the smell of freshly baked bread.

"Go ahead."

"Siem, it's like this. You'll remember Karin was supposed to go on that talk show tomorrow on TV, but I've just heard she's got flu. Lost her voice. My question is: can you take her place? Personally I think it's a golden opportunity to squelch all the grumbling about that school plan. What do you think?"

"I'm standing on a ski slope, Hendrik. To be honest, I'm not doing all that much thinking." What he does think is: don't leave me alone. Talk to me.

Hendrik swears. Then he laughs: yes, he thought he'd seen the call was being forwarded out of the country, now he remembers Sigerius mentioning spending the holidays in France. "That's that, then, Siem, never mind. Have yourself a fine vacation."

"You too, Hendrik, you too." Apparently something in his tone keeps the other from hanging up. A hesitant silence fills the air. Hendrik is a boat floating far up above him, he must swim up to the surface, and fast. "What are you going to do?" he asks.

"Me? Oh, this and that, tie up some loose ends. I've got a lunch with that new parliamentary reporter, kid from the NRC."

"Actually, I meant for Christmas, Hendrik." Between sentences his teeth chatter, he pulls in his lips over his teeth. "And New Year's Eve."

"Nothing special, Siem."

"The children? Doing anything with them?" His teeth chatter.

Hendrik pauses. Then, reluctantly: "My wife's daughters are coming for Christmas. The youngest one has a new boyfriend." He coughs, waits for another fraction of a second. "A boy from former Yugoslavia. My wife's dreading it slightly, I think. So. Siem."

As soon as they've hung up he sinks back into the depths of an abyss, cold and ever darker.

• • •

He scoured himself clean with gritty gel from a small tube. The stuff grated the top layer of skin on his neck, on his face; everything had to come off and get washed down the drain. With every fleshy little snot he cringed in self-loathing and disgust. The hot water ate into the places hit by the nunchuk, there was an enormous bruise under his armpit and another elongated one on his neck. He washed his hair twice with a handful of shampoo, his fingers like a steel brush over his scalp. He squeezed toothpaste onto the brush that lay on the small glass shelf and scrubbed his teeth, spat the froth between his feet, and then scrubbed again until his gums bled. He removed the showerhead from its holder and squatted down. There was a soft pink substance on the drain that he pushed through the holes in the copper plate with the back end of the toothbrush. Why, he didn't know, but as he was doing this he thought back to the full living room in their house on the Antonius Matthaeuslaan, the week after the birth. All his in-laws were there, smoking, bantering, munching the biscuits with sprinkles that he and his older sister had prepared in the kitchen while Margriet's father sat on the john, for a good long time, he remembers thinking. He could smell the old Wijn. That lout behind the bathroom door bothered him: a reminder that their little boy up there in his crib carried the genes of the guy on his toilet. He was unhappy.

You sawed him up. He tried to stand up, his ribs cut into his chest like sabers, he had to grab hold of the aluminum doorframe. The devastating force tearing into him was not localized, not something on the scale of his life—it was immense. *You murdered him and then you sawed him up.*

The unease *and* the happiness when the baby was born. He

was happy, because now he had something over the Wijn clan. His own parents were dead and buried, it was him versus them. The unease was stronger, it arose from mixing his genes with these Utrecht low-lifes—but the child was still a Sigerius. Whenever he fantasized about running off, leaving Margriet, in his daydream he always took his son with him—

His frozen son, Siem Sigerius's sawed-up son, lay like bait in his shed, a hunk of meat that would soon thaw and stink and betray him. He would be devoured by the scorn of politicos, his disgrace would be broadcast nationwide, his nervous system evoked images of the gray colossus of Justice, in no time it would be established that it was murder. Then visions of something even more merciless: the media, the fucking media, the drooling press, the *international* press, newspaper headlines in thick ink, dripping columns covering his trial: the mathematician and his children, blackmail, nude pictures, a circular saw. He pressed his chafed chin to his chest and let the water splash against the back of his head.

Keep on thinking—please. He turned the hot tap halfway off, the water went lukewarm. Tepid water allows him to think clearly. That's what he did at MIT when he'd drawn a blank: take a shower. No way is he going to just give up. There was a forgotten, primitive shower at the end of the Mathematics Department corridor, beyond Quillen's room. When he was stuck, like now, he would take his towel and walk down to that cubicle. That sawing, he just couldn't go through with it. He wanted to turn the hot water back up, but restrained himself. Hot water was for chickens, he needed to cool himself off. Think cold. His shoes made a high-pitched ticking noise in the corridor, on the walls hung portraits of the greatest mathematicians in history: Euler, Gauss, Riemann, Hilbert, Fermat, Galois. He stands motionless under the tepid stream, goose bumps on his body. And now? Get rid of him. *Make a puzzle of it.* He'd stand there in the MIT shower, up to his neck in Von Neumann algebras, not to mention physically bricked in, until his brain underwent nuclear fusion. The puzzling-together of those algebras and the knot theory, he had to support himself against the tiled shower, his fingers spread, to keep from falling over. But now there's no fusion, on the contrary: his nucleus splits. First comes panic, then the urge for survival. *Fission yourself first.* He turned the hot water off entirely. *Freeze yourself.* The coldness, Wilbert Sigerius's coldness. A son who waits until his father is naked and then attacks him with a lead truncheon. The cold, merciless marrow of that bastard, he drank it up like liquid nitrogen. He ran his hands over his scalp one last time and got out of the shower.

He walked back to the workshop and untaped the corpse from the board, pried the upper leg out of the saw. He thought for a moment, then threw the wooden door all the way open, stuck his arms under the dead weight and dragged the pillar of flesh into the backyard. Picking up speed, he followed the blind wall of the workshop where chopped hardwood was stacked under a low lean-to shingled with barked planks. In the fresh snow he could see the outline of the oak stump where Tineke chopped wood. He hurriedly kicked the snow off the trunk and laid the stiffened body over it, the waist in the middle of the round platform, head and heels draping into the snow. There was enough light from the outdoor lamp above the terrace. He walked back to the workshop, pulled the roll of garbage bags out of the backpack. In the left corner of the shed, propped in a sooty fire basket, was an axe. He took it with him outside.

It was an enormous axe with a red-painted steel blade and an elegantly curved, almost athletic handle. First he kicked the left hand away from the groin, and then tugged the leather jacket up a bit. He had brought this dangerous piece of garbage into the world. He had to repeat it a few times before he raised the axe—*You brought dangerous rubbish into the world.* The first blow was aimed at the saw wound in the thigh, but the axe bounced off something hard and lodged itself in the chopping block. *And now you'll clean up the mess.* He crouched next to the leg, wriggled his hand into the greasy trouser pocket. It was his duty. First he pulled out a pack of Sportlife chewing gum, and almost cut himself when he pried out an open jackknife. The kid was three years old, Karin was staying with them, Margriet's youngest sister. Problems with her father. A lethargic girl in polka-dot frocks who sat there the whole day chewing Bazooka bubblegum. The house was littered with those waxy wrappers with cartoons on them. One Sunday afternoon they heard breathless shrieking on the landing. There he sat, with a gob of bubblegum the size of a golf ball lodged in his throat, Karin had stuck it to the edge of the kitchen table, "a whole pack," she screamed, while little blue-faced Wilbert lay there choking to death. He should have cleaned up that mess right then and there. He looked at the weapon, the blow must have knocked the blade open, there was a deep groove in the wooden sheath. Should've let him choke.

But he rushed over and gave him a few punches to the belly, held his unconscious child by the ankles and eventually managed, with three fingers, to fish the sticky, bright pink glob out of the toddler's throat.

The axe struck the upper leg. With four or five overhand blows—raising it with hate, chopping with hate *and* gravity—he cleaved the half-sawn-off leg the rest of the way; the flesh was as grainy as sorbet, he heard the bone snap. It became a weird loose thing with a sneaker on it. Dark blood welled up out of the ragged open cut, which he absolutely did not want to stare at, but did anyway; the vivid red surface agreed with what he imagined the cross-section of a leg would look like: skin around flesh around bone. Numb, he stuffed the object in a garbage bag that he then wound shut with the silver-colored duct tape, and carried it to the workshop.

His gamble paid off: the tent bag was long enough. He carried the backpack back to the chopping block. The darkness seemed less deep. Against his better judgment he gauged the opening of the backpack and then the breadth of the shoulders. The torso was indeed too large, his son had his build, stocky and massive; the good arm simply had to come off too. *And the head?* Keep your shit together. No time to lose, when would that Teeuwen girl be coming by? Always start with the least fun stuff, that's what he had told his daughters their entire youth, get it out of the way. The dishes first, then TV. Homework first, then horseback riding. First the head, then the limbs. He fought back the sudden urge to grab the axe and fling it against the sunroom—he could hear the tinkling of the glass already. *The awful thought of the head.* Wasn't there a bigger bag upstairs? A *taller* bag, so that he could leave the head attached?

What he'd most like is to close his eyes, just for a minute, but he is too agitated. The backpack—got to go to the car. Taking short steps, he climbs out of the hole and makes his way back through the tree trunks. Even without the thirty-kilo load he stumbles against roots and branches, his toes are frozen, the sound he makes is unnaturally loud. As soon as he has spotted the Audi, its silver finish sparkling in the winter sun, he picks up his pace; for the last fifty meters his eyes water from the stabbing pain in his ribs. Without looking either way along the path he gets in on the driver's side. He locks the doors. In the glove compartment he finds a road map of France. Soon the drive southward, through Reims and Dijon, to his family. But first, the backpack. He turns on the engine and drives, too aggressively for a dirt path like this, toward the country road. He turns off toward Charleroi.

From the viaduct the long, desolate street looked abandoned, but now a boy is walking alongside him. He is scrawny and wiry, like a stray dog. The boy is wearing clothes that do not suit him: a filthy, oversized quilted body warmer that hangs below his knees, white nurses' clogs with tiny girlish holes in them. On his hand is a large black-and-red-leather motorcycle glove. It is clothing that doesn't look good on anyone.

The boy walks on the gritty, gravelly asphalt and he up on the raised sidewalk. He can't be older than twelve, and yet his eyes, barely visible, are sunk deep in their flaking sockets: black drain holes that keep a continual and close watch on the backpack. It has started to drip and weighs heavily on his shoulders. He keeps a close eye on his car, the Audi is parked half off the road, half under the viaduct.

He looks around, pretending he does not notice the boy. Much of the already rundown street has been demolished; around the few derelict houses is an empty lot littered with rubble and plastic bottles. They are about thirty meters from their destination: a small dumping ground for household refuse that he'd spotted from the ring road. Old sofas, TVs, mangled bicycles, garbage bags—especially lots of disgorging garbage bags. Answering the boy's attentive gaze, he points to the dump. A look of dismay shoots over the old-ish, serious face, the purple lips move like worms. "*Non,*" the boy commands, "*non*." He gestures with the huge palm of his leather glove. "*Venez!*"

But he does not want to go with him. He has to dispose of the backpack. It appears that the boy understands this, but still knows what's best for him. He walks up alongside him, and in a flash the enormous glove grabs him by the wrist. The boy gestures with his small, round chin to the opposite side of the street. To oblige him he nods and steps off the sidewalk, the asphalt crunching under his soles. The boy tugs him diagonally across the road, they are nearly running, the white clogs clack like horses' hooves on the decrepit blacktop. He is worried about the backpack, the load bounces unrhythmically up and down. The straps dig into his shoulders. The blood drips faster, he is leaving a trail behind. *Soon the head will be rolling down the street.* Why did he put it in the bottom compartment? Is the zipper shut?

He braces his foot against the curb, but the boy pulls him with the strength of a mule up onto the gray-paved sidewalk. They enter a café with a burned-out beer sign above the door. The boy pulls aside the velvet curtain and what they see is a ruin. The building has no back, blinding sunlight almost knocks over the crumbling cavity walls. His mouth agape, he walks over a wooden floor that gives onto rough grassland. A panorama extends out before them: he sees a sun-drenched railway yard stretching the entire breadth of the horizon, its countless parallel rusted tracks overgrown with nettles, dandelions, poppies. Here and there, dusty coal cars and abandoned passenger carriages glisten in the sunlight. You'd almost think it was spring. Beyond it, in the distance, is a gray canal, or maybe it's a reservoir. On the horizon, a steaming industrial complex with wide gray towers that spew out thick columns of yellow smoke.

"*Allons*," the boy says, followed by something in high-speed

French that he does not understand. He is standing on the third tread of a stairway, his body warmer looks like a kind of dress. The eyes roll insistently in their rusted sockets. Only now does he notice a rudimentary upper floor. Above his head is a half-demolished ceiling, loose copper pipes and tattered insulation material stick out of it. Blood is now pouring out of his backpack, it is too warm here, it seeps along the floor planks. "*Bouffer.*" The boy mimes eating and quickly takes hold of the peeling handrail—with a shock he realizes the other arm is missing. Just under the shoulder is a pale, sewn-up stump. He struggles up the staircase after the boy.

Upstairs, a man and a girl are seated at a fully set table, eating a sort of dark-red stew. He smells cooking grease. A stout woman crouches before an open oven. The room has no roof, but is furnished nevertheless. There are floor lamps, a dark oil painting hangs on the wall. The boy has already sat down next to the girl, who helps him remove the motorcycle glove. She is the spitting image of Janis, the same cropped hair, the close-set eyes. She stares past him toward the railway yard.

"I'm Siem," he says.

The man—a former Tubantia dean, he sees now—looks up and nods. "*Asseyez-vous.*" He suddenly realizes how famished he is. He'd like nothing better than a helping of that mashed food. He could almost cry with gratitude.

He tries to remove the backpack—the bleeding has stopped, maybe there's no more blood?—to take a place at the table, but he gets the shock of his life. The straps feel different now, they aren't straps anymore, but arms that resist. Thin fingers clamp themselves to his shoulders. He screams with fright, but the others watch him impassively. No sooner has he wrested the one bony wrist loose than the other hand clings tenaciously to his coat. "It's me, Simon," he hears close to his ear. "Your mother. You don't want to desert your mother, do you, boy?"

Even before he opens his eyes he realizes where he is: in his car, he is lying on the reclined passenger seat, wedged against his skis. He is in a rest area just outside Lyons. He is shattered. The dashboard clock tells him it is quarter to five in the afternoon. He has slept for forty-five minutes, tops. Dusk is already settling in. His nightmare clings to him for another ten seconds or so, then the previous twenty-four hours jolt through him like an electric shock.

The effect is dramatic. Of course he didn't book a hotel, which is why he is trying to get some shut-eye here, to put an end to the night of horrors that was bleeding into the morning. Usually things seem less catastrophic by day. But not now. The night has deepened.

He pulls the seat upright, crawls over the gear shift to the driver's side. He clamps himself to the steering wheel. While he is driving he catches his brain doing more or less the same thing; it clamps itself to practicalities, he's got his brain's strategy figured out. It neurotically goes through the whole checklist. Is the workshop entirely clean? No blood on the tree stump? Why did he throw away the chipboard at home? Did he put the garbage bags back in the utility room? Had anyone see him walking through Charleroi? *Why'd you answer your phone in the middle of those woods?* The suspects in the fireworks case were traced by their cell phone calls. For seven years you're the rector of a technical university and you happily answer your cell phone in those woods?

These are diversionary tactics. The manic rush he experienced between Charleroi and Lyons, pedal to the metal, 160 kpm the whole way, *Mingus at Antibes* coming full-blast out of the speakers, his wild, lawless, furious, frenzied mood—it's gone, evaporated. As though it never was. Within a minute of opening his eyes he feels something opening under his soul, a terrifying void, above which his most inner core, the man he is, the man he has to remain, tries to keep afloat. Thermal.

His car eats up the asphalt that separates him from normality. He can be in Val-d'Isère in an hour, *one more hour*, and the sketch that will become the rest of his life can begin. But he's losing altitude. He tries everything. The elbow, the scraps of flesh—they are spent, they are what they are. What he wants to do in The Hague, that letter to Joni, one more try. Can he call Aaron? Isabelle Orthel, he tries to recall her face—but raw, nocturnal images overrule his haphazard fantasies. That feverish dreaming has exhausted him, in traffic near Lyons he took a shallow curve too wide and nearly hit the guardrail.

It went all wrong. He botched it. He had shoved the gruesome torso backward onto the tree stump; the head still hung back and off to one side, he had cut away the scarf with shears—enough exposed neck to finish the job. But that rum he'd drunk. The rum, coupled with what he asked of himself. The first swing fell wide. There was more than enough room to hit the pale, outstretched neck, but he wasn't paying attention, or perhaps he faltered; in any case the blade of the axe landed too high, struck squarely into the lower part of the face. It cut a deep gash in the left corner of the mouth, through the upper lip and a bit of nose—everything gaped, he heard teeth, maybe even molars, breaking off. For a moment the axe appeared to be stuck, lodged deep in the upper jaw. He gasped for air. When he had jiggled the blade loose his arms, his hands, his entire body started to tremble.

It's all going so fast. Got to find thermal. Mathematics. Absolute clarity, synchronicity of beauty and insight? The ecstasy it could make him feel. Yellowish bone and flesh. The diagonal gash welled up with fluid: blood, but something grayish too. The Erdős problems he used to have at his fingertips. During receptions when he felt completely lost, during bad movies. When they lived on Bonita Avenue and he'd sit in the YMCA canteen during Janis's and Joni's swimming lessons. But now, Erdős ran through his fingers like fine sand. Joni was totally wrapped up in those lessons. *What is going on?* Not Janis: she'd keep looking over at him, smiling and waving. The sight of the jawbone, the hacked-off tongue, the mangled face. He tried to raise the axe a second time, but the thing weighed 100 kilos, halfway up he had to let it drop back. For a few moments his head was totally empty, until the clattering sound of breaking teeth returned, the strange overtones in the sloshy blow of the axe. The teeth. *Scattered everywhere.* A pathologist needed only one tiny piece of tooth. Shovel all that crap into the garbage bin, that was his first impulse, he was about to get the spade but was suddenly overcome with panic. Fell to his knees, tore off his gloves and began to grabble wildly in the snow. The pain in his frozen feet.

He was burrowing in the snow like a truffle hog when someone walked into the yard. The Teeuwen girl—he still can't remember her first name—came into view. Black spots filled his vision.

The ring road is busy, he approaches the exit for Val-d'Isère. He's got the route down pat, they've been coming here for years. He's known her since she was born, the Teeuwen girl. Was it that time already? She took her bike around the back, her full school bag strapped to the baggage carrier. She snapped out the kickstand, checked to see that the bike stayed put, precious seconds he used to stretch out his legs and lie flat in the snow. There he lay, prepared for utter ignominy. His eyes wide open, he peered past the bloody torso, his face pulsated. Thirty meters away, the thickly clothed girl walked toward the back door, the utility room. He could see her stop short as she approached. Her gloved hand briefly touched the taped-up windowpane. What was her name again? She looked around, he squeezed his eyes shut. When he looked again she had opened the back door. Her voice was dry in the morning air. "Hello?" she called out. He begged, he *prayed* she would go inside. To get to the cats' food bowls she would have to cut through the living room to the front hall. Had he cleaned up properly? She disappeared into the farmhouse.

Get off here. Chambéry exit. The will to carry on, the survival instinct that now leaks from him like alkaline from a spent flashlight battery, brought him to his feet. Swiftly he scrambled up and lifted the torso off the stump, dragged it to the workshop without breathing, and went around the back of the large workbench. Drunk with adrenaline, he laid the monstrosity behind the veneer press and lay down next to it. Wait. Don't move. That girl has to go to school, she'd feed the cats and cycle off to school. What was her name, damn it? Joni looked after her, Joni used to babysit at the Teeuwens'.

It's another quarter of an hour beyond Chambéry. But what he's known all along, happens: he keeps driving. The two of them, they were at the Teeuwens' together. *He misses the exit and keeps on driving.* Joni and Wilbert babysat that girl *together.* His Audi is a droplet gliding toward the Mediterranean Sea.

Pushkin Press

Pushkin Press was founded in 1997, and publishes novels, essays, memoirs, children's books—everything from timeless classics to the urgent and contemporary.

Our books represent exciting, high-quality writing from around the world: we publish some of the twentieth century's most widely acclaimed, brilliant authors such as Stefan Zweig, Marcel Aymé, Antal Szerb, Paul Morand and Yasushi Inoue, as well as compelling and award-winning contemporary writers, including Andrés Neuman, Edith Pearlman and Ryu Murakami.

Pushkin Press publishes the world's best stories, to be read and read again. Here are just some of the titles from our long and varied list. For more amazing stories, visit www.pushkinpress.com.

THE SPECTRE OF ALEXANDER WOLF

GAITO GAZDANOV

'A mesmerising work of literature' Antony Beevor

BINOCULAR VISION

EDITH PEARLMAN

'A genius of the short story' Mark Lawson, *Guardian*

TRAVELLER OF THE CENTURY

ANDRÉS NEUMAN

'A beautiful, accomplished novel: as ambitious as it is generous, as moving as it is smart' Juan Gabriel Vásquez, *Guardian*

BEWARE OF PITY

STEFAN ZWEIG

'Zweig's fictional masterpiece' *Guardian*

THE WORLD OF YESTERDAY

STEFAN ZWEIG

'*The World of Yesterday* is one of the greatest memoirs of the twentieth century, as perfect in its evocation of the world Zweig loved, as it is in its portrayal of how that world was destroyed' David Hare

JOURNEY BY MOONLIGHT

ANTAL SZERB

'Just divine… makes you imagine the author has had private access to your own soul' Nicholas Lezard, *Guardian*

BONITA AVENUE

PETER BUWALDA

'One wild ride: a swirling helix of a family saga… a new writer as toe-curling as early Roth, as roomy as Franzen and as caustic as Houellebecq' *Sunday Telegraph*

THE PARROTS

FILIPPO BOLOGNA

'A five-star satire on literary vanity… a wonderful, surprising novel' *Metro*

I WAS JACK MORTIMER

ALEXANDER LERNET-HOLENIA

'Terrific… a truly clever, rather wonderful book that both plays with and defies genre' Eileen Battersby, *Irish Times*

SONG FOR AN APPROACHING STORM

PETER FRÖBERG IDLING

'Beautifully evocative… a must-read novel' *Daily Mail*

THE RABBIT BACK LITERATURE SOCIETY

PASI ILMARI JÄÄSKELÄINEN

'Wonderfully knotty… a very grown-up fantasy masquerading as quirky fable. Unexpected, thrilling and absurd' *Sunday Telegraph*

RED LOVE: THE STORY OF AN EAST GERMAN FAMILY

MAXIM LEO

'Beautiful and supremely touching… an unbearably poignant description of a world that no longer exists' *Sunday Telegraph*